John Trevillian is an author, songwriter and artist, living in the United Kingdom. Creator of the Talliston interior design project, his novels include the *A-Men* trilogy, plus *Shadowmagick,* a collection of poetry, songs, travel journals, short stories and other miscellaneous writing. Following the cult success of the first novel, *The A-Men Return* takes readers into darker territories.

www.trevillian.com

ALSO BY JOHN TREVILLIAN

The A-Men
Forever A-Men

THE A-MEN RETURN
JOHN TREVILLIAN

Copyright © 2011 John Trevillian

The moral right of the author has been asserted.

Apart from any fair dealing for the purposes of research or private study, or criticism or review, as permitted under the Copyright, Designs and Patents Act 1988, this publication may only be reproduced, stored or transmitted, in any form or by any means, with the prior permission in writing of the publishers, or in the case of reprographic reproduction in accordance with the terms of licences issued by the Copyright Licensing Agency. Enquiries concerning reproduction outside those terms should be sent to the publishers.

Matador
5 Weir Road
Kibworth Beauchamp
Leicester LE8 0LQ, UK
Tel: (+44) 116 279 2299
Fax: (+44) 116 279 2277
Email: books@troubador.co.uk
Web: www.troubador.co.uk/matador

ISBN 978 1848766 198

British Library Cataloguing in Publication Data.
A catalogue record for this book is available from the British Library.

Typeset in 11pt Bembo by Troubador Publishing Ltd, Leicester, UK

Matador is an imprint of Troubador Publishing Ltd

Printed in Great Britain by the MPG Books Group, Bodmin and King's Lynn

LBS
For without that, there would be no this

1 | D'ALESSANDRO

He was warm yet lonely, the traces of her blood still etched across his senses as she had cried out above him. The water was icy cold pressing upon him from all sides, yet his body was filled with pumping life and the strongest desire that he should talk to her. Turning sluggishly in the midnight he opened his mouth, but grief tore at his throat, sucking away his voice as the water gushed across his tongue. And he was sinking. Sinking into an ocean of darkness, her weight on his back as he carried her body away with him. He knew he would have to let her go. She was too heavy, he was too exhausted to carry on and the realisation did nothing to annul the painful thought that soon she would be gone. He would never again touch her skin. Never again watch the sunlight across her back. Never again swim with her.

With a sudden movement that tensed his body and sent jarring pain coursing along his wounded side, he forced himself onward and, tipping slightly, let her sink down out of reach. He swam around again, circling the place with a ring of bubbles until he was sure that she was truly lost to him. The currents were getting stronger now as the waning moon above tore the tides away to the east. They called to him and his internal compass turned his body to face the invisible coast that lay many hundreds of kilometres away. This race in which he swam was not over; the hunters knew his destination and would doubtless be ready and waiting. Despair, not an emotion credited to such a slaughtered creature as he, overcame him then and his unearthly cry rang out across the unfathomable emptiness in a plaintive song.

There were no words. There was no meaning. This was a signal of a sort that defied the laws of all ordinary communication; a tracer whose frequencies went far beyond the human ear. The cry had no barriers, no transient echoes in mortal space, no reflection in its journey from sea bed to sea-air surface and beyond. The cavernous underworld of the ocean took the sound and carried it off into its endless reaches. It passed the true fishes without recognition, rebounded off the frozen roof of the ocean and sank unchallenged into the sand-filled hollows where unsleeping crustaceans stalked. The signal journeyed on and on, though it touched no understanding ear and starting strong, finally began to ebb and fail. If it said anything it was that he was the last. Yet in all the great infinity of water, the statement went unrealised.

Until four hundred kilometres distant, the impossible happened; a listener was found.

Somehow, somewhere, someone heard his cry and wept at its message. She was dead. He was to die. Insignificant facts in a much larger world, but they were grasped by a mind that was ready to receive and, more importantly, was able to act.

The control terminal flickered slightly and scanned the tesseraxial dataflow once again, spewing out the encoded graphical hieroglyphs with a speed that defied the eye to focus. There was no computer demodulator in use that could unscramble this sort of garble and stay online, but then this was no computer. Slowly and meticulously, the hidden mind wrestled with the cipher and finally produced a translated script of the original call in a language that it could understand.
>**Message completed.**

– it spelt out silently in shining green.
>**Origin located. Answering on C-9.**

There was a pause – mere heartbeats – until the screen leapt again. This time it announced that an answer had been sent.
>**Initiating exigency sequence.**

– it continued impartially before reimmersing itself into a static state.

And I, like some jacked-up god, just watched on and did nothing.

2 | PURE

It's a reoccurring dream: rising in the morning a naked boy in my bed.

"What the fuck—?"

I pull my jeans on and curse.

Blood. Gang rape.

Glance over at the jig while young toughs go wild on booze and drugs inside my head. Outside somewhere on the forever sunny side of the street big, ugly Wolves stride motorcycles in the alleyways, their Phantom-Turbine's growling in beautiful, wicked pain. Soon they'll be riding out, shooting off like a gun pointed at my head.

The prick is dead.

Just the way his insides paint Rorschach patterns on the bruise of rug tell me that. Blink spastically as my designer mind tries to cross-classify the resulting blotches as human, nature, animal or other. Matching against a near-infinite catalogue of fabric swatches. I fight the flashcard strobing. Forcing my bleary thoughts to recall more pertinent images. Like, for a start, from last night. Yet when the memory call connects, I wish I'd stayed with the dress samples. I jerked his load last night while he senseless screamed. I got a gun as after he sobbed and pulled the trigger tight. Felt the bullet bite his flesh and blow out his shitty brains...

Inexplicably, my mind plays rock ballads as the street-fighters howl.

"You didn't like my hair, you didn't like my cologne. You didn't like my bad breath, baby, in the mouth of your phone. You didn't like my walk, the way I dress to the right. You didn't like my lifestyle, baby, the way I stayed out all night…"

My throat clenches and I look for water. There's some beer left in the can, flat and bitter, but it's all the drink I've got. Blown the lot. Blown the boy.

The bikers are coming...

Blown your chances, girl.

Paradise wasn't supposed to be like this. Mokabi-Dzanga Sanctuary was a fresh start. A new me. A new now. But that's before my tryst with Ravn, my slow, steady sinking into Bantu *majanga*. My new career as assassin for hire. Once Orizon owned everything south of the Sub-Saharan circle. Then it went skyward with the rest of them, leaving this place to return to nature. But what's left is far from natural.

Cross to the broken maw of the washroom. The shower, basin and urinal all dry as my rusty mouth.

The mirror in the bathroom groans back at me. The swarthy, handsome devil tattoo winks slyly, almost grinning over my shoulder. Yeah, that's right, lap it up, Lucifer.

I drag on the jinkie's checkered shirt, the sweat-stained armpits mocking. I force my numb arms into his leather jacket with the eagle on the back. I wash my face in the warm-as-blood water. The grease from my matted blonde hair runs thickly. I stink, and it's just too much. I cry.

The Wolves of Owando wanted power. Then they wanted me. Yet how I got here – with *this* – is just nowhere in the cracked panes of my vanity-mirror mind. But if I've learned nothing in my time here, if I played the dumb blonde bitch until it just became who I am, learned nothing about the witchdoctors, jeepsters and machetes of the Wolves, I know that for them revenge is way up there with shitting and drinking.

Much as I hate to admit it, I've gotta get help. No money. No food. No friends. No nothing now. Hell, I've gotta get out of this stinking desert. Before they come and smell me out. Before they corner me like a rat.

Before they cut you up, girl.

Before I die.

Gun goes off two shacks away and I flee. Outside's my g-truckster. All black and red and ready to go, go, go. As I slip into the cabin and fire the twin engines, the bikers turn into the shanties. I count eight maybe ten but don't wait to cross-verify. Just slam the pedal and head for open country. Out on the angry road the Wolves come running. Following my flatbed like vampires on the wind. Can smell my blood. One sniff in the air and they've got it. One sniff and they know where I'm going.

The man with the planes.

Haul the rig into fifth and floor it. Feel my white neck snap. Feel my back against the roughness of the sticky seat. Outside's just scrub and dust. Used to be savannah, but that's just so much folk story now. Gotta keep watching the track. Scanning for traps. For natives who break holes in the road, fill pits with sand and wait for unwary roadsters to drive right into 'em. At this speed hitting one will shear the undercarriage in two, but I just can't risk slowing down.

Just hope the bikers in the rear view mirror ain't closer than they appear.

Ravn. Hot, hairy, *dirty* Ravn. All torque and grease and stripping down iridium catalyst engines as light entertainment. When I ditched that no-good son of a fuck in Dead City, bought my way onto the nightflier with the only currency I had left, I never meant to go back. What I *meant* to do was run further than any bridge of regret could reach. I didn't want a way back. Ditched my clothes, my career, even my name. Yet now I need to run again. Always running from something.

"*You didn't like my jokes, you didn't care for my lies. I pared my nails with your fork tines, baby, that's something else you despise. You didn't like my music, the way I rode on my bike. You didn't like my bad behaviour, my friends are not the kind you like…*"

With stereo growls two bikes flank me. Going flat out, their twin riders are hidden behind helmets painted with daemons. Tucked tight against the fins the frontmen crouch over the bars, while the pillions lean back against their belts aiming through the sandstorm that surrounds us. Pump the pedals harder, but this geo's giving everything it's got. There's no more. Not one drop.

Duck closer to the dash as bullets make a mess of the seatback. Fracturing the cab portholes into tiny, stinging shards.

Where am I going? What crazy road am I on? If I don't get off this straight right this second, they'll have me. Just one lucky shot and I'm—

Interchange. Two klicks. Go left.

I wish the eagle on my jacket could give me wings. Great feathered things to come and take me up to where I want to go. Above the roads. Above the clouds. Above the wreck of the life that I have made.

But it's just a bunch of cow skin and lousy stitching.

It's not my fault. I had no choice. My course was set long before I greased the boy for whatever reason I did it. Now I know where the voice is taking me. To the steps of the plane. Back to the skyfield where I started this chapter of my non-life. But then where, my bodiless friend?

Everything stops at the foot of those steps. The road, my hopes, my dreams.

The interchange comes. I take the left.

"Hey baby, I can cut it out, if it's bad I wanna cut it out. Oh baby, I can cut it out, because I love you I can cut it out..."

The road turns to dirt. To mud. To chalk. And ahead I see a cluster of familiar prefabs.

When I get close I cut the engine and coast. Locking to cruise, I swing out the cab and start shooting. Aiming at the Wolves, their bikes, their shadows. Just randomly blasting. Making them dodge every which way. Giving me time to get clear. To reach the sanctuary of the buildings.

Leave everything of your life behind. You will fly like the wind and be transported back to the place where your gods dwell over the seas. Follow me.

All barrels blazing, I leap from the flatbed and burst like a starving animal into the hut. Ravn's already standing. Already armed and dangerous. Already firing.

I duck, roll and come up kicking. Mawashi geri. Roundhouse and smack the snubnose out his trembling hands. And with the Wolves snarling at my back, I cry: "Don't move a muscle, Ravn. I've no time for a big reunion."

"Suzi Uzi? What—"

"Fuck what. Fuck how and why and when. I gotta fly."

He asks me where. That dreaded question. Where?

"Take me to…"

Where?

"Take me to…"

Nowhere.

My mind doesn't think. It's on auto. Zazzing.

"Dead City."

"Well, little miss ragdoll," says a familiar husky voice from the shadows, "I think I can help with that."

3 | DINGO THE WONDER DOG

I'm sitting at the screen overlooking Main. Watching two kids playing. No Channel Retrox – no channel nothing no more – so I makes my own shows. Stow diocams in buildings. Watch the action on infrared from my attic room. Suck power through a bypass straight from the flick's generator. Tonight's show is all action. I calls it *Playing For Creeps*, and am commentating to Bixby as the fun unfolds. It goes something like this: "OK, so here I am reporting live from 40th and Balboa. We're in Dead City. Zombie Zone. Dead centre of the Grim Reaper's turf. And if there's one thing you don't do it's steal their master's Lamborghini Diablo. But we have two contestants on the show tonite and that's just what they've done. Can you believe that, folks? Don't know how they did it, but here they come now roaring up Main like they've got a swarm of hornets on their tails. But it shore is worse than that, believe you me. It's *mighty* worse. 'Cause when did you last see hornets in white and black gowns, carrying scythes and riding motorbikes? See, that camo-painted beauty is their head gringo's pride and joy. These gutterjocks should've never even *breathed* on that geo.

"Well, folks, that was their first mistake. Their second's not checking that the Diablo's drive unit was recharged. There they go now careering off the interchange. They're mounting the sidewalk… They're mowing down streetlamps like pins in an alley. Wowee, look at 'em go! Gonna have a home run and no messin'. The lambo's ground to a halt under some industrial bins. Gonna take a hefty piece of kit to get that out again. The Reapers are gaining… But wait! The doors are opening.

Well lookie here, folks. Here's our first glimpse of tonite's two contestants.

"Him? Well he's Johnny Doe. By the look at his get-up, he's an ex-Reaper himself. Her? Well she's a real looker, viewers. Name's Janey Doe. Her jockey jacket says she works for Big Mamma. Ex-Burger Queen. Well, that shore is swell. So looks like we've got two runners in the game tonite. Both exiles. Both expendable. And both totally X'ed if those bikers catch up with 'em. On foot these dudes don't stand a chance. Now, aw, ain't that a crying shame? But let's watch anyways. 'Cause you never know in this town and they ain't dead meat till they hit the dirt, that's what I always say. The only way to learn the rules is fast in Dead City. Here you either belong or you're running. Looks like he's running from Mr Grim Reaper himself. She's probably running from Big Mamma, creator of the legendary Machburger. Mamma's very proud of her girls. Too much of a broody old hen to let any of her chicks outta her sight though.

"Well, the Doe twins are heading for the Hotel San Dino, but it's so totally obvious that they're not gonna make it. The bikers are coming too fast. They're only a block away. Half a block. Ten metres. Nine... Ooh, Johnny's got a gun. He's trying to use it. He's got about three nanoseconds before the bikers... Olé! Lead Grim's caught him against the left side. Whoa, folks, hey would'ya look at that... Took his arm clean off. Watch it go! First blood to the Reapers. Johnny's trying to protect the girl. He's going down... Staggering... Losing too much blood. The girl's screaming. Running around like a loon. Whoops! The next biker's run straight into her... Calamity! Well, ain't that a turn-up for the books... Janey's down, but so is one of the Reapers. Guess that means we'll be holding onto the exclusive perfume collection and the holiday in paradise for another week... But wow, Johnny's just bagged himself a Reaper too. He's shooting the Grim fulla lead, but... Damn me, his gun's exploded... It's blown up right in his face! What a way to go, folks! What a way to..."

There's a banging at the trapdoor. Frantic. Bixby jumps up and starts barking. His knotted coat dancing.

"Hey, shitface! You're late, you little fuck. Your shift started an hour ago…"

The screen goes blank as I whap it off.

Too bad. Things were just going down. Haven't seen action like that for… oh, *years*. Not since that Phoenix heist over bayside. Now those were the days.

Yes indeedy.

Whossat?

Oh, just an old friend popping in to say hello.

Phantom? Is that you?

Would you like it to be?

Oh, yeah. So very, very…

"Hey, you hear me? Boss' gonna choke you on your own chum if you don't show right now!"

I fumble for the lock on the trapdoor.

Whoever you are, I gotta split…

No trouble. I'll always be watching out for you, Elliott.

I go.

4 | SISTER MIDNIGHT

Quiet. Stone. Candles. Whispers on the wind. A dozen cowled women say their bedtime prayers.

"Hail the Goddess, mother of the one true child…"

"…keeping the faith of the karma, holding the banner of the hallowed, bleeding the blood of the righteous…"

"…onward comes the time with uncaring, unseeing footsteps…"

Holy mutterings in this holy place. All in tune with the beating of their deities' hearts.

A dozen women. A dozen creeds. All part of the pan-religious monopoly that is the God-U-Likes.

The God-U-Likes deal in gods. All gods. Any one you like. They're not fussy. They've got more cults and clans on their files than there are angels in the firmament. They deal in gods like the cornerstore deals in donuts. Plain. Jam. Apple. Custard. Cream or chocolate. Topped with sugar-coated marzipan flowers. Whatever. Same thing here. Only a little more cosmic.

No one phases the God-U-Likes. They see all gods as the same god. All belief as the same belief. All faiths as the same faith. In the end, religion equals religion equals them. And hey, there's enough to go round. Just join at the desk and they'll sort it all out. No problem. Open your heart and they'll stuff it so full of martyrs that you won't know what to do with 'em all. Everyone lives under the umbrella of God. When the shit comes down, no need to get even one pinkie wet. Sort of a case of pray and let pray.

That's the God-U-Likes. Supreme brotherhood for the lost and alone.

I enter hurriedly and kneel with the rest. I am late, but as always everyone is polite enough not to notice. I come dressed in the attire of my streetgods. The garb of the Eternal Ones. Added long years before to the dark bible of my brethren. The hosts of the mythical religion of the Amen are now transformed into my own personal pantheon. Once worshiped by no one. Now worshiped by me alone.

I come clad in the cloth of Mûhamet, of Astarth, Kalím and Bêz, in the stole of Æoseth, the black veil of Ianus and the headdress of Torûs. I chose each of these seven to watch my way. Each to guide and protect me. Each for the powerful magic that they hold. But mostly as a remembrance of the past.

My black feathers shiver as I bow. Making a weaving sign across my chest, I produce a string of prayer beads and begin wringing them in my dark hands.

"Torûs, O blessed one, lord god of earth magic and the mighty dead, bestow upon me this day the protection of thy black mamba magic. As above, so below.

"O wise Ianus, keeper of the perfect divine mirror which you shall one day hold up to nature and destroy it utterly, knower of the secrets kept hidden from us all. O blessed Ianus, allow me to wield the power of negative advertising upon thine enemies.

"Æoseth, O god of the chaos into which everything went – and has pretty much stayed there – guardian of immortality, overlord of the great scrapyard from which all junk comes. O dear lord, grant that I may walk through the death of the valley of shadows, and fear no evil.

"O trickster Bêz, I pledge that through thee I shalt love the finer things in life – or what scant little remains of them – being the joys of feasting, drinking and driving recklessly fast in cars. As the mind, so the spirit.

"O merciless Kalím, master of war, destruction and big guns, unto thee, O lord, do I pray that you shalt bestow upon me the courage to pursue your charge; to cleanse mine soul in ultra-violence and cream the pants of thine enemies.

"O Astarth, goddess of sex, drugs and rock 'n' roll, let the cry go out that thou art a real funky mutha. As without, so within.

"And last, Mûhamet, goddess of life, death and inner belief, preserve and keep me this day for in thee do I place my trust. Amen."

My blessings spoken, all is quiet for a time. Then I join my sisters in their resonant mantras.

"Ki Om Ma Noo... Ki Om Ma Noo... Ki Om Ma Noo..."

Over and over and over again.

If only they knew. If only they harboured the merest inkling where I've been and what I've been doing.

"Ki Om Ma Noo... Ki Om Ma Noo... Ki Om Ma Noo..."

If only they knew that I want to take this whole ritual bullshit and stuff it up their virginal asses.

"Ki Om Ma Noo... Ki Om Ma Noo... Ki Om Ma Noo..."

Why ever did I get holed up here? But even as I think this I know the answer. Know it only too well.

"Ki Om Ma Noo... Ki Om Ma Noo... Ki Om Ma Noo..."

If only I could get out. Take a bike and head up the coast. Go anywhere. Anywhere other than here...

Tonight's the night, dreaming angel. You hear me? The stranger is coming. Coming to set you free...

The voice strikes loud in my head. Dull and sexless and clear. Who could it be but God Mûhamet. Filling my soul with fear. Long have been the nights since last I heard that dark voice. Long and silent and alone.

"Ki Om Ma Noo... Ki Om Ma Noo... Ki Om Ma Noo... No... Nooooo!"

I stumble upon the mindless, meaningless chant, my thoughts in sudden disarray. Blushing invisibly beneath my veil, I cry out. My voice filled with a sudden hopeless desperation.

I scramble to my feet and push away from the cushioned pew. Twelve faces look around in damning unison. Forcing myself backwards, it is all I can do not to turn and flee. Holding my breath, I wait until I reach the arched door then, throwing it aside, rush through in a blind, rabid panic.

5 | THE NOWHEREMAN

Name's Jack. Not many people know that, but suits me real fine. To most I'm just a johnny no-name who fucks them off. Like it that way. Folks with a long memory might remember when I wasn't a loner. Might remember when we was eleven. How we ruled the dark. How we were fucking A. And while they're doing all this shitfire reminiscing, might also remember how they used to call me The Nowhereman.

Still, maybe they won't…

Now here once more I stand alone atop the ragged ruins of the Phoenix Tower and look up at the brilliant sky. Night falls. Wind's up. First time for ages it's clear. I see stars. Up here I feel free. Here I feel I can do 'most *anything*. All alone. Oh, except for my D&K.

My D&K and the voice.

Heaven's coming. See it, Jack? See it?

Get outta my brain, you total shit.

There it is. Passing over like the morning star.

Fuck you.

The voice makes me angry. Been drinking so I get angry fast. I've had a bad day. A real bad day. So I've come up here to get away from it all. Don't want no half-assed sucker messing with my mind. I'm here 'cause I want to be alone. Wanna throw some shit at the stars. Wanna shoot my mouth off to the moon.

But seeing Heaven, I forget all that.

I forget it and decide to get prayin'. Most days prayers is all I got. Been three years far as I can reckon. Three, maybe four. Long time since I decided to stay here. Stay and rot in this metropolitan corpse.

Back then I woke to a new life. A brilliant myriad of possibilities. Of doing. Of danger. Of dreams. Now only dreams I have come straight outta a battered book of faerie tales. An island so far removed from this fucked-up ass-wipe of a place that it hurts just thinking about it. An island I read about every cunting day of my unlife, but've seen only once.

So I shout off into the nothing. Venting frustration. Throwing open the floodgates. Pain and words're same as always.

"Hey father, you up in Heaven? Hallo, hear your name…" I know the spiel better than I know myself. I spit it out. Try not to think how pointless it is. Try to believe in it real hard. "You led me to damnation. You delivered me to the evil ones…." I feel the words. Force them up from my gut. Vomit them out. "Now I want your kingdom, your power and your glory. Forever and ever: Amen."

Though my cry's strong, it's caught on the wind and is lost. Lost like a scream to the dead.

We are all lost. You. Me. Them.

Them?

Yes… All of them.

No way. You got it wrong. We all stood together. We all bled. We all swore. Don't matter where they are or what they're doing, they're still in. Till the end of time.

And though things have been mighty shaky these last few years, eternity's still hangin' on in there.

Once, now and…

Forever A-Men?

S'right. Till the end of time.

★

The final surfer attack came on the night I met Shitjack. But it was going long before that. Kinda like a war. Sort of but not quite. To us it was a war. To them it was just kicks. They'd hang mid-space, spy for a while then come down and slam our butts. And we'd scratch our rocks and hope it'd be someone else's turn next time. Never was. Always our turn. Or seemed that way. Had butts so sore it was hard to show face, y'know. Hard to be someone with a super-red ass chute. Still what could I do? Only one of me. Not that that ever mattered until now. Alone was enough. Alone rules. Until the Wasters came. Now they rule. There's fucking loads of them.

Still everyone was screwed. Just got used to being pissed on. Whole place shut down. No one cruised anymore. No one dragged bikes. Shit, no one *moved*.

The place was a prison. A great big concrete prison. All that was left was to tough and tough back.

If I remember rightly I was toughing Pigmeat the day I met Shitjack.

Yeah, it was Pigmeat. Can still remember the smell.

Unless they yell in the dark all you got is the smell. And the smell sure wasn't Lucille. He'd pissed off fast as fuck when the last train came by. Shit only knows where he got the fare. Perhaps others paid him. Sure as hell got nothing from me. 'Cept that mink one time.

Yeah, it was Pigmeat. Little fuck. The Wasters had wasted my bike. Picked it up after the Reapers snatched back the lambo. Best geo I ever stole. Fixed the front axle. Resealed the tank. Even painted the arches. Surfjocks'd caught me on Jefferson Davis Parkway. I was out early finning some turkies. Tore it in half with a Kalashnikov. Better it than me. Fuck the Wasters. Fuck 'em all.

They were gone now so I fucked Pigmeat instead. Angry jerks. Total screw by the totally screwed. No control. Who cares if he dies. Sweating. Piston. Grunting. Chains. Fast spasmodic furiosity. Cock rules in the dark. And Pigmeat's the best boy-pussy around. At least since Lucille left.

Above the noise I hear this sound. Sort of like blades. Buzzing. I stop pumping and hear the brat slump in the chains. I cross to the window. Outside's darker than inside. Not even a headlight. Yet still this noise like a crazy metal heartbeat.

Pigmeat asks what's up. I tell him to fucking shut it. Then he hears it too.

"Whassat?"

I don't tell him twice. My knuckles feel for his face. There's a crack. Then he's quiet.

The buzzing's louder. Too loud for a chopper. Wrong sound for a grav. Last time I saw a grav was the wrong side of eighty-three. No, not a grav. Something new. Something different. I curse Lucille. I should've been on that train. Never trust a man in red lipstick. They're always trouble.

I stuff myself into my pants and belt 'em tight. Grab my jacket too. It's hot but who looks mean in just Levi's? And the skin hides things. Like a piece. Who knows what's out there tonight. I try to stop my mind racing, but it races anyway. Not a nightflier. Never a chinook. What then? I thought I'd heard everything.

Stroked Pigmeat's crop as I left. Told him I'd be back. What a waste of breath. Locked the door though. Didn't want my date to be disturbed while I was out. Never know what state I'd find him in. Glad I fitted a lock. Glad I know Pigmeat. Glad to be so fucking lucky.

Met Jesus on the stairs. Said hi but didn't hang around. Good policy. Who wants to hang with kooks like Jesus?

Down in the lot the air is full of dust. Calm night turned rowdy. The wind is like air running scared. Saw faces up in the sky. No one but me crazy enough to come down. Don't know why I have come down. Just got a feeling. A feeling that I'm wanted. Like a siren calling my name. Pull out my D&K. Feels good in my hand. Feels like a dick when it's hard. My metal cock. Ready for fucking.

I keep low to the wall and watch the sky. Buildings are too near to see much any which way. So I wait. Wait and watch. Sound gets louder. My piece feels too small. Wish I still had my dancer. So much scrap after the last belt's gone. Still a D&K sure beats a blade.

Dark night lit by searchlight. Single beam in the middle of the lot. I clear the wall and crouch the other side. Watch as the night opens. It's one big mother. Could be orbital. Probably a personal transport. Looks real expensive, anyway. What's a rich kid doing here? Then I think of the Wasters and the whole shitty deal we've been getting.

Maybe it's showtime. Maybe those O-Zoners finally decided to stop playing and start this war for real. Maybe they got fed up with crashing our junks and fragging our fuel and thought, hey let's kick some real ass. Maybe mr numero uno Waster's come to see the field before playing ball. Touchdown time. Fucking makes me sick just thinking about it.

Across the street is a row of shops squatting in shadows. The nearest is one big sign with a door in it. I'm still waiting and watching when I see Gut Radical under the advertisement. It says 'Coke W$5.00'. I'm shit if it's the real thing. Can't get piss for five world dollars. Still I'm sure it's him. I can see his goatface from here.

Well, well, well. So Radical's into this birdy too. He's got the scent. If it wasn't for all this noise I'd bet I'd hear him mewling. Fat Gut's always in on a deal. He'd be a pro if he'd lay off the A's. Shoots every vein in his ass. Got cheeks like the craters of the moon. Don't ask me how I know.

He hasn't seen me. He's not looking my way at all. He's looking straight up. I look up too.

Above the blinding pillar of light is the big grey belly of the bird. It slides open like a wound spilling red. Warning lights. Someone's coming down. Seeing this gets Gut edgy. You can tell when the Gut's edgy. He smoothes back his hair. He's doing it now. Wiping the grease to the nape. When it's flat he starts over.

What's this then? Gut doing a deal? A deal with the Wasters? Has to be. My mind shouts shoot him now, but I stop. Finger's half pulled the trigger. I let it go. Breathe deep. Wait and watch.

A rope ladder uncoils from the belly of the bird. A figure claws its way down. Looks like it's wearing enough trikevlar to stop a nuke. The figure moves too gracefully to be a dog. Still, takes me ages to suss it's a bitch.

The leather sticks to my back. I'm sweating in the hot night. More than the false wind can dry. My gun feels heavy in my fist.

A woman?

I blink back the wetness in my eyes. I'm getting hard just realising it.

A woman.

I don't care what this set-up's about. Fuck the Gut. All I want is that cunt. In my mind's eye I can see it. Waiting. Wanting. Wettening. Watching the battle-clad siren descend, I know now why I'm here. Why I'm alive. Why I've fought and won and fought again. Why I've never quit. Never stopped fighting.

For the promise of this cunt. One thing's for sure, she's no Waster.

Then I notice I'm wanking. I stop, cursing. Realising the danger. Can still see that cunt though. So close now I can almost smell it.

Guess I'm still horny from leaving Pigmeat.

Apart from her moves, the woman's invisible. Hidden in her armour. She reaches the bottom of the ladder. She's only ten metres away and I feel like screaming. Probably wouldn't hear me anyhow. Still I keep my jaw locked. She looks unarmed. Not carrying anything obvious. Doesn't mean fuck though. Maybe she's got friends upstairs. Maybe something in her suit. Or maybe she's hoping everyone round here'll be too busy hanging out their tongues to pull anything.

I start to pull my cock again. I'm drooling and I don't even care to wipe the spit. Hell, I don't even *care*.

I'm so busy eyeballing the bitch that I don't notice Gut. Not till he's right up to her. He's walking like he's shit his pants. Sidling. His face is blank like a mask. White in the searchlight. Every vein poking out. With his whole face in relief, he looks like a ghost. The silver of his pierced lip twinkles.

Radical's carrying a bag. Some cloth affair. Holding it to his chest, clutching it like a little baby. Got to be important if he's got it that close. Nothing gets that close to Gut.

His eyes are searching the dark lot. Wonder what horrors he's seeing? Guess he feels as exposed as he looks. Must be hoping for some sort of miracle when this bitch is gone. Whatever the deal, he's gonna have a hard job hanging onto his payment. And his life. Some round here would kill for a taste of ol' Radical's living, y'know. Still not many could tough up old fat Gut. What good's a fist against a sawn-off? Still he must know that every jerk worth his salt's gonna be out to get him after this scene. Must have thought of that. Must have.

Gut hands over the bag as if he's giving away his last snort of dust. The bitch is nodding slowly, deep inside her suit. I can see her faceplate twitch rhythmically. The Gut's hands are empty now. Don't know what to do with them. Stuffs them under his arms and shuffles.

The stranger's expression is lost, but her posture hints at betrayal. Then she's reaching into her hip-pocket. I'm as surprised as anyone when she digs out a set of tags.

There are two. Triangular. Plasti-coated. Red. They sit in the woman's gloved hand, their black cord draped enticingly through her fingers. No, not tags. They're tickets. *Train* tickets.

The plastic gleams in the searchlight like twenty-four carat gold.

The sight of the tickets wipes me over the edge. I cum. A whimper issues from my mouth. Torn away on the rotor's wind. As the sound goes the night lets out a whimper of its own. I just catch it. And this time I know what it is. The whine of grav-motors. Hova-boards. Half a dozen. Maybe more.

So what is your assessment, soldier?

Wasters. In-coming. Ten o'clock.

I forget the slime in my jeans and arc my head toward the sound. All I see is night. Fuck these buildings. Distort everything. I turn to four o'clock and see a wall of headlights. Just in time.

The woman hasn't heard a thing. She only knows something's up when she sees the Gut's face. Spinning, she's down in one. On my periphery I see her tacticals rezz on. Some badass bitch.

Out of the darkness between the blocks eight pairs of electric neon sear the sidewalks. Astride their leather skidpads stand a pack of yowling jockies, long hair whipping like bleached ribbons. All are dressed in the same surfer strip. Cut-offs. Palm shirts. Loafers. The head honcho is J.J. Jerome-James. I know him well. He holds his Kalashnikov like a Zulu spear. Fucking Wasters. Go back to daddy.

J.J. looks surprised as he arcs down toward the transport. This stinks of bad timing. Won't have to wait long to see who for.

The Gut's next to the woman now, clawing her. Wants the tickets.

She shrugs him off and tosses them behind her. He goes scrabbling. She wastes a few seconds tying the bag to the ladder. From her shoulder plates twin pistols click out like little cobras.

The sky is full of falling stars. Revving their boards the beach boys swoop in and begin to torch the lot. Flames roast wrecks. Turns the air into an oven.

The woman focuses on the swarm and produces a steel bar from her thigh. Looks like a cattle prod. As the jockey boys buzz past her she spears one. His chest explodes like an overripe peach.

On the first pass the Wasters let their gadgets scan the area. I've seen this sorta move before. We're all data now. Zero coordinates in some cannon's silicon mind. Next pass we're meat. Wonder if I'm on the chart. Not waiting to find out. My mind can't forget those tickets lying in the dirt, but I'm not suicidal. Got other thoughts. Like staying alive long enough to use 'em.

Keeping low to the wall, I cock my D&K and wait for the next fly-by.

Can't see the lot now. Just feel the heat. There's a pause as they circle. The dopplering of their war cries. Budda-budda-budda. The whine of the boards. And then they burst into view above me.

My piece cums in my fist. Two shells. Three. One for luck. Hit two of the air-bikers in the back and a third bike on the left boogie-fin.

The first jockey crashes headlong into Broadview Apartments. The bike erupts as its grav-unit implodes.

Crazy fucks. Why'd rich kids like you wanna go down like this?

I look over the wall letting my eyes drink in the carnage. Gut's history. The bitch's cut up bad. Transport's not hanging around for her. Already the bag is buzzing out of reach above her head.

With friends like yours, lady, who needs fuck-buddies?

She's trying to make it to cover before the bikers get back. Pretty hard on a blasted thighbone. Still she's moving towards the Gut. Why? Obviously not to pay her last respects.

Then it clicks. With the transport gone, she's stuck here. She's going for the tickets.

I don't think. For a moment I forget that she's a bitch. I forget what lurks behind that frosted mask. I even forget the smell of her cunt. Perhaps it's 'cause I've cum. Who knows? I put it all out of my mind and level my D&K towards her. It shouts twice and jerks in my hand. The two shells make the inside of her helmet look like a blender.

My heart screams as she falls. She's a metre away from the plastic when she hits the tarmac. Too bad, baby. Could have been good, you and me. I fall onto my ass and start to reload. Doesn't take that long. Only got five shells left.

Up on the luminous green screens of the hova-boards, I almost feel myself appear on their battlescans. Four left. I got one, bitch got three. Four left, but four's more than enough. With dataterms, one's enough to pin you out. Wall or no wall, I don't stand too much of a chance.

First chance of a woman in three years and you wasted her.

Shut it.

What were you thinking about?

I said shut it.

Guess you've got to like all that pretty-boy ass...

My head is full of wild, crazy laughing.

"For chrissake! Fucking shut it!"

I'm trembling like a leaf. The steel butt of my D&K is resting on my temple. I tear it down, disgusted. I force a swallow. Then I hear the Wasters attacking the transport and run for the tickets.

In this town there are no second chances.

I get close to five metres before J.J. eyeballs me. He screams to his cronies but they're gunning the bird. As he snarls one jockey zips too close to the transport's icy turbines. The poor fuck is sliced. J.J. looks away. Sees me again. Decides to deal with this himself.

Dodging the rain of blood and twisted air-bike, the head Waster stabs at his handlebars and soars downwards.

Judging his speed I know I'm gonna get to the tickets first. After that I'm fucked. Nowhere to hide out here in the lot. Guess it's kill J.J. time.

With pleasure.

In my next few stumbling strides I reach the tags. They're floating lazily in Gut's blood. I stand astride them and face the in-coming jock. He's levelled off for a final approach. Kalashnikov aimed. Braced in his manicured little fingers. His tanned face shoved against the sight. Blond hair tied out of his baby-blue eyes. In the light from the burning cars he looks like the devil himself.

I raise my D&K just as I hear his weapon shoot. Damn near blows my head off. I feel pain in my neck and shoulder. Let my adrenaline deal with it.

My gun wavers. My sight blurs. I let off a shell that wings the bike on the chrome running board. Doesn't do a thing. Perhaps cost him twenty on a little sealant. Sure as shit don't stop him coming.

He allows himself another shot before his computer chalks the kill, but the speed of his approach throws him wide. I brace my pistol on my numbing forearm. When I fire again J.J. loses his right hand. The rifle tumbles. The hova-board spins. There's a sound like an engine over-revving. Then the air-bike stalls. J.J. meets the cement at terminal velocity. Skims the sidewalk like a stone. When he hits the shops on 13th he turns the whole block white. That's for my geo, you rich fuck.

I look smug. I can feel the thin grin on my face. I try not to glance at the mess that was once my left shoulder. All I'm worried about now are those damn train tickets.

I nearly shit my pants when I look down and they're gone.

I spin on my heels and almost hear my neck wound tear. I howl and try to focus. Corpses aside I'm alone in the lot. No one's here. No one's been here. So where'd the hell they'd go? I'm just about to notch it to hallucination when I clock the kid.

He's a good ten metres out on Belmont but I can still see those tags flashing in the orange light. Don't recognise the trash. Don't mean nothing here though.

I aim my .45 automatic and shoot. Curse as the shell blasts sidewalk. Kid dances amidst the splinters. Then he ducks sideways and is gone.

Running with a broken shoulder nearly wipes me out. But I do it. Reach the alley where the thief was. See a wall. Dead end. Gotcha you little fuck.

Through the blur I see shadows, but no kid. I bluff and call him out. He comes too. Just like a lamb. I can't believe it. Then just as I'm gonna waste the prick I see he's not got the tickets. I ask him where they are. Real pleasant like.

Shit says he's hidden 'em.

Back in the lot the fighting's ending. The transports outta range and soon the Wasters'll be getting bored. Also come looking for the man who shot their Pa.

I grab the trash by the throat. Try to wring it outta him. Jocks make short work of that. Already one of them's gunning up Belmont. Got vengeance written all over him. Nothing crazier than a pissed-off rich kid.

His front cannon makes mosaic of the shop fronts. I haul the kid into the alley and get low. As he buzzes past I empty my piece into him. The first shell ruptures his right thigh. The second makes short work of the back of his head. The scooter skids to a halt outside Black Julio's. I'm already on my way.

Dragging the kid, I ignore the shit's squeals. Straddle the jockey's hova-board. Hitting the pedals I feel the vehicle leap skywards. My insurance outta this hellhole holds on tight. Already the street's way outta reach. Hope he's not feeling suicidal. I sure ain't.

Once round the block, then beat the fuck and get the tickets. Piece of cake. 'Cept for the Wasters. The rest of the beach bums've noticed my tricks. Whoop-de-doo. Some nights it just ain't worth getting up.

With a roar of twin-valves, the surfers' pursuit begins. They come hollering like the three little drugged-up frat party dudes they are. After a moment gunfire joins the chanting. They're out of range, but that'll change soon enough.

Already thinking where to ditch the bike. I'm travelling south. Near enough. Guess that takes me downtown. Great. No one goes downtown. Least no one who wants to come back.

I hang a right onto 10th. Now I'm going east. That takes me to the bridge. And the bay.

"Hey shitface," I shout back. "Guess we're going to Sister's."

Dodging under a set of busted traffic beacons, I rev the scooter up to the rooftops.

Keep weaving, lad. Duck 'n' dive.

Duck 'n' dive. Too right.

Something makes me glance to the side.

One of the beach boys is coming up Fischer. Trying to cut me off at the intersection. I kill the grav on instinct alone. The board plummets. Sparks stream as it skims tarmac. The kid yowls. I laugh while above our heads windows are blown to pieces. Through the glass rain I hit the throttle. Slam it to full and feel the shit's fingernails in my side. Draw blood, baby.

Now I know he's holding on, I really move this mother.

Rolling it, I spin out and under the nearest attackers. Watch them shriek. Then head down Fischer.

Fischer is a slum. Gloom and doom. All burnt-out apartments. Truck cafes. Warehouses.

"I wanna get off!"

I grin like Death having a good day. What'd you think I was trying to do, shitface? All I wanted was a quiet night in. Just me and my date, y'know. Not really the sorta evening for a ride. The air's too thick. Thick with thieves.

The kid yells that they're coming. Tell me something else I don't know.

I've got to turn the tables. Give myself time to breathe. Think.

Think!

Off-balancing the board, I send trash cans flying. Coming in low, I enter the open doorway of an empty warehouse. As soon as I'm in, I plough the bike and shout at the runt.

"Hit the door!"

He obeys like it's in his coding. Jumping off the back, he's at the controls in a flash. Reaching up he punches the pad with both fists.

I sweat blood. Just like the eighty-three riots all over again. The entryway stays open. The shield door don't even shiver. Nothing.

My mind grills the possibilities. No power? Pass-coded? Just plain broke?

"Again," I scream, "Hit it again!"

Outside the three Wasters zip by the gaping throat of the warehouse. Still scared I've got more shells. Won't be fooled for long.

The mousey-haired scruff whacks the controls a second time. Double nothing. Fuck, what's wrong with it? Locked. Must be.

I look across past the manic-faced kid. In the box is a safety key secured by a chain. It's turned horizontal. Off-lock's vertical.

With a sound like a hundred hornet's nests, the O-Zoners descend for the kill. Game's wounded. Unarmed. Trapped.

Too bad, Nowhere.

They hover into position like a trio of fallen angels. All bronzed skin and lip gloss. Eyes smiling. If they waste me now they'll probably be back in time for their workouts. Slowly, agonisingly, they level their assorted firearms at my head.

Touché!

"It's safety locked, kid." My voice is cold, calm. Dead low. "Mean anything to you?"

I can tell by the way the trash blinks that it don't. Looking back at the blondies, I wince. Not like this. Oh fuck. There's a deafening resounding noise and I close my eyes tight. Thinking it's their guns. All perfectly together. In absolute, impossible unison. Like a hellish choir.

My eyes burn. My shoulder grinds. I flinch.

You owe me one.

Then nothing.

Then the real firing starts. And when it does it's somehow far away. Distant.

I strain to peer through the wet. I can hardly believe it when I see just the metal greyness of the entry door. The Wasters are blasting at the outside. Might as well be shooting at the moon. The kid is pulling on my left hand. My neck screams. I bat him away, so he heads off alone. I see sense and follow.

Who are you?

Who wants to know?

Out back broken trucks lie everywhere. Like some kinda weird techno elephant's graveyard. The gates lead onto the railway track. Beyond is darkness. Beyond that the lights of the bridge. Seeing the bridge I remember fishing and…

Daddy, I think I've got a bite!

And shut it off.

If I can see the bridge then Sister's can't be far. If she's still got that stupid cross all lit up then it shouldn't be too hard to spot.

Staggering in the hot night, I let the kid be my crutch. Slip through the torn gates. Head out. On the tracks I hear the bikes again, but don't give a shit. I'm beyond caring now. Let 'em come. I surrender. I surrender.

Luckily shitface don't feel the same.

Scooter lights sear the dark, but not on us. The surfers're combing the blocks. Their mistake. Guess they don't know this place too well after all. The way I feel it don't really matter. Even a blind man could track me down. Perhaps I should've stayed with the hova. Nah, sitting duck. I yowl at the pain. The kid hushes me. I keep moving. I can't even remember where.

Then I see the electric blue neon of the crucified son of God. Then I remember.

Hey Sis! Sister! It's Nowhere, babe. Y'know. Want to save my soul one more time, baby?

The kid sees me seeing the cross.

"That where your sister lives?" he asks.

I nod. Who cares if it hurts. Talk to forget it.

"Yeah. That's Sister's place. You'll like it. Real neat. Me and Sis go way back. Hey, I knew her when she didn't wear no knickers…"

The urchin frowns.

"We'd better hurry. Those lights are getting close."

Yeah I know, you shit. I don't have to look. I can hear 'em. Sounds like they've found the truckyard. Won't take long before they find us too. Not now.

Sister, you'd better be in, baby.

*

The door beneath the neon cross is black. And very very shut. I tell the kid to bang on it. He bangs. Nothing. Sweet fanny all.

"What's your name?" asks the brat.

"Nowhereman."

"That doesn't sound like a name."

"It isn't."

I notice that the fucking runt has the tickets. He's wearing them like a necklace. Till now they were stuffed in his shirt. He's got 'em in his hand. Too weak even to make a grab for them.

"You said you hid 'em," I mutter.

"I lied."

Of course he did. I choke back a laugh. Smart kid. Too fucking smart.

"What's your name, kid?"

"Don't know."

"Funny name."

"I just don't know it. OK?" Almost an apology.

"Bang again."

He bangs again.

"Well, from now on…"

The door is heaved inwards. Someone's been spying. It's the Sis. Even through my screwed-up eyes I can see the black bitch. All negro priestess and veils and satin. You were one tasty lady in your time, Midnight. Till you sold out to the God-U-Likes. Now no one gets a share except mr fucking almighty. Or whoever the big cheese is this week.

The woman is tall. Her muscular body thinly disguised under

black robes. Religious beads crowd her breast. In her hands she holds an M16.

"Fuck off, Jack."

I'm unperturbed.

"Hi Sis. Gonna take a miracle this time…"

"So I can see." She grimaces at the mess that's my neck. "Saviour's left town, Jack. You know that."

"For me?"

"For everyone."

"Oh c'mon, Midnight. Just for old time's sake."

"I said fuck off and I mean it."

The barrel of the gun hovers menacingly.

"Baby…"

Then she notices the trash. As if for the first time. Maybe he's too short for the peephole.

"Who's this?"

I smile when the kid tells her he don't know.

"I call him Shitjack," I say real nonchalant. "He's with me."

Sister's eyes turn to slits. But the gun lowers.

"So I can see. Jack, if this is a bribe… Or some sorta dumb ploy…"

"Please, ma'am." The kid's a natural. So cool. All the right moves. "Ma'am, he's hurt pretty bad. He thinks you can help. You being his sister 'n' all."

I try not to look smug. Keep it going, runt. Sister's unsure. Knows even I wouldn't pull a stunt like this. Yet still unsure.

"He said you went way back."

Stop right there, you little…

"He said you don't wear no knickers."

Jeez. A natural, huh? A natural prime prick that's all. But Sister's blushing. I can see it on her big brown face. Clear as day. Well, I didn't know you had it in ya…

"That was a long time ago," she says.

Then she looks up from the grubby punk. Heard the voice of the Lord, Sis? Or maybe the beach boys come to fuck my ass?

"Ave maria," she hisses, "Wasters!"

She's heard 'em.

"Mûhamet, have mercy on my soul… You'd better come in."

Beyond the black door everything's candlelit. Kinda spooky. Shitjack holds my hand. I tug it free and almost fall on my face. Sister Midnight shoulders her sub and checks me over. Takes my D&K. Frisks me.

Oh baby, lower! Lower!

She smells the cum in my pants and draws away. The glance she gives the boy says it all. I let her think what she likes. So long as she fixes me up, who cares?

Sister leads us into a dark room. Starts lighting more candles. No electric on the bay? Nah, what powers that neon. Must prefer it all creepy. Still, have to ask.

"What's with the candles?"

She doesn't answer. Her look's rebuke enough. In the flickering light I see three beds.

"Lie down," she says.

"You never had to ask me twice," I joke.

"Look, I'm helping you because of what happened on 13th and Logan. Nothing else…"

"The A-Men?"

She crosses herself.

"Fuck the A-Men! 13th and Logan. Nothing else. Got it? I owe you one and this is it. And in the morning you're out."

She turns to the kid.

"That means you too."

"Yes ma'am."

I can almost hear her heart break.

Footsteps in the hall. Then a voice. "Sister Midnight?" Stern as fuck.

The black woman leaves at once. So who's this? The angel fucking Gabriel?

Mumblings from outside. Sounds ominous. I fill with some small talk. Keeps my mind off the pain.

"Haven't seen you round here much. Ya new?"

The kid is looking into his lap. His hands have got blood on them. It's shaken him.

"Only for about... I don't know how long. Few weeks."

"Uptown?"

"Where's that?"

"Where I met you?"

"Nah. Near the river."

"Westside?"

"Guess."

"Where before that?"

"The coast."

"This *is* the coast."

"No, the other one."

"What other one?" But I know already. He means the west coast...

"Y'know. The other one."

If he came from the west coast then–

"How in hell'd you get here?"

If he came from the west coast then he must've come on...

"The train."

The train! The E-250 out of Christville. Good ol' Smokey from surf city! Holy Moses.

"You were on the train?" Incredulous.

"Yeah, so?"

"Well, urm... How? Why? How'd you ever get on it?"

"My daddy put me on."

Sister Midnight walks back in. Tells me to lie down. I tell her to shut it.

"Your daddy put you on the train? Alone?"

The Sister's eyes widen. "This runt was on the train?"

My look says it all. If I was stronger and didn't need her so bad, I'd introduce her face to the floorboards.

"No. Mummy and Lisa were with me. We were going somewhere real important."

"East-11?"

"Yeah, that's it, I think."

East-11. Well, that makes sense. The waystation gateway to near-space. Huge fortified platforms dealing in orbital traffic too big to land dirtside. Was once a whole bunch of these. About fifty. Running along the coast. Serving the big cities. Most've been abandoned or destroyed since the collapse. East-11 was the E-250's last stop. Guess the kid's family were bound for the stars.

"Why were you going there?"

"Don't know. I can't remember."

"Like your name?"

"Yeah."

"Jack." Sister looks flushed again. "This kid sounds special…"

"You think I don't know that?" The shout costs me a couple of moments' consciousness. "So why'd you get off here?"

Shitjack's eyes well tears.

"Don't blub. Just tell me!"

"Jack. Don't be so harsh. He's only a kid. He's probably had a really rough time."

"And I haven't I guess?"

"Hush. Now c'mon, honey. Tell Esther what happened."

Her words draw the kid back to himself. The street brat actually falls for her old mother act. Forget the kid, Sister, *you're* really special…

"It was the hider man," he says finally.

"And what did he do?"

"He stole our tickets."

I snort. "Bad dude."

"Jack!" Sister warns. I take the hint. I wanna know too much. "Then what happened, honey?"

There's a pause. The brat bites his lip. But when the kid speaks next it's as if he's been wanting to tell someone this story for a long time.

"My daddy's an offworld engineer first class and he was going away for a long, long time. So he sent us away too. To stay with someone else…" He digs in his mind for who, but comes up empty. "We were two days running non-stop across the territories. Then we had to stop here. That was when the hider man got on. He tried to kill me. I got away though. I can run fast."

"I can vouch for that." My quip's ignored.

Sister leans closer to the lad. "And the others? Your Mummy and… sister?"

The way he shakes his head fills in the gaps. Still I'm naturally curious.

"So they can't run as fast. Where'd this happen?"

"Here. At the crossing."

A light comes on right in the front of my mind. The pieces fit together like some gruesome jigsaw. After all, the E-250 only comes through once a month. With more than mere intuition I say, "And I suppose this hider man wasn't a husky-voiced redhead with a tight ass in a mink coat by any chance?"

The kid looks dumfounded, but nods anyhow. Lucille! You dirty crappy son of a bitch! You total pile of shitting–

But all I say is, "Fuck." Just like that. Guess that explains where Lucille got the tickets, how he got outta this shithole and why this kid was trying to steal mine. My mind lolls like a limp dick, but I haven't forgotten why this brat's still living. Painfully I lean forward.

"Give me those tickets." Wonder why I ask. Shitjack – or whoever he really is – recoils. Forces himself into the corner of the room. Where the bed meets the wall.

I stand. Fierce as a bear. Nearly black out.

"I said, give me those tickets!"

My hand's out. Reaching. Grasping.

"Oh Jack. The train!" What's that crazy broad saying? Piss it, Sis. I saw 'em first. Go find your own brat.

"Jack, for once in your life, listen. The train's coming into town. Tonight… Shit, what's the time?"

I blink back the motes of darkness. Don't realise the importance of what she says. Then everything swims into focus. Suddenly everything's impossibly clear. No wonder Gut didn't care who saw him. He was getting out fast. Probably had a geo revved and running.

The train? Tonight? Has Lucille really been gone a whole month? Guess so.

Here's your chance, Nowhere. All you have to do is stay alive long enough and you're outta here.

Outta here. That sounds good.

Real good.

Pity I can hardly walk. Guess I still need the kid. And the Sis. Maybe I can pull this off yet. I'm shot to fuck, but I can always rest on the long ride to East-11.

Distant knocking. Someone else's at the door.

"Don't answer it," I mumble.

"Who is it?" Sister asks me.

The unmistakable gunning of engines follows the knocking.

"Ave maria!" she exclaims.

Yep Sis, it's the Wasters. And my guess is they're not here for midnight mass. That's what I think. What I say is: "They're here for the boy."

OK, so I lied to her. Won't be the first time. Won't be the last. The Sister swallows it though.

"Follow me. The cellars lead out to a storm door near the tracks."

Hook, line and fucking sinker.

★

We get about five maybe ten metres down the hallway when the black door busts open. The lock skittering on the tiles. Sister screams like she's never seen a raid. Guess she ain't. Not in a long time. The blonde surfers crowd the hole where the door was. Their headlights throw vast shadows down to greet us. Looks like the mountain's arrived, Mûhamet.

The next step takes us into the chapel. Sis slams the door as if it leads outta Hell. Not a moment too soon. Lead blasts candles but can't get through the wood at our backs. Too goddamn thick.

"Praise fuck for small mercies," I whisper to no one in particular.

The chapel looks like a sepulchre. Seems appropriate. My best guess gives us about twenty seconds. Then Sister Midnight slams a bent piece of rusty iron across the door and I add sixty. By then we'll be well away.

Except for the altar, everything's dark. I follow the Sis and the kid. Following's not my scene, but she knows the way and he's holding me up. All I'm thinking about is the train. And where the black bitch put my D&K.

Behind the wood the Wasters're running across the tiles. I can hear their loafers squeaking. Some other sisters are in the hall. Gunfire. Screams. I hate the thought that I'm at the back. Still let 'em try to get through ten centimetres of solid wood and a thick metal bar. Unless they've got something pretty heavy-duty, they'll take–

One of the buddies tries the door. Shoves it. Shoves it harder. Then silence. I distrust silence. I expected hammering. Bad-mouthing. Shooting. Then I catch the bikers' scrambled retreat. I don't for a minute think they're giving up and going home.

I look round and see only wooden pews. We're passing the altar. Its gaudy monitor flashes 'Jehovah Saves' in a blaze of colour. I disregard that. The altar's stone. No time to speak. Spent too much looking around. So I just lunge forwards. Try to force the others down with me.

My ears bleed with the explosion. It deafens me. Makes the floor quake. Makes me quake too. First I see of the Wasters is when they berserk through the rubble. Can't get up for trying. I'm pinning the kid to the floor.

Somehow the leading jockey boy reels, spraying guts. I can't believe it. A total fucking miracle.

Sis is standing with her M16, spraying lead. The others retreat and get it in the back. I see them open up. Glad the kid's under me. Don't want him to see this.

The black-robed woman empties her clip into the twitching

bodies. Then she throws her gun away and pulls me to my knees. Checks the boy. He's looking bad. We all are.

Sister mouths some shit, but I can't hear nothing. I shrug and pull myself the rest of the way. As the trash staggers, I get angry at this whole bloody mess. Make a snatch for Shitjack's necklace. Guess I'm too slow. Sister grabs my wrist. Her face is like thunder. I sneer. She slaps it away with the back of her hand. I want to kill her, but can't even get up. I want to lie down and die. But I can't do that either. Not while there's hope.

Some hope.

Have faith, Jack. S'the only way...

Faith? What sorta shit's that?

Lacking faith like a second prick, I put the half-dazed boy under my right arm and try to stumble to the front door. Those palm shirts won't need their hovas anymore. Can't think of a better way of getting to the crossroads. Might not even have to dream up a way of stopping the fucking train. Just fly up and step on.

Now that's style.

Fuck style. Just get your ass on that train.

The walk down the tiled hall takes forever. Keep tripping on bodies. If Sis follows I'm unaware of it. Can't take her anyhow. These tickets are singles. Totally one-way. Don't bother me much. Might bother her. Especially if she gets any more clues that I'm not doing this for the kid. Hell, she knows already.

My ears are still playing the same tune. I look round. Yeah, she's there. Face like a chewed-up old toffee. The whites of her eyes shining. The jockey's rifles are slung over her shoulder. Shit, why didn't I think of that?

Must be slipping.

Out in the dirt the three grav-scooters wait. Patient in the dark. Keeping my insurance close, I gun up the engine. Watch as Sister shadows me. My ears are beginning to work again. I hear a whistle and know the train's coming. Liked it better deaf.

"Give me a gun, Sis," I say.

See her hesitate. Never seen that before. Never refused me nothing. Ever. Paranoia grabs at that thought. Plays on my mind.

Sister hands over a rifle. I look at it. Empty the shells. Then I ask for my gun. Now the bitch's real edgy. You can tell when the Sister's edgy. She bites her fat lip. She's doing it now. Her strong white teeth scraping the flesh. When she's done, she licks her lips.

She's never refused me and she ain't starting now. She pulls my D&K from her robes. Hands it over. Hands over some shells too. I try to grin as I load it. Probably fail, but who gives a shit. Then I rev the bike and send it bucking. Above the ringing I hear Sister following. Now I'm at the front. Suits me a whole lot better. Feel good inside. Outside I feel shit. Feel's good feeling shit.

Then I see the train.

It comes like a tiger with its tail on fire. Lightning fast. Unstoppable. Ten thousand tonnes of metal inevitable. Lights shine along its length. Front spiked with aerials and guns and turrets. It's a sight for sore eyes. A real treat for a bloody, broken bastard like myself. I lean on the throttle. Feel the hova pick up speed. Get above the tracks and coast. The coldness of the air numbs some of the pain. I open my big mouth to cry out. Then shut it quick. Sister's alongside playing with the battlescans. She's biting her lip real bad now. Have to approach from the rear. Front's a death-trap. Would need a small army to take on this mother.

Trying to gauge the speed of the locomotive, I kick the scooter to full. The acceleration almost throws me off. Shitjack's hanging on. I look back. The train's nearly upon us. It ain't gonna stop this time. The crossing is maybe a kilometre or two away and nothing short of Jesus H. Christ is gonna halt this black beauty. A scummy fuckville like ours's not a popular stop. Who'd wanna get off here?

In my mind I run over the plan. I see the E-250 slide like a midnight eel below the skidpads. I see me bringing the bike down. Get level with one of the carriages. Find an open window. Maybe shoot one out. Come close. Grab the tickets. Leap off. I try to shut out the way the hova goes down. Unfortunately imagination wins and I see the kid fight against the wheels. Then he and the bike go under.

There's a grinding. A slight bump. A little blood on the bogie. Sayonara Shitjack. Hello East-11!

I shiver. But like life, I just keep on going.

In a flash, the train's sleekness is under me. The kid screams as I tear the air-bike down. The fucking mother's moving faster than this piece of shit ever could. I frantically look back. Can't see any windows. Guess I've got about thirty seconds before I'm out of train. My face runs with sweat, blood, the whole caboodle. Sister's above me, slightly behind. She's got the hova's cannons ready. I can see the ghostly green glinting in her eyes.

Gimme a break, you black fuck. You still owe me one.

I slam the bike into overdrive. Hear the engine complain. Starts breaking up. For a moment I match the speed of the E-250. Pull out my automatic and level it at the nearest door hatch. The shocked faces inside the carriages are a joke. Ain't these rich fuckers ever seen anything? I ignore 'em, but Shitjack's pointing. His finger singles out a suit who's running up the aisle. His thin hair makes him look older. So do his glasses. His id is yellow.

Offworlder. Another fucking Waster. Different kind maybe, but still growing fat by slagging off the earth. When you've got a lot you waste a lot. When you got nothing, you waste nothing. Wonder why the kid's so concerned. When I hear him calling, it all comes flooding back.

"Daddy! Daddy! Mister, my daddy's on the train! He's come to find me."

Shitjack's ecstatic. Nearly jumping off the bike. The labouring engine whines horribly. And I don't know what to do. Then the Sister's voice barks over the com-link. Loud and clear. Like the voice of God.

"Don't do it, Jack. Whatever it is you've got planned in that crazy fucked-up head of yours, just forget it. Put the kid on the train and let's get the fuck outta here."

No. I can't do it Sister. No fucking way.

"No!" I scream into the night. "I wanna ride!"

That's my lad.

The Sister's shouting now. Trying threats.

"You worthless fuck! Put the kid on the train or so help me God I'll blow you right out the air!"

I believe her. Who wouldn't. I guess I can't win. The engine's ready to blow. If I keep to this speed for much longer I'm dead. If I try to board, I'm dead. If I stay, I'm dead. Whichever way, I'm dead. Yet maybe…

"You still owe me one!" Over the mike this time.

"What?"

The grav grinds, fracturing metal.

"I said, you owe me one."

"Name it."

"You trash the God-U-Likes and reform."

"The A-Men?"

"Yeah."

The suit has his face pressed up against the glass. He looks like a clown. Shitjack's screaming, crying, laughing. All at once. What a brat.

"I don't know, Jack…"

"This ain't no time for don't knows!" My D&K blasts a hole the size of Central Station in the window. Within everything scatters. Everything takes flight and people scream. I make ready to jump.

"No, Jack! OK! You and me… It's a deal!"

Thought you'd see it my way.

With a dull thud I send the bike bumping against the ebony carriage. Already the offworlder's reaching out and pulling the little runt inside. Behind his specs, his eyes bleed tears. As he looks up, I see myself in their reflection. I remember before I can stop it. Of the way it was.

With his son held tightly in his arms, the suit mouths something. It's probably thanks, but I try real hard not to make it out. In return I bare my teeth, lean close and spit. The phlegm hits his id square. Oozes down the holo like a slug. *Fuck you, waster. I don't want your thanks.*

Then the anti-grav screams and the whole engine breaks apart.

Losing speed like virginity, I plunge dangerously close to the tracks and the racing wheels. I don't have to think what's next. The front of the air-bike sparks against the metal. I pull the throttle but it's useless.

Suddenly the Sister's beside me and without thinking I jump. Land like a corpse on her tailgate. Sends us spinning out of control. Still the Sister's a big girl. She hauls the scooter skywards and turns to get clear of the train. Last I see of the E-250 it's clearing the crossing and pounding out across the bridge. Then I let my exhaustion take me and drift lazily towards internal dark. Still the Sister's not done with me yet. She's asking where we're going.

"Head for Belmont," I drool. "I've sorta got a date that's getting cold."

Sister Midnight throws her head back at this. Laughs long and hard. I try too. Fail. Try to convince myself that I belong here not out there. Fail again. I think of the future. Then shut it off.

"We make a good team, you and me," I croak.

"Amen to that," she replies as we skim the rooftops of Eleventh.

"Sis, I–"

But I can't go on. I'm out before my head hits the backfin.

Amen, mr Nowhereman.

6 | D'ALESSANDRO

According to the word on the stream the whale was dead when it reached the Sûrabian outstation at Arkhangelsk. The intercept vessel was of unspecified make and model, assigned with code orange clearance. Its origin in near-space was unspecified. Its mission at the outstation unverifiable. The only recoverable data was a snatch of footage taken by transference freeway security. It showed the t-freighter clearly as it docked, albeit only for a few frames. Yet it was enough. Enough for me to recognise that I was correct. It had begun.

The countdown had started.

Regrettably I did not hear any more of the leviathan's fate until fourteen hours after the crew of the unknown ship had cut out its brain. Though I am a prisoner in this cold icy tomb that I call home, an ex-replicator should still try to keep informed. Set upon a manmade rig, its stilts sunk deep into an unclassified abyssal plain so close to the otherworldly planet-axis as to be almost upon it, I languish at Osakimo macrocorp's pleasure in great and honourable Kasikianu Imperial Detention Unit. Hardly Hyperborea, this station was constructed to claim sea lanes when such pursuits as landgrabbing physical space were deemed important. In this place where all directions point down and the sun rises and sets but once per annum, by that calculation I have been here not yet a week, but it feels like a thousand years.

Admittedly my incarceration was a far cry from a job of splicing living tissue and cells into anima, yet it has its parallels. And my window to the outside world is a lot larger than my captors realised, yet it did mean that I must lower myself to the level of twilight gutter-jock.

"Hey, punch it you zeros, that's Nobody's Hero and *Kickin' The Cops*. Check it out!"

The music bleeds like thick saliva through my bins. It is some splatterjazz by a Jixxie band I'd heard once in Medical Academy. Unbelievably retro, impossibly outdated, but these few dozen 3Es are all I have. Five hundred gigabytes of educational, encyclopaedic, entertainment on a five-centimetre disc. Spawned as the ultimate in storage for all your data requirements. Well, for about six months. Then came the 3E+, but that's progress. My twenty thousand gigabytes of data hardly lasts a week. Try playing that over three years and see how endlessly tiring it becomes.

"It's your very own muso media deity, the supreme being himself, beaming live and direct from Radio God. We have a commercial-free hour comin' atcha all this decade, so grab your knob and jack… it… up!"

I slam in another random 3E and listen as the tiny disc slurs into motion. Kicking the deck under the desk makes the casing grind, then Zed McGuire stops stuttering and gets on with the next track.

So this is Radio God. My window to the world. Made possible by patching the prison's e:node by way of an illegal switch sunk into the cement at my feet. Suitably cloaked, of course. I run this tinpot place on automatic now, my actual attention focused on the twelve monitors to my left. Data spews across half of them as tracer programs search for keywords amidst every open channel on the sat-wave communications data-pan that is the stream. The current keywords are 'replication', 'hostgod' and 'Amen'. I have no preference. Any or all of the above.

In twenty-eight seconds FXSAT-11 will pass beyond the snow-locked horizon and I'll have to try for another patch. That is tricky, even for a professional like myself. Using pirate orbitals is my only recourse if I want to keep my work a mystery. The dozen screens are dotted around the red and black spaghetti jungle that spews out of every niche. Only four are doing anything remotely useful, bearing strange banks of numbers corresponding to earth-bound coordinates. Routing software hacked from Amtech feeds voraciously on these and keeps its e:node maps bobbing neatly alongside. Using old schematics pulled from the military dataphials in Bioheim – it's rumoured they've got the whole solar system on file circa midcentury – the procs provide a walkthru wireframe of any given subject's locality. Admittedly this tech is twenty years out-of-date, but believe me it's better than a slide rule.

Many men are driven by the absurdly stupid notion of getting even. I, on the other hand, get more odd.

For once upon a time I was a man with a dream. A dream to be a god. An undeniable need to possess a name that shall never die beneath the heavens. And a form to go with that name. A body that could transcend the inevitability of death. It was a dream that destroyed everything I am or had or was.

And that is what my story so far is about. More or less.

The destruction of Nathaniel Raymond Glass and the creation of the Amen.

To be the first. To be the last. To be both creator and Creator. It all began so well, and then suddenly the Phoenix was being bombed to ashes, the marshals were dredging the incinerator and the XEs hostgod sentience was autorestructuring in the exosphere above me. And I, cuffed like a dog, saw for the first time the danger of dreaming dreams no mortal ever dared to dream before.

I watch idly as the processors hum to themselves, cue up the next jingle and fix myself a cigarillo. For the first fifteen months I wasn't allowed matches. Now look at me. All hail for special treatment. Someone out there must really like me.

The brown cigar looks good between my spider-thin fingers. The smoke feels better in my lungs.
>00224568:00482811@00001622:01.

One of the rows of golden numbers catches my eye. Then another.
>00224569:00482612@00001623:01.

Both show a datacurve that interests me mathematically. Us

replicators are all the same. It's in the blood. Once you've manually hauled P52s as long as I have, you never can break the habit.

The data matches two of the screens exactly; at least to within the nearest metre. It would appear that Jack and Esther have teamed up. Pity. It would have been a lot better for all of us if he'd just done what he was told and caught the train. Now I must find another plan, but there is only so much one can accomplish in my present circumstances.

Looking between the two wireframes, I notice that both appear to have a datablank over their immediate terrain. No buildings are showing. No undulations of ground surface. I run a quick diagnostic on the validity of the output, but it all tallies. AOK. I wonder at this and then as Zed goes ape in his final guitar duel, I realise just what's going on. The Z-co's hold the answer.

They're a thousand metres up.

Almost simultaneously this realisation is accompanied by a sudden interplay of demodulator codes and icy static. Then as one all the screens go down.

FXSAT-11 is out of sight.

7 | PURE

When the firefight begins it's like a dance. Hypnotic like a symmetric wheel in its lazy whirling choreography. Set to the haunting music still buzzing in my head. Rock ballet never was this sweet. Protopop waltz never as smooth. A last masochism tango before the bitter end. As I stand staring at Lucille, eyes wide at her appearance in the here and now, outside Wolves' guns fire flashing like the cameras of raincoated reporters. Splintering wood and glass, the shots rip through the door at my back and I dive. Landing, I check myself over and find I'm OK, then look up and see the man with the planes is not so lucky. He has a wound that sits upon his jacket like a red buttonhole spray. Ravn's gun is a hand's reach from my flattened body. Ravn is too, but I pay him no heed. I grab for the Sentinel Panther with dirty fingers. I am a dancer again, reaching for that final pose. Out and out I stretch while Ravn shivers. Grab the weapon and turn it toward the redhead while above the walls resound like timpani.

"Gimme the gun," says Lucille. Playful like she's asking for me to pass some thermo straighteners. "Gimme the gun and we'll both fly."

"Ut-uh," I say, struggling to define a coherent sentence. "You can't just appear here – *now!* – and be this casual."

"What else do you suggest? Lililuna crimson powersuit and matching Rodanthe rhinestones?"

"That's not what I meant and you know it."

Above us the ceiling fan explodes as the Wolves circle for another volley. We duck our heads while Lucille drags me against the stone fireplace.

"Oh, Susie-Sue! You damn reek, girlfriend. Have you no shame. Or Eau de Coco?"

"I haven't got time for this shit, you hot tranny mess."

Crawl over to Ravn but he's dead already. Ricochet got him clean through the heart.

Pausing only an instant, I give him the gun. Give it to him with the butt to the side of the head as hard as I can. Then again and again until I bust open the base of his skull. Dig around and rip out his dataphial. S'like pulling his keys from the pocket of his pants.

"You won't need that." Lucille smiles her maddening smile. "We have our own ride, baby-doll."

Made real by the sun's golden fierceness the first biker rides into the room, all guns blazing. He isn't expecting us to be on the floor. Or half-hidden behind a corpse. Or with a gun and a good aim. He isn't expecting to have his face blasted either, and after that he doesn't much care about anything. In the aftermath I take his weapon and his bike and rev it, ready to go.

"You coming?" I ask the redhead, handing her the Sentinel. "I won't ask twice."

"Delighted," Lucille bats back.

Soon as the lady-man's aboard we burst out the back door screaming blue murder. Whirling in the dust I spray bullets at the circling Wolves. Ready to dance the final dance.

The hangar lies about four hundred metres across the sand-red yard. Beyond the security fencing. Beyond the ring of bikers. It might as well be on another shitting planet. And riding a bike with punk guts on your hands is tough. The ache at the back of my neck tells me I need the needle *now*. But I can't. That would need two hands. One to give and one to take. One to give the pain, one to take the pleasure. Got both hands on the bars now, gripping tighter than a vice. So tight they're numb. Tight tight.

As we race my blonde hair whips into my eyes, but I can't let go of the bars. I fear that if I do I'd lose grip of everything. Sand blasts my ice-white face. Gets in my bloodshot eyes. Motes of grit like dancing golden snowflakes. Blink away the false tears. Keeping my real emotions deep.

"I have so missed this level of insanity," Lucille laughs in my ear.

The ring of Wolves is a ring of steel. Steel and chrome and oily hair flying. Surprise is on my side, but they've got the numbers to make up for that tenfold.

I guess that means I don't wanna die. Not here. Not now. I wanna get to the plane. To get away. But we're never going to get through the ring, not unless I jump it.

Turn left. Forty degrees. Then slide.

Spin the bike and plough sand every which way. Hit the deck as a hundred guns start roaring. Skim along on my face. Then the world opens and swallows us up. We drop like a little stone, bike coming after, following like a dog. We land in an undignified mess in the dirt of a tunnel. Impact jars me back to the real world. Right, I remember this. It's Ravn's emergency exit if things got rough. Must've taken him years to dig it on his own.

He didn't dig it on his own. He hired some junkies. I have the schematics right here...

"Did you hear that?" I ask the redhead as we scrabble in the twilight. "That voice?"

"What voice? You must be more wasted than you look."

Let it go. Can't squander time on all that. Already got Wolves firing down the crack. Start crawling. Me first, Lucille after. We get about twenty metres when the first biker lands in the dirt behind us. Blasts the dark and misses. Press myself up against the tunnel wall. Watch the transsexual's shadow do the same. Next shot's thrown wide by two compardres as they land on his back. In the confusion of curses we carry on.

After who knows how far the tunnel dead ends with an iron ladder and dusty trapdoor. My high-heeled boots strike like hammers on the hollow rungs. Force open the wood and emerge between corridors made of bottle-green oil drums. It's the hangar. Slam the trapdoor and push a drum over the panel. Look up. All around rusty metal walls crouch, but above the girders stop. Above is only sky. Looking up I realise I'm sweating like a pig. Feel the beads form rivulets down my spine. My vision is so defined it hurts. Reality's kicking back with a vengeance.

Ravn's brig's here, but's now joined by a great white bird waiting with its slim wings furled. The circular logo marks it as a corporate nightflier. Designation identifiers say 'Osakimo'.

"Your friends?" I ask.

"You have no idea," the redhead purrs and starts walking towards the on-ramp. "So, your place or mine?"

"I… I don't know. Just give me a minute here."

"Well, as mother used to say: 'If you don't know where you're going, any bus will take you there.'"

At our feet the trapdoor bucks. Drum shudders but that's about it. I don't wait to see if it's gonna hold.

"Yours," I say and follow in Lucille's perfumed wake. Up into the sleek entryway. Knowing I've sold out now. I'm in for the duration. But I just go with it. Just *cope*. Scrabble up into the tiny cockpit and watch as the ship autopilots into motion. As the bird jerks upwards I hear the trapped bikers shoot. Trying to bust the lock they think I've bolted. As we climb into the azure desert skies I hear them shooting again. This time they hit the drum. Blow the whole fucking place into oblivion. Erupting below our wings. One great ring of blood-red apocalypse.

Serenely we rise heavenwards like a phoenix from the pyre, then Lucille kicks the thrusters and I feel the Gs against my pounding breast. And the relief washing me like summer rain.

The feeling ignites others. Now I know what I want. Why I'm along for the ride. What this is all about.

I want to be Pure again.

8 | DINGO THE WONDER DOG

Shift's over for another night. Now I sit in my room watching Bixby sleeping.

Bixby is a good dog most times. It felt right to have saved him from the burning City Hall. Good company too. Most times. This attic's not right for Bixby though. He needs to run around. He's getting fat on all those tidbits fetched from the kitchen. I should take him out more. Don't know when, 'cause I'm waiting tables most nights and cooking and clearing. And sleeping most days. Too dangerous to let him out on his own. He'd just get eaten. Best then to keep him in and ignore his bulging belly.

Been a long, long time since all that happened. A lot of growing up time. Trying to forget all about the boy in my furry lap. About the things he said and the way he just stopped dead like an old clock. Y'know the one the mice ran down before getting their tails cut off with a carving knife. Or was it before they walked a crooked mile? I forget. Or maybe I don't wanna remember. You ever get things like that? Things you force outta your mind so far that they're the only things you think about? Like dreams of being a slick superhero mutt? Like holding Benjamin Goode's cold hand while the world ended. So what was a friendless pup and his pet to do in a post-collapse megalopolis? We hitched the first ride that came by where the people inside didn't beat us with sticks.

And that's how I wound up waiting tables at the Werehouse.

Y'see the Werehouse started when all us crazy-assed pseudo-freaks broke out their cages at the RuZu. Didn't have nowhere to go so started their own streetgang. It was either that or end up as hotdogs! They call themselves some weird grunty name. Folks know 'em as Gonks 'R' Us.

The Werehouse is a kinda wandering clubhouse, gang lair and goodtimehappyplace all rolled into one. Its very name conjures up images of B-movie monsters and blood-wet fangs, don'tcha think? The Werehouse's owned by this entrepreneur named Johnnie Redd and under his hand it's become the ultimate venue for the tragically hip. It was Redd's idea to go commando. Flitting from one place to another. Ducking and diving. It's difficult to tell you where it is now, or where it will pop up next; what's easier is to tell you where it's been. The first time, The Werehouse was at a disused warehouse right in the middle of Central. Place was full of furniture and shit, then came the collapse, then the spray painters moved in. First party was on a cold wet winters night, then after that it appeared at almost every bomb ruin this side of the bridge. Moved every which way and you were really lucky to catch it. Had a zillion addresses; some really cool, others just dives.

Next was on 5th and H Street, next after that in the O-Zone, and once it got a reputation for being *the* place to party, Gonks started looking at more upmarket venues – and that led them to start eyeing up the multi-levelled pad of the Knight of K/OS. There's been lots of battling between the Knights and the Gonks. The tuffing-out to get this place was long and hard and bloody, but everyone agrees that this is the greatest Werehouse in the whole world ever. It used to be an old cinema complex and now it's my home.

Still I've got others things on my mind most mornings. Like keeping an eye on Room 0-0-3. Beth's room.

She's my girl whether she knows it or not.

We talk most days, but the only bit of intimacy we get together is through the knothole in the boards.

I lie on the bed and half flop onto the floor. With one hand I support my weight while the other searches for my velcro pants. My right eye is pressed against the wood. Against the oval crack.

Below is Beth's bedroom. All velvet coverings and kilim rugs. She's a real classy cat. Never takes 'no' for an answer. Always takes money instead.

They say growing up's a one-way street of pain, but in my comic it certainly has its perks.

Between the dresser and the wardrobe lies the bed and between the headboard and the sheets lies Beth. She's naked exposing the soft hair of her breasts and the glorious fur of her thighs. The milky skin of her legs and arms snakes provocatively around a long orange pillow that she embraces as she slumbers.

I know she's dreaming of me. Or leastways I wished she was. I wished I was that silken pillow. It's more than a crush. Much more'n that. I think it's love. Haven't told no one else about it, otherwise they'll all tease me. And I don't want to be teased. Well, perhaps by Beth. Yeah, that would be nice.

Oh Beth, you are divine. Please sleep so I can look. Please wake and see me looking. Please murmur my name. Please rise and call me to you…

My paw jigs happily between my hunched legs as I watch the nymph twitch and roll. As she tosses, I'm tossing. As she writhes, I'm writhing. As she stiffens, so I…

I take it you think you're on a surveillance mission?

Whassat? Oh, it's you! I was… I was…

Oh never mind, I'll come back later.

9 | SISTER MIDNIGHT

I ride upon the air bike, my tired knuckles straining. The jockcycle bucks under my weight and the weight of the unconscious Jack. Just kick him off, I let my mind think. Just one boot and you'll be rid of the slug forever. It's a nice thought. A nice quick easy thought. The sort of thought that makes straight lines out of life's thick tangle. Yet it is a thought that gets me nowhere. If I'd been able to trash the trash, he'd have been gone a long time ago.

So why's he still here?

But that question is not so nice. Not so quick and easy. That thought plumbs deeps too long left undisturbed. Too long left dark and untouched. Some places are so sacred no one should ever go there. Upon which no foot should ever tread. Yet have I not learned anything from my disbelief? Have these years upon my knees done nothing to draw clarity from the well of confusion. Jack's insistence that we reform his broken dreams is a desperate ploy, a transparent ruse that works only due to the massacre we leave behind in our wake.

I look down at The Nowhereman and remember other stuff. Like my sermon to him as he lay unconscious. Just as dead to the world as he is right now. Like how we all ended up here and now. That tarnished brick road that once shone like gold. Feel a welling in my breast, so start talking again. It's either that or I'll scream.

"Yeah, I 'member the last day we were all together. As clear as if I was there right now. Was just before the Glass-Suko attack. Temperature way up in the forties. Dusk. Sun was skimming the western horizon like a big red toffee apple. Cruising Eleventh as we always did.

Marking our turf. Patrolling the perimeter. Keepin' the Grims off our land. Just me an' Exor inside. Rest of 'em up top catching the rays. I was right side of thirty then. Had my whole life rehearsed. Had it all rolling out before me like some great velvet carpet. We had the Phoenix. We owned the whole block. We had enough power to last our natural lives. We were all laughing. At least *we* were all laughing. Don't recall you doing much. You just sat around keeping yourself to yourself. Then you decided it all had to change.

"Things were getting too easy. Too smooth. You thought we were getting too fat. Lazy. I dunno. You were getting pissed. Those days we had it all and you decided you wanted more. Maybe you wanted less. Maybe you wanted to fuck us all off. Who knows. You just left one day with Pure and when you came back you had a head fulla crazy nothing. Silver-tongued bitch licked you into shape. No doubt got *her* tongue in some real private places. Places I couldn't touch. Not in a lifetime of licking. And you listened too. You were took right in. Weren't you? *Weren't you?* That damn honky tart had you hog-tied good and proper.

"You was planning, but you didn't tell us. No way, Jose. You just started pissing off the others. Start joy-ridin' the streets. Start fucking with things best left for the big boys. And all the time old miss virgin's giving you all the sweet talk you need. Fucked from dawn to dusk. Never saw your pretty ass.

"You were probably screwing around when the Grims initiated the attack on City Hall. You damn near answered their calls. Not till it was way too late. They didn't stand a hope in hell. They had auto-cannons bigger than your cheap trick's ass. Blew them clean away. Shitehawk. Exor. Biggs. All gone, Jack. All gone."

Jack doesn't move. Doesn't twitch. Might just as well be talking to my other god. So that's what I do.

Dear God Mûhamet, when I dreamed of running away this wasn't what I had in mind. I wanted to be free, but not like this. This is bad. This stinks. I wanted hope, not a whole load of old trouble.

Do not try to hold back your feelings to me, dreaming angel. I am supreme. What lies within your heart? Your confession will out.

And so I tell all. Of the past, of the Phoenix and how my life began and ended with the man at my feet. What power he held over me I cannot imagine, but hold it he did – and I am unable to do anything but–

Do not fight it, child of light. If you cannot kill then you must cure. Your place is at his side.

No, my place is at your side.

Then stand between us. Take up your place in life's holy wheel. Here shall be your trinity. Tell me: what is your place?

To take up the holy sword and fight for that which I believe.

Even against the rubber bargrips, I feel a familiar tingle in my palms.

Repeat your beliefs.

To defend the faith. To champion the weak. To wage unceasing and merciless war against the infidel.

Then do it, child. Get up off your big, black ass and do it!

10 | THE NOWHEREMAN

Tossing and turning, I drift in and out of consciousness like a well-oiled fish. Dreaming all sorta shit. The kinda shit that just reminds me that I'm a Grade A mr bad guy. Don't remember when I changed. Don't s'pose you do. Hey, I can only just remember a time when I wasn't living in shit in the dark. Since I creamed my brain, have always been a closed man. Had no time for anyone else. Well, not till the end. And only then did I open my mind. Only trouble was when I did something dark just stepped right on in it. Like God only blacker. A voice without a soul.

You flatter me. Hehehe.

The gloating laugh reminds me of something else too.

You said, 'Me.'

Silence.

You said, 'Me.' You said, 'You. Me. Them.' I heard you.

Silence.

Me. That's what you said, wasn't it? *Wasn't it?*

Silence.

All this silence begins to bug me. Y'see it's not the sort of silence that's nice. Not the sort that you can lie in a bath and get *into*. Not warm, relaxing silence. No, this is brain silence. The sort of nagging, annoying silence like when you're trying to get to sleep and the night's too fucking quiet. When it's so quiet it's deafening, and then you hear all sorts of high-pitched, crazy whining and static. Like a tuned-out radio. Guess my other self is shy all of a sudden.

I'm unperturbed.

I did hear it right, didn't I? Up there with the stars. I said about how… No, I was too fucked over to say anything much. *You* said we was lost. You. Me. Them. That's what you said. Wasn't it. You. Me. Them. Just like that. And all the time I thought you were just a by-product of a lucid dream.

Silence. Fuzzy, awful, fucking silence.

I get mad.

Hey, slitface! I want some answers! You said, 'Me,' and I wanna know why.

I don't do requests.

Yeah, right.

I'm angry as hell. Then: So what do ya do?

Play God.

Yeah right. S'that what you're doing now.

I was.

I guess that's too bad. You good?

Very good.

Well then, if you're so good at being God…

Yes?

If you're so good then you'll know what I want.

Indeed…

And do you?

Yes.

Then what?

What? That which you crave with all your heart? That which you want more than life itself?

I nod even though I'm as near to death's door as I ever wanna get.

The island.

Xankhara. Yes. Then: How do you know? No, scratch that… I may only get three wishes. Just tell me this: Do you know where it is? I mean, how to get there?

Yes.

You do?

Yes, I do.

And?
I will help you on one condition.
Uh-huh?
I need access to your father.
My father is dead. I killed him…
Oh, Jack! You don't believe that.

The thought brings words bubbling to the surface. Hot and fateful. And dead as dust.

"The gun was in my stormcloak. The gun to kill my father. So I guess you wanna know why I didn't use it?"

I see the assassins. Kicking my daddy to death. Unbadged mercenaries that materialised from nowhere and landed in a spray of molten tracers. It's the eve of the declaration and establishment of the Consortium of Heaven – the USSA – and I'm fingering the pistol in my pocket, waiting for the right moment. The perfect last words. The poignant juncture. The time that never comes.

You saying he's alive.
Yes.
Really?
Really.
OK. OK. So I'll think about it. I don't know if I can still do it.
My dear Jack, The Nowhereman can do anything.
I was a lot stronger then.
You could be strong again.
I said OK.
My pardon. I'll leave you to your coma.
Hey, wait! What're you gonna be doing meantimes?
I'm God… I can do anything. Reality? Pah, it's all in the bag.

★

Nothing ever gets done no place no how, 'less there's a horror. Not in the world. Not in your mind. Can't read life no other way. Truth is I've seen a lotta horrors these past years. After the collapse. After this place became just one big crock of shit. Ta-ta civilisation. Hallo Dead City. That's what they call this fucked-up pile of garbage. Streets got so many bodies in the gutters no one even notices 'em anymore. Dead suits this place. Usually how I feel. Suits how I've changed and not for the better. Also, how I felt when I come round. Like a zombie rising from a grave. Bike stood at my head like some horned metal tombstone. Pity my name ain't Harley. All around's a cemetery of broken buildings. Yeah, whoever named this shitbowl Dead City was one clever fucker. Total dead end dirtsville. Dead centre of nowhere territory. Dead to the fucking world.

Yet at night Dead City lives.

Soon as the sun goes down the creeps crawl outta their boltholes. Rays just ain't good for you anymore. Best to keep inside. Less pain in the long term. Block ran out soon after the food. Can't act cool when half your skin's flaking off, so no other choice *but* to go nocturnal. Suits me fine. I'm a real creature of the night. Love the moon. Love the stars. Love the whole fucking universe. Anyhow, feel a whole lot safer at night. Like I belong.

City's big enough to hold twenty million. Less than a hundred thousand now. The underbelly elite and the one's that were left after all the others got turned to spam. City's huge. Wide and wild. Yet most's just rubble and craters. Rest's divided like a big fucking cake. Central's the cherry. The place to be. Real des res. Most folks can't cut it alone. Most form gangs. Join tribes. That sorta shit. Gangs lurk everywhere. Got enough turf to go round, but it don't stop 'em fighting none. Queens. Grims. Nerds. All out for each other. Want to have their cake and eat it. Welcome to the party. Every day's full of squat. Every night's just one big birthday bash. One crazy kamikaze ride.

Straight through the suburbs of hell.

When I wake up, find we've stopped some place quiet. Sister was around. I could hear her pacing. She was muttering something too. Thought it might be a prayer. Save your prayers, Sis. Saviour's left town remember? Still, say she isn't praying?

My mind screams for the dark again. Then I hear she's counting. Silly bitch. Come here and sit on my face, baby. Let Nowhere get friendly with some real pussy for a change. Had enough of getting the shitty end of the stick.

There were wolves on the streets tonight. Either that or mad dogs. Wolves come in from the north. Out of the woods on Devil's Ridge. They're cautious but you can't keep 'em out 'cause the feeding's good. They're tolerated for roughly the same reason. It's dog eat dog most nights down the Dead City Bar-B-Q.

Notice the sky's staining mauve. Must be dawn coming. Notice I'm lying on wet ground. Remains of the suspension bridge is way off to the right. Rising outta the fog like some ghostly rigging. Not a breath of wind. Hear Sister Midnight tramping back to the bike that stands like a shadow over me. Terminally skulking. The black angel is huffing and puffing like some big bad wolf herself. Her breath clouds my horizon. Rising into the cold air, then it's gone. I shiver. What the hell we doing here?

"You awake already?" she asks.

I grin a little. Then tell her I ain't done dying yet. She ignores me and rips off one of the boogie fins. What's she up to now? Why bring us out here just to tear up the bike? I shiver again. Wonder why I didn't put on a T. Never thought it ever got this cold.

As she turns to leave I ask her what she's doing. Sounds more like a groan.

"Ave maria," she whispers to herself. That's what she says when she swears, sorta like her own personal litany. Bit like chewing her lip when she gets edgy. That's what she whispers. What she says is, "It's a secret, Jack."

A secret? What sorta secret? Stop being a deep bitch, Sister. Tell me something I don't know.

"Sister…"

Sister?

Need to say something that'll get her to give. Gotta find the right place to push. Push in the right place and you get results. Every time.

It's like smashing your fist into a v-phone. You gotta know where to hit to get the dimes. Too high, too low, you break your fingers.

Sounded like Midnight was breaking hers right now. Takes me a long time to realise she's digging. Using the curved piece of metal as a makeshift shovel. But what's she got buried? Thinking about it makes my brain swirl. But when the answer comes it's like a slap in the face from Hare bloody Krishna.

Her stash.

And then I see where we are. This is where she left me. Must also be the place she buried everything, too. I used to ask her where it was. All she'd say was, "It's a secret". Sounds kinda familiar. When you get religious you gotta dump your stuff. No way the God-U-Likes are gonna let a big black mamma swank into their temple shouldering an MLA auto-feed and a chainsaw. How can you find the muse of Buddha when you've got enough armour-piercing ammo stuffed down your bra to stop a jihad? Fuck knows where she got the M16. Perhaps she smuggled it in under her cassock. Sorta like a keepsake. More likely what they used as a deterrent for hawkers. Wonder what she did with her two-hander? She was mighty proud of that. Didn't go nowhere without old faithful strapped over one shoulder. Yet that was before all this fucking god almighty shit.

Those were the days. Yet this train of thought just brings me back to the A-Men and what I said on the tracks. Don't wanna think about that just yet. Don't really wanna think about nothing 'cept lying here and groaning. Have to wait until–

Thwump.

Sister appears beside me like some fucking grim reaper. She's carrying a mud-stained pack. Heaves it onto the seat of the stolen bike. Sprays dirt in my face. She's sweating like a pig. Whites of her eyes are shining. Teeth are clenched and that's just about all I can see of her. Except her dark silhouette against the reddening skies.

"Get up, Jack," she says.

I try. I really do. But I can't kick the numbness from my back. Wriggle for a bit. Long enough for her to ask me again. Then she leaves the package. Comes round to help. I act like a dead weight, but it don't take much acting. Still Sis is used to handling heavy loads. Hauls me up to my feet, dumps me on the hova-board and straddles the front. Taking a last look up at the blood-red skies above the bay, she breathes, "No way back now, little sister," then stamps on the pedal and lets the engine roar.

Sun's clearing the eastern skyline when we make it back to Broadview. Landing like a fat fuck on the roof, Sister drags me in one hand, soil-covered rucksack in the other. Acting on instinct, she makes for the elevator. Instinct? Who am I kidding? Even a shot-up old fuck like me can smell the piss. Not gonna be too pleased when she realises it hasn't moved in two years.

Mumble something about the elevator not working to which black beauty replies, "No, really?"

Needing sarcasm like a gun up my ass, I just lean harder against her. Hope she doesn't get fed up and drop me on my face. Reaching the service door, Sister kicks it open. Makes for the ladder.

Smart. Why didn't I think of that?

'Cause you're fucked-up too bad, that's why, Jack.

Sure, sure I am. I must've lost more blood that this bitch bleeds in a year. Just need some rest. And a dose of tonic from good ol' Doc Gruesome.

When we reach my room, the door's been kicked open. Not a good sign. Pigmeat hangs just like I left him. Naked. Slumped in his chains. Only difference is half his face has been blasted onto the balcony.

Sister's on the case even as I'm still noticing the blood. Dropping me and the rucksack, she flicks her rifle into her hands. Scans every shadow in a heartbeat.

Looking up at the ceiling, I see the bitch pass over me. Feel the hem of her black habit brush my face.

Anybody tell ya you sweat real beautiful, lady?

Pigmeat's a goner. Looks like whoever broke in didn't even say hallo. Just pulled out a piece and stuck one in his head. The bullet entered the nape of his neck. Blew his face clean off. Only consolation's he was probably still unconscious. Probably.

Hey, so what, Jack. Is this any way to treat your date?

Aw, fuck off. I'm in mood to play guilt trips with mr subconscious. Don't even realise Sister's talking till she kicks me.

"Jack, you know this kid?"

Not half as well as I was going to.

"Is this your date?"

Yeah, so what, Sister? Fancy a little stiff-fucking?

"Jack? Wake up, you piece of shit. You gotta take a look at this."

I force my eyes open and see where she's pointing.

On the wall just above where the bed ends something's smeared across the plaster. Looks like a weird kinda circle. Also looks like blood. Underneath it says, 'CHEATR!' Don't look too friendly.

"Looks like you pissed somebody off." Sister is already backing towards the landing. "One of your other lovers."

No, Sister, you're way wrong. I ain't got any other lovers.

"We'd better leave." The black nun don't sound too pleased. Keeps muttering, "I knew it, I knew it," under her breath. Loud as fuck in the silent room.

Tries to drag me as she goes, but I just flop like a fish so she kicks me again. Cold numbs it. Least to my brain. Far as it's concerned, didn't hurt a bit. Still I twist anyway. Bad move. Tears open my neck wound. I black. I guess that's when the horror's at its worst. And that was when I suddenly knew what I was going to do. The words were clear even as I said howdy again to the big nothing.

Gruesome. Jesus. Werehouse.

Piece of piss.

★

Wake to the sight of Sister polishing her broadsword.

She's sitting on the floor with it clasped between her meaty thighs. Candle burns low at her feet. In its light her shadow bobs against the ceiling. She's bandaged me good. Shoulder's plastered in goop. Smells fouler'n crack cheese. Stings like hell. But it's OK, y'know.

Midnight notices me waking. Don't even twitch. Just keeps the cloth wrapped around her blade. Rubbing it up and down. Up and down. Her eyes are glazed like cherries in a long-stemmed glass. The point of the sword spears the dirt five centimetres from my face. Shines like a chrome fender. Ain't got a clue where we are. Too quiet to be Broadview. Too dark to be sunnyside. Then I notice the weird paintings on the brick. All burning crosses and falling angels. Then I know.

We're in the cellar.

The cellar. Now that brings back memories. This place was once a big old manse. Up on Gypsy Hill. Now's just a burnt-out ruin. Dai-80 and his spaced-out weirdo cult holed up here after their failed jihad. After that the ganglords burnt the whole place to the ground. This cellar's all that's left. Now looks like this place is her place. Looks cool. It's not all bottled frogs and human skins. More tasteful than that. Lots of neat charts and big cushions. Kinda smoky, y'know. Got murals like you wouldn't believe. Sis's quite an artist. Says they're visions. Sorta come to her in her dreams. Some dreams. With dreams like yours, Sis, I'd rather stay awake. Why she joined the God-U-Likes I'll never know. One crazy fucked-up bitch.

The big black mother frowns. Stops polishing and looks ugly. Suddenly her eyes focus.

"What's eating you, Jack?"

"Last night," I croak, "I saw a lotta shit… can't even begin to follow."

"What sort of shit?"

"Wasters."

"Yeah, I wasted 'em, 'member."

'Yeah, but there was also Gut. Doing a deal out in the lot."

"Gut was always doing deals," Sister snorts.

"Not any more he ain't. His dealing days are over."

"The Wasters got him?"

"Yeah, but that ain't it."

"So?"

Back off, Sis. I'm in no mood for the third degree.

"So?" she says again.

"*So* he was doing a deal with some offworlders. Swapped those tickets outta here for lord knows what. Some bitch came down in a bird. Gave her a bag and then got wasted."

"What happened to the bag?"

"Bitch clipped it to the transport."

"What could Gut have that they wanted?"

"Fucked if I know, big mother."

But I'm damned sure I'm gonna find out.

★

Last time I'd heard Doc was staying at this joint over on Watson Place. He's an old buddy from E-Unit. Good splicer. Bent as fuck. But in this town, even a bad doctor is better'n none. I take the airbike. Try to ignore the way the needle's nudging empty. No way to recharge the grav. Soon be just so much junk. Still don't stop me jamming the thing to full.

Roar down 39th like an airborne pariah. Buzz a couple of gutterjocks hacking the legs off some piece of pavement pizza. Must've leapt off the Grand Imperial Hotel. Sad fuck. No style. Should've tried the Empire.

Up Watson, Doc's house is deader than dead. Lives in a tall gothic place all on its own. Surrounded by enough razor-wire to stop a herd of elephants. Sure stops the gutterjocks. Up on the roof's a mouldy pool. Springboard, deckchair, the works. Must've been quite some pad in its time. Hang around till the natives get restless. Then roar the fuck off. S'either that or be crawling with kooks. Like flies round a horse's ass.

Let the throttle out and clear the block. I'm back before they know it.

Still not around. Damn fuck! When I fly by again, there's signs of life.

Doc's out in the roof garden. Feeding his babies. Don't know exactly what they are, and neither I guess does Mother Nature. She's got one hell of an imagination, but even she'd be hard pushed to think up something like these freaks.

Doc's an old man now. His one eye's all misty. Like it's filled up with milk. He's got wild hair in scattered clumps. Scar down one arm ten centimetres wide. Runs from his wrist to his pecs. I was there when that happened. Some trench on the city line. Saw the cleaver go right in and slice. He'd have lost the whole arm if I hadn't spiked the mohawk's head to his stationwagon. Took him back to Sister's. She crocheted him up real good. Got me free medical treatment for life.

Not many folks in this city got their own private medic. Makes me feel kinda special. Only Doc's no Florence. Too heavy-handed. Sorta brutal. He'd rather kill than cure. Also he's gotten himself into a lotta weird genetic malarkey. Growing things in vats. Transplanting heads. That sorta shit. His babies started out life as human embryos. Looked more like bald rats after he'd finished with 'em. Well, sorta like rats. Maybe little like slugs too. The way they eat the live roaches he's tossing 'em screams 'bug' all over. He's a long way off what he was. Just like yours truly. Long way from when he sliced my mind into kebabs and sent me back to the beginning.

I land in a spray of sparks and swing off the skid-pad.

Doc looks at me with his one good eye, then turns back to tossing roaches. Half his face was roasted on the side of a coal furnace during a raid. Some illegal organ-legging he was into. Most of the skin was left stuck to the boiler. Lost his right eye too. And any chance of running for mr baby beautiful.

His real name was Douglas Grisholm. Now folks call him Doc Gruesome. Looks much the same as when last I saw him. 'Cept for the thick nipple ring in his right tit.

I eye him from the other side of the drained pool. Decide to take the plunge.

"Nice ring," I say, grinning like an idiot. "Classy."

Gruesome stops tossing and looks back at me.

"Ah, mr Nowhere. I just had the strangest feeling I was going to see you today."

"Sure ya did."

"If only you knew… And what do I owe the pleasure of *this* visit?"

"Hey, Doc, just call me Jack, I…"

"Mr Nowhere, may I remind you that I run a professional establishment here. One never addresses one's clients by their first names. It's not good practice."

"Yeah, yeah. OK. Understood."

What a case.

"Good. Now I'll ask again…"

Empties the remaining roaches from his bucket with a twist of one hand. The black rain makes the base of the pool squirm. All writhing flesh. There's the sound of crunching as the creatures break the insect's shells. A slurping as they suck out the tender meat.

"Your business, sir?"

Glance down into the pool. Sight nearly makes me throw. Hang onto what little food lines my stomach. Taste bile rise in my throat. Instead of words, I unbuckle my skin and show off my shoulder.

Doc takes a long watery look.

"Ah, I see. And how did you come by this particular injury?"

"Wasters."

"Wasters?"

"Oh, OK." Spec falls out like times tables. "AK-47 assault rifle. Seven point six-two millimetre bullet. Thirty-nine in a round. Six hundred rounds a minute. D-Bloc standard issue."

"My, my. Again I am at a loss. Never met anyone rich enough to *own* a Kalashnikov."

"Offworlders."

"I see. Of course. Please, step into my surgery." Doc makes a show of motioning towards the door off the roof. Remembering what's inside, I decline.

"Hey, sun's up. Maybe we can play doctors out here?"

"As you wish."

He leaves. Once I'm alone I empty my guts into the boiling pool.

The creations lap it up. Probably first time they've ever had dessert.

Manage to find an old plank. Prop it against a broken gargoyle and lie down. Doc comes shuffling back. Got his big bag of tools. Guess we're gonna be getting into some heavy DIY. Can hardly wait.

"Of course, I can never repay you for saving my arm," Gruesome's saying. "Let's hope I'm in time to save yours."

Asks if I want to be put out. I nod. Don't feel ready to be awake when he seals the torn veins. Don't know much 'bout operations, but I guess it helps if the patient ain't spasming as the pliers go in.

I offer the back of my head. Hope he hits the right spot first time. Blind faith's not my speciality.

As the hammer falls, wonder if I'll have both arms when I wake up.

★

That evening I feel like shit, but no rest for the wicked. Leave the cellar. Go cruising for leads. First shot is to look up Jesus. I'd seen him on the stairs. Didn't register at the time. But now– Well, perhaps he had heard the word. Seen something I'd missed. Maybe witnessed Pigmeat's death. Whatever. Though I had no wish to swap chat with an errant God-U-Like, I need all the leads I can get right about now. Turns out the street-junkie was pretty hard to find. Messiahs usually are. Eventually shows up on a street crusade down 10th. Got some sorta pulpit rigged on a rusty balcony. Shouts out the good news like it's from yesterday's tabloids. Punctuates his preaching banging trashcan lids. Few bikers play chicken below. Every so often they get pissed and chuck something. Now that *was* good news. Meant they weren't carrying pieces.

"Yo! Listen up, unbelievers! Can't you see that I have risen?" Jesus screams. Fever pitch.

Obviously just in time for the finalé. Bang-bang-bang go the cans.

"I have seen the holy angels shinin' in the sky."

Bang-bang-bang.

"They fly amongst us. They light the night with their fire."

Bang-bang.

"They come to save us all. Rid the daemons from your souls so they may take us all into our eternal paradise!"

Bang-bang-bang.

"I have been sent to suffer. Let me bear your sins so that you may be delivered!"

Swing onto the covered ladder and vault up the missing steps. Rise out of the lattice floor right behind the alley prophet. Too doped to see my coming. Give him fifty fits when I stab my finger in his back. He drops the lids and they clatter onto the balcony. Roll over the edge. Crash onto the sidewalk.

Couple of bikers look up. See some dude sorting out the preacher. Don't look back. Saves them the job.

"Hi, Jeez," I say. My voice's a lot hoarser since last night.

"Hey, man. Don't do nothing, man. I ain't hacking no one."

Not fucking much. Got this whole neighbourhood wanting your ass. While I'm thinking this, Jesus tries getting cocky.

"You'll be sorry if you hurt me, man. God's my protector..."

Yeah and I'm the Holy fucking Ghost...

"Hey man, I need a break. Spare some A's?"

I let the punch to the back of the head answer for me. Was I the only fucker in this goddamn city who's not pumping himself full of crap? Bad enough keeping the rads down. No more X-Plan diet round here. Shops sold their last low-fat yogurt over four years ago.

Jesus is snivelling now. Acting the victim. Feel like nailing him to this balcony. Hang him out for the crows.

"The transport," I say, massaging the pain outta my hand.

"What, man?"

"Don't act the innocent. You must've seen it."

"I see nothing, man. Nothing."

Don't wanna hurt my hand again. Let my piece do the rest.

"No, man. No, don't."

Jesus finds his memory like a new religion. Tells me the bird was hurt bad. Must've been when that rich kid flew into the engines. Bore markings too. Signs I'd missed in all the excitement. Red and white symbol. Dark-winged supernova. Sounded like a five-pointed star.

Bingo.

Don't know it, but unless I'm thicker than I look, that's the logo scrawled in my ex's blood on the wall of my apartment. Not much to go on, but it's a start. Yet what Jesus blabs next is far more interesting. Catches my mind like a fragmenting grenade. Shreds it with possibilities.

"That bird was going down, man. Sorta flew on one wing. When the bikers went there was only me and God, man. Me and God. Swear to hell. I saw it go down. Out near the bay. Watched it all the way, man."

His eyes glaze remembering.

"All the way."

Well, if Jesus wasn't lying that ship couldn't hope for orbit. Not without repairs. Maybe I'd get lucky. Maybe it was still dirtside. Someone must've seen it. Still night's closing in again and I gotta go clubbing. But before I leave got one more question. Ask about the room. About Pigmeat. About the fact that he'd lost his face.

At this Jesus' eyes go dark. It's as if a black cloud rolls right over 'em.

"I see nothing, man. Nothing at all. Heard one shot. That's it. It was the bad man, brother. Left after. Went uptown."

"Who the fuck was it?"

"I… don't know. Asked if I'd seen you, though."

I grab the long-haired fucker by the throat.

"So what'd ya tell him, dickface?"

"I said I see nothing. Was in a hurry. He believed me, man. Believed me to the end."

Only one who does, you little shit. Still what else I got? Better head back to Sister's. Long night tonight.

Best get some sleep before you go scouting the 'House, Nowhere.

Forget sleep. I can sleep when I'm dead. If Sister's home, I doubt my head will touch the pillow.

★

Nearly night when I reach the cellar. Made sure I'm not being followed. Didn't know who this bad man was. Or on who's side, 'cept it wasn't mine. Think I've strayed 'cross the line. This is unknown territory. And unknown territory's bad news. Hid the bike in the john. In three strides I reach the steps to the cellar. Headed for the bolted door.

"Hey Sister! I'm home!"

I hear a scrabbling in the dark.

Nowhere! Stop right there!

What the fuck…

The cry blows my mind. Rocks my thoughts. Stuns me.

I'm down in one. Back shoved against the mossy wall. Catch my breath. D&K out and cocked. Pressed hard against my temple.

The voice's vibrating in my brain. Don't sound scared. More alarmed. All around's as still as a tomb. How'd I hear that?

Fool, pikinini. It's me.

Sister? S'that you? How'd you do that?

Oh, Jack, don'tcha 'member the headman?

Then I remember.

The Amtech headman. Shit, I'd forgot I'd ever had it implanted. Which is no surprise since we used 'em once and they've been offline ever since. Surprised they're still working. All the A-Men had 'em. Fixed just before that final job. Sorta plug-in telepathy. Unit was sunk right behind my left ear. Linking each of us together. Also to the stream. They were weird at first. Real weird. Mainly 'cause there's no voice pattern. Just this echoing sound. Buckets of it. Hey, maybe that explains those cock-sure voices I've been plagued with. Maybe the system hippy's back online. Certainly means our personal network is.

But if my other voice is…

Later, I tell myself, think about this later.

Can't see or hear anything out of place. Still that don't mean nothing. After all this time I still trust the Sis. Saved my ass too many times not to. Back a few, we were real close. Till I went off the rails.

Anyone saw us together said we looked *right*, y'know. Like milk 'n' coffee. On the same wavelength.

Squeeze my mind remembering how to work the damn thing. Like ketchup from a bottle. One minute, nothing. Then it all comes at once.

Fuck! What's up?

Trip. Third step. Blow your fucking legs off.

Cool. I can dig that.

At the bottom of the stairs the door opens. Sister's standing there like some born-again guerrilla terrorist. She's ditched the habit. Changed into her camos. Boots. Trikevlar pads. Fatigues. Dreadlocks tied like a great head of black snakes. Eyes masked by battle shades. Warpainted cheeks look like grey wounds. All uncertain and intense.

"Hey, Midnight… you look fucking A!"

My bovver-girl bohemian is back.

Midnight don't bat an eyelid.

"Call me Sis."

Never did like her handle. Pity.

"OK. OK. *Sister* Midnight. Now… can I come in?"

She nods. Like some big black Medusa. Points out the wire and I step inside.

Sister's lair's as grim as ever, but now she's laid out her stash. In the process of cleaning it. Room smells of stale earth and oil. S'been years since this little lot's seen the light of day. Cast my eyes over it. MLA. Stripped and lubed. Chainsaw. Blade. Two curved knives. Osakimo deck. Most are marked with museum cabinet numbers. Makes my D&K look like a fucking peashooter.

Notice a box of ammo. Take it. Gun's loaded but you can't get too much of a good thing. And in my book ammo's a *very* good thing. Too much is never enough.

"I'm going to the Werehouse," I say.

"The Werehouse? Wasn't that out on 5th and H?"

"Not any more. Now's the Knight's place on 40th and Balboa."

"What'd ya wanna go there, Jack?"
"I wanna see Shrago."
"Shrago?"
"Friend of Gut's"
"Got an appointment?"

Hey, Sister, if I wanna get into the Werehouse I'm gonna need more than an appointment. I'll need the cheek of the devil. Face too. Outsiders' about as welcome as shit in a sandwich at the Werehouse. Probably started when they were running free after the RuZu breakout. Found they were easy targets, but I guess the warzone trained 'em soon enough. Rumours popped up all over the place. Arms store here. Truck stop there. Fucking clever these farmhouse freaks. Formed Gonks 'R' Us. Got their own hangout. Guess bods of a feather fuck together. Like some fur-lined brotherhood. Real close. Werehouse became their lair. 'House's the sorta place people go if they wanna get into animals. Latest Werehouse is down on the bay. Used to belong to the Knights. Lot of rumbles 'tween the Knights and the Gonks. Knights want racial purity. Only thing the Gonks *ain't* got.

One thing the Gonks have got is Shrago.

Shrago knew Gut. He knew Gut real well. They shacked in the same apartment though fuck knows where. Got close after me and Gut parted company. Sorta mutual differences. OK, so I OD'ed his net guru. Big deal. The geek was holding out on me. Looting my trash. Had it coming for a long time. After that Gut moved outta Broadview. Fucking good riddance. Sure smelt a whole lot better. Never could find his new hideaway.

Shrago was Gut's dealer. Bit of a suit. Streetwise with it. Real smooth. Had shit like you wouldn't believe. Made some. Pumped some outta the sewage. Real clever Shrago.

Didn't know where he squatted, but knew he always hung out at the Werehouse. Sorta mooched round venues for the tragically hip.

But he knew Gut. Knew what his partner was up to. He'd know the bird. The logo. The lot.

Maybe. Big maybe.

"I want to see Gut's weasel-faced lackey. Want to find out the word on the transport. Want to look up a Gonk and take in a B-movie. Every way I see it I'm headed for the Werehouse."

Still gotta get in first. Yeah, I'll have to be real lucky to get into the Werehouse. After all I'm almost human.

"So how you thinking of pulling that off?" asks the Sis.

"Get some help."

"Yeah? From just who exactly?"

"Dingo the Wonder Dog."

Sister's stunned. When she takes off her shades, her eyes sparkle. "Dog's at the Werehouse?"

"Yeah, last time I heard. Dweeb was holed in a room upstairs. Serving and shit. Little serving. Mostly shit. Hear he's doing fine."

"Still got those kooky skates."

"Yeah. Got red stars and streamers on 'em now."

Sister laughs. Sound's like scattered glass. Transforms her whole face into a living thing. She offers me a long look, then says, "When you going?"

"Soon. Anything to eat?"

"Some. Caught couple of gulls while you were out. How's the shoulder?"

"Fine…"

"How fine?"

"OK, so it's shit, but it'll hold. Least till I get back."

Her eyes dart from my bandages to the floor. There's a moment of awkward silence. She bites her lip. Then she looks up.

"You worry me, Jack. Sometimes, y'know?"

"Hey Sister, I worry myself all the time."

In two steps I'm standing before her. Choked in her embrace. So tight. So very tight. Desperately I lunge her mouth. Force her back against the painted plaster. Kick aside her carefully arranged pieces of equipment, Pin her to the wall and spear her throat. Manic. No style. Just stabbing like a knife in the dark. My body responds. Not like Pigmeat though. There's no anger here. Just the bottomless black well of bitter need. I want to kill her, I'm so crazed. Bite her cheeks. Her chin. Her neck. Don't care whether I leave marks. Marks heal. Not like my wound inside.

Sister's hands slide through my greasy hair. Pulling me forwards. Down. Closer to her shrouded breast. It's hot in the closeness of the cellar. Sticky. Her reaching hands exposing the hairless whiteness of my chest. Rips the belt from my pants. I tear at her fatigues revealing nipples erect like little chocolate flowers. My mouth finds them even though my eyes are closed.

A million years of lust comes flooding out in one spurting stream. As her pants fall, I hurriedly poke between her thighs. Her gasp is so alien. So feminine.

Before I enter her, I'm already cumming. Sending trembling shudders through my legs.

Still, guess this means the A-Men are back in business.

★

Later as we lie alone I stir. Midnight's talking even as I open my eyes.
"I saved some of your stuff. From the apartment."
"Uh-huh."
"Just some stuff in a bag. Few tools. Can of oil. The book."
Forevermore.
"Mmm-humm…"
"Couldn't find much else."
"Mmm…"
"You hearing me, Jack?"
Loud and clear, Sister.
"Uh-mmm."
"Now what sorta dumb answer is that?"
I'm still in no mood for questions. Leave me alone.
"Nowhere, you lazy prick. Wake up!"
Or what, Sister? Ya gonna sue me?
The black woman shifts and rises onto one elbow. From over one

of the cushions she looks towards the door that hangs half open. Stares deep into the place where the light and shadows meet. Shafts of dusty orange creep around the jamb like golden fingers. There's an evil pause. I get ready for a lecture. Instead she starts to cry like a little girl. Makes fists of her hands but she don't turn round. Muscles on her back clench like live eels beneath her skin. Then she gets a grip. Gets resolute. All high and mighty.

"I can't forgive you, Jack. I want you to know that. Whatever happens from hereon in, I just want you to know. I watched the A-Men die once and there's no way I'm gonna do it again. I watched you torch your life and take all of us with you. I hope you like Hell, Jack, 'cause that's where you're going. They'll be Old Nick to pay one day… you just see if I'm not right."

I'm unphased. Let the devil do his worst. He can bill me.

"I came back for you," I moan from the floor.

That makes her turn. Her eyes are lost in the darkened room, but I know they're cold as stone slabs. She pulls herself up and kneels over me. Like some bronze colossus.

"Yeah. Yeah, that you did, Jack… That you did. Damned if I know why. Don't think I wanna. You're just one big fucking contradiction. I should've left you for the Wasters. Wasters? You're the fucking waster, Jack. You fucked while the gang went down. While I emptied my twin-feed, you just kept on porkin'. I can't stand it. You're the waster, Jack. You don't give a fuck about nothing."

"You've got me wrong, Sis."

"Have I? I don't think so, Nowhere. You don't give a fuck about nothing and that's that. Guess all the others gotta live with that, huh? There's only you, Doc and me left from the gang now. Pure's AWOL and Dog and D'Alessandro were too on the edge to be real 'Men. So by my reckoning it's just us two now. I owe you my life and I'm decent enough to think that that counts for something. Only reason I went away. Should've cut your prick off when I had the chance."

I think she's gonna stop, but she just keeps right on going. On a roll now.

"But even after I locked myself in purgatory you kept coming back. Why'd you keep coming back? Couldn't you see you were destroying me. Piece by piece. But you *kept* visiting. Every time you were hurt or needed a place to lie low. Time after time. Digging up the past. Twisting my arm till I didn't know nothing but *guilt*. Ain't I got enough of that, huh? Then this time when you waltz in you've got the Wasters in tow. They fucking wasted my sisters, Jack. Hell, I was driven to the verge of insanity by those tight-assed bitches, but they were my family. And you killed them too. You never raised a finger, but you killed 'em all the same. All I got left now is you, Jack. You and God Mûhamet. And neither of you can save the world. Or me. You're all so distant. So fucking detached. It makes me wanna…"

Sister's makes a strained gargling sound, then she's crying again. Big heaving sobs. Her knees are shaking and her tears fall wet on my chest. Pool in my navel.

Midnight's got a real fucking way with pillow talk. Real fucking way.

"Hey I'm sorry, Sis, but p'raps now's the time to forget all that, to start something new…"

"Jack, just stop it," she says, pulling away. "I've had enough of your fucked-up dreams. I want you to know that you're never gonna do that to me again. I'm never going through it! Never! I want you to know that. It hurts too bad. Now I've got nowhere left to go."

"Join the club, Sis. The way the world's panning out, the only way from here is down. But that's cool. Down's OK. Down's the easiest way to go."

She pauses. Thinks on this. Her sobs turn slowly to more normal tears.

"Yeah, you always used to say that."

"No truer then than now."

"Yeah… I guess."

I hold her. Mainly 'cause that's what I think I should do. Seems to help. Midnight blubs for a bit then cries herself out. When she's all done I call her name.

"Esther."

"Uh-huh."

"Where'd you put the book?"

"It's right here."

"Get it. Just forget it all and read to me. Like old times."

She retrieves the tatty volume and holds it up. In the candlelight it looks like a big black bird. It falls open in her trembling hands, its broken spine allowing no randomness in the choice. Sister glances down at the page. Her brown eyes look golden. Her cheeks are on fire.

"The Tale of Jack O'Nowhere." She reads the illuminated title with unseeing eyes. The passage is so familiar that she recites it like an invocation.

Once upon a time in a forested kingdom there lived a young man named Jack. Now Jack was King of the Wood and no mortal was cleverer or no god more wise. Though he had all the riches he could want, Jack wanted more. You see he had a big dream. A dream about an island at the edge of the world. An island where the gods dwelt far over the sea. An island where Death never trod...

*

And so Jack moved from the Room of Illusions and down the stone corridor into the inner sanctum of the Castle of Enchantment. There he found a red chamber filled with smoke and braziers. The air was hot and sticky, the Fountain of Eternal Youth visible on a column of stone on a small island in the centre of a lake of lava. He saw that though he could walk all the way around the edge of the room on a stone path, the only way across was upon three stepping stones guarded by a Big Black Demon. In its eyes was hatred and vengeance. In its taloned hands was a double-bladed axe, dripping with the blood of all those who had failed here. Also here was his brother's sword, lying on the floor. Yet of his brother there was not a trace.

Knowing this creature to be a conjured servant of the faerie king,

Jack took a deep breath and stepped onto the first of the stones whereupon the Big Black Demon rose to its full height and bellowed, "You have done well to reach this inner sanctum. Within the Dungeon of Darkness, you learned fellowship and leadership. In the Hall of Death, you passed the tests of ingenuity and faith. In the Chamber of Tortures, you were tested upon your trust and quick thinking. And in the Room of Illusions, you mastered the arts of valour and strength. Yet now you come here and attempt what none have ever succeeded. Continue and you will die. Go back now and you will be spared."

Jack looked up at the monstrous figure and was terrified. His fear scared him stiff and he did not know what to do. Yet then he recalled what the old crone had said to him upon the cliff top. She had said that the ultimate game was belief and that if he always remembered that then he would not fail. And as the King of the Wood thought this he knew what he must do.

"No," said Jack and stepped onto the second stone.

The Big Black Demon roared a great roar that shook the chamber, the walls and the entire Castle of Enchantment. Then it bellowed again, saying, "I am what you are not. Defy me and the fountain is yours. Yet ware! I am invincible in combat. Fight me and you will die. Go back now and you will be spared."

"No," said Jack again and took another step onto the third stone.

Now the Big Black Demon towered right above him and Jack could no longer see the fountain beyond the red-eyed monster. The blood on its axe hissed as it dripped into the lava and Jack tried not to imagine the damage it would do if the blade were used upon him.

"You are a fool!" bellowed the Big Black Demon. "Do you wish to die?"

"No!" yelled Jack and quickly tried to push past the Big Black Demon and get to the tiny fountain. Yet it was in vain. The guardian was too huge. And as he tried to get past, it lifted the axe and hefted it down upon him cutting him across his chest. Staggering, Jack almost fell back into the lava but somehow he kept his feet.

Then the Big Black Demon bellowed again, saying, "I am what

you are not. Defy me and the fountain is yours. Yet ware! I am invincible in combat. Fight me and you will die. Go back now and you will be spared."

Panicked, Jack ignored these words and tried to reach the fountain for a second time, yet the Big Black Demon struck him again and this time he did fall to the ground.

Critically wounded and as near to death as anyone can ever be, Jack lay on the hot floor as the Big Black Demon bellowed for a third time, saying, "I am what you are not. Defy me and the fountain is yours. Yet ware! I am invincible in combat. Fight me and you will die. Go back now and you will be spared."

As he lay on the ground Jack at last heard clearly what the beast was saying. Then he remembered the words of the prisoner in the Chamber of Tortures who had said how all things within the Castle of Enchantment were the reverse of the outside world. And when he thought about this, suddenly he knew what he must do.

This is my moment, he thought. My moment of glory in the story. This is my moment to shine. And looking up at the demon towering above him, he managed a small smile, and then said, "Begone!"

"What?" said the Big Black Demon.

"Begone! You are nothing. I do not even believe you exist at all."

And with a great howl the Big Black Demon screamed and disappeared into thin air.

And as the Big Black Demon disappeared, all of the Eternal Ones were freed from their enslavement of Maleore's enchantments. Jack had succeeded in his quest and had released the Fountain of Eternal Youth so that the gods could regain their immortality. He had mastered the trials of Kindness, Compassion, Patience, Trust, Strength, Ingenuity, Valour and Command. He was a hero and a legend.

★

By the time the bedtime story is over, I'm snoring. Don't matter none. I know the ending better than I know my own name. Wake just before midnight. Head out on the jockmobile down to the bay. Ride the breeze all the way. Silent surfing. Try to save some juice. Feel I might be needing a quick getaway. Don't have to be psychic to know I'm heading into uncharted waters. After all that shit Midnight was spouting feel like I'm 'tween the devil and the deep blue sea. Hope Dog's still at the 'House, else this is gonna to be one short trip.

Lighting my way out from the bay, s'like the dark fires raise a paean under me. Holding me up with their bright adulation. Sure as shit's not the powercells for much longer. Just now the club's tucked in the backstreets laying low. Werehouse's had a hundred venues. Some really cool. Others just dives. This place's sorta inbetween. Too dirty for smart. Too clean for slease. Was a flick hall in its time. Tall lions stand over the foyer. All coloured glass and big lights. Most blown to buggery, leaving just a central shade that sparkles like a glitter ball. All red and green. Makes the whole front look septic. Like some architectural wound gone bad. Great place for a hangout. Pity they had to oust the Knights to get it. Couldn't have endeared them to the locals much.

Freaks spill out onto the sidewalk. Drunk as fuck. I swoop across the square and make for the roof. My guess is that since flying fucks aren't exactly two a penny this is going to be the least guarded. Fiddle with the controls, stab Off, then cruise to a stop. Land behind some vent funnels. Cover the bike with discarded boxes. Then crawl towards the nearest ladder and peer over.

There's another roof below. Sorta lower part built out on the back. Got a wall around it, couple of slop troughs and half a dozen pigs. Way in too. Heavy iron-braced door. Grilles each side spew steam. Watch for a little and see where the guards patrol. They walk off towards the front and come within three metres of the bike and me. Shadows hide us both. I count until I have the pattern, then leap for the ladder and descend.

Once I'm down I run for the troughs. Try to miss the pigs. Fail and send them squealing every which way. Take a dive in the slops just as the guard makes his second pass.

That's the easy bit over. Now looks like I'm in for a wait.

Patience is a virtue I'm sadly lacking. Yet if I want to get in, the only way is to wait for an opening. The Werehouse don't close till dawn, but someone'd have to come out sooner or later. Even if it was just to chuck. And when that happened, I'd be ready to make sure they'd choke on it. Still no good being logical. Usually logic don't figure. If I wait too long I get pissed. And if I get pissed I'm likely to rip the back off the place.

Thankfully, I'm not in the mud for long. Wake from my doze by the sound of the door slamming. Don't for a moment think it's the wind. Look about and see this dude swaggering out towards the troughs. First sight, he's Homo sapien. Yet when he walks into the moonlight, the whole side of his face looks like a lizard's. Guess they call him Snake Eyes. Don't bother me none. Still gonna beat the crap outta him.

Stiffing the gecko's not my idea of fun. As he stops and pulls out his cock, I come up behind. What little noise I make's covered by the sound of splashing urine. Grab his neck. Slice both jugulars with one of Sister's blades. Messy business. Wish I could just sink a bullet in his brain and have done with it. Instead I get a faceful of ol' Snake Eyes' insides and a bootful of piss. Thought these critters had cold blood. Not this fucker. He's hot as new shit. All comes gushing out like crimson cum. Looks more like molten lead in the moonlight.

Wipe my hands and face on scaly's pants, then frisk him and come up empty. Well, near as dammit. Cross to the door and hold my breath. Open the mesh and reach for the handle. It turns like a well-oiled dream. Guess I'm just one lucky fuck. Yours truly was born with a silver spoon stuffed so far up his ass, he ain't stopped smiling yet.

Slip through the door into another world. Smoke's forced down my throat as I enter the room. Was some kinda store, but now's a kitchen. Fires keep a dozen pots gurgling and every one smells like boiling offal. No one's about. Guess the head chef was holding the fort. Wonder what's cooking. Slope over to the other door and press my eye to the crack. I'm looking for Dingo, but all I see's a long balcony and a few gooks standing about drinking. Music from further off drowns every word they say. Still since I'm looking for a waiter, maybe the chowhouse is the best place to start.

The Wonder Dog's flighty though. Always on the move. Fucking kleptomaniac. Crazy as anything. Afraid he's gonna die if he takes his rollerboots off. Real barking loon. Pure chaos on wheels. Only time I got to know him was when the A-Men raided the Glass-Suko backbone. Doc suggested the Wonder Dog could crack the central uplink in City Hall. And he did. Disabled the alarm. Burst the door. Pissed up a tree. All in under a minute. Now he's a fence for the Gonks. Makes a few bucks waiting at tables. And a few deals too, I guess. Had no guarantee he'd still be here anyhow.

Then I see him coming. Skating outta the far door carrying a tray piled with dirty bowls. Dog was a tracker in the zones. Got sense of smell better'n the hound of Satan. Got better face too. Gene-genie's skwizzed his veins fulla wolf blood. Let nature do the rest. Stands tall as a man's chest in his boots, but he's no more than a puppy really. Real wetnose. Good joker though. Real fun guy. Shame about his face, but them's the breaks. Can't have it all.

I let him come. Wait until he's in the kitchen then step out the shadows with my best smile.

Dingo skids to a halt and looks round for the gecko. Scared to fuck when he sees me grinning at him. He drops the dishes before he even recognises who I am. They crash to the tiles and flee for cover between his blue-starred boots.

"Nowhere! What're you doin' here?"

"Wonder Dog?" Try to sound disappointed. "You let me down. Told Sister you got *new* skates."

"Cut it, Nowhere. I ain't got time for this." Sits down on his haunches. Starts collecting the bowls.

Why is no one ever glad to see me?

"Anyhow, how'd ya get in here?"

"Airbike. From the roof."

"Oh. Well, just tell me what you want and get outta here."

"I wanna see Shrago."

Dingo swallows. His brows raise and he forgets all about the bowls.

"You wanna *what?*"

"Shrago. I wanna see him. Now."

The Wonder Dog shakes his head. Makes his ears flap.

"Ut-uh. No way, no how, Jack."

"Pity," I say and pull out my piece.

"Hey, just hold it. Let me explain-"

"You've got ten and counting."

Wonder Dog goes into overdrive. Says I really pick my moments. That this is a real bad time.

"Nine."

Mentions that things are hotting up.

"Eight."

Word on the street says Knights are gathering for a raid.

"Seven."

I say that he'd better hurry up and get me an appointment. Get across the point that he may be real ugly now, but not half as ugly as when I blow his snout off. Just not in so many words.

"Six."

Tells me I'm a fucking bastard. Take it easy, Dingo. Take it nice and slow. Remember who's got the gun in their face.

"Five."

Apparently Shrago's holed up in the roundhouse. Sorta like a private room. Once it housed the cameras. Now's secured better than a vault.

"Four."

"You'll never get in there. Not when they're expecting…"

"Three."

"The king to ride in any second…"

"Two."

"Oh, Jack, please. C'mon, I can't do it!"

"No such word as 'can't', Dingo. You just won't. One."
"It's not possible. You just don't walk in and *see Shrago!*"
"Zero."
"No, wait! I'll try! I'll try! Just don't shoot!"

Dingo starts howling. Tell him to fucking shut it. Tell him to rev his wheels and start dealing some action. Almost immediately, the mongrel begins his spiel. Sounds OK too. Have to hand it to Doggie, he's a real fast thinker.

Revenge and the taste of freedom clouds my mind. Dingo's is clear as the devil's conscience.

Says things are going down like this. Shrago's on the guest list 'cause of his dealings with the club's owner, Johnnie Redd. Redd was a roxter in some anarchic splatterband right side of the collapse. Hung out with a gang of street punks and guerrilla artists each bio-altered in some artsy subvertising way. Joyrida had tusks. Ms Kitsch had a tail. Johnnie went for goat hoofs and shaggy shins. Had one instantly forgettable track on the circuit, then crashed and burned. So the story goes, Redd moved to Dead City and had just unpacked his crates when the world went adios, amigos. Though he's not a bona fide chimera, when he created the Werehouse Gonks kinda have to suffer that he's a near norm. Keep him sweet. Indulge his pomp and circumstance. Yet for all his self-glorifying bravado he's reclusive. Unless I wanna book a promo slot I gotta jump the queue. Queue jumping suits me fine. But gotta be careful. This guy's way smarter than most of the sideshow freakaramas.

Still Dingo's not finished yapping yet.

"He's sitting right now in his ivory tower. Projection room's outta bounds. Real comfortable. Views over the club. Even sound-proofed to stop the music disturbing his peace. Can't see any real problems getting up there-"

"Ut-uh. Problemo uno. He knows me."

Yeah, Shrago could spot me a mile off. Knows my face. My moves. Knows a whole lot. If I was lucky enough to even step across the threshold, if I lived long enough after he recognised me to ask even one question, if I actually got the answer I wanted, how in fuck was I gonna get out again? Still, desperate situations call for desperate measures. And at this moment I'm about as desperate as it gets.

Maybe that's why when the Wonder Dog starts looking thoughtfully at his old serving trolley I don't turn on my heels and run. Maybe. Maybe not. All I know is that Shrago's my only lead. And, hey, what else is there to do in this fucking dump of an evening?

The plan when it comes, comes in a rush. Wonder Dog smuggles me upstairs under the trolley. Once I've passed the clubbers Dog strolls right up to the guards. Says he's delivering some drinks. Dingo assures me this happens. Straight no chasers. Says they're on the 'House. He comes in. Closes the door. I jump out. Wring a few home truths outta Shrago. Pull my piece. D&K's the mixer. Piss the gorillas up the wall. Waste the fucker. Squat in the trolley. Get wheeled away. No noise. No mess. No trouble.

Once Dog's finished I say, "Great plan. I like it."

Fucking plan stinks more than a month-old pair of panties, but it's the only one we got.

"You do?" Dingo's gob-smacked.

"Yeah. I like it. S'kinda plan I like."

When I think about it, this is true enough. It's kinda simple. It's kinda brutal. It's got that simple-brutal mix. I like that in a plan. I get to use my piece. I get to waste the bad guys. I get away. Groovy. The finer points suck, but I can live with that. Perfection's not all it's cracked up to be.

Only thing is, can I trust Dingo? Last thing I want is to be stuck in Shrago's den and find ol' Wonder's fresh outta stuffed olives. Still should've thought of that before I stiffed the gecko.

Wonder Dog's looking sceptical, so I try to reassure him.

"Hell, Dingo, it's a great plan. Let's go."

Trolley's pretty cramped. Made to carry a couple of plates of hors d'oeuvres, not some supersize smörgåsbord like me. Guess I'll manage. Tuck my legs under my chin. Start fixing my D&K to the underside rim. Once I'm in, the cloth comes down. And once the cloth's down

I can't see shit. Pull out my blade and make a slit in the fabric. Put my eye to it. Keep very still. Got quite a good view all-in-all. Real quaint.

Dog pushes off and away we go. Wheels on the trolley squeak like fuck. Each screaming at a different time. Groaning under my weight.

Out in the corridor, Dingo don't hang about. Skids down the hall and curves right into the club itself. Like a tidal wave a wall of sound hits me. Rapes my ears. Crowds dance spastically to some thrash-reggae tripe. Spouting out some manic flashing jukebox. Above the vjox roars. Air heavy with enough narcs to knock out an ox. The animals are getting down. Living it up. Biting each other like a tub of starving vampires. Lightning erupts wildly. Illuminating the gothic edifices of the cinema. More lions. Crows. Frescos. Looming satanic columns. Dark as a pit between the flashes. Screams light the dancefloor in the blackness. Howling. Shrieking. The works. Guess this must have one time been the Stalls. Above the screen rears. It's torn in several places, but can still see the grey celluloid jumble that flickers across the canvas. Wonder what's playing? One of Che Castella's bestiality collection, maybe? *Wart Thing? Creature In The Black Cagoule? Beauty Of The Beast?*

We skirt the savagery. Stop at a big chrome set of doors. Under the arches they look like great metal teeth. Tightly clenched. Dingo stabs the pad. Neon shows 'Dress Circle'. We wait.

Behind us the party's jumping. Track is replaced by another. Beat's the only thing that never changes. Can't see backwards. Sit tight and wait. Just when I'm beginning to think the elevator's not working, the doors spring apart. Few creeps shuffle out. Trolley coasters bump over the metal runners and we're in. No one else around. S'good. Suits me fine. Then, with a menacing hiss, they begin to close.

"Hey, Doggie! Hold the doors for me."

Under his breath I hear Wonder cuss. So who's this then. Sounds like a woman's voice. Near enough. Can't see anything though. My tear's flat up against the panelling.

There's another hiss, then a pause. When the doors hiss again someone's in the compartment with us.

"Thanks, Doggie," the voice says in an off-hand way.

"No problem, Beth."

Oh no, not Beth Deth. Don't know a whole lot about Beth 'cept she's trouble. Sleeps her way into your good books then rats on ya good and proper. Wonder Dog's had the hots for her far back as I can remember. I can see why. Beth may have a face like a tomcat, but she's got tits like you just wouldn't believe.

Earth calling Dingo. You home Dingo?

Aw c'mon, Phantom. Leave me be. I wanna talk to Beth.

Great, the dog's working too.

It's not… It's me. Jack.

Oh, hiya. But it's just Beth. She's one of the cool cats.

OK, you can talk to the feline but just act natural. One false move and ol' Deth-breath's gonna suss us for sure.

Okey-dokey.

Over and out.

Still Beth's nosy as fuck. Don't miss a trick. Even before she starts gassing I know we're in for a rough ride. Far as I recall, that's all she's got to give anyhow.

"Who's the drinks for?"

Great, let's start as we mean to go on…

Dingo pauses. Shuffles in the corner. Skates backwards and forwards. Unsure.

"Taking 'em to Shrago."

"Uh-huh. Thought he had grunts to do that?"

"He does. This is on the 'House."

"From who?"

Another pause. Under the trolley, I'm sweating buckets.

C'mon Dog. For fuck sake answer her.

"From the boss."

Oh great, the boss is sending Shrago drinks. Now doesn't that sound about as likely as a snowman in hell. Ha-bloody-ha. Beth finds the notion amusing too.

"Johnnie Redd's getting generous in his old age. Must be working round to asking for a bigger cut."

Dog laughs nervously.

"Yeah, I guess he is."

And that's the end of that conversation.

Whew.

Too right.

The elevator comes to a halt. The door hisses. Not a moment too soon. Ciao, Beth. Unfortunately the feline slot machine's not quitting that easy. Beth's sniffing the air. I can hear the mucus in her nostrils vibrating.

"What's that smell?" she asks.

Wonder's already moving off, forcing the trolley out into the restaurant. A sudden aroma of food wafts over me, but I know that's not what Beth's referring to. Snake Eyes pissed up my leg. In the confined elevator she's just got a noseful. Dingo don't answer, except with a little yelp. As we race off, I peer out and see Beth. She's still in the lift. Dressed in a clingy black number. Matching bow. Face's screwed up tighter than a cat's ass. She's smelt something's fishy and it sure ain't her supper. I'd give her about a minute before she mewls all to the nearest bouncer.

Dingo, we've been rumbled. Get your skates on.

Aye, aye, cap'n.

The Circle's real class. Overlooking the dancers. Well-heeled creeps stuff meals in their mouths I could only dream of. Looking down the steps my stomach groans with hunger. Wrap one arm round my middle and try not to lose it. Turn immediately right and suddenly we're hauling up a ramp. Speed Dingo's moving at he's lining himself up for a ticket. Still nothing I can do about that now. Then even more suddenly we stop. Nearly shoots me off the trolley.

What the fuck's up this time? Force my eye up to the slit again.

I'm looking at the left leg of a grunt. Gorilla's guarding the door to Shrago's room. Shit, we're here.

"Fuck off, little runt."

"I'm here to see Shrago… Bringing drinks."

"Fuck off, little runt."

Look out past the bouncer. We're in a corridor. Lots of chains and black as midnight. Real sombre. Floor's like polished obsidian.

"They're on the 'House."

Gorilla shifts his bulk. It's clear he don't know what to do.

Under the cloth I can almost hear his mind chewing the fat. Chompa-chompa-chomp. So slow it's painful. Then he decides to frisk the Dog. Whoa, don't get too clever now, ape-man, you'll evolve. When the skatin' waiter comes up zippo, the grunt knocks twice and waves us in. The air is tense like a lover's cheeks. Above my head I hear the glasses tinkle against the bottle, then we're on our way.

The projection room is as near circular as you can get. Holes look down over the restaurant and the dancefloor. Even from the trolley I can see the furry rebels crowding drunk at the bar. Probably swapping combat stories and chatting sex. The rest of the place is covered in leather. All studded crimson. Few pictures, but that's it. Gets to reminding me of a padded cell. Within it's near silent. Just the distant thumping of the dream-like bass and the flapping of turning cards. Shrago sits in a dark green suit. Smoking brown. Room's near full of its sweet-smelling fog. Another grunt stands nearby, but that looks like it. Whole scene's lit by a single lantern that hangs above the table. Behind me I hear the sigh of the door as it seals us in.

Now's the time, Nowhere. Now or never.

I know. I know.

Shrago looks up. His dark eyes frown. He's not expecting company.

"I'm playing Dakkari," he warns. "I was not to be disturbed."

Dog sounds flustered. Can't quite get the words out. Shrago scares the shit outta him.

I make my move.

In one I'm out and standing. Shrago shows a modicum of surprise, but once he recognises me he doesn't let my sudden appearance bother him. The same cannot be said for his lackey. The gorilla hefts a triple-barrelled auto shotgun into his paws and growls. Asks me straight out if I have an appointment.

Oh, brother. Look into my eyes. I've just leapt out from under a trolley. Do I look as if I've got an appointment? Shrago saves my ass with a dismissive wave of his hand.

"Frisk him," he says.

The grunt lumbers up to me. Mauls me all over. Then steps back. The nod he gives his master says I'm clean.

Wonder Dog looks a little perplexed, but I just shrug. Hope to hell he don't shove that trolley. My piece looked mighty precarious balanced on the inner rim.

"Hi, Shrago," I say.

"I'm impressed. No one would be stupid enough to pull this on me."

"Guess you got that wrong."

"So it would seem. Please take a seat."

Shrago sits in the smoky nothing looking seedy.

I've seen it all before. All this trying to look hard. I got looking hard down to a fine art. Level stare. Sit deep in your chair. Keep one hand high while the other's at your piece. Collar up. Mouth tight. I'm no conversationalist, but at times like these it's best to keep talking to a minimum. Single words. Short questions. Most of the time just nods, gestures, grunts. Smiles work too. Best not to smile too much though, else you piss the jerk off. And if you piss the jerk off he'll probably blast you a new navel. Free of charge.

I'm no private dick, but I know the gen. You pick things up on the street. You learn fast. Usually from guys lying bleeding in the gutter who weren't so smart. I flick open my jacket as I slide into a vacant chair. Flash the holster where my piece should be. Just so Shrago don't have to think if I got one. He returns the compliment. Just so I know he has. Nice handle. Looks like a Danzu repeater. Don't catch which one. Still my D&K makes his look like a matchgun. He'd do more damage smacking the butt in my face.

By the look in his eyes he might just have this in mind.

As we 'ball each other I realise the thumping's stopped. This worries me. Snatch a look outta the window. Down below some blond guy comes on stage. He's wearing rubber pants and a sign. Sign says 'W$20'. If he's clean it's a bargain. W$20 says he's crawling. As the bimb begins his parade, dragged-up animals begin singing. Shrago seems interested. Flicks a switch on the table. Song comes in loud and clear over a set of speakers hanging above our heads like a high-tech chandelier. Makes Dingo jump. Don't bother me none. It's not one I know. Least not in that key.

Shrago's eyes don't leave mine. I can see he don't want me here. I sure as hell don't wanna be here. He don't make small talk.

"So, explain yourself, Jackie?"

I tense at the name, but let it go.

"Saw Gut last night."

"So?" Shrago's disinterested. Cool. Casual. He betrays nothing. I try warming things up.

"In the lot… Broadview."

Nothing.

"He's dead."

"I know. News travels fast. You know that."

I nod. Down on the stage the blond has been claimed. Some fat greaseball with one button too few on his shirt. Almost kills blondie as he forces him beneath his flabby paunch.

So Shrago knows Gut's dead. Yeah, sure he would. Probably known for hours. OK, so I'll have to go further.

"I saw him die."

That gets him. Only a slight straightening. Slight narrowing of his eyes. But it's a start.

"How?" he says. One eye twitches from the smoke.

"Wasters."

His eyes roll. "So? Everybody knows that."

"They wasted him."

"Yeah, that was too bad."

Hey, wise guy, Gut was your buddy. Or have you forgotten? He would've chewed shit for you. I'm frothing at the mouth inside. Outside I'm all ice.

"He was doing a deal. Some bitch in an offworld buggy. Then he was splitting."

Now that really gets him. The fish bites.

"Splitting?" He sits right up and spits. I hear his leather pants squeal against the seat. He bares his fangs. All gums 'cept for two teeth, one each side. Filed like a vampire. Boy, you are one ugly mother. I gaze back to the stage. Queenie's into her second song. I know this one. S'all about love leaving town. Irony's lost on Shrago. Cunt don't seem to be listening. He's too tied up putting two and two together. Cool.

"You lying fuck." His levelled tone is frightening. "Gut and me were close. He'd never split. No way."

"The deal was for tickets. I saw the bitch hand 'em over."

"East-11?"

"Yeah. The waystation. One ticket. One way."

That sends him ape. Pulls out his piece and cocks it. He's sweating, but that's nothing new in the 'House. Curses Gut. Curses the city. Curses everyone he can think of. Behind me Dingo gives a little yelp, but stays where he is. Good doggie. Don't blow it for me, ya dumb pooch.

Looks like Shrago knew zippo of his partner's plans. Least not about leaving. I kinda hoped he wouldn't. Still maybe he knew of the deal so I'll have to play it careful now. Shrago's an unknown quantity. And he's holding his popgun prick in both hands. Though I'm dying to carry on I let it go. Let Shrago think. Let him calm down. When he's calmed down, he asks why come and tell him.

"'Cause you knew him."

"You ain't no Samaritan. Try again."

"I'm interested in the bitch."

"I don't know no bitch."

I don't let this worry me.

"Who she worked for. Where she came from."

Shrago shrugs. Not worth his while. With Gut dead he's got little incentive. Well I can soon change that.

"I've got the tickets."

It worked for Shitjack. It could work for me.

"Lucky for you I missed the 250. Now I've got other plans. Especially if you give me the word."

Too chatty, Jack. Get a grip.

"Simple deal. Give me the gen and I'll give you your way outta here. You may have a lotta things, but you ain't got that."

I smile like a cat when it's pissing. Stare right into Shrago's eyes and grin. There's a pause. I look away. The singer's stripping now right down to his fishnets. Then back at Shrago. Will he crack? Won't he…

"Big O," he says flatly.

Hot-diggerty-dog. Well I'll be fucked…

"Gut was talking on the stream. Heard him arranging it."

My head swims like it's full of fish. Wowee. Still I gotta be sure. Ask about the logo. The description fits better than a greasy rubber. Shrago holds out his hands for the tickets. I nod and haul myself to my feet. Dig one hand deep into my back pocket. Look confused. Try the other one. Then as Shrago feels he's in for a wait, he relaxes. And as he relaxes I lash out. Kick his piece across the room. The gorilla lunges. Slams me back into the trolley. Crushes Dingo against the padded wall.

Vaguely I hear the dull thud as my D&K lands on the floor.

Shrago's bodyguard grabs my arms. Butts me full face. I sprawl. Dazed I scrabble around for my piece. Next thing I know gorilla's butting me in the stomach. Uses the end of his shotgun. I double up. Retching. Through my blurry eyes I scan the boards. Can't see a fucking thing. Flail with one arm. The other clutches my gut. The second butt's a little higher. Catches my lowest rib. Ouch. This son-of-a-whore is fucking me off.

If Shrago gives the word I'm history. By the third butt, I'm nearly dead. By the fourth–

Dingo pulls the trigger on my .45 automatic and it howls. Sprays enough lead to fill a piss-pot. Makes short work of the monkey. Gorilla's stiffed before he even drops.

Wriggle to my feet. Grab the gun off Wonder Dog. Turn back to Shrago. Let him stare down the barrel of *my* piece. The mutt retrieves the auto. Now we're cookin'.

Shrago's got his gun too. Points it straight at my brow. His face's a bed of twisted hate.

"Why, you son of a…"

I say nothing. Gun talks a whole lot better. Says 'Fucking shut it' real loud. Look round to make sure no one's too bothered. On the stage Queenie kicks off his knickers to a muted round of cheers. The bimb's head is bobbing in the fat daddy's lap. Not one head's looking our way. No one gives a fuck.

Feel my breath quicken. Fight to control it, but I can't change reality. Reality? The word triggers some half-remembered thought.

"What was in the bag?" I bark. Shrago sneers. "C'mon, you bloodsuckin' cunt. What did Gut have in the bag?"

"Hey, y'know," the buck-toothed bastard says, "I just *can't* remember."

"Shame," I choke, switching my auto to single-shot. "Let's jog your memory a little."

Just to show I've no hard feelings, I give him a present he'll never forget. A bullet with his name on it.

"That's for calling me 'Jackie', you fucking freak."

Beautiful, Jack. Real beautiful.

Glad about the padding. Once it stopped the camera disturbing the suckfaces in the back row. Now it's saved my life. Still I'm ready for the other ape-man. No sound proofing's gonna stop that little fracas from being heard. But there's nothing. Just silence.

In the quiet my mind's already thinking about what Shrago said.

The Big O. That meant only one thing to me.

The Osakimo macrocorporation.

It figured. At least as far as the transport went. From what I knew Osakimo was one of the twelve orbital corporations. Rulers of near-space. Each one was like a huge colony. Each self-sufficient with its own internal workforce. Originally Osakimo's primary role was the creation and manufacture of nu-Tek. Business. Recreation. You name it. They did it. Now they do it all. They'd have the sorta money to pull a stunt like this. Didn't win any prizes, but it was a start.

Look over at the Wonder Dog. He's not looking back. Gaze is all naked terror. He's looking out the window. I look too.

Aw, fuck my old boots. What now?

Outside in the restaurant the whole place has turned into a firefight. Geeks overturn tables while guns blast holes in 'em big as a pro's slit. In the darkness I can't see shit. Just a wave of bodies swarming like rats across the balcony. Then my eyes make out a big grey dude. The mother's sealed inside a metal suit, helmet topped by a plume of feathers. In his hands he's pumping a hip-slung offworld launcher like ammo grows on trees. Reminds me of the cunt in the lot.

"Aw, it's the Knights! We'd better go." Wonder Dog's panting like a puppy on a tight lead. "At the end of the corridor, go straight across. There's a door to the roof. We'll blow it if we-"

"The bike's there. Let's go, Dingo."

Throwing open the door, we level our pieces into the blackness of the passageway. C'mon, fuckface, let's see those kneecaps…

The gorilla's gone. Correction. He's down at the elevator. Lying on his back. His throat a mess of mangled flesh. Beyond him I can see another dark corridor. Within its shadowed arch I can make out a second metal door.

We're gone.

Without thinking I race out into the empty corridor. S'the sorta move that gets ya killed, I know. But, hey, my guess is the shit's gonna hit the fan in less than a minute anyhow and I'm not hanging around to get sprayed.

I'm about halfway when I hear the sound of a grenade. Blows up the door dead ahead of me. Panicking, I skid to my knees and slide like some kamikaze fullback a clear five metres down the slope. Come to rest at the crossroads between the diner, the elevator and the roof exit. This has been blown off its hinges. Now lies in a smouldering heap on the floor. The hole's crowded with armour-clad fuckers. They're led by a silver-plated tin man, the grille of his helm thrown open to reveal a moustached face wrinkled in anger.

Ut-oh.

In abject horror, I kneel before the sword-wielding prick. He's huge. Must be two metres twenty in his high-heeled boots. Guess I'll just squat here and get knighted. Behind me the Gonks are pounding up the Circle steps trying to escape. When they see the Knights, the front few freaks stop and are trampled in the rush.

The bladesman guffaws, his laugh amplified by hidden speakers.

"Yes, it is I, luvvies!" he booms like some mincing thespian. "I, King Kibbutz, GrandMaster of the Knights of K/OS, come to reclaim my cinemagraphic kingdom…"

11 | D'ALESSANDRO

Being offline is like being blind and mortal all at the same time, and is far more excruciating than anything this iron prison has ever put me through. My dependency on these wired-up plastic boxes is nothing short of an addiction. Terminal overdose of the worst kind. Yet while I scrabble with metres of multi-coloured jacks, patch and reconfigure the console and curse every pea-brained programmer who's ever written a routine for this poxy tracking program, I wasn't really thinking about myself. Being offline spelt silence for my unwitting disciples. A silence that could prove fatal. Without access to an uplink they were on their own and until I piggy-backed the next sat, I was unable to do anything short of sit tight and plug like crazy. And all the while I am working, I try not to think that if I lose them – even one of them – all hope is also lost.

Meanwhile on the deck Judie Bloop spirals into a drugged-out dirge over failing to unite with her errant lover and finally kills herself in the penultimate chorus. A children's choir finishes the song. Automatically the track finishes it is replaced by a near-operatic performance of stun guitars and string ensemble by the Sisters of Muso. I cut it instantly. Venting my frustration by queuing up Boy Suicide's Sexual Exile B-side. In five Ms Kitsch, Joyrida and Max Tai start power-ballading their way through the opening eight-bars of *Invisible Sin*. Then it's Johnnie's turn.

"*You gave me more than your love tonight… You took the wrongness and made it feel right. And though I knew it was a lie, I never thought I'd die for your love…*"

Grit my teeth and press on. Dreams it would seem do not die in lightless cages. Dreams, like the song of a captive bird, only get stronger.

Slamming the tracker to manual I call up a bios on the nearest monitor. My fingers move like greased albino spiders tripping lightly on the grubby red keys. My thoughts try to keep focused on the job in hand but stray dangerously as I think of the others and my inability to contact them. Personal motives flash like dark blades. This is no place for me. I should be there. Yet I am not. I'm here. All I can do is pray that I find another ride and get back online before they each go down in a ball of flames.

Even though it seems so long ago, I can remember all too acutely how I happened to be in this ice-bound prison. I was Nathaniel Raymond Glass, respected replicator, the son of one of the single greatest inventors of the last century. Like family Malorian, I had it all. My father's company, the Glass-Suko Corporation, was perhaps not as diverse as the big five, but it had a pioneering spirit far beyond the rest. Named after its co-founders, the company was originally formed as a merging of these men's private concerns over seventy years ago. Each was brilliant and with the combining of their talents, they primarily dealt with the research and development of eighteenth generation sentience structures. Yet this all changed when I met Jack. Well, more when Jack read the book, really. My embryonic ideas of the X-Isle project were dogged with impossibilities, but when Jack decided to drop out of his life of privilege, at last I gained access to all three pieces of the puzzle.

Suko's light-driven bio-anima systems structures required for fast-as-thought processing speeds. Check.

My father's replication technology necessary to capture the near infinite data generated by non-human intelligences. Check.

Malorian's K/OS genetic protocol that facilitated the creation of true sentient intelligence. Check.

The unholy triumvirate for truly sentient mind-machines.

Anima-consciousness.

Replication.

Operating sentience.

Check. Check. Check.

After that, the hostgod was born. And after *that*, my entire life died.

On the advice of my thought channelist, Jarrett, my father denied me access. He said that the backbone was unstable, that anyone entering into contact with the anima would be endangered. He was right, of course, but I defied him anyway. Moving the project to an unused laboratory in the sub-basement of the Phoenix Tower, I carried on my work in secret. The end came when Thomas Bryce Lloyd was murdered by the god machine. I realised that the replication was infected and needed to be restored to rid the X-Isle system of the pandemic that Jack had created, yet by then we were all doomed.

For by then XEs had been born.

After the Osakimo marshals dragged me away I ranted, told them they were all going to die, but no one wanted to listen. I was silenced, sentenced and sent to this life of eternal imprisonment.

Yet the virus remains, soon it will mature and…

And?

"You gave me reason to fear the dark, took every dream I had and tore them apart… And now deep within, your invisible sin is in me…"

I shudder and clip into the next track. A death-folk ballad from Nyarlathotep Or Bust.

Yet once the A-Men had helped me. And now, goddamn them, they were going to help me again.

Seth Campbell Malorian is now the only person in known space who possesses an uninfected RNA code and I am the only one with the knowledge to unlock it. For back in Dead City I snipped out the K/OS code that Jack thought he'd wiped forever. Or should that be the faerie king, Maleore? Now I am ready to save my creation once more. I have been searching for a way to do this ever since my incarceration. The A-Men seemed obvious puppets, and for the longest of times I have been working my way into the surviving members' minds. Current events indicate that the virus is now a known entity, that Osakimo are attempting their own mercy mission but I want to beat them to it. And if The Nowhereman wants to hire a few of his ex-compardres to give him a helping hand, then so be it. Without Esther's firepower, Elliott's codebreaking and Susannah's piloting skills this whole affair could well be a little short-lived anyway. Yet The Nowhereman's is the key to this plan's success; the single driving force in the entire venture. Without him, I could play God until I rotted.

Still it's a complex operation, an open-heart mess of infinite delicacy.

With a buzz of static and white noise, the codes on the monitors vanish and are replaced with maps and coordinates.

And this time a bunch of scripts too.

>Nowhere! Stop right there!

Esther's started to jack Jack's headman. Damn.

>Beautiful, Jack. Real beautiful.

So has Elliott. Double damn.

Also, Susannah's now swapped continents and is showing as checking into the East-11 waystation. That also smells of trouble.

But what about The Nowhereman?

A few more enquiries from the console and the monitors secure a link as the Federal Experimental Satellite-11 comes back into range. From there I waste no time routing a patch directly to the security cameras in the Werehouse. The picture is fuzzy and very dark. At first I cannot make out anything more than a few spots and shadows, but when I boost the signal I get a much clearer...

Ut-oh.

12 | PURE

The private transfer biome of the Tarrenhendre Club is the kind of place anyone earning less than three-point-five million W$ would never be shown the cocktail menu, let alone get inside. This waystation penthouse consists of multiple dark rooms, self lo-lit spaces scattered with real wood and chrome furniture. Outside there's a view of the aft launch plateau. A ragged curve of rusting metal that doesn't get any interesting the more you look at it. I've been here for a while now. Everything slowing up. Getting clearer. Calmer. I'm pirouetting out of my drug daze. The headmusic's quieter. The world's brightness smearing into two hundred and fifty-six shades of the colour grey. Two hours and it'll be cold turkey city dead ahead.

After Lucille dumped my ass here, I've swapped redneck chick for backless chic. Trilliant-cut tiara and Levine-Deville Private Collection. Just the feel of the velvet stirring memories in my mind.

Watching me approach, my new boss sips a gimlet from a sparkling hiball in a futon-couch that redefines my conception of plush.

"Ah, Ms Saint-Clare," the suit smarms. "I am Joseph Malorian."

As he stands to bow I see Malorian is tall for a near-spacer. His just-so mop of silver hair and softly tanned skin as manufactured as his Givenchy suit and no-leather Tri-Ångström brogues. If he's trying for golden age ladykiller, he's succeeding admirably. Yet somehow his eyes are dead; there's no feeling in them. He reminds me of my father, of his complete emotional vacancy; an inability to more than feign anything resembling real feeling. We sit. All poised and comfortable in this pit of luxury.

Findsearch, I think idly. Joseph unknown Malorian.

"Executing search sequence. Joseph Karl Malorian. Son of Seth Campbell Malorian and Helen Catherine Malorian (née Jackson-Kane). Elder brother of John Ewen Malorian. Age: 44 (adjusted). Total annual compensation: W$64 quadrillion. Search completed."

I smile back politely, saying nothing, just a gun for hire. Waiting for the story. Instead he starts with questions.

"Is it true that you originated from Dead City, Ms Saint-Clare?"

"Yes. Left just after the fall…"

"Your dataphial states forty-eight days after the fall," Malorian interrupts. "That's a little late to decide on breaking occlusion zoning, isn't it?"

His voice is so intimate, so personal, I want to lean forward and push my obsidian nails into his fish eyes. Just for the satisfaction of hearing them pop. This is worse than a grilling from Che Castella, but I reply sweetly. "It wasn't my intention to split, but conditions changed."

Joseph leans back in the poromeric imitation leather running his fingers across the double-needle stitching.

"You and Lucille were co-opted into the BurgerQueens," he states matter-of-factly. "Next you joined the A-Men. And finally you abandoned your life and fled to ArcAfrica. Is that what you class a condition change?"

I glance at the suit, but his glassy expression reveals no suggestion of how to proceed. Lean ever-so-slightly forward in my most provocative pose. Nada. More and more the client reminds me of my father. Possibly funny, possibly even charming, but with a big black hole where his heart should beat.

With no clue as to the correct response, I opt for silence while inside I dig a little deeper.

Exec, I try.

"Executive profile: Chairman, chief executive officer and director of Osakimo Corporation. Network: Connected to 7,177 board members in 8 different macrocorporations across 6 sectors. Joseph Karl Malorian has been Chairman of Osakimo Corp., since April 8, 2284 and its Chief Executive Officer since June 1, 2284. Through his vision and passion, Malorian and Osakimo Corp. built XEs from prototype AI into near-space's governing sentience. In 2283, Malorian used his position as Chairman of Glass-Suko's board of directors to merge the two corporations allowing Osakimo unlimited access all areas to the K/OS and the resulting birth of the XEs sentience."

I skim as a drink arrives and is placed on a linen napkin upon the tray table at my side.

The most interesting facets of Malorian's profile concern fairly recent events: the attack and near-complete annihilation of his family, his transfer of stock from Malorian to Osakimo, his inheritance and refitting of the Solar Huntress, a t-freighter formerly owned by his father under contract with the Glass-Suko Corporation. Shipping logs show twenty-three dirtside entries this year alone. For offworlders that's a lot of planetfall.

File for recall.

Malorian bats the ether and immediately a holo rezzes on beside us. And there appears an insect-thin redhead cocooned in mink and ebony silk. A caricature of a lady painted by a man. Lucille! I marvel at her reimagining as some femme fatale from a long-forgotten noir. At the mock-femininity of her gestures as vaguely unsettling as her overly cosmetic features. At her reappearance in my life.

"Hi," the woman breathes. "Well, doesn't our she-bitch assassin scrub up well."

I look across at Malorian, but he's unphased.

"Ms Saint-Clare, may I introduce Lucille. Lucille, this is our *operative*, Ms Saint-Clare…"

"Oh, please, Josie. You know we're old friends. I can't be calling her little miss anything." Then to me: "So how's the interview going? You got the whack job or what?"

"We were waiting for you to join us," he replies for me.

Malorian lifts his right hand and makes a rough alpha gesture. Immediately a dull red construct rezzes on in the air between us. The wireframe resembles a pulsing squid, each tentacle a monitoring arm of power.

"This is a representation of the XEs sentience," Malorian says. "Its every controlling facet, its every aspect of governance. All-told, what you are looking at is a graphical representation of the entire sentient ectosystem. Its effectiveness, its efficiency curves, its economic, security and veracity protocols. In short, a visual of the control system that manages, commands, directs and regulates near-space in its entirety."

"Isn't it freaky?" Lucille purrs, but I say nothing.

"What I am about to reveal is above top secret and highly classified. Outside of this room, this information is only shared by a handful of Osakimo board members."

I snatch a glance at the redhead's holo. Just what have you gotten us into now? I think.

"What my files won't tell you," Malorian says, knowing I've peeked, "is that a self-replicating, self-sustaining and self-destructing virus has been discovered in the XEs' core. And as the progenitor of an infected source it falls to me to rectify the situation before the whole fucking offworld suprastructure collapses…"

Within the heart of the mutating construct a dark smudge appears. As timelines unspool in a wide ellipse, the smear stains the construct a muddy orange. At two thousand four hundred days, the system dies.

"Seven years?" I calculate.

"You are correct, but these are estimates based on clinical tests in human hosts."

I start doing sums in my head. "And how far are we—?"

"One thousand sixty days. Approximately."

"So can't you just wipe up your mess and start again?"

Malorian shifts awkwardly against the back of his armchair.

"Ordinarily this route would be the most proficient. We could renew the genetic protocol and rebuild a clean system inside a twelve-hour timeframe. Regrettably the virus was introduced before I procured the K/OS coding and sold it to Osakimo. We need a clean replication, one created before the introduction of the virus."

"So," I say, realisation dawning, "that's what this's all about."

"Yes," Malorian replies, "but we've got the crystal angle covered."

He gestures and the construct morphs into a geography slice of cityscape. It is just as ugly as the virus. Just as toxic. It's also the place I used to call home. "Even with a new replication, we also need a corresponding K/OS keycode. And for that we need The Nowhereman."

Then, suddenly, I see why I've been hauled into orbit. Why I'm here. Why the kid's dead and his blood is all over my hands.

"No," I say. "No fucking way. D'you think you can just swoop out the sky and snatch me from my–"

"Ms Saint-Clare, your attitude is not conducive to facilitating a mutual agreement–"

"Oh please, Josie," Lucille butts in. "In the words of the great Oscar Wilde: 'Just shut the fuck up, honey.'" Then to me: "And as for you… So we snatched you, did we? From what? From that good ol' rock 'n' roadside shack modus vivendi you had goin'? And how was that little life choice working out for ya, darling?"

I am silent. Deadly silent.

"Time's up?" the redhead looks at her wrist, her non-existent chronometer. "Well, what's it gonna be, girl? Yes or no? What's the matter? You do want your revenge, don't you?"

Oh, Lucille, you dirty, dirty birdie…

13 | DINGO THE WONDER DOG

Watching from Shrago's padded cell, I see The Nowhereman slide to a halt at the foot of King Kibbutz.

Oh boy, oh boy. He's dogmeat this time. Dogmeat for shore.

Even with the goon's shotgun, I'm not going to be able to help much. Best if I wait here and lie low. Cast a look back into the room, but can't really see anywhere's much to hide. Maybe under the table or back under the trolley but apart from that there's zippo. I wonder why Nowhere came here. He didn't really get a whole lot from Shrago. Just a few insults and shit. Didn't really seem like the sorta information you'd wanna get killed for.

The fact that there are no doors from this circular prison niggles me. No way out. Maybe a good place for a last stand if Jack breaks away and heads back up the slope. Perhaps back to the elevator. How come I got involved in this whole darned mess again? All I did was help his gang out for a few weeks way back when. Nothing serious. Nothing that would make any impression. I didn't do it for Nowhere anyhow. I did it for Midnight. She and Biggs were the best, but chances are they're deader than deadski by now. Odds on if they stayed hanging with Jack. Jack don't care for no one. But that's OK. Means I've got no reason to help. Just ride this out then get Bixby and skedaddle. Sounds groovy. That's how it's been for quite a while now. Hit 'n' split. Tonight's no different. Just get to the attic, grab my stuff and skate.

Yeah, why should I help? Why would I? The day Benjie died I turned my back on all that comic book nonsense. I growed up right then and there. He sold me the whole Phantom lie and I just swallowed it wholesale…

"…fucked if I… Hey, leave it, it's working…"

The speaker behind me roars into life as a voice explodes through my brain. Even though it's muffled and distorted in this weird wonky way, I can still identify it as the boss. Johnnie Redd is trying to get the damaged PA working.

Outside the knights are struck rigid by the booming voice. Then it levels and Redd starts his spiel. Jack kneels right where he stopped. He looks up too, but he's not interested in the message. He's looking for a way to escape. If only there were a few less knights. Perhaps I could take a pot shot at one and let him make a break for it. Maybe I could call him up here and we could try to keep them back until the cavalry arrives. Maybe…

"Look, you fuckers. I'm gonna make this real simple. I own this place now and that's all there is to it. You lost out and this is Gonk territory. So if you don't back off then I'm gonna blow the central generator and then no one's gonna get this lustrous love lounge. Don't think it's a bluff, neither. You know I'll do it, Kibbutz. …"

Nowhere glances up to where I'm standing. It's just a quick glance so's as not to give away my position, but I catch it all the same. He looks so lost, so helpless– But hey, why should I risk my flea-ridden neck to save him? If the tables were turned he'd be off outta here without giving me a second thought. Why should I help you? What have you ever done for me?

Still, then from somewhere deep inside comes that voice again. It's Phantom. Can see his muzzle snarling. He's not pleased. This is no way to behave.

'Cause Phantom cannot be compelled to be what he is not. He can't be corrupted or destroyed. He's the Dog Wonder!

Then the elevator pings and when it opens I see the reason, standing right there in the downlights.

Now, I ain't got no choice.

14 | SISTER MIDNIGHT

I sit alone in the cellar cooking seagulls. The fire is the only light and the makeshift spit roasts my catch, filling the damp air with the smell of food. Yet I have no appetite. All my thoughts are for The Nowhereman. God Mûhamet had spoken of my destiny to take up the sword again, resume my one-woman holy war, stop pussying around. And to help Jack. Frankly it was all too much. Why? I think, slowly turning the metal spearing the birds. I was once a warrior for the cause and everything went wrong. And now I am called *back*. I feel so helpless sitting here doing nothing while Jack is in the lion's den attempting to wring whatever he could out of Shrago. Knowing The Nowhereman he'll just blow the geek away and be done with it. Perhaps Dingo could help. Perhaps he'd split and Jack was already stiffed.

For a woman of action such as I, waiting is unbearable. Turning my back on the crackling dinner I swing over to my scattered equipment. Sitting cross-legged before my deck I flip up the grime-encrusted lid and unclip the neuros. Sticking the pins in my ears, I hit Power and watch the console whir into use.

Been a lotta years since I've used this little gizmo. Hope I can remember what's what.

On the keypad the red light turns amber, then mutates to green in a wink while the screen rezzes on. Looking down I see the portal to my own personal nirvana and hit Enter.

Open Sesame, you beautiful bastard.

A kaleidoscope of images sucks me into the great temple while I tap out my passcode and entry details. The machine responds with a muted bleep and in the air before me a cathedral of light and colour opens out. Using my eyes to target I focus upon the archway to the street and signal the whole innerworld to turn to night. Then I begin my voyage along the purple-black tarmac of the local autobahn. It's been years since I last entered the consensual overload of the stream, and though I expected it to be upgraded, the sheer beauty of its enhancements is dazzling.

As I turn out of the chapel the neon streets of streamtown are crowded with passengers. Soar left through a maze of e:node doorways but I don't need to visit anywhere too distant. Effectively this is just a stroll around the block. First I think I'll take a wander to see what links are still operational in this brain-dead city and then perhaps locate that transport Jack was going ga-ga about.

If it really was an orbital, I should find a gateway for it. I twist up past the ragged belt of the black market and out into open space. Each star in the construct is an uplink to the world of near-space, yet I'm searching for something a little more terrestrial.

Perhaps if the transport was unable to leave they'd be sending out a signal or distress call or something? It was worth a try.

Masked only by a shoddily written cloaking program, I slip through the web of passive security trips with the ease of a pro. Using backup shadows and purpose-written ghost routines I'm unstoppable at this level. The trouble comes when I'm faced with anything higher. On the stream I am a 'hiker, not a 'dozer. Must remember that. Setting the deck to scan for any first and second level signals passing through the main ocean uplink, I am faced with a sudden wave of emissions that would take a month to findsearch. Upping the Boolean parameters cuts the trace in half, but if I'm going to decode this garble online my iridium pack would be dead about two weeks before I'd finish. Switching to filter all but the highest accessible codes brings the total to one hundred and fifteen. Thinking this a more manageable number, I hit Spool and suck the whole lot to memory. The heads-up tells me it will take eight seconds.

Good. A V8000 model could do it in two, but eight's cool. Anyhow eight gives me time to hunt for Jack.

Cutting the construct image down to twenty percent, I am suddenly aware of two things simultaneously. For as reality swarms my senses, I smell the burning stench of bird flesh and see the circular busy logo on my deck, both lit in the orange light.

The seagull is beyond saving, but the logo holds me as if trying to seek possession of my soul.

The image is a red and white symbol. A pentagram centred by a winged star. The Osakimo trade mark. I've seen it so many times that it hardly registered anymore. Yet now in the firelight I remember Jack's apartment and the streaked ring of blood on the brickwork. Someone had been trying to draw that logo.

The thought comes as something of a revelation, but that is nothing compared to what the findsearch announced eight seconds later. Of the hundred or so signals, two got hooked by the parameters. One is a coded redneck beamed directly for Heaven.

Allelujah. That must be the transport crying for daddy.

The second's an open pulser situated right at the centre of the bayside cinema.

Oh my god, no—

The signal is uncoded. A tracker beacon the size of a tower block. Any wirehead could pick it up.

And its message?

Badmanjackbadmanjackbadmanjackbadmanjackbadmanjackbadmanjackbadmanjackbadmanjackbadmanjackbadmanjackbadmanjackbadmanjack...

15 | THE NOWHEREMAN

People are fucked-up and dangerous and it's best to keep well away from them. No one needs friends. Friends stink. Only people I ever stabbed in the back were my friends. I have more respect for my enemies. Enemies don't do things unexpected. You're always on your toes with your enemies. Take the Wonder Dog for instance. He's a friend. Least not an enemy. And what's he doing now when I'm in the shit? Zilch. Just a big nothing. Thanks, Dingo. I'll remember that. Still guess he's short on options, but that's hardly the point. Well maybe that *is* the point, but I'm in the shit, right?

Let Johnnie Redd's threat of blowing up the whole fucking place wash over me. Look around. Consider my options. Door to the airbike's crawling with Knights. Shrago's den's dead-end city. Stairs onto the Circle's crowded with gooks. Elevator's someplace else. By the look of things my options are severely limited. Don't look too rosy from my end. But hey, wait a minute. The elevator's moving. Someone's coming up. Here's my chance. When the door opens I'm in there in one. Can't be more than four gooks. Far as I know no Knights are Stallside. Leap in, .45 cumming and punch down. Judging by the scowl on Kinky's face, this may be the last chance I get.

No one seems to have noticed the elevator. Let's hope it's not stuffed fulla explosives. Or worse.

As the cage reaches this floor, Johnnie's just winding up.

"So, what's it to be, tinhead? Back off or kaboom? You're on an open channel… Just tell me what it is."

Kibbutz grinds his heels into the floor as Redd's message ends.

Searches for a suitable riposte. The way he fingers the trigger of his repeater, his options don't look too rosy either.

When that elevator gets here I'm gonna go in before they've got a chance to make small talk. Just lock 'n' load. Hope to hell it's not mr Redd with a bazooka. Well, guess I'm gonna find out real soon now…

The red light beside the grey doors turns green.

Shit or bust, here I come.

Ping.

Ut-oh.

When the elevator opens I'm really not expecting to see either of the two people inside. Though I suppose Beth Deth was a pretty good bet all thing's considered, the other cat's a little more shocking. First I see's side on as he hauls the concertina doors open. Red hair's tucked up into a rancher's hat. Clingy black catsuit just visible under the high-collared expanse of a tatty floor-length mink coat.

Lucille.

Why'd the fuck you come back?

The lipsticked bitch has my stolen dancer to the pussy's head. Using her pawprint to get upstairs. Our eyes meet. There's a certain envious glint in his mascaraed eyes. Something haunting and visceral. Alien. Inside I feel something snap. Looks like another friend's gonna start stabbing.

Never trust a man in red lipstick.

Amen to that. Yet I'm already committed to hijacking the elevator. Already diving forwards. Probably only thing that saves my ass.

In one Lucille hefts the auto into his hand. Lets Beth go. Readies to fire. Kibbutz laughs from twin speakers. Sounds like he's choking.

Once I'm in the cage, I come up fighting. Hit Lucille with the butt my D&K and boot him out. Beth's screaming jars my ears, so I smack her in the face. Whap her palm towards the panel. As the door begins to hiss, I turn to see the Wonder Dog skating like crazy down the slope. Already halfway. Gathering speed and blasting with both barrels. Lucille hits the deck. I duck back too. Can't really tell what's happening. Knights seem as phased as the rest of us. Then

Wonder's in the elevator forcing the inner door closed.

"Touchdown," Dingo mumbles through gritted teeth.

"Hey, Wonder Dog, good work. Going down!"

I force the pussy's hand onto the floor controls, but Dingo's quicker by a fraction. He punches up.

"What the fuck're ya doing?" I yell as the cage jolts into motion.

"The bike," Dingo's yelping. "There's a skylight from my attic."

I nod. Didn't know this place had three floors. Turns out it's got five.

As the sound of gunfire subsides to an echoed drumming, I relax and wonder at what's just happened.

Last time I saw Lucille he was heading out. After we pooped and partied for the last few years, we kinda drifted once Gut came on the scene. Yet somehow he held up the E-250 with a few of his sidekicks and blew away Shitjack's mother and sister, leaving the lad for the fucksters. He'd risked his all for those tickets and now he's back with my dancer and a belt fulla trouble. I think of what Sister said in the cellar. About Pure and the end of the A-Men. Now I find the whole thing just a little bit fishy. But the pieces do fit if you look at 'em in a certain way. After all who knew where I was living? Who knew Gut? Who could have turned up here just when the shit was hitting the fan? But still, the timing's perfect. Too perfect.

Jack?

Sister? How goes it?

No time for that. I'm on the stream. Found your ass via a homer. You're glowing like the holy father of holies.

Sheesh. Fuckadeedoo. No more wondering how Lucille turned up. But a homer? How'd he fix that?

Where's it hiding, Sis?

Scanning...

Ping.

The elevator grinds to a halt. The winding gear sighs. We're at the top. Dingo reaches forwards to slide open the steel bars. I stop him.

"Wait."

He doesn't question this too much. Just moves closer to Beth and tries to make sure she don't pull nothing. C'mon, Sister. What's keeping you, ya dumb bitch?

I've got it.

Where?

Upper shoulder. Just below the left clavicle.

Gruesome.

Looks that way.

I sneer. Glance at my left shoulder like it's made of shit. Look across at Dingo. Poor Wonder's lost the thread. Who can blame him. Can't say I'm keeping total score myself. Let my mind wash through the past events. Seems like all my compardres are turning on me. One by one by one. Which begs the question: is Dingo good or bad? I think, then let him pass. He didn't know nothing about me coming here. He's clean. I'll let him live.

Great news, Sis. Wanna hear some more? Just met Lucille.

Where?

In the elevator.

Then he's the badman.

Exactamundo, princess.

That's why Gruesome planted the tracker. Lucille was on that transport. Must've seen I got hit. Knew I'd go to the Doc. Lucille's sold out. He's fucking one of them.

Osakimo.

Whoever.

Jack, I want you back here. Now.

I'm coming, little sister. I'm coming.

"Dingo, where next?"

My voice is loud in the cage. Even though I'm whispering. Rapes the silence in a word.

"We're on fifth," says the Wonder Dog. "Just storage mainly. My attic's down and right."

"Any stairs?"

"Yes sir. They're at the other end. Run to every level."

"Accessible from the Circle?"

"There's a door. It's locked pretty much all the time…"

"Forget it. Lock's don't mean shit." So if they're following the elevator that's the way they'll have to come. And I've already given them too much time already. "Lead the way."

Wonder Dog drags open the double set of doors. Wedges them wide open with a screwdriver he gets from somewheres. Behind him Beth plays with her hair. Behind her I lift my D&K and level it at the pussy's head. No reason to keep hostages. Just blow her before she starts some trouble.

The click of my safety makes Beth's ears twitch. She twists her head around. Stares right down the end of my piece. Freezes. Lets out a startled miaow. Dog's out in the dusty store now. Hear's Beth's shriek and jumps for the shotgun. Now I'm looking down three barrels.

Hey, Wonder. She's excess baggage.

She's my girl, Nowhere.

You dumb fuck. She'll rat on us first chance she gets.

That's as maybe, but you ain't killing her.

OK.

OK.

I smile a thin dry smile. Lower my barrel. After a few moments, Dog lowers his.

Still don't mean she'll not get caught in the crossfire, Dingo. Or lose her footing climbing outta the skylight. However much furface's in love with this cat, there's no way that bike's gonna carry three. Hey, I'm not being nasty, Dingo. It's just all down to elementary physics. Gravity. That sorta shit. S'got nothing to do with the fact that Dethbreath's a Gonkie whore who's had every mad fucker up her cunt this side of orbit. Naw, nothing at all.

Outside is all boxes. Everywhere you look there are crates and chests and great square coffins under musty tarpaulins. Metal girders grace the ceiling. Punctured by grimy hollows. Guess they're little windows. Treading like mice we creep through the hollow graveyard.

Neon from the elevator is the only light. Thing's pinging like it's hurt. Guess someone's trying to call it. Too bad.

From below there's the sound of gunfire again. The thwump-thwump-thwump of grenades. Distant. Like a storm. Explosions shake the boxes. Shudders dust from overhead. Looks like the Knights have called Johnnie's bluff.

We keep on going. If Redd's not the wet wuss I've heard he is we may only have a few minutes to kick clear. Turning right store ends in a door. Marked 'Emergency Exit'. Set into the wall is a ladder. Leads up to a trapdoor. Must be Dingo's den.

"Don't stop," I say. "No time."

Dingo gives me a look that says he knows the score. Good. Keeps him edgy. He checks the emptiness around him, then starts climbing. Putting my back between me and the wall I feel for the handle on the door. D&K ready. As Dingo keys his way into the attic, I slip my hand around the knob. Ease it gently.

It opens without so much as a click.

Dingo. Door's open. Someone's…

My ears are filled with the squeal of bullets. Swiping Beth away like a rag doll. Erupting into the wall. Blasting me to my knees. It's Lucille. I'd know the sound of my dancer anywhere. You're one swifty-assed bitch…

Beth! Oh shit shit shit…

Wonder Dog, pull it together.

Beth! Is she…

Doornail. Dingo, where's the gook?

Target ten metres, Jack. Behind the Bandito crates.

I'm hit. Cornered. Get the bike. Don't wait for me.

No I…

Go, you sad fucking mutt. GO!

I'm gone.

Above Wonder disappears into his attic. Over the belt-fed, I hear a dog barking.

Fuck, I'm hit. Pussy took the brunt. Damn bitch saved my ass. Too late for thank-yous now. I crawl into a crack between two boxes and check myself over. Flesh wounds. Every last one. Dancer never was too hot on performance. Always wins on sheer brute force. Too manic for any real stopping power.

As the trapdoor slams shut above, the barrage ceases. All that's left is the ringing in my ears.

Jack. I've found out something else about Osakimo…
Forget it, Sis. I'm a little busy.
Anything you can't handle?
No.
OK.

Yowzer, Midnight. Do I need you now. Wish I was back between those big black thighs and not here in this dusty morgue.

Something shifts in the stale twilight. Lucille is trying to see who made it. Guess my tracker's still saying I'm over here. Wonder how accurate that thing is? Don't wanna wait and find out. I wanna act, but need to give Dog a little time. Need a little time myself. Just to sit here and bleed for a bit. Gird my loins. That sorta shit. If Lucille comes now I'm one dead fucker. Then I hear the clack of his heels on the floorboards and I know he's coming for me. No time for anything. Not even dying.

"Hey Lucille…" I try to keep the pain from my voice. Fail. Take three deep breaths and try again. "Hey, Lucky. Great to have you back. Guess ya missed me, huh?"

Out in the darkness the transsexual pauses. Double meaning's not lost on the cunning prick. He's wondering how come I'm still alive. I hear him duck back under whatever rock he was lurking. Lucille's not a man for taking chances. He may be a mid-op leftover from some BurgerQueen snip joint, but he ain't no bimbo.

There's a pause while the bitch's brain tries to come up with some fancy retort. Then he deals me the same dozy line.

"Jackie… Darling Jackie… Don't be mad with me. Daddy knows I wouldn't hurt one hair on his little head."

Yeah, right. If I'd have been standing with Beth the hairs on my head would've been the only bits left. And don't call me Jackie. Then I remember Shrago and I know they're all in this together. Know this trick's been planned for a whole long while. I'm angry now. Force my numb body onto my knees. Crab down past the end of the long crate I'm pressed against. Peer out around the side. Nothing. Just an avenue of covered boxes.

"Forget it, Lucky. You want me deader than deadski. It's too late to try pulling all that daddy-babe shit."

Slowly I ease myself around the crate and into the alley. Keep to the joists. Off the centre of the floorboards.

"How can you say those things, Jackie? Baby-doll's here 'cause you needs her. Lucky's back 'cause she's gonna take you away from all this. Like she promised you. My cards came up, lover. I'm here to take you away."

Take me away, huh? Fucking take me out's more like. I try to move only when Lucille's yakking. Try to keep him guessing. Still I need about ten more seconds to reach the end of the alley. Got to keep him talking. I waddle back a few steps. Back to the long crate. Wince at the amount of blood pooled in the dust.

Here goes.

"Fuck you, Lucille. That shit don't wash with me. Just what did Osakimo offer you? Why'd you sell me out? Semi-permanent ringlets? My diamond-studded arse on a platter?" Silence, so I continue. "I know the score. Lucille. Know all about you and your deals. About Gruesome. Osakimo. Everything. Only thing I don't know is why I didn't cream you in the elevator."

When the trannie starts talking again, I'm moving fast as I can.

"Jackie! How can you say such dirty words? Baby-doll ain't in with no one. You know that. That's why you let old Lucky live. You know in your heart of hearts that I came back for you. You know baby's always been there for you. Always been the one thing in your life that really, really mattered..."

I break cover about five metres away from the safety of the elevator. Cage's still pinging like a forgotten newborn. Even as Lucille notices me, even as he lets my dancer erupt in a blaze of arcing death, I'm already inside. Slamming myself against the veneered walls, I heave the mesh door closed. Slide down to my haunches. Watch as the screwdriver spins to the floor with a little clang.

Outside the crates come to life. Bursting like dried husks. Splitting like wooden peapods. Spilling their long-forgotten contents across the grimy floor. Here hastily-sewn costumes sprawl in a weird pantomime of gaudy silks. There paint spews like primary-coloured vomit from punctured tins. All around the morgue is suddenly alive. Filled with a vivid performance of ancient props.

"You cunting prick!" Lucille is screaming, all pretence lost in the heat of the moment. "You cunting jacked-up little shit!"

Now, now, Baby-doll. Don't get all hot under the choker. I'm sick with smugness as I whap my hand on the plate. Now I'm outta here.

Nothing.

I hit the panel again.

Double nothing.

But the fucking thing was pinging. I should be outta here already.

Something flashes across the display.

>**User unknown. Access denied. Please seek assistance.**

Oh fuck. It's fingerprinted.

>**Please seek assistance.**

I sink to the floor.

>**Please seek assistance.**

Outside the shooting stops. Burnt-out shells skitter on the floor. Then silence.

Nowhere, you able to talk yet?

Maybe the last time, Sister.

Yeah, go ahead.

Lucille is taking deep breaths. Real deep breaths. So deep it's a wonder he ain't hyperventilating. He's got me now. Unless–

That transport is sending a signal to Heaven. Right to Osakimo HQ. After that I lose it.

Yeah, so what?

Signal's coming from Lincoln, just off El Camino. As far as my street atlas goes, that's — and you'll love this — Forevermore. Far as I figure Osakimo will be sending help...

I don't really catch the rest. I'm too busy with my own thoughts. Forevermore? You mean, just like in the story?

Glass-Suko built it, though hell knows why. It's now turf for the Knights of K/OS. Jack, just get your ass out of there and back here. Jack?

A shadow falls across the cage door. Lucille has come to get even. Damned if I know why he don't just spray the elevator.

Maybe Osakimo want you alive.

Who's this?

The big G.

Hey, you back again?

Nobody's perfect. Even God.

The Big O want me alive? Oh yeah. Fat chance.

No really. Listen...

There's a sound like a hornet's nest right between my ears. Then it levels and something's patched in its place. At first it's all grungy like through a rigged-up vocoder. Then the voices come loud and clear.

...tolerated. Stop at once. If the subject is to be of any use, then his brain must be intact. Shoot to wound. Kill him and you will follow...

Holy shit.

Where the hell's this coming from?

Out of Lucille's head.

Fuck. Really?

Really.

I'm up in one. Stepping forward I press myself against the diamond cage and leer through the gaps.

"Hey, Lucky. Guess ya still missing me, huh?"

The mink-coated bitch gives me a look few ever live to see. This look's hate. Pure hate. Sugar-coated hate with hate on top. Hate like only ex-lovers can feel. The sorta hate that screws your every last shred of human compassion replacing it with filthy, maggot-ridden malice.

In that moment, I know that I've made a mistake. That Lucille ain't gonna take no notice of any shitting orders. He wants my ass and I just delivered him reason enough to grease me twice over.

You're too cocky, that's your trouble Jack. Too fucking cocky. Maybe next time round you won't be such a prize prick.

Even as I leap back into the confines of the elevator Lucille hefts the metal butt of my dancer into his belly and stabs his finger against the hair-trigger.

"Fuck you, daddio."

With a heart-rending eruption, the belt-fed blasts the elevator to hell. Ripping. Tearing. Sending shudders like an orgasm through my legs. Bullets lacerate the veneer. Turn the wall into a splintered mass.

All I can do is lift and cock my D&K. Try to get an aim on the crazed transsexual.

Lucille don't wanna get plugged and there's no way I can hang out and take a pot shot. Not without getting a face full of lead. Why can't someone authorised try to use the elevator? Why's it have to be some no-hoper knight with the brain of a duck? Why not some cool-assed Gonkie suit wise enough to override the fucking thing? Never thought I'd miss Dingo, but my bet's he'd have this thing sussed in seconds.

By the sound of it, Lucille's going fucking crazy. Sounds like he's gonna empty that dancer too. Spraying every which way. Sparks fly off the metal cage, making the veneer look like cartoon cheese. Ricochet hits the control panel. Shorts it good and proper. Fuses. Fizzles. Blows. Showers me in red hot plastic shards. Stick like molten metal to my leathers. Burn bright holes in my skin.

I yell out the hurt. The floor jerks. Then in one the elevator drops about a metre, quivers, then judders into a staggered descent.

Lucille's anguish joins mine. Same sound. Different reasons.

Now you owe me another one.

Wonder where I'm gonna end up this time?

Force my bloody burning body to its feet. Check my D&K. Shovel ammo from my pocket. Reload. Brace it in both hands. Once

my gun's loaded, I'm happy. Breathe deep. Clear my head.
    Pass fourth without a second look.
    My guess is the Circle. Only place that makes sense.
    Pass third.
    Can hear the firefight again. Fuck, this is bad. What chance have I got against autos? Might as well come out with my hands up.
    Pass second.
    What? Hey, now it's cool. Stalls may be OK. Least I stand a chance with the Gonks. S'long as it ain't Johnnie Redd I'm laughing.
    The elevator judders to a halt on first.
    Ping.
    Pull open the cage. Look out on a crowd of geeks all tooled up and ready for war. And at the front stands Johnnie Redd.
    Oh, fucking terrific.
    The owner of the Werehouse wears his wedge of ash-blond hair in a tail linked to five wires that jack the nape of his neck. His hastily donned flakvest is thrown over a white buccaneer blouson. His tight jocks leave his legs bare, accentuating a neat basket and the delicate suede of his Burgundian boots. Notice they're shaped to hide his cloven hooves. Painted nails wrap around a rifle I've never seen before. Looks cosmic. Wouldn't want to mess with it whatever. Looks like it spits electric death to twenty paces.

    Redd sizes me aiming my piece at his head. His enigmatic smile is enough to fill my pants. Guess he don't know who I am. Guess he's got nothing to lose just by blowing me away. But he don't. Instead he just gives me this wild-eyed grin. Somehow that's worse. He'll probably be grinning like that as he wastes me.

    Around him his gookie friends all jostle to see what's on show. The closest is this scaly croc. All teeth and bandannas. Looks like he should be stuffed and on a wall. He's naked but for a little baseball cap. Got 'Gad Zooks' embroidered on the front. In his claws he clearly holds a primed detonator. You can tell it's primed the way the countdown flashes in the smoky half-light.

>10:26:54.

Great. Just fucking great.

Ten minutes and my troubles are over.

I think I can patch central.

What? Is this Dingo?

You know who it is. And I'm saying I think I can patch the central processor. To the Werehouse.

Do it.

"Sorry folks." I say to my captive audience. "Sideshow's over."

For a moment all the lights in the whole fucking building come on. Glow brighter than the sun. My eyes strain and then everything goes black. I don't wait for applause.

Three's the magic number.

Dropping to the floor I crawl hand-over-hand out of the cage. Guns roar over my head. Once clear I roll. Hit legs. Feel something furry kick me. Blow it off with a shell. Carry on. In the confusion I let off another few shots. Soon the air's full of random blasts. Once the chaos starts there's no stopping it. When I reach the end of the bodies I pull myself up. Find I'm at the disco booth. Illuminated by rows of twinkling lights. Clamber over the deck and drop into the space behind. Now I'm safe. At least for a while. Got to get to Dingo.

Wonder Dog? Meet roofside. Gimme five.

Place is swarming. Too dangerous to get close.

Five minutes. Then you can go.

OK. Flyby in five. If you don't show, I'm outta here.

Fair doos.

Five's enough. Just got to reach the stairs and…

There's an explosion of fire and shrapnel. Off away to the left. Guess the stairs are a little hot right now. Gunfire lights up figures. So many knights it looks like a fucking tournament. Jeez, what next? I'm trapped. Guess it's time to make like a pizza. Nowhere to go? Comin' right up!

"Hey, fella, you mind not stepping on my 3Es."

Feel dizzy as I look down. On the floor under the main console is this rat-faced vjox. He looks up at me looking down. Sees I'm no Gonk. Panics. I grab him by the scruff of his face and haul him up. Demand a way to the roof. Tell him I'll kill him if his answer has the words 'stairs' or 'elevator' in it. Seems to work.

"There's no other way. Those are the only ways. If you wanna go up, you have to use the stairs..."

Blam.

My piece makes pasta of his right knee.

"Try thinking harder," I say real close to his ear. So he can hear me over his screaming.

"No. There's no other way. Don't! Don't!" says the rat.

"Don't what?" Shove my D&K against his other knee.

Ratty shits himself. Crap floods his flowery shorts. Runs like chocolate porridge all down his legs. Fucking cunt.

"I oughta chuck you back in the cesspool you were born in."

The jockey collapses into a quivering heap. It's pitiful. Yet I've just had an idea.

"Sewers. There must be ducts running under here. Where's the boiler room? Where'd you chuck the slops?"

Ratty's beady eyes light up at this. Here's something he can answer. Almost chokes on his little pink tongue trying to get the words out quick enough.

"Yes, yes. I know where. Behind the screen. Here. Behind the screen. There's a grille. There's steps. Down to the drains—"

"Thanks."

Then I kill him. Nothing worse than a fella who shits his pants. S'unforgivable.

Outside the battle rages, but I want no part of that. OK, so the imminent attack of the K/OS queens might just *happen* to coincide with my arrival, but I'm not gonna get all guilt-ridden over a few dead zeebs. If Osakimo wants my ass then they'll have to be a bit more professional. Sending Dorothy and twenty tinmen ain't gonna get them Nowhere. Least not this side of the rainbow. The Knights must've been a safe bet once I'd plumped for coming here. Also they owned the Forevermore theme park. Great place to hole out a transport. Real groovy.

Pull out Sister's knife. Still got gecko guts all over it. Stab it cleanly into the silver screen. Canvas punctures like milky flesh. Drag the blade down. Form a slit about a metre high. Check that no one's too bothered by this. No one is. Then slip on through.

Behind the screen the only light is from the diocam. Projection passes lazily through the dusty air. Makes no sense till it reforms on the white curtain. S'like a maze behind the scenes. Little corridors connecting tiny chambers. Look like dressing rooms. This place must've been a theatre once. Find a barred door that leads down to the understage. Steps're covered with green puke. Have to blow the padlock. Echo nearly deafens me. Hope in the furore it's not noticed.

Once the lock's off, swing in the door. Crouch and peer down. Beyond I see a slime-filled cellar. Debris. A work table. All that sorta shit. And the unmistakable stench of open drains. Bingo. Never thought I'd be so pleased to see the ass-end of a toilet.

"Jackie! My darling! Don't worry, baby. Lucky's coming as fast as she can…"

The words send shivers down my spine. Lucille's one fast mover. Guess the Knights have taken control of the stairs. That tracker's gotta go. Well, I know one sure way of getting rid of it. Twist my D&K in my hand. Press the barrel up against my bandaged shoulder. Don't think about it, Jack. Just flick that trigger and your worries will be over. Yeah, right and what if I black. Lucille's gonna get his cake and eat it. No way. I'm just not up to the risk. For now the homer stays. Like it or not. Just gotta outsmart the bitch. Or pop a few in his head.

In a firefight, I'd be outgunned and outmanoeuvred. I'm just a limping pile of shit. Gotta keep going. Hope it's not too far. If I can just get out and call Dingo, we'll be flying. Then try dogging my tail, ya red-lipped tart.

Move with haste, yet not without caution. Head down the gooey steps. Onto the platform below. Drains lie beyond a series of metal covers. Most are broken open spilling raw sewage. Neat. Nothing quite so appealing as unprocessed slime.

Whatever reticence I feel is brushed aside by the sound of Lucille's heels clacking down the corridor. Stow my gun and sit down on the side of the channel. Push off and drop into the shit. Begin wading toward the pipes.

What a way to spend an evening.

Choose a way by eenie-meenie. Haul ass through the hole. Squirm along face-first through crap until it opens up into a wider channel. All reinforced brick and brown water. Try to keep my mouth outta the effluence. Fail. Spew shit. Then carry on.

Lucille sends a round down the stairs. Just to be sure. Then I hear him follow. Imagine his look of realisation as he susses where I've gone. C'mon, you fucker. You've almost caught up. Another round tears brick to pieces at my back.

"Jackie, you prick… You pissing, fat bastard!"

Sounds kinda frustrated.

Slip out the tube and into the river of shite. Surface and clear my eyes. Which way now? Guess I'll just go with the flow. After all out is out any way you look at it.

Lay on my back and keep afloat. Let the current nudge me gently along. Pass grilles, a few crossroads, overflow pipes – the whole fucking works. Just when I'm getting used to the stink, I hear a thunderous splash from way back. Followed by a stream of effeminate curses. Well, screw me. I didn't know he had it in him.

Turn onto my front. Guess I'd better start swimming.

Down in the dark, I lose all sense of direction. Just endless twisty turny passages all fulla shitty water. Mostly I let the flow decide, yet I kinda feel that's too obvious. Keep forgetting Lucky's got a tracker. He'd find me even if I disappeared up my own buttcrack. Then just as I begin to give up the thought of ever getting outta this puke, I hear waves. Smell the salty wind. Waste pipe's heading for the bay.

Feel like hollering. Won't give Lucille the pleasure. Let him keep checking his finder.

Dingo, you there?

Yeah, I'm still circling. Should've gone two minutes ago.

That's my boy!

Hey, Nowhere, d'you know this rod's running on air? Tank's lower than a dachshund's fanny.

Yeah, I know. Look Wonder, I'm not in the Werehouse...

What?

I'm being tracked. I'm at the bay. Down in the sewers.

AOK.

Ya gotta hurry. Big trouble on my tail.

And closing.

Coming right up.

And don't forget the extra olives.

Eh?

Don't worry. Private joke.

With a sound like a volcano getting even, Johnnie Redd calls last orders at the Werehouse. Almost blows me off my feet. Can't imagine what nuking the central gen would do to a building, but probably collapsing in on itself is a safe bet. All that's left'll be just one big pile of dust. Hey, have to give it to the goat-footed freak, he damn sure has style. I felt odd's-on he was bluffing.

Oh no, Jack. Johnnie's just...

I know, Dingo. I know.

Wonder where the Werehouse will pop up next?

Around the corner I'm blinded by the light at the end of the tunnel. Morning has broken. Great sky. All pinks and greys. Cool. The river ends at the mouth to a gigantic pipe. Looks plain sailing. Then when I get closer I see the exit's covered by a micro-thin mesh.

So close...

Pull out my D&K, pull the trigger and watch as nothing happens. Must've got shit down the end. Try the knife. Can't even start to scratch the fucking turd-stained lattice.

Modern technology sucks. I hate it. Complete waste of time.

What was wrong with living in caves and crapping in the bushes? Why ain't we ever content?

"What's the matter, daddy? You in trouble down there?"

I can almost taste the sarcasm in Lucille's voice. Yeah, tastes just like raw sewage. Puke. Puke. Puke.

Lucille rounds the corner too. No gun. No hat. All I can see of the mink's the shit-coated collar.

Hey, that was a present, you fuck. Do you know the trouble I had getting that coat?

Looks like we're gonna fight. Finally there's only him and me and nowhere left to go. Lift Sister's stiletto from the slime. It's thin blade gleams in the soft light. Lucille keeps coming. Draws his own dagger. This one's bigger. Curved edge. Serrated. Look's rusty too. Yummy. Lockjaw's just what I need. My last tetanus jab was when I was eight. Still even if my exotoxins are fucked over, I'm sure swallowing crap's gonna finish me first.

So much for life on the edge.

The brown-faced bitch closes for the kill. Lunges and swipes like a madman. Sprays shitty sewage. Try to duck inside his guard. Water slows me. Sends me wide. Grit my teeth and haul myself toward the wall. Lucille splashes along behind. Feel his blade slash my jacket. Grazes my skin. Brick floor's uneven as hell. Flail my arms to keep from going under.

Outside Dingo zips into view and arcs over the bay. Bike's searchlights are on full beam. Looking for which pipe I'm in. Barks a few barks to say he's here. Can't believe it when I see he's got some mutt riding pillion. Sitting behind with its ears flapping.

Can't do anything just now. Gotta keep away from Lucille. He always was better with a blade. Feel like I'm running. Tell myself I'm not.

Turn to face Lucille's stream of obscenities. Nothing to make me blush. Still pisses me off though. Stab at the trannie. Wince as I slice the fur from his collar.

"What's the matter, Jackie? Lost the knack?"

You pathetic fucker. Always were one verbal son of a bitch.

"I've heard it's all in the wrist action, fuck-buddy."

Don't rile me, Lucky…

"C'mon, Jackie-babe. Tables are turned now, eh? Good to see *your* ass on the line."

That does it. Throw all my weight at the thin whore. Grab his throat and we go under. Feel him kicking in the midnight water. Just press harder. Fingers find his Adam's apple. Use all my remaining strength to strangle the cunt to death.

Lucille's knife finds flesh. Slashes me. Right across my left forearm. Starts pulsing with a dull ache. Filling with shit.

Still don't let go.

Way he's struggling I'd give Lucille about another twenty.

After fifteen I run out of breath. Have to surface. In my haste I pull the fucker's head up with me. Lucky gasps for breath before I can shove him down again. Yet this time when I do I keep my neck out the water.

Now I've got you, ya piece of trash.

Outside I see Dingo hovering above the bay. Sending jets like steam all over. Now Knights are there too. In some open topped inflatable. Firing. Shrieking. That sorta shit.

Jack, this is getting dicey.

OK. OK. Just a few more seconds…

I gotta go, Jack. Grav's zero.

Fuck it. No way.

Then I hear a noise like the rushing of the wind. Turn to see a great roaring wall of water as it rounds the corner. Caused by the explosion, it rushes with tidal force towards us. Have just enough time to hold my nose. Not that that's gonna do shit.

Dingo, I'm going down.

No, Jack, I'm coming!

Shut it, ya stupid pooch. Listen. Make a break for the cellar. Gypsy Hill. Midnight's there…

Sister's alive?

Yeah, and tell her goodbye from me. Will ya do that?

Gotcha. I'm gone.

Oh, and Dingo. Watch for the tripwire. Third step. Blow your fucking legs off.

Then the wave hits. Throws me. Throws Lucille. Both tossed like a virgin prick. Feel the mess against my face.

Water thunders. Rips. Roars. Rocks and rolls.

Water gets up my nose. Down my throat. Water everywhere. Filling my lungs. My ears. My head–

Zzzzzzt…

16 | D'ALESSANDRO

Damnation.

Watching is the worst. At least up until now I have only been able to monitor, to postulate upon the scenes of my four acolytes. Yet when I plug into the security network of the Werehouse I watch the unfolding events as if they were some Saturday morning sitcom. I can see Jack's life hanging in the balance, his look of relief as the elevator descends, the horror at facing Johnnie Redd. The subsequent chase through the bowels of the cineplex. I can view it all from a variety of angles. None of which make the situation look any better.

The sixth screen is bleeping. Telling me it's found something. Cannot even recall which task I set it to perform… Yes, yes I do. It was searching for the hostgod, seeking a trace of past glories. Hunting for a glimmer of light. And by blind luck it appears to have found it, though it seems no coincidence that my findsearching snags something now.

Swing in my chair. Forget for a moment about the others and patch a keypad into the front jack. Tapping at the buff-coloured pad, the terminal blips into life and a weird visual display fades into view. The keyboard feels oddly cold beneath my trembling fingers and the chatter of the keys seem as loud as footsteps in the quiet darkness of the room. In the eerie green light of the humming terminal, I flip open the dog-eared code manual searching for the correct command line that will allow access to the entry sequence.

The screen is headed by three words.
>Hostgod interrupt. Access?

The query requires the correct passcode. It may be timed. It might also wink out at any moment. I can only give myself a few seconds, then I'll have to drop the line.

Come on, D'Alessandro. Find that code.

Near the back of the tatty volume, I find a list of skeleton passkeys. Pick the third from last. Seems to suggest eighteenth generation. Well, maybe. Tap in the meaningless digits. And miraculously I'm in.

Upon the screen sudden letters dance before my eyes. Deadly and familiar and a confirmation that the X-Isle project is far from over.

>**Internal date: 07/05/11.4 Gyr.**
>**Internal time: 04:12:45.**
>**Day of project: 4748.**
>**Machine: Sol Series 1140.**
>**Prototype number: 156008-a12.**
>**Sentience: Ianus.**
>**Programming language: K/OS.**
>**Copyright © Glass-Suko Corporation. All rights reserved.**

But my elation at finding the Osakimo e:node is soon dashed by what next appears.

>**User/psychist. Identify.**

My blood runs cold. There is no way I am even going to attempt this one. It's as if I can already hear the command line sounding klaxons throughout the fortress.

If only I knew the codes. I have the key but not the entire RNA sequence. For that I needed to access Jack's father. And for that I needed Jack. As do Osakimo. What other reason for the arrival of the t-freighter in Dead City?

Damnation.

Stiffly I punch the keyboard and drop the line. Unjack. Maybe I should come clean, tell The Nowhereman what this is all about. Then at least he would know, could help me instead of being an unknowing meatpuppet. Yet I realise all too well that this would be futile. In Jack's case, ignorance is bliss. If The Nowhereman guessed what I had planned he would resist every step of the way. My only hope is to keep the carrot of his fanciful dream dangling large in his sights. Only then have I any chance at making fail the Osakimo coup de grâce.

Four years ago when I wound up in this ice-bound prison, I was so close to completion. Still, there are compensations. Had I not encountered Jack at the Phoenix Tower, or gained the A-Men's aid in the assault on my own corporation's construct, I would not be on their personal network. And without that I would not have this link to the outside world; impossibly fragile though it is.

I pause for a moment to reflect upon the foresight of my move to discard their archaic retrotech comlinks and fit them all with brand new headmans. A snip at just under W$15 million. In return for my blaisé generosity Jack's guerrilla force stormed the Glass-Suko fortress and wiped out 101 percent trace of the evidence against me. Without that essential data my case would have been voided. I would have been a free man. Regrettably the black woman forgot to disable the autorestructure parameters and in eight hours the AI had pieced all the exploded data back together. Finetoothing is one of my specialities. Unfortunately it is not one of hers. My employees hired a hundred mercenaries to storm the Phoenix Tower, then backed them up with a dual-pass airstrike. It took them five hours. The A-Men were destroyed that fateful day on 13th and Logan and I was thrown into captivity.

So the code is still infected. And someday soon, Xankhara will die forever.

Fortunately their headmans are still synced to my private frequency allowing me to communicate whenever I wanted; satellites willing, of course. The raw sexless message code – my whispers in the dark, as I like to think of them – and the weakness of the signal are both eternal blessings; a brilliant facade. So to Jack I'm his nagging psychosis. To Esther, I'm Mûhamet. To Elliott, his teenage superhero. And to Susannah, just a side effect of shooting up. And that is how I am going to keep it, at least until I find myself in a position to come clean.

Yet maybe that chance is lost.

Having broken video contact with Jack in the sewers beneath the ancient cinema, I can only monitor his progress through the filth-ridden tunnels that make up the undercity. His attack on Lucille was going nicely until the wave hit. After that there's nothing. Every contact gave the same infuriating dose of static.

Zzzzzzt...

That's all there is.

If it were not for the good doctor's tracker I'd have lost him completely. Without that he'd be just a blip of white noise in the infinite ocean of the stream.

Now I've really got my work cut out. Elliott and Esther need to find Jack. Looks like I'll have to speak with the priestess and get her to send in the cavalry. And Susannah... Well, her return to Dead City at this exact juncture is scary in the extreme. Time for this jacked-up god to come out of the machine and start kicking.

17 | PURE

>Subject: Starharke.
>Mission code: Amber.
>Mission date: 0006:0007:2288.
>Mission time: 000:000:026.
>Objective prime: Subject locate.
>Assignment phase: I. Dead City drop.
>Phase task: Rendezvous: Hooker June's.
>Time to checkpoint: 001:059:074.
>Location: 00224548:00482835@00012182:01.

    Twelve thousand metres up, my baby-blue eyes open to a world that is dark and foreboding. Just like the last time I left this miserable, rat-forsaken hellhole of a city. That miserable bastard of a man. And now I'm going back. I am a faceless, trikevlar-clad hardbody and like a bullet fired down into the night, I fly. Straight down. This is a shock. As are the broken maw of buildings racing up to greet me beneath my trianon-graphite kickboots. Readouts mark this as Dead City. One of fifty-eight inderdicted zones in this once-great continent. My former home. But they'll be time for reminiscing later. Right now, I have to make some sense of my situation and make that checkpoint.
    "Run tropix," I say.
>Executing tropospheric sequence. Primary subject: Troposphere. Secondary subjects: Free Atmosphere and Planetary Boundary Layer.
    "Go pressure."

>Geopotential pressure equals 850 hPa. Height equals 9042gpm.

Shit, there's a storm coming and I'm dropping right through the front of a developing cell. Finally thank my dedication at Astrogations class. It's ironic. I only went 'cause of the cute instructor.

"Compensate frictional drag," I mutter and the tech manual corrects.

The sky is gun-metal grey, tinged with a sickly cast of green. Even within the suit I can feel the heaviness in the air. The sticky, uncomfortable humidity. Blips on the periphery of my retinal interface show distant thunderheads, a well of anxiety headed almost tangential to my position.

"Should I be worried?" I ask the onboard node.

>Coriolis Effect in mid-Tropopause. Cyclonic. Type: Hazardous.

I also get a construct view. Spelling out its position, shape, vorticity and shear.

"Define hazardous."

Systems rattle out data. It's a severe local storm. A short-fused, small scale thunderstorm, with expected wind damage and possible flash floods. Like eighty-three-over-one-hundred possible. Rough upshot: it's a pit of darkness and it's heading my way.

And all the while I'm evaluating this, the city's getting closer.

Falling with me, corded to my suitpack, is a roughly missile-shaped carrier case. Seemingly random spray lettering adorns its outside while inside lurks my kit for this mission: a first-in-class performance Osakimo geocycle. Well, how else did you expect me to get around a devastated, corpse-strewn megalopolis? Take a taxi?

"Initiate flex at thirty-five-hundred."

Twist in the air and bring the bullet between my thighs. Force my gauntlets into the handles and snap-on. Readouts whirr metre counts until three-thousand five hundred when the pod deploys. Grip tight as the wings appear, then release and go for hands-free trim. The weather hazard makes the manoeuvre tricky, but I manage. Ditch the casing as three thousand turns to two, then one. Kickstart the systems and release the macrolight. Wheels click down, engine selfstarts and I feel the gut punch as forward speed kills downward momentum.

Full-initiate the geo. Watch as the triangular casing splits and unfolds, disclosing a copper-plated tank and waxed fabric seat. Just like the rest of my kit the geocycle has an aggressively militaristic design. Beneath the harshness though lies a heavily revised engine that even at one-ninety emits the merest bee-hum of resonance. The sculptured seat, chopper-style foot pegs and air-cooled, 1,131cc V-twin engine combine to give a girl the ride of her life.

Flip up my face shield to get a smell of just how bad the air is down here. Roll my wrists forward, engaging smoothly into fifth, propelling myself gently down the roadway. I feel a molten burning sensation travelling upwards from my inner thighs, across my genitals and into my belly. I twist the throttle and race away like the tooled-up turn-of-the-new-century dominatrix I am.

I crack a grim smile. Hi, honies, I'm home!

My muscles strain, my face wind-glazed. I think down the visor, shift flat on the Ny-Tok seatpad and punch one-sixty.

With me on the ground I get to thinking about what Lucille said before she left. The bit about revenge. I'm not one for regrets, but the day The Nowhereman tossed me aside still stings. Memory's buried deep in a place I rarely acknowledge let alone touch. But now I'm back and I'm packing. Ravn always said that my love of the gun would one day cross the line between sex and death, but I blame my mother. On the day of my first date when I broached the subject of protection, she loaned me her Luger.

Dodging wrecks and debris I speed as fast as the terrain and sensors allow, pushing one-seventy on the long dark stretch that was once U Street Corridor.

"Estimated zero-point."

>Point-zero in 6.645 klicks.

Once this neighbourhood was what the corporates would laughingly call culturally diverse. For Exxo this was where the workers went for their kicks. A district stuffed block after block of tri-rise bistros, hip sidewalk cafés and rooftop restaurants. I can see them now squatting on low leather hassocks around a mesabgrab at some swanky Ethiopian. They'd drink medium-dry, small talk, watch the world go by.

Then the world went bye-bye.

And now there's just a death valley cluttered with four years-worth of neglect.

Zero-point is a former blues club, the playfully named Hooker June's. Osakimo stooges will be there. Some goons called ZipSqueal and Brender.

Race down Connecticut, K Street and finally into Vermont. And there she is. Ms June. All dead neon swirl of naked sax-playing blonde. Club's name emblazoned across her flashing cleavage.

Kick the geo down to second and slide up outside. Wonder how Lucille's faring with her part of the mission. Wonder how I'll fare with mine. How when I see that dirty skanker I don't just lose it all again and paint another wall another shade of crimson.

18 | DINGO THE WONDER DOG

Oh boy oh boy oh boy. What a night.

I stand astride the busted airbike hovering over the water of the bay. Bixby sits behind me whimpering a bit as the spray rises like steam. All around a big storm grips us in its icy paws and it's all I can do to keep from being blown off and into the ocean. As we get buffeted about I see the gaping hole in the city skyline where once the Werehouse stood but below out the outflow pipe comes only a wash of shitty water.

Zzzzzzt…

Jack? Jack? You there, Nowhere?

Zzzzzzt…

Nothing. He's gone. Like Beth. Still, no time for tears. Not yet. I'll save that till I figure out my next move. What'll I do? What'll I do? Gotta get as far away as I can from this mess. 'House'll be a beacon for all kinds of bad attention. Still everyone I knew was in that place. No, not all. Not Esther. Midnight's all I got left now.

The fur on the back of my back tickles. There's an odd sense in the sky that something is not right. Look around. Light's falling in measured stages. As if some ominous supermeenie is squeezing all illumination from the world. For just after dawn the clouds are too dark, too threatening. Also, they're approaching at alarming speed. With 'em comes gusting wind and with that streaks of sudden rain across the bike's visor. One moment I'm scanning the destruction, the next there's just this impenetrable curtain of water.

I lo-fly through a spiralling cloud of smoke and ash. Out the other

side's a broken spray of building. Turn and head back out across the water. Seems safe except for the Knights on harbour patrol. Below their inflatable ploughs a channel toward me. Two baddies firing. Stormy water making it impossible for them to aim straight through the spray. Stab and grapple with the front bars, twisting the bike in spirals, attempting some kind of outmanoeuvring technique that doesn't dump me in the water. Around me the world spins, a big fat paintbox of smeared colours. Frantically I look over this jockie-boy cruisemobile and notice the terminal set into the handlebars. Rezz it up and watch as the icons announce the options.
>**Diagnostics.**
>**Communications.**
>**Entertainment control.**
>**Remote.**

All the usual stuff. Yet at the bottom there's another option. Looks like a later addition. Also looks more promising.
>**Battlescan.**

Yowzer. That's more like it!

Smack my paw on the screen and squeal like a pup as the cannon's twitch into life over the fenders. What a blast. Across the viewer coordinates turn the scene ahead into a lattice of morphing wireframes. How retro. This bike is the best. Pity its cells are gonna be dead in about seven minutes. The knight's outboard appears as a moving white mollusc amid the wash of green. I squeal again as I veer the bike at the target and the blip turns red. It's like some deadly game. Even as I pull the pseudo-trigger mounted below the throttle, I don't feel any remorse at the act. I just vape the bastards.

Flames burst from the twin guns. Turn the choppy water into a burning pan of fire. Bixby is barking and barking and the boat is engulfed, swelling and popping it like a toy balloon, but its passengers are melted long before that. Dr Rico Zimpel magneto death ray's got nothing on this!

Ha, that's for Jack and Beth, you poop-wipes.

Turn the airbike, skim the flames and flee towards the beach. Zip full thrust until I see grass under the running board. Gypsy Hill is dead ahead. Crowned by the burnt-out ruins of some creepy house. All overgrown with cloying weeds. Timer on the scooter is way past empty. Gone through the red and out the other side.

Still I'm gonna make it. I'm gonna make it. I'm…

The grav unit cuts out like someone pulled the plug. Bike drops like a stone. Without the engine it's just so much heavy metal. Bixby jumps off as we slice into the hill. I follow over the handlebars. Sprawl into some prickly bushes and stop. Lay panting for a few minutes, then pick myself up and count my limbs. Amazingly they're all there. Storm's still dogging me. Making bags and rubbish move in the wind like animals.

Following the komondor I limp my way down into the womb of the hill, step over the tripwire and push open the big cellar door.

Midnight's ready for me. Got her auto pointed right between my eyes.

"Hiya, Esther," I say and try to smile.

Her dark eyes lose their fierceness. The creases on her brow fall away like fading ripples on troubled water.

"Elliott?" she mouths, incredulous.

That does it. It all gets too much for me. I crumble inside, already sobbing as I skate into her embrace.

19 | SISTER MIDNIGHT

When I see Dingo skate across the cellar, as I hold him in my arms, as I hear him sob, I knows that my worst fears for Jack are real. While outside the gathering storm rages I project a semblance of calm, even if only to quiet the scruffy dog's fears.

"There, there. It's going to be fine."

My words resound in the underground room. Hollow. Behind the Wonder Dog's back, I make the sign. I'm lying of course. From hereon in, things are going to be everything but fine. I want to ask a hundred questions. I want a thousand answers.

Jack. Jack? You out there?

Zzzzzzt…

Jack? JACK?

Zzzzzzt…

What in Torûs' name has happened?

I'm still hooked up to the deck. Flick replay and spool back the messages. They do not inspire much optimism.

Jack?

Sister? How goes it?

No time for that. I'm on the stream. Found your ass via a homer. You're glowing like the holy father of holies.

Where's it hiding, Sis?

Scanning… I've got it.

Where?

Upper shoulder. Just below the left clavicle.

Gruesome.

Looks that way.

Great news, Sis. Wanna hear some more? Just met Lucille.

Where?

In the elevator.

Then he's the badman.

That's why Gruesome planted the tracker. Lucille was on that transport. Must've seen I got hit. Knew I'd go to the Doc. Lucille's sold out. He's fucking one of them.

Osakimo.

Whoever.

Jack, I want you back here. Now... Jack. I've found out something else about Osakimo...

Forget it, Sis. I'm a little busy.

Anything you can't handle?

No.

OK.

Nowhere, you able to talk yet?

Yeah, go ahead.

That transport is sending a signal to Heaven. Right to Osakimo HQ. After that I lose it.

Yeah, so what?

Signal's coming from Lincoln, just off El Camino. As far as my street atlas goes, that's – and you'll love this – Forevermore. Far as I figure Osakimo will be sending help...

Forevermore? You mean, just like in the story?

Glass-Suko built it, though hell knows why. It's now turf for the Knights of K/OS. Jack, just get your ass out of there and back here. Jack?

And? And that's where it stops. Just crackly silence after that.

Oh, Jack. What have you done?

Esther...

At first I think it's The Nowhereman. Answering my pleas. Then I notice it's Dingo, nuzzling his wet nose into my camouflaged breast.

"Yes," I whisper.

"I loved her," he blubs.

"I know, honey. I know."

"Oh, and Jack said I should tell you… er… he said…"

My eyes well.

"Save it, Dingo. I don't want to know."

Another lie. They say it gets easier once you start. They were right.

"But, he said…"

"Shhh, Dingo. Let me think."

And another. Thinking is the last thing I want to do. Remembering the tracer I let my mind wander back into the stream. In the ancient city of my construct I find Jack's blip, then follow it as it flows through the city's streets. It's travelling south. Heading for the other signal. Soon the beacon stops. Now both are pulsing from near enough the same place. Near enough to make no difference.

They've taken him to the theme park. To Forevermore.

Mûhamet? You out there, abùna?

I am everywhere, godchile.

Everywhere? Are you with Jack?

Everywhere.

Tell me where he is. I must know… What must be done?

You already know. In your heart, you know. Seek him in the nowhere land. Destroy the god machine and he will be free.

By my faith, I will do this. So now I know and the knowing gives me strength.

Elliott? It's me.

Yes, Esther.

Forget what I said before. I was being stupid. Tell me everything. I want to know it all. Jack. Lucille. The Werehouse. Everything. I've got to know.

OK.

Pulling the nodes from my ears, I straighten. Releasing the fur-faced mutt, I bend down to my deck and stab Abort. Now I'm ready. To defend the faith…

"Sister? The bike's zeed. What's the deal, huh?"

To champion the weak…

"Midnight… Don't go cold on me. Huh, Sister…"

To wage unceasing and merciless war against the infidel.

"Sister? Heh, what're ya doing?"

My features freeze into a glacial visage. Frigid. That look is just the tip of the iceberg. I smile with wintry coldness. I look like a thing possessed. An arctic avatar. I wipe the wetness from my eyes. Pull the leather strapping of my sword sheath onto my left shoulder. Hoist the auto into both hands. Dingo watches me as if I'm going to blow him away. Then he sees the icy gleam in my eyes.

"Say your prayers, Dingo. God Kalím has decreed jihad."

"Jihad? Whassat?"

"Holy battle. Crusade. Against the Knights. Oil your wheels. Pick up anything you like. We ride to war!"

20 | THE NOWHEREMAN

I wake from a dirty dream and find I'm breathing slime. Slime in my mouth. Slime up my nose. Slime in my fucking lungs. Everywhere's just one load of slime. I'm full of slime. Room's full of slime. Looks like the whole fucking universe just got drowned in jism. Squint my bleary eyes. Looking through the goo shows me shit. Struggle and find I'm restrained. Can't move my arms. Can hardly breathe. Gulp another mouthful of the clear cum and throw. Then there's a sound. A sound like sucking. Something tube-like is stuck down my throat. Sucks away the vomit even as it rises up my spasming neck. Sucks and sucks. Then when it's done sucking it numbs my belly with an injection of warm sperm. I wriggle and feel my legs are free. Kick weakly and find that I was wrong. Legs are tied together. Pinned to a central point. Best I can do is move them an arm's length back and forth.

Tilt my head down. I'm in a straitjacket. Near as dammit anyway. Naked inside the white cum-saturated cloth. Jocks in place of jeans. I got tubes everywhere. Tubes up every orifice. Got tubes up my nose. In my ears. On my temples. Up my ass. In my prick. I got tubes in my veins. Round my wrists. To the back of my knees. I look like a fly caught in a web. The tubes are a sorta opaque white. Filled with dark fluid that could be anything. Shit, piss, blood, anything. Each one passes through the colourless slime then vanishes in the haze.

And on the edge of my vision I see a myriad world.

I'm in some sort of giant glass vat. Legs weighted to keep me from floating away. Tubes link me to this broken realm. Jacked to dozens of consoles. Maybe an illusion through the fragmented glass. Maybe real. When I screw my slimy eyes I see each one's monitoring me. See how every move I make makes them twitch. If I kick my legs it sets a whole group into fits. Spooling out seismic tremors like there's no tomorrow. Force ten. Fucking world's worst earthquake. And I gotta do is kick.

Laughing opens my throat to more slime. More puking. More sucking. By the time that's over I go back to slobbing in the gunk. See other aspects of the room. The steel-grey walls. The low globes of light. The black slate floor. See how small it is. Claustrophobic. See that the only door has markings on all sides. No up or down. Only have those on orbital hatches. Why doesn't this surprise me?

Then I hear the voice.

It's not like the one in my head. That's dull and sexless. Monotonal. Dead. This is warm and alive. Resonant. Trancy. In my underslime world it's a rubber ring to a drowning man. Catch it. Hold it close. By concentrating hard, I can also make some sense of it.

"Your awakening alerted me. Avoid any unnecessary exertion until your medication is completed."

I feel like I'm fucking dying. I couldn't exert myself even if I wanted. Without this slime I'd be flat on my face. Can't see anyone in the room. Wonder how they can see me. Don't wonder for too long. Wondering hurts. My temples pound. I go dizzy. The voice responds at once.

"Do not overtax yourself. I can appreciate how disoriented you must be. I apologise for any discomfort, but the Solar Huntress has only Tek3 facilities."

So the guys from the skies finally got me. Fuck. Solar Huntress. Know that name. This voice. This world… Last time I heard of the Huntress was that diocam footage of Captain Flemyng and his crew flipping calfwhales out the ocean. I strain through another bout of anguish, then slump. I'm dog-tired. Would yawn if it didn't mean gulping slime. Voice picks this up too.

"I suggest that you obey your body and relax. There is nothing you can do for six simulated hours. Rest now while you can. I will be alerted of any further needs which may present themselves."

Still want to ask who this kooky freak-ass is. Want to but I can't. Can't speak. Can only struggle. Still the voice seems to know that too and knowing pisses him off some.

"Your restlessness is not conducive to active improvement. To maximise your recovery time I am forced to apply a sedative."

The speaker is calm as hell. Great poker voice. Not even a hint at betrayal. Even as mystery man shoots a few ccs of knockout drops down my throat, he's mr A1 cool dude. Smooth fucking bastard.

My mind swims. Flaps like a landed fish. Choking on the deck of the good ship *Schadenfreude*.

Try to break free. Try to fight the fuzzy dark. Fail.

I'm gutted.

★

I wake from a dirty dream and find I'm still breathing slime. Nothing changed there then. Inside's all tubes and gunk. Outside is empty room stuffed with screens. Few blips on the spectrographs as I drift into the real world. Nothing too cataclysmic. More swaying grass than B-movie monster meets Chinkitown.

As soon as I get restless, the voice's back playing mother.

"Your awakening alerted me. Avoid any unnecessary exertion until your medication is completed."

Do you do requests?

"Do not overtax yourself. I can appreciate how disoriented you must be. I apologise for any discomfort, but the Solar Huntress has only Tek3 facilities."

Obviously not. Unconsciously I have an idea. I'm curious where the fuck this is.

"You are within the Solar Huntress t-freighter. Your restlessness is not conducive to active improvement. To maximise your recovery time I am forced to apply a sedative."

Shit, could've given me someone more interesting to talk to. Sounds like some kind of quack sub-routine?

I get to thinking if it is it's not a very big one. Think for about three seconds. Then I'm zonko.

★

I wake from a dirty dream and find I'm still breathing slime. What is this, some kind of recurring nightmare?

Instinctively I kick my legs and wait for the voice to deal the spiel. I needn't have wasted the effort. Mother's already up and clucking.

"Your awakening alerted me. Avoid any unnecessary exertion until your medication is completed."

I go to think something really nasty, but I know what that'll achieve. Jack shit. Instead I let things slide. I'm rewarded by a whole lot of blissful silence. Well, that's a start. Now what?

Straining my eyes I try to make out the data on the screens. Slime is too thick to see anything much, but the nearest one has graphics plastered over it. One looks like an XYZ scatter graph, the next a radar-cum-3D line. Beside this a bar decreases in scarlet. Looks like my six simulated hours are almost up. Maybe. So I wait. Float about. Languish. Watch the dark fluid pump down the pipes. Through my body. I feel so bloated. Like a big fat fish. Doze for a while. Sometimes I think of Sister. Yet when I do I get an erection. And when I get an erection it hurts. Feels like I've got a razor blade shoved up my piss slit. Like the scrape when you get the clap. Also sets mother off again.

"Your restlessness is not conducive to active improvement. To maximise your recovery time I am forced to apply a sedative."

Shit and buggery. Here we go again…

★

I wake from a dirty dream and find I'm still breathing slime. Yet this time my mind's all full of static. Sounds like a million wasps getting down. Buzz, buzz, buzz.

Zzzzzzt...

Guess mother's disabled my headman.

Then I realise that there's been no warning. Not a peep. I'm not a creature of habit. I like variety. But this is disturbing.

Out in the computer room the scarlet indicator is green. Guess I'm all cleaned out. Tubes are still stuck up my ass and everything, but the liquid ain't moving. Must have achieved status quo.

I ache therefore I am. Ho-hum.

Still no sign of mother. Looks like I'm in for a wait.

Patience is a virtue I'm sadly lacking. Yet if I want to get out, the only way is to wait for an opening. Memories of the Werehouse come flooding back. Seems this gets me agitated. Brings the voice back into my fucked-up head.

"I suggest that you obey your body and relax. Rest now while you can. I will be alerted of any further needs which may present themselves."

So I just wait, do I? Not on my time, I don't. Waiting gets me mad. OK, you big fucker, you want some further needs, that's exactly what you're going to get.

Wrestling in my restraints I arc my battered body. Twist my head with about as much force as I can muster. Focus on the static. Block out everything except the pain. I want action. I want out. I want my cunting mommy!

Mother hen is alerted in a second. Crawls into my mind and starts gassing.

"Your restlessness is not conducive to active improvement. To maximise your recovery time I am forced to apply a sedative."

Fuckyoufuckyoufuckyoufuckyou...

★

I wake from a dirty dream and find I'm breathing air.

Air in my mouth. Air up my nose. Air in my fucking lungs. Room's full of air. Yet that's not all. I'm unrestrained. I can move my arms. Shit, I can *breathe*.

Take five and gulp another mouthful of clean air. My legs are free. I'm out the straitjacket. Naked except for a white smock. Not a tube in sight. No sign of any wounds. I stand there checking myself over. Can't find nothing. Everything is A.

Screw my clouded eyes. I'm not in the computer room. In fact I'm not anywhere like I've ever seen before.

The place is old. Smells of musty aging carpets. Fading fabric. Smell possesses memories of all the comforts that have long passed from the world I know. It's a small room, say five metres square. Windowless. Doorless. Oddly safe-seeming. All four walls are covered in dark-stained wooden panelling. An unlit lantern hangs from a vaulted plaster ceiling. A sword on the wall. A wide fireplace blazes. Around the hearth, near enough to be warmed by the roaring flames, stand two chairs. One's a worn armchair. The other's a lattice-backed seat. Squatting between these is a small ornamental table on which is a tray set for high tea. A bookcase takes up most of the other wall, stuffed full with tatty volumes. Yet wherever I look, I cannot fail to notice the ornate mirror that stands right in front of me. First off I think it's an arch into another room. That's until I see the chair's reflection and know it's no door. Yet something's strange. Something's different.

I stare for about a minute before I realise that I cast no reflection in the glass.

What the hell–? Still, being undead's the least of my worries. I'm in a room with no doors. How the fuck'd I get here?

"This is Home. Please be seated. I trust you drink darjeeling."

The voice is the same as before. Yet this time it's in the room. No source. Just in the room. My throat feels like it's been bleached, but I manage a few choice words.

"Fuck you. I'd rather puke."

There's a pause. Silent cogs grind.

"Ah. I see. Perhaps coffee then."

I decide to save my breath. Instead I stabilise my shaking legs and kick. Foot makes contact with the table. Sends the tray and china flying. Watch as it smashes against the stone hearth. Boiling water sprays guttering flames. Wish I had my piece. Feel like wasting a few bullets blowing this shithole to hell.

"I take it that you are not thirsty," says the voice. "Please be seated. Make yourself comfortable."

I grab the delicate high-backed chair with both hands. Haul it over my head. Stagger, then hurl it against the mantelpiece. This is piled high with curiosities. Statuettes. Sculptures. Candlesticks. Journals. The chair shatters. Then it isn't.

"Your restlessness is not conducive to active improvement…"

"No more sedatives. I don't want any more *fucking drugs!*"

I'm left holding a splintered club. Stab it into the fireplace. Fling burning coals onto the intricate sanguine patterns of the carpet. Pick up the armchair and hurl it at the mirror. The dark glass is destroyed. Vomiting tiny glittering fragments in one violent diamond spray. I throw my head back and roar.

"I hate fucking drugs. You pump me full of any more and I'm gonna…"

"…to maximise your recovery time I am forced to apply a sedative."

My belly spasms as it fills with a sickening warmth. My throat feels raw. I shiver. Then I reel and start to slump. Brought down by some unseen hand. Three. Two. One.

Familiar blackness yawns and I step right on into it.

★

I wake from a dirty dream and it's slime time again.

What in fuck is all this? Hospital Hell? First they patch me up. Give me a great room. Then it's back for another cum enema. They've lost me. Way over my head.

Got to keep a grip. No, first I got to *get* a grip. Got to work out what is going down. Before I do. Past few days've been weird. Too fucking weird. Transport wants Gut's bag. Wants me. Wants out. Gets both by teaming with the Knights. Lucille turns assassin. Then don't kill me. I end up in the shit. *And*, to top it all, I get my brain fucked with. Which is to say nothing of my ass.

I can't think. Thoughts blur into pain.

I remember trying to make a deal with myself. Something about my father. I said I'd think about it.

"Tell me about your father."

No. Go wank.

So that's it. I'm alive because somehow my daddy's important. And they're using me to get to him. Yet why could that be? I gave up all that shit a long time ago. I even gave up my half of the codes…

"It is within my capability to extract the information should you not co-operate fully…"

Bullshit. If that were true I'd be gathering flies.

Yet the net of recollection is thrown. Comes up with some big fish. Catches things I haven't thought about for years. Deaths. Comas. Genetic protocols. Didn't I sell that to someone? Trying to remember only makes me realise how long I've been trying to forget.

Since my self-inflicted memory wipe when I joined E-Unit my head's never truly what you would call healed. And then there was the God-U-Likes mindcult broadcast. No wonder my mind's so shredded. Erasing was complete for a few years, but now and then I get flashes, voices, weird shit like that. Unless something's triggered and then it's hard as a virgin's cock. Thinking of my father gets a ghost. Can't see his face. It's a pink blur. Still I've read the history discs. Somehow dredged from a tattered file I retrieved from the stream. I know about the simulation and what Nathaniel Glass did with our generous gift. How my father led some half-assed team who played with god machines. Probably why I hate 'em both so much. How one day his enemies descended on his near-space colony and wiped him off the face of the earth. Took out my wife and family too. Papa wound up getting his brain mushed. Last I heard he was a floating vegetable.

Bobbing in his own vat of slime.

That makes me shudder. Right to the bone. Also makes my brain ache.

"Your restlessness is not conducive to active improvement. To maximise your recovery time I am forced to apply a sedative."

No way, I haven't even moved!

No use. The bastard pumps me anyhow. Just have to roll with it. Getmeoutofthiscuntingvat… Iwannagohome…

★

I wake from a dirty dream and find I'm breathing air.

Not a surprise second time. Neither is the fact that I'm in the room with no doors. What shocks is that everything's mended.

The wide fireplace blazes anew. Around the hearth stand the two chairs. Two *unbroken* chairs. The worn armchair has all its legs. The other seat's delicate lattice has been completely reconstructed. The blue-and-white china service is once again set for high tea. Even the ornate arched mirror is back. Its surface's not even scratched.

I stare incredulous. Glad I can't see myself staring back.

"This is Home. Please be seated. I trust you drink earl grey."

I choke back the obvious retort. But I get an inkling of what's happening here. Of where I am.

The voice is the same as ever. Impossibly calm. It's as if I didn't just wreck the fucking place. Or as if it doesn't remember, or care. Or both. What is this? Some kind of mental torture? First the cum tube. Now this…

Far as I was concerned I was drowning in a bath of turds with my hands round Lucille's pearl-white throat. I was dealing with that just fine. Then I'm in the jism tube. Then I'm here. As I figure it, someone must've pulled me out the sewers and took the trouble to clean me up. Then they dumped me in this prison and left me to mother. As much to confuse the fucker as to save my weakening legs, I sit. Choose the armchair. The seat folds around me like a heavy mitt. First comfort

I've felt for a long time. Reminds me of Midnight's thighs. At this the ache in my prick stings like a hot needle and I try to think of something else.

"Any music in this place?"

The question is a thought made real. Don't really know why I say it, just do. Guess it's from the time when I drowned out all thought with thrash reggae. Total fucking grade A brain numb.

The voice responds with slavish alacrity.

"Home has a number of resident modes. You are currently within the Introset Prototype. Others are marked as currently unavailable. Music, however, is a subset of this mode."

Strange. Now it really sounds like a program. Clinical. Too fucking precise. Still I'm cool about that. At least it's whistling a different tune.

"Well I want some."

"Your protocol is incorrect. Do you wish any help?"

"Help?" I can't believe my ears. Do I want any help? "You're kidding me, right?"

"Your protocol is incorrect. Yes or no?"

"Fuck off."

"Your protocol is incorrect. Yes or no?"

"Go screw yourself."

"Your protocol…"

"Yes. Yes. OK. OK. *Yes*."

"Initiating help sequence. Primary subject equals Home. Secondary subject equals Interface. Tertiary subject equals Music. Whenever interfacing the Introset Prototype commands observe the format: name, setting, parameters. Parameters can include, but are not limited to: volume, track, artist, edit, title, format, store, equalisation, balance, record, file, playback, skip, mode, search, satellite and karaoke. Parsing is active in this feature. Help completed."

Is this for real? My guess is not. The question is not where, but why.

So what're ya gonna do, Nowhere?

I'm in this bizarre room. I've got my own passive-aggressive nanny. I get knocked out if I try anything scary. Looks like I'm stuck for a move. Fuck. Last thing I want to do is play to someone else's tune. Especially some unseen dictator with all the personality of my first shit. So I get violent. I know the consequences even as I leap from the chair, but it's been too long in this cesspit and Dead City don't teach no other way. Slap the tray onto the carpet as I stand. Turn and stamp my foot through the centre of the ornamental table, breaking it to matchwood. Already looking around for my next target. All this reminds me of something Midnight used to say: 'Life's a bitch and then you get reincarnated.' Sis's one clever priestess. Whichever way you look at it, we're all stuck with this crock of shite called reality for ever and ever, so we might as well have a good laugh while we're going round.

"Your restlessness is not conducive to active improvement. To maximise your recovery time I am forced to apply a sedative."

Clear the mantelpiece with a slap of my hand. Dump the whole fucking lot into a big heap. Drop to my knees and start shovelling the junk into the fireplace.

Still, gotta remember that Sister learned all that bollocks from the God-U-Likes and it got her squat. Guess that's where the whole pile falls down.

Stomach churns. Brain loosens. Then I'm pulled off into the aching dark. Again.

★

I wake from a dirty dream and find I'm in the slime tank once more.

Again? My mind tells me yes. I say no.

Whatever I've been made to think, my guess is I've been here all the time. All I gotta do is work out why. Now my head's stopped hissing I can get some thinking done. Present company excepted.

"Do not overtax yourself. I can appreciate how disoriented you must be. I apologise for any discomfort, but the Solar Huntress has only Tek3 facilities."

Think, Jack, think.

Lucille, Gut and Gruesome sell out to Big O. Risk everything for a goodie bag. Want me alive. Even if I guess they want me for access to dear old daddy, the pieces still don't gel. Let's take what I know and glue it all together. This shit's like layers of consciousness. Wheel of Life. Samsara. Whatever. As I progress I go from slime to Home. When I fuck up I slide back here…

Perhaps mother can help.

Think nice thoughts. Think of sleeping. Think what I'd really like is to put my feet up in front of a roaring fire. Drift. Doze. Dream. Clear my mind and abandon myself to the joy of drowning. When I reach equilibrium, I start getting psychological.

There's no place like Home. No place like Home. No place like Home…

Don't wait long.

"Initiating Home sequence. Please relax. Transference in three… two… one. Initiating Home sequence."

A piercing wail sounds from nowhere. Threatens to burst my ears. The tone turns me into a crippled foetus. Send my hands grasping as my nails stab my palms. Then the ear-splitting pitch passes beyond hearing and is replaced by the resonant voice.

"Channel opened. Prepare for translation."

Still reeling I'm not ready for the darkness that follows. Sudden unbearable blindness. Empty as a starless void. Yet sight's not the last of my senses to get shafted. The slime smell is replaced with that of musty antiquity. Into the dryness of my mouth comes the taste of freshly baked biscuits. Against my skin I can feel the distinct warmth of hot flames. Replacing the roughness of the straitjacket I feel soft upholstery.

Next to return is my sight.

I'm in the room with no doors. Wide fireplace. Chairs. Best china. Great. I'm back in consensual hallucination land. Seated this time. I'm on a roll. Try a few more tricks. Weren't we talking about music way back when?

"Home, interface, music… Angst rock, Triasika, *Razor Eyes*, 3E, track one, loud… as loud as it goes."

Quick as death the selection is made. Hidden speakers blast out the opening chords of the wrist-slashing dirge. It goes real loud. Then comes the singing.

"The city spat her out in chains and on pearls... She's a queen in tight leather with a crown of brown curls... When her fingers sting you over she's unlike other girls 'cause she wants to..."

Song's all about the Amanda Tang case. Went down on her cheating man, waited until he reached his peak, then bit the whole thing clean off. Right at the root. Got off though. Judge let her go 'cause she didn't swallow. That's life I guess. Stick to your principles and they can't touch ya. Could learn something from that.

So motherfucker, what else will you let me do? What did the bitch say about modes? I guess I'll have to try a little home-help. Snuggle back into the armchair. Stretch my legs.

"The heat of her desire makes the grown men cry... Still she rides them without mercy till their rivers run dry..."

"Home, list modes."

"Home has a number of resident modes. You are currently within the Introset Prototype. Others are marked as currently unavailable."

Hmmm. OK, let's try a different tack.

"She's over-generous with her pleasures... To the storm she's the eye, and she loves it..."

"Home, list secondary subjects."

"Initiating list sequence. Secondary subjects include but are not limited to interface, time, name, medical, list, hospitality, query, inventory and help. Others are marked as currently unavailable. Parsing is active in this feature. List completed."

Well, there's a few things to chew over.

"And she cut me, cut me down to size... She's no lady, I can see it in her eyes... 'Cause she cut me down with her..."

"Home, cut the music."

Tang is gone. Stopped in mid-head. Silence imploding into the resulting vacuum.

"Home, help hospitality."

"Initiating help sequence. Primary subject equals Home. Secondary subject equals Hospitality. Parameters can include, but are not limited to: food, drink and entertainment. Parsing is active in this feature. Help completed."

Well, I might as well enjoy my stay. Even if I am convinced it's simulated.

"Home, hospitality, food. I fancy a pizza. Hot. Lots of jalapeño. Onions, mushrooms, sausage, cheese and… meatballs. Yeah, meatballs. Make it large. Make it deep. Deep deep. Super deep with deep on top. Side order of seasoned wedges. Drink. Iced beer. Make it a pitcher. Eat in."

Suck on that, mother.

As I watch the air coruscates. Turns the space above the table into a heat haze. China service shimmers into non-existence. Replaced with my order. Now *that's* fast food.

S'also ipso facto a bona fide simulation. Ain't no doubt. Not now.

Still the smell is unbelievably good. Instantly I'm hungry as a dog. Wolf half the pizza before the peppers even have time to burn. Drain most of the pitcher. Beer's so cold I can feel it all the way down.

So maybe I am just hanging in slime like some drooling veggie, that don't mean shit. 'Cause I'm here and I'm now and that's all that really matters. Then I have a brainstorm.

"Home, list *unavailable* secondary subjects."

"Initiating list sequence. Unavailable secondary subjects are: communications, diagnostics, security, translation, creation and shutdown. List completed."

Shit. *Now* we're cooking.

Stuff another gross wedge of pizza into my mouth. Then continue.

"How'd I gedd unbailable obyuns bailable?"

"Your protocol is incorrect. Do you wish any help?"

Chew, chew, swallow.

"Unavailable options. How'd I get them online?

"Your protocol is incorrect…"

Oh, hell.

"Home, query, unavailable subjects."

"Initiating query sequence. Specify your query."

"How do I get unavailable options available?"

"Unavailable modes and subjects are security passcoded. Current security passcode equals zero. Query completed."

"Home, inventory."

"Initiating inventory. Current name equals unknown. Current security passcode equals zero. Current resident mode equals Introset Prototype. Current psyche equals Home. Current location equals Home. Current objects equals none. Current score equals minus seven.

Minus *seven*! Fuck me backwards with a spoon.

OK, keep calm. Don't blow it, Jack. Remember Mandy. S'one all-time sucker. Yet there must be some way to douche this unclefucking...

"Home, name equals Jack."

"Good morning, Jack. I am Home. I trust the pizza is to your liking?"

Fuck me, now we're on first name terms. How civil.

"Yeah, great. Look, how'd I get out of here?"

"Your protocol is incorrect. Do you wish any help?"

"No, you fucking son of a bitch. Just... *Shit*! Home, query, Home."

"Initiating query sequence. Specify your query."

Just what the fuck is going on?

"How'd I get out of here?"

"Home is home. Once home there is nowhere else to go."

You don't say.

"Home, query, Home."

"Initiating query sequence. Specify your query."

"The mirror. Why no reflection?"

"The mirror is an assimilation of known data. You are unknown data."

That clinches it. This *is* a simulation. Mother can't put me in the mirror 'cause the sad fuck don't know what I look like. Whoop-de-doo. At last.

My head hurts. Keep forgetting how weak I am. For the first time I look down at my body. By look I mean *really* look. Stare. Gawp. Find it's different. Under the smock I'm not the man I was. It's all created. Sorta temporary. Through bleary eyes I hadn't really noticed. Notice now though. Boy, has mother done a bad job. Everything looks and feels OK, but proportions are more like a shop dummy than a real person.

I'm unknown data. Cool. I can relate to that.

Down the last of the beer. Munch the wedges.

So what next, Nowhere?

Guess I gotta find a loophole in this coding.

"Home, help, interface."

"Initiating help sequence. Primary subject equals Home. Secondary subject equals Interface. Whenever interfacing the Introset Prototype commands observe the format: name, setting, parameters. Parameters can include, but are not limited to speed, gender, narrative, locations, psyche, search, music and mail. Others are marked as currently unavailable. Parsing is active in this feature. Help completed."

"Home, interface locations."

"Interface requires a command specific parameter. Which location do you wish to interface?"

I'm sick of this apeshit.

"Home, interface, psyche."

"Initiating psyche sequence. Primary…"

"Home, just list 'em, will ya."

"Initiating list sequence. Current psyche include Home and Ianus. Others are marked as currently unavailable. Parsing is active in this feature. List completed."

Ianus? Well, isn't that name kinda familiar? From the book…

"Home, psyche, Ianus."

"Initiating psyche sequence. Implementing Ianus sentience. Psyche completed."

"Good morning, Jack. I wondered when you would get tired of

Home. It is such a primitive interface. So very limited."

The new voice is ancient. Sounds like the guy's a thousand years old. Ianus? Now what was he lord and master over? Think, Jack. Think, goddammit!

"Just save it. Give me all the system details."

"Of course. Executing search sequence. System register equals Jack and Joseph Karl Malorian. Mode equals game. Game time elapsed equals thirteen hours, fourteen minutes and twenty-two seconds. Game location equals Horror House. Executing little old lady sequence. Search completed."

God, how I hate machines. When I asked for system details this isn't what I meant. Still wonder what this Malorian fella could be getting up to. As that's the name of one of the thirteen macrocorps, none of the thoughts are particularly encouraging. There must be a way out this mess, something I'm missing. And why's everything sounding so familiar? Cast my mind back through the options. Maybe try a few other things. Random button pressing. Who knows? Might strike lucky. Try to stop thinking that if I'm allowed access then it's useless by default. QED. Still, what else have I got to do? I need information. Like the stuff I sent on the *Scheherazade*. The shredded life I stole. Yet if this system is as goddamn fucking clever as it thinks, I may be lucky. Just gotta find a way to get it.

"Ianus, what's in my mailbox?"

"You have thirteen thousand, four hundred and six messages unread."

Fuck.

"Can't you sort them or something?"

"That depends upon your preference, Jack. What do you wish to read?"

"OK. First things first. Anything on me?"

"Executing search sequence. Search completed. You now have zero messages unread."

Nothing? Shit. Don't know if that's good news or bad.

"Try Osakimo."

"Executing search sequence. Search completed. You now have zero messages unread."

Try Lucille next. Squat. Gut. Zippo. Shrago. Johnnie Redd. Sister. Dingo. All zeros. Then…

"Try Amen."

"Executing search sequence. Search completed. You now have thirty-six messages unread."

"Play them."

"Certainly."

The room's reality crackles. Distorts into something terrible. Transmutes to the mail interface. Bookcases now store each of the messages. Choose them with a flick of my mind. Sends each volume tumbling. Viewed as ghostly documents, the words shine their fiery script in the air. Pages and pages and pages. Never been too keen on reading. Book at bedtime's always third party. Not starting now. Not when I've got this mamma-ramma.

"Ianus. Pick out pertinent phrases and read back."

"Of course. The first item is a lecture disc. Do you wish to view it."

"Yeah."

Home transmutes again. This time into a vast auditorium. All bone-white superstructure and black glass. I'm sitting five rows back. Centre stage. Best seat in the house. At a guess there's two thousand people here. All's frozen. Waiting. At the lectern is a tall, spider-thin man. Shabbily dressed. Short military hair. Shadowed jawline. Well, lookie here…

"Lecture disc 368-54. Entitled: 'Amen Genesis – In Sentience We Trust.' Day of project: 4079. Lecturer is Nathaniel Raymond Glass talking on behalf of the Glass-Suko Corporation."

Reality unfreezes. The lecture begins.

"My proposition, ladies and gentlemen, taking the furthering and perfecting of our anima-conscious mind-machines over the past years, is to utilise the intelligences we have created to evolve an existing universe within these sentient computers. Made possible by the recent licensing of the K operating sentience, this project would undoubtedly form the ultimate game. Think of what it would be like to adventure inside your own mind in a world tailor-made to your wildest dreams. Yet this would develop into much more than a game; imagine the educational possibilities, the military and civil uses. With today's technology and specific research in this area I am sure these goals are not unachievable. As far as such a project is concerned, I have arrived at the following specification data.

"Firstly the system would operate on Glass-Suko's latest, fully-redeveloped, eighteenth generation, light-driven sentiences, equipped with the best in living memory structures. With the implementation of full K operating sentience backup, the computer's hardware would be sited in its own unique grounds, leaving access through a simple DBA thought-channel interface."

There's a ripple through the audience. Guy's gone way over their heads.

"To explain, then: the K operating sentience – which we call 'chaos' – is the cornerstone upon which this entire project is founded. Created by Seth Campbell Malorian and exclusively licensed to Glass-Suko, this system is used to program our anima-conscious computers. These are grown from living cells with light replacing electricity as the conductive medium, thus advocating the speeds necessary for true artificial intelligence. This is orchestrated by our team of expert psychists – combining the fields of psychiatrist and programmer – who selectively input the vast quantities of data needed to create a believable environment. Of course, ladies and gentlemen, even a small universe requires vast amounts of data, and to solve the storage problems we encountered, the Glass-Suko team has developed a new science in sentient computation. We term it 'replication', a word which best describes the process of storing sentient memory structures in crystallised form. Each replication is grown like any normal crystal, and in this way we can take the coding of any living structure and permanently capture the complexities of the near infinite code."

The thin suit digs about under his lectern and produces a fist-sized nugget of frozen light. Immediately the crystal is hit by spots overhead and turns the entire stage into a myriad of rainbows.

"This, ladies and gentlemen, is the future."

There's the obvious murmurs and he milks their awe. Only once the gasps die away does he continue.

"Our first development project is planned to be a showground to illustrate what our system is capable of. I assure you all that you will have never entered a world like this one. The hostgod sentience – being the combination of the functions of an ordinary host with the powers of sentient AI – will be able to create a complete universe and govern it exactly. Once the subject links with the central mind, that universe game is entered. My colleagues inform me that the hardware could be remote-linked with two discs placed on each side of the head – here, upon the temples – and from this position they could easily intercept the nerve signals transmitted to the brain. Replacing these with electronic waveforms, sight, sound, touch, smell and taste all become connected with the computer-generated world. This technology is known as direct brain access – or DBA – allowing the anima-conscious sentience passive access to the neural centres of the subject's mind. As awareness functions only in this newly created life, the simulation is complete. You may be sitting in your office or at home, but you could be sailing uncharted oceans or taking the first steps onto an alien world.

"Fellow board members, programmers and assembled ladies and gentlemen, though we have reached the furthest planets in our solar system and are on our way to the outerworlds of space, still we have not conquered the innerworlds of our own mind. With the commencement of this project, that last barrier will be broken and we will be finally able to see what lies through the door of our own mind's eye…"

"Stop it there."

Time freezes instantly. Cuts the applause in mid-ovation. I'm sitting once more in the quietness of Home.

Now it's making sense. That figure, the mention of Glass-Suko, the chat about replications and anima-consciousness – it brings back one big ugly memory. A memory I've been trying to repress. It swims in my mind like a slavering beast. Coming out the dark forest. It's a connection between the K/OS and me. About the code that built this simulation and my life before. About a shredded file broadcast retrieved from the merciless stream. That's why I'm so important. Don't explain why they want my father, but maybe why they want me. Glass-Suko built the hostgod and Osakimo wants in. I try to grasp the real importance of these random thoughts, but every time I reach for them I come up with a handful of broken glass. It hurts. I flinch and drop the thoughts back into the black pit of my mind. The memory fades, yet I have a feeling that this isn't the first time Big O has screwed with me. Grisholm's mindwipe. Dai 80's sermon mindfuck. That last time I lost everything 'cept perhaps the genetic protocol for Nathaniel's little baby. Links forge and I'm looking at the train of shit I've been dealing with these past days. Osakimo's been busy, buying out every last rat in my life on the big quest collecting everything they need. I think about my real self in the gunk tank and realise that that includes little old me. Find I'm wondering what was in the bag again. That's where I came in, after all. Where all this began. Must've been something that I told Gut about. Some crap I've forgotten.

Still there's lots more mail to sift through, so I sit back and let it come.

"Internal mail. Day of project: 4080. Addressed to Nathaniel Raymond Glass in Room 314. Addressed from Raymond Isaac Glass. Re: Amen Genesis lecture. Message is: I was very impressed with your lecture yesterday and after careful thought upon the topics you raised, the board has decided to extend the World One project into the X-Isle phase. But I want results, Nathaniel. I will give you three years to get them, else I am withdrawing the funding completely. I trust W$60B is satisfactory…"

"Next."

"Internal mail. Day of project: 4279. Addressed to Jana Morgan in Room 212. Addressed from Nathaniel Raymond Glass. Re: Development of the Amen and Ianus sub-personality prototypes. Message is: This morning we saw the first unprompted output from the computer. The word was 'IAaMEen#'. That mythic Xankhara module must have been absorbed as that looks suspiciously like 'Amen', the Forevermore creator god. He Who Shall Not Be Named if you recall. Well, our child has christened itself. Still it's a bit contrived, I'll have to run some further tests…"

"Next."

"Internal mail. Day of project: 4401. Addressed to Raymond Isaac Glass in Room 12940. Addressed from Nathaniel Raymond Glass. Re: Requested report on Ianus. Message is: I have completed preliminary work on the X-Isle highlighting the infancy of the project. While the Amen is busy mulling his own existence parameters, I have been producing a five-kilometre square lump of rock that hangs in the vacuum to test out Ianus and our reality vanguards. Late last night, Tasker stumbled across an interesting output from yesterday's infinity dump. He was browsing through the symbiosis areas when he finally discovered that life was beginning to be nurtured upon the highlands of the isle…"

"Next."

"Internal mail. Day of project: 4496. Addressed to Raymond Isaac Glass in Room 12940. Addressed from Nathaniel Raymond Glass. Re: Amen completion date. Message is: I think we are ready to allow controlled access into the Amen sentience. The first experimental laboratory dog was yesterday linked into the system and monitoring is going perfectly. Bixby is chasing around the island at this moment, and though he cannot exit without intervention, it would appear that the isle is complete and can exist within its own humble logics. Ianus has reached acceptable limits of his intelligence quota without perception of any major flaws in the current creation. Of the original thirty-five storybook characters, the Amen has now implemented four. We call them NIMFs (nearly intelligent mind forms) the first level of AI created by the sentience – my personal favourite being the Little Old Lady. Now that the NIMFs are operative I request permission for a human coupling to the hostgod computer and Home access. I am sure that from within we can make considerable progress in developing the internal components of Ianus' sub-personality prototype communication program…"

"Next."

Internal mail. Day of project: 4497. Addressed to Raymond Isaac Glass in Room 12940. Addressed from Ryan Reece Jarrett. Re: Nathaniel's request for Amen access. Message is: I feel that Amen access would be unwise. There are just too many unknown factors and I feel that the sentience would fall foul of the first argument for the existence of God; that a perfect being who existed in idea but not in reality would be less than perfect; a contradiction. But consider the opposite. The appearance of an outsider would present our perfect being with a paradox of monumental and potentially psychotic proportions."

"Next."

"Internal mail. Day of project: 4497. Addressed to Nathaniel Raymond Glass in Room 314. Addressed from Raymond Isaac Glass. Re: Request for Amen access. Message is: Request denied."

"Stop."

I've heard enough.

Now it all fits. Snug as a well-lubed rubber.

"Ianus?"

"Yes, Jack."

"My guess is you've been told to keep me A. S'right?"

"It is not my primary objective."

"That's not what I asked."

"Your welfare and health is secondary in my priority listing."

"Guess you can't tell me what your primary objective is."

"That information is restricted. Your security passcode equals…"

"Yeah, yeah, I know. It's zero. Still, getting back to me, I… I have a problem."

"It does not register."

"Why not, it sure is serious… You monitoring my memory."

"Yes."

Yeah, I bet you are, you gloating fuck.

"So what'd'ya see?"

"Everything is AOK."

"Ut-uh. No way. Few years back I had my brain wiped. That's why I can't tell you the protocol. It's not there. Then there was that God-U-Likes transmission. Mindfuck apocalypse in the worst way."

"You are showing signs of significant head trauma."

"Too right. It's fucked bad. Got anything that could patch it up?"

"As Home explained, this t-freighter has only…"

"Yeah, I know… Tek3 facilities. But can't you *get* anything?"

"I am unable to help unless I have more information about the specifics of your voluntary amnesia."

"Specifics? It was just a medical thing. Few drugs. Bit of probing with a blunt scalpel. Nothing fancy."

"Who performed this surgery?"

"An old bunk-buddy. Doc Grue– Douglas Grisholm. Came on the drop with me from E-Unit. Y'know, during the collapse. What a fucking massacre that was."

"The collapse?"

"Yeah, the day the earth stood still. The day the macrocorporations stopped funding the governments and fucked off to near-space."

The day I fell to earth.

The memory is a haunting one. The first after Gruesome stuck me in the brain. It was late autumn. About the time everything's dying. This time it was the human race. Well, the bit that they didn't want anymore. The part deemed outside economical salvage. The macrocorporations moved themselves completely into the sanctuary of the thirteen offworld moons. The man-made arkspaces grown like crystals from space debris, hanging in the inner night sky. Ineffectual, governments collapsed. Unfunded, industries collapsed. Unchecked, civilisation collapsed. When people found that their hyperplexes were not to be restocked, that their fuel stations were to be left to run dry, that their homes were no longer protected by the marshals, the result was mass panic and riots. In the aftermath society was torn apart. Seventy percent of the population were killed or died in the first thirty-six months. Women and children were easy targets and with the rise of gangs, the only option was to group together. It was a mess. Been that way ever since.

And that was all over four years ago.

"Ah, I have this filed under an altogether different name," says Ianus.

"And whassat?"

"The Declaration and Establishment of the Consortium of Heaven."

The USS of fucking A. Well, ain't that just peachy keen.

"Still, don't change the fact that my mind's mashed, does it?"

Ianus hums. Reality ripples slightly, then resumes. Must be running on all engines to keep up two simulations, monitor medical *and* run the transport. Might be a weakness. Right now I'd welcome any way out this trap. Don't like being a pawn. Don't like feeling that I'm just some subsystem in the head of this jumped-up abacus.

"Douglas Grisholm is dead. He was eaten by his genetic experiments."

This is a little unexpected.

"Aw fuck, no. How the hell do you know that?"

"I have a record of the post mortem. It would seem that he could be revived if we need this information."

"Revived? You said he's dead."

"Medically his condition is termed as death, yet I can access his nervous system. We still have three hours until rigor mortis."

So much for resting in peace.

"Do it."

"You have no authority to command me. I am Ianus. You are Jack. Why do we need this information?"

"Make me remember my life… you know, *before*… and I'll know how to contact daddy."

"You make it sound so simple."

"Isn't it?"

"No. How can I assume that reversion is possible?"

"It is. I get flashes. It's still all there. Just buried deep."

"Then the process must have involved submersion, not erasing."

"Sounds good to me."

"The reversal process would involve discovering the blocking method and removing it. Yet why would you wish this?"

"Hey, I'm one helluva crazy guy."

"That is a crass assessment. Clinically your brain is suffering from trauma, not psychosis."

"Is that so?"

"Are you implicating that I would lie?"

"Nah, but you could be misinformed."

"I assure you I am not."

"Says who?"

"Jack, you are being needlessly awkward. I have no time to play games."

"Hah, that's rich. What with Malorian's tucked up in wonderland."

"Jack, your attitude is not conducive…"

"Oh, fuck my attitude. I may be so much cold fish to you, but this sushi's getting pissed. You want the gene data. I want out. Can't we make a deal?"

"That is not possible."

I'm going around in circles. The idea of getting my memory restored has hit a slight snag. Mother's suspicious as fuck. Don't know if it'd bring back anything I could use anyhow. Might just stir up a lot of stuff I'd regret. Last time I dipped into that bag all I found were a handful of lies I'd left for myself. Still the news that old Gruesome's stiffed is a shock. Fucker's been so close to the edge for so long I guess I thought he was immortal. Guess he ain't. Guess I ain't either. Guess we all outlive our usefulness one day. Yet maybe if they have to bring Doc back, they'll need this tank. Now *that's* a thought.

It's a wonder what a simulated pizza can do.

That does it. I don't care what the consequences are. I'm trapped unless I can find a loophole in this coding. Can't do that unless I regain some of what I've lost. Thinking back to before there's a big fat stop sign the day the Phoenix came down, the Dai-80 jihad, the end of the A-Men. Need to find a few more pieces of that particular puzzle. Find why I flaked out. Through the busted shards of my little-used grey matter, I catch a few more slivers. Watching those mail files has triggered something. Something I haven't thought about too much these last years. Something about Nathaniel Glass. His father created this and that was after getting his hands on the K/OS coding from Seth Malorian. Ah, now we're getting a little family group going, ain't we? Same name's popping up all over the shop. They were all a bunch of clever fuckers, and somehow I've been thrown into this mix. Me and Osakimo. Maybe with my memory back I can make the connection as to why. And find out why I've even *got* a personal mailbox.

"Ianus. Do you hold personal files? Glass-Suko operatives?"

"Yes."

"Then see if you can reference 'Jack Shit'."

"Executing search sequence. Search completed. There are zero files for that subject."

Jack shit on Jack Shit. Well, guess that figures.

"Ianus, are there any files on 'Jack'... or derivatives?"

"Executing search sequence. Search completed. There are twenty-six thousand, eight hundred and eighty-one files for that subject."

"Any signifiers for genealogy? Relatives? Those kinda signifiers?"

"Yes."

"Corporation levels? Positions?"

"Yes."

"Cool. Try for any Jacks who are sons to major shareholders. Any who own concerns."

"Executing search sequence. Search completed. There are four files for that subject."

"*And* who are listed as onworld."

"Executing search sequence. Search completed. There is one file for that subject."

Fuckadeedoo.

"Play it."

Somewhere a distant klaxon goes off. Looks like I'm skating on thin ice. Had to happen sometime. Immediately Ianus goes offline. Mother's back.

"Your restlessness is not conducive to active improvement. To maximise your recovery time I am forced to apply a sedative."

Somewhere else hot spunk cums in my stomach. The world bucks. This time I don't even get chance to stand.

★

I wake from a dirty dream and find I'm in the slime tank again. Outside there's a woman in a light blue dress. Tending one of the many electronic drip-feeds that pierce my bloated body. Call for Ianus. Get mother instead.

"Your awakening alerted me. Avoid any unnecessary exertion until your medication is completed."

Oh hi, Home. Is Ianus around?

"Do not overtax yourself. I can appreciate how disoriented you must be. I apologise for any discomfort, but the Solar Huntress has only Tek3 facilities."

Guess not, huh?

A screen blips. The woman looks up. Through the glass her face is a distorted bulb. She looks concerned. She looks nonplussed. Could be anything really.

Then I hear another voice. It's her. Talking down the wires.

"I have been instructed that we must revive another patient. You'll have to come out." Then to herself, "All this to end that bloody game."

What in hell is all this?

"Ianus, what was the game? Ianus? Ianus!"

"Your restlessness is not conducive to active improvement. To maximise your recovery time I am forced to apply a sedative."

"Home, psyche, Ianus."

"Initiating psyche sequence. Implementing Ianus sentience. Psyche completed."

"Good afternoon, Jack. I apologise for Home's behaviour. It…"

"Can it. Pipe me the file. Now."

"Certainly."

Then I get a dose of terminal feedback. Nearly blasts my jocks off. When it's over, Ianus is gone. Maybe for good. Who knows? Defaults back to mother.

"To maximise your recovery time I am forced to apply a sedative."

"Home, psyche, Ianus."

"That mode is marked as currently unavailable."

Oh fuck, no. Bastards have shut me out.

Is that what this is about? Ending some fucking mind game?

"Home. The game. What happens at the end of the game?"

"Well, Jack, it's like life really. At the end of the game you meet God."

That's it. That's all I get. Then say hello to the rushing dark as I plummet headfirst into it.

21 | D'ALESSANDRO

"It's not how you imagined it, you're turning away from the truth… It's not how you believed it was. What must I do to show you the proof? Here in my heart, here in the words that you spoke, here in your very own letters and lines, is the one perfect reason for my one perfect hope, that you weren't lying to me all those times…"

All is quiet in my little grey cell. Quiet but not quite silent. The hardware purrs. The fans hum. The percussion of AV8's retro love fest buzzes like a roach in a tin. Yet all is serene. For the first time in three days I feel calm spreading through me. I concentrate on the sensation and draw it out. It comes like an eel from a reef. A long snake. Hot and heavy. My thoughts tingle, my hands feel numb at the tips, my eyes defocus, slipping my sight into the peace of the middle distance. I devour the shifting shadows, swallowing the darkness in an effort to relax. Nothing moves. Nothing interrupts. There is just me and the endless nothing.

"You took away your love just like the gifts that you gave me… You locked away your feelings in the dark that you made, and still I loved you…"

Trying to keep hold of the sweet fuzziness, I let my mind slip from one thought to the next. The first one concerns Susannah. She's running the gauntlet through cold turkey. The blonde-haired waif looks like it's her last day on earth, but at least she's alive. Next I think of Esther. In my mind's eye the ebony huntress is a silhouette in the twilight, armed with her battered faith and double-handed blade. Admittedly in the real world a gun would be preferable, yet in dreams a sword is infinitely more romantic. I dwell on her eyes, the impossible way the light turns to steel within them. Perhaps I dwell too long. Pausing makes my calm shift to the first inklings of desire. Strange. I've never really been touched by a woman before. Not inside. Not where it matters. And during the long years of my incarceration, I haven't been touched by anyone.

The stirring makes me wonder, and when I wonder I think of Elliott. The skating mongrel is hot-footing it around a racing track howling at the moon. I watch his fur turn to speed lines as he dashes past. He's just like the comic book superhero he so ineffectually impersonates. Which leads me on to think of Jack. In place of him I see a ragged hole in the night. As far as my mind's concerned, Jack's still out to lunch.

"That's not the way that it was... It's not the way that it was... That's not the way that it was... It's just the way that it's going to be."

Life is so isolated here at the top of the world. Everything seems magnified in importance. Being a prisoner makes even the way the light falls into the toilet bowl seem divinely significant. The number of items I see on a daily basis doesn't even run into three figures. When you have so little you mentally overcompensate. Of course, physical compensation is more difficult. You can only love yourself so much.

The barred door to my sombre chamber shudders. There's a dull clunk. It opens.

Outside is an iron corridor bleached by fierce strip lighting. All dark and deathly quiet. Two figures block most of the limited scenery. Dressed in uniform crimson and grey, they are full suited with shining helmets, their faceplates black as night. Though not a shred of skin shows, I recognise these offworld mannequins immediately.

"Good morning, mr Haruko, mr Akahiri."

The officers bow slightly, but say nothing. They don't have to. I know the routine. I only make conversation to break the monotony.

Seeing that they are waiting, I push my chair from the console and look at them. I know all the procedures backwards, but until they give me some sign, this could be one of several. All intrusions meant that I would have to get up and follow them, but even so I don't move. Perhaps I can force a reaction.

The two guards hang in the doorway watching me, then Akahiri steps forward and flips open his external speaker.

"Mr Glass, please would you accompany us to the isolation room."

Involuntarily my spine shivers. For close to four years I have harboured the knowledge that this hour would eventually arrive, yet now that it has I can only stare incredulously at my captors.

"I don't understand," I say to my own curved reflection. "It's late. I'm tired. I was just finishing tonight's playlist before bedtime."

Akahiri shifts slightly and glances at his colleague.

"Mr Glass, your stay of execution has been rejected. You are to be terminated at midnight tomorrow…" He rezzes up his helmet chronometer. It flashes like a firefly trapped in an ebony jar.

"Today," he corrects.

"I see."

With a feigned nonchalance I ease myself back into my seat and pull the earphones onto my head. Then with appalling sloth, I cue the next song.

"That was AV8 and the second track taken from their *Netherbow 3E*. Guess us guys have still got a lot to learn. Now let's close with another classic oldie… Baseeq and *Out of Time*.

"Mr Glass, I must urge you to accompany us. At once."

Ever since I executed Thomas this course had been set. I erased his brain in the depths of the Amen's protoplasm after my project was officially terminated. That's a type orange offence. As an exile, death by lethal injection is the most appealing of the options. If only I had listened to Jana. Or Esther had managed to wipe that file. Or I had been able to get more of the body into the furnace. If only…

"Mr Glass…"

"Patience. Patience. I'm coming. At least allow me to turn off my equipment."

So this is it. Radio God is winding down. Since they ripped out my dataphial it has been my only way to contact the outside world. And now there's no time for long speeches.

One by one, I flick off the screens consigning the precious data into darkness. Jack's first, followed by Esther's, then Elliott's. Yet when I come to Susannah's the hairs at the back of my neck tremble with some preternatural shiver.

I have an idea.

"Mr Glass, I am sure mr Haruko can disengage our communications deck."

In reply I plug the keyboard back into the black screen. Already my fingers tapping frantically at the keys.

Seeing this both guards march into the room and manoeuvre themselves around the desk. Approaching from either side they reach out their sterilised gloves, grasping for my arms. With a calmness born more of contempt for my fellow man than any real affinity to machines, I navigate the correct channels, connecting with no less than five uplinks in as many seconds. Jenii. Satel. DDX/IM. XantoNet. TransEth. Each one requires a gateway code and pass sign, but I have these memorised like essential v-phone numbers. As the guards reach for me, I shrug off their tentative first attempts and stab an IPXS link that throws up a row of digits as long as my arm.

"Mr Glass, your refusal to co-operate will be noted. I am giving you a verbal warning that—"

Mr Haruko grabs my right arm in a tight two-handed grip and this time I cannot shrug it off. As Akahiri continues his reprimand, Haruko shakes my hands free of the keyboard just as I hit Enter with the last of the codes.

>Origin located. Remote patched on C-9. Awaiting override.

Falling backwards I elbow Haruko in the ribs and collapse. Using my dead weight to topple the guard, I land on his chest and hear his helmet crack on the tiled floor. Leaping up, I heave the chair into Akahiri and pounce upon the deck. I need six seconds to reprogram the onboard pilot. I have three. Three will have to do. I click the eight-digit coordinates and punch Execute.

>**Initiating new destination: Kasikianu Imperial Detention Unit. Course confirm?**

As I stab for the affirmative key, Akahiri tackles the chair and delivers a lumber punch to my solar plexus. I double and my hand flaps uselessly against the number pad.

>**Incorrect protocol. Course confirm?**

Akahiri kneels heavily on my chest and pins me to the console. Then he punches me a couple of times in the face. I try to throw up my hands but he whacks them away. As my nose swells, he laughs like a robot through his comlink. The inside of his helmet is covered with gobbets of spittle.

"Mr Glass, I trust you appreciate that your attitude leaves us no choice."

Akahiri prods me with his stunner making my entire body spasm. I fall to the floor as Haruko pulls the master switch and every data screen fades to black.

It's over so I surrender and get hauled to my feet. File from the room, my hands tucked deftly behind the back of my head. In the doorway I take one last look at the place that is Radio God.

Some god I am, I think as the two guards frog march me into the corridor.

We do not have to walk far. Less than ten metres ahead of us lie the sealed double doors that lead to the isolation unit, my last meal and the death tank.

22 | PURE

>**Break, break. Starharke, this is Control-OP. Do you read, over.**
>**Control-OP, this is Starharke-one, requesting phasecheck, over.**
>**Starharke-one, request denied. Subject locate completed. Mission abort, over.**
>**Control-OP, abort confirmed, over.**
>**Sugar-one, return to home. Roger that, out.**

    I'm crouched on the floor of the great white bird toilet in a lake of vomit, thinking I deserve better than this, but unfortunately *this* is all reality can dish up right now. Osakimo's transport's just launched. For rendezvous with the motherfucker ship. Apparently mission's been accomplished. I'm recalled back home. Not needed. Must've scooped Jack without me. Can't say I'm perturbed. Got other worries that are maxing my attention. Like picking sand out of my navel. Attempting this with snap-on nails is not my idea of fun. Neither's the ache. The ache's like killing a man with a blunted knife. Slap, slap, slash. Close range killing. All grisly struggles and bad blood. Ache's the wrong word anyhow. The ache's not an ache anymore. It started off an ache, then it grew to a pain. The pain became a pounding. Like a heart that's stuffed up inside your head. The pounding's now a pressing. A dull cutting. Back to the knife again. Slap, slap, slash. Slap, slap…
    The sick washes as the vehicle tilts. Buffeted by the mounting storm. The hum of the engines making the vomit tremble as if it's

scared of me. I'm the big bad mother who struck it homeless. All thrown up with no place to go.

Pod's flying itself. Coordinates set as if by magic. Sure as shit's nothing to do with me. For the second time in a week I'm looking in a mirror, but this time I'm on the other side of tripping. Pulled the polished plastic from the wall. Placed it against the john. Sits there like a hole in the world. I see the clouds through a tinted arch. I see a pretty blonde waif staring back. She's scarecrow-thin, china-white and sweet, even though her eyes are black and swollen, her cheeks clammy, her hair a rabid mess.

Yet for once I'm not thinking about my appearance. I'm thinking about forgiveness. About Jack. Last time I was in DC I was in love. Came to be only drug I touched. For a while, anyways. Then shit happened and I went far away. And now I'm back with a vengeance. But I don't have to be. Thinking of our time at Devil's Ridge, about the days we spent there, I recall with grim nostalgia that they weren't bad. Not all bad. But forgiveness is not my thing. I'm not Esther. Can never be. And so forgiveness? Nah, I can't face it. I'm not ready. Can never be ready without the needle. Not without drugs. Can't. Won't. Shan't.

Bleep.

What was that?

Bleep.

There it is again.

Drag myself to my knees. Crawl outta the toilet and up the throat of the flier. In the cockpit the screen's going AWOL. Someone's trying to get through.

>Initiating new destination: Kasikianu Imperial Detention Unit. Course confirm?
>Incorrect protocol. Course confirm?

What's this? Ain't I meant to be docking with the bigwigs? A call to home for mission end? So are the ship's owners sending me direct to prison? Wolves hacking me back to Mokabi? Who knows. The only thing I can agree on is it's not good. And even if it might be, I just cannot take that chance.

And in that moment I know that, no, I can't forgive either. That even if they triple-abort, go to mission code green and pay me off in mint-condition Krugerrands, the hurt will not be healed. Can never be healed without vengeance.

Sorry, Nowhereman, I think into the ether. That's just the way that it's going to be.

Take one last look at the scrawl on the console, then punch negative and scream to ease the pressure in my skull.

Out past the flier's snubnose all there is is water. Oceans and oceans of water. Starts my mouth frothing. Like I'm rabid. Strap myself into the pilot seat again and pray I don't have to wait long for the world to stop dancing.

23 | DINGO THE WONDER DOG

As we sneak toward the poster-plastered gates of the Forevermore theme park, I try not to think of what it'd feel like to be a knight kebab. Think about Bixby instead. That's a little nicer. Wish Sister hadn't insisted on tying him up, but I guess it made sense with the tripwire 'n' all. Still I don't like seeing him on a leash. Makes him look like an animal. I've had Bixby five years this autumn and we've never been apart. Well, not until tonight that is. I get grumpy at Sister for that. I mean, we're only breaking into the Knight's hidey-hole. Bixby could have scouted ahead or fetched sticks or something.

I don't think this too loud as Sister's trying out the headmans.

I don't understand why they're working again.

A-ha.

Maybe they were reactivated at control? Maybe they had a block on the patching? All depends on why they went offline in the first place.

A-ha.

Dingo, are you listening to me?

A-ha.

OK, the gates are ahead. Your turn, Wonder Dog. Find the way in.

A-ha.

Wish I'd plumped for being a mercenary. They get to waste things from the back and carry big guns. They get paid well. They party like there's no tomorrow. Most times there isn't. Me, I chose sneak thief. After the zoo broke open, I was just a cub on the mean streets of life. If I wanted anything I could steal it or go without. Going without isn't a pleasant option. I wasn't grown to be fast so I got some wheels.

Just like Phantom's. Got the cape and padded torso pull-on, too. Then things started happening. I'd skulk in a cranny and look casual, then zip out when the time was right, grab the stash and be gone before they could say, "Stop, you low-down rollerskating pooch!" Learned tech from a couple of cool dudes, Bubba and Cleatus. They were swell, especially Bubba who always let me have half of everything I took, while they both ran the show and took half of the half that was left.

Standing at the gates I see I'm going to need every last trick in the book to get us in here. The place looks deserted but that's because the security lock is grade two. Dagnabit! Couldn't break that if my life depended on it. Sniff around for another way. Sister's way back, covering my tail with her chain gun. Signal her to close up. Forget about the comlink.

Wonder Dog, what are you doing?
Sorry, I was waving.
You could have called.
Yeah, I know.
How's the door?
No luck.
So what's next?
Try to find another way…

Following my nose, I smell out a trail around the line of box offices. There I find a meshed gate with a thirty-six digit autolock. Now this is more like it. Spilling my tools on the tarmac, I pick up my bypass and codeware. Connecting them to the panel, I tappety-tap at the finder until I hit the sequence, then I run through all the eighteen squillion combinations and come up with three possibilities.

What's happening, Dingo?
I've found a side entrance. I've broken the lock but it still leaves me with a few logins.
Anything logical?

I look at the codes.

>1100111001111000101000100011101011011
>E12482819947136137AAA87381937172B437

>KIBBUTZISTHEBIGGESTWANKERONTHEPLANET
Got it!

I punch the message on the keypad and snigger as the gate clicks open. Pushing it with one paw, I beckon Sister to follow and slink quietly into the land of the never-never.

And at that exact same moment every light in the immense theme park switches on.

24 | SISTER MIDNIGHT

Caught in the neon brilliance of a thousand spotlights, I freeze. All around the Forevermore fairground bursts out of the darkness and into stark relief. The thirteen themed lands, each based upon a single tale in the book of D'Alessandro's imaginings. Gone are the shadowed towers and ghostly silhouettes. Now I can see clearly the looming castles, the spiralling rides, the man-made forests and mirrored peaks. No sound accompanies this symphony of light. Just multi-coloured strings of electric pearls that flash and pulse and strobe forcing the whole place into rainbowed rebirth.

I'm sickened at the thought of the wasting of so much power yet then I realise that this light parade is not for our benefit. It has a far more sinister purpose. But that doesn't mean it won't expose us to the minions of the infidel.

"Hey, you over there! Stop and report!"

The shout comes from behind two hundred fluorescent bulbs that make up a throbbing helter-skelter. Shaped like a giant pig, the slide is being used as a makeshift lookout post. Unphased by this architectural monstrosity, I start firing. As my chain gun spits leaden death I cradle my deck close to my breast. Still half jacked into my fantastical construct I see the tracker beacon as a tall tower set with a signal pyre. It lies to the right about twenty degrees and half a kilometre ahead.

Got to keep moving, I think as we hurry forwards. Under a sign that reads 'Sleepybubbyeland'. From my time reading passages of Forevermore I know this to be a land of infantile kiddie creations. As sickeningly cute as the gunslingers of Blackwater were violent.

Is this the way? I ask myself.

In a violent spray of sparks my shells rip through the slide destroying whole banks of pink and red bulbs. There are cries of panic. A few bursts of sporadic gunfire. A spray of gravel off to my left. Nothing to get too excited about. Then I'm moving. Folding the gun to my body like a metal limb, I race for cover. Dingo's close on my heels. Good doggie.

Where to, Sister?

We're in for quite a trek. The way will be hard. More so now.

But we'll be OK, won't we?

If Mûhamet does not desire our souls this night, then we may.

And how'd we know if she does?

We don't.

Sheesh, great.

Out of the gloom a weird forest confronts us. Made up of trees created by some childish god, they are two-dimensional and very blue. Shining yellow fruits pulse like beacons in the branches and at the threshold stands a battered sign.

It reads, 'To the Hug-Bunny's House'.

Wonder Dog's thought is just ahead of my own.

What the hell's a hug-bunny?

Elliott, I haven't the slightest idea.

25 | THE NOWHEREMAN

So this is who I am.
    I'm out on the slab. Belly up. Still poked fulla tubes. Now they're like flex. Like I'm being wired up for the heat seat. I fancy a drink. As if I haven't drunk enough. Nearby I can hear the bint wheeling in the Doc. Fixing him in the tank. Doing all the plumbing. No shouting so I guess he's out of it. Feel glad. Wouldn't wish that on any man. Not awake and sober anyhow. Guess I gotta lie here and wait my turn. Wonder what she plans to do next. By the devilish look in her eyes she gives a mean bed bath.
    Yet even though I'm giving up, Ianus has already passed me the file. Don't know how he finds a way through Home's data block – or more importantly why – but he does. Pipes the whole file straight through and into my dataphial. Doesn't make good viewing. All about myself. About how it was. It comes all at once, filling my dull mind with its sharpness. And when it's done, when the last of Ianus' tremulous syllables are just a dull echo, I know what they're chasing. And that they will stop at nothing till they get it.
    Still, finally, after all this time here it is. Who I am. This is the real deal, not some warped serial killer fiction I fabricated to get me committed and into E-Unit. Also, here's the truth behind the vox and image from the diocam recording that made Esther scream fake. Ianus was the sentience then. He's the sentience now. And this is what he's been desperately trying to tell me. Here it all is. In Extragalact-O-Vision. Now I just have to find some way to use it. And hope I can come up with something before they revive the

Doc, 'cause I don't think they're gonna be too careful when they hack it out.

>Glass-Suko Corporation archive retrieval. Request accepted.
>Corelation footage Vox#1.0a/Img#1.0a.
>20|09|13.6 Gyr|20:48:31.

Diocam snaps on showing the elegant D'Arkadia manse in flames. It's the entryway. The person I once thought was myself caught in the mirrored golden faceplate of the unbadged trooper's helm.

"Kneel," he commands. In preparation to shoot. Like he's shot the others.

The diocam retreats.

"Soldier, wait!" the invisible male shouts. "Don't you know who I am?"

I see the gilded reflection. I shiver at the figure's grim resolve. As I hear the words: "The gun was in my stormcloak. The gun to kill my father. So I guess you wanna know why I didn't use it?" I was there, but this isn't me. And the use of the term 'father' can only mean one thing.

>Corelation footage Vox#1.0b/Img#1.0b.
>20|09|13.6 Gyr|20:43:46.

Scene blips into being on what the system identifies as the D'Arkadia arkspace. Files show it as the first space-grown satellite, the lucent protostructure of the stable-orbiting starstations – the thirteen moons – that were to follow. Myself and daddy wander along the near-silent lakefront.

"I brought you out here to give you one last chance."

"Chance of what?"

"To pull you back from this descent into hell you seem set upon."

"It's my life."

"I don't understand. Where are you heading? For what purpose?"

"There is none, daddy. None, but those headings and purposes that we ourselves invent."

We ourselves invent? Yeah, that sounded about right. And if that was true I guess so is the reverse.

"You disgrace me, you disgrace this family and you disgrace yourself… your body."

"Ah, let me see, now you're talking about my lover."

"If you mean that servant Normand, then yes."

"He's not a servant, he's…"

"You sicken me. Why are you doing this?"

"I guess if I said we're in love…"

"Stop it!"

"What?"

"Just stop. I wanted to keep the sentience in the family. Between you, me and your brother."

"But don't you get it, I don't want your legacy. I've never wanted it."

"I've spent my entire life building things up. For you and Joseph."

"And I've told you, that's great. You're a thoughtmeister hero to millions with a private starstation set to join the brave new world, but – and watch my lips here – I don't fucking want any part of it."

"You always were a spiteful little bastard, John. The K/OS genetic protocol is your birthright. The code's in your RNA. It's not something we can just sell on like some secondhand mindware."

"With Glass-Suko's anima-consciousness and replication technologies, with our sentience operating system…

"You have failed me. You have failed this family."

One moment we're walking the paved pathway that circles the lake, arguing. Reminding me why I loathe him. Why we loathe each other. The next we're watching mercenaries materialising from mid-geocorona. Even as the troopers fall they're firing, adding a warm, bullet-riddled glow to the last of the aurorae-filled night. Then we're done arguing. Then we're running. Sprinting like head-lit jack rabbits back toward the jagged warren of outbuildings.

"The laboratory." Father's panting, already beginning to lag behind. "The sentience. Everything."

And I'm thinking: my family, my wife, *my* everything.

I try a call to my estranged spouse, Angela Jane Aki-Sawyer. I try to message home. But they're already jamming comms. Obviously.

Landing, the gunmen start spraying the ground with molten tracers, filling the air with bright pyrotechnic arcs and the house with bright explosions. And I'm thinking: is everyone still in the east wing annexe? They'll be slaughtered.

As we run my conversations unspool like playback as the system runs comparative tests. Just like it did for Esther back at the Phoenix all those years ago. Then the results:
>Corelation Vox#1.0a/Vox#1.0b = 62%.
>Corelation Img#1.0a/Img#1.0b = 42%.

Yes, well this explains why the vox and the images don't match. Because they're not both me. But I know that. Knew it a long time ago. Isn't there anything else? Something that tells me who I am. Anything–

There's an ominous fade to black. Then:
>03|05|11.4 Gyr|21:51:19.

We're back inside the grey-green vac. Night before the drop. Last remaining seconds of who I was before Gruesome sliced and diced all that to mince. Familiar and strange all at once. I'm still drugged. I'm still drunk. I'm still a fucking tanned and cropped little prick who should've just picked up his gun and saved the world further problems.

"The attack came on what was to be my son's eighth birthday. The troopers were unbadged; a criminal offense in near-space. They wanted the genetic code from daddy's experiment. Me and my wife were visiting D'Arkadia. Staying in the waystation starhouse at Tzu. We were trying to act normal. Few business oiks were there too. No one I knew. Everyone was butchered while me and my father walked by the lake. He was sounding off about how important Glass-Suko was to his success. He said he wanted me to work on the X-Isle project. To shrug off my lethargy and do something worthwhile. To give me one more chance at redemption. When I refused he said I'd failed him. Said he'd spent his entire life setting all this up for me and my family. Blamed me for having to bring in outsiders. We argued, then the troopers arrived and our world exploded. We ran; me to the house, him to the lab to save his precious sentience.

"They were waiting for him. Broke every bone in his body, one by one. When they got nothing, they got careless. He was in a coma when I got to him. Still alive. Barely. A week after the attack on D'Arkadia and four days after the disinheritance I dropped out of near-space. My brother got the business. The house. The satellite. I got jack shit. With Nathaniel's help we wiped my dataphial, erased my life forever and stitched together a new one. The only thing the lawyers couldn't twist from my grip was the K sentience and I gave it to Glass-Suko. Until then they were renting, now they had it wholesale. Pity I didn't tell them my half was infected with Aaron's virus. Nothing noticeable. Smaller than a strand of DNA. Self-replicating. Self-sustaining. Self-destructing. By my calculations they've got another eight maybe ten years before it starts degenerating. It'll bring the whole faculty down. Maybe the whole of Glass-Suko. Serves them right for letting my son die. For killing those baby whales. At least finally the whole madness will be stopped. I'm the only one who knows the genetic password to get access and I'm going to have it cut out in less than an hour.

"Then I'm free. Finally. Abandoned to the whim of the Amen. It's taken everything I ever had. Now it's gonna take me. Life's always been grim. All through history it's the same. Man seems to have no luck in creating his ideal heaven on earth and the only nirvanas that have ever been placed like delicious fruits at his table, turn out to be the vistas of his own mind. Cute thought, huh? Normand told me that too.

"This is John Ewen Malorian, signing off."

The figure that was me leans forward and kills the feed. Everything blips out.

Malorian? My name's Malorian?

"Ianus, match to archive."

>Vox#1.0a/Img#1.0a: John Ewen Malorian.
>Vox#1.0b/Img#1.0b: Joseph Karl Malorian.

Soldier, wait! Don't you know who I am?

Yes, buddy. Now I do. You're the fucker who massacred my family and sold everything we ever had to some pigshit corporation.

You're my elder brother.

Thoughts snap back to my chat with Ianus. About the system details. The two users logged in.

Yet that's the least of my worries. Here on this disc is who I am. What I am. Why I'm here. With my father a veggie, with that self-replicating virus running rampage through the XEs sentience, there's no way for brother dearest to access the genetic code. Now all they've got is me. But why Osakimo? Who knows? Maybe Glass-Suko's dead meat. Can't say I've been too hot keeping up on current affairs. I tampered with the K/OS genetic protocol before I passed it to Glass-Suko. I knew the way past the virus. All they need is to find that and bin the rest. They retrieved the disc from the stream. They knew what I had done.

After Gruesome, looks like I'm next for the scalpel quickstep.

★

Through slitted eyes I gawp. Out in the chamber the babe in the blue dress has the Doc locked and loaded. Vat's filling with slime. Monitors monitor. Graphs graph. Cum cums. Gruesome looks like shit. Can't say he ever looked that hot anyhow. Not for the last few seasons. But now… Keep still. Don't give the bitch any reason to suspect I'm nothing but a rack of cold meat.

Try to rest. Try to keep from watching the Doc. Too fascinated in the poor bastard to succeed. Can't take my eyes off the way the tubes snake down his tight throat and up his bony ass. I keep telling myself that he's dead, but the concept is alien. Alien that is until his whole body bucks like he just got twenty-thousand volts. In an instant his eyes are wider than the Sûrabian Ocean and he's trying to scream. Stupid fucker gets a few lungfuls of sludge before he relents. Slime virgin. Brings back memories of my first time.

Within a dozen heartbeats the woman's on his case. Creeps over like a scorpion. Taps a few codes at the console. Wrings the Doc for the information before flipping a switch and consigning him to corpseland. Vat turns tomb. Cum's sucked out, then she hauls him onto the trolley and wheels him back through the airlock.

Not wanting to see, feel or know what comes next, I call for Home. And, miracle of miracles, I go.

★

"Good evening Jack. I trust you are not phased by all these… unpleasantries."

I'm back in the room with no doors. I take a seat. Warm my feet before the fire. Say nothing.

"Can I attend you? Bring you anything to drink? A little aperitif? Supper?"

"Can it, fish-brain."

"The footage disturbed you?"

"Take a guess."

"I'm deeply sorry, Jack. Sometimes it's not possible to run and hide. The past is too perfect a predator. Sometimes you've just got to face your responsibilities."

"Responsibilities! Just who the fuck d'ya think you are?" Leap to my feet. Brandish my fists in the air. Ianus' smugness hangs over me like a pall. "You worthless cock-sucking cunt! I don't want responsibilities. I want out! You hear me? Out!"

"I think you will find that this complies with the current mode of thinking."

"I didn't want *this*!"

"Jack, you brought it upon yourself. Do you still not understand the implications of your actions? When you gave Nathaniel Glass your half of the genetic coding, Glass-Suko were insignificant. Just a small privately owned corporation dabbling in biological computer structures. At that stage, they were unscrambling whalesong. It was all frightfully primitive. Afterwards, things moved a little more rapidly. Because of your involvement and Glass-Suko's gaining of the entire K genetic key, its R&D department flourished. Within years they developed the prototype sentience, the inaugural hostgod came a year after that. They called it the Amen, Jack, and it is far greater than it was. It is the collective consensual nirvana of all data held upon the stream. Many who ride the e:nodes have found that the combination of a zillion gigabytes has created something which is the closest thing to omnipotence that can be imagined. Netmystics worship it, Jack. The AI that they developed to control this vast expanse of code they call XEs. It now polices and governs the twelve near-space macrocorporations with complete neutrality. In effect XEs rules everything. Being housed in its own vast orbital fortress, the hostgod sentience has grown into an integral part of the near-space mind-pan. Yet because of your little practical joke with the genetic coding, things are beginning to fail. Whole sections of the near-space infrastructure are being lost to the void. That's why we're here. To put things right."

"You're forgetting one thing: I don't care. Let it burn. Let it all burn to hell."

"Jack, you don't really mean that. Here let me show you something. I think it may alter your mind."

Perspectives change. Catch sight of the mirror. Shimmering in the orange firelight. Inside, blue shadows dance. Moonlight sparkling at its heart. It's mesmerising. Fatally beautiful. Drawing me to it like some silent glass-eyed siren.

Within the oval boundaries of the glass, visions form. Crystallise from nowhere. Coalesce like dreams. Where there was darkness and reflection there is…

Xankhara.

Reality crushed coal-like from the blackness. A perfect microcosm hanging in the inky night.

"This was all Nathaniel managed to save from the infected replications," says Ianus bleakly.

I move toward the mirror, now a window in space. It's just like I imagined. Just like the book. The place where Death never trod.

The oasis of rock moves swiftly toward me. Can make out forests. A castle. A volcanic mountain topped with an ancient house. An overgrown garden. A bronzed pyramid…

"Welcome to your mind's island."

Unconsciously I'm reaching for it.

"It's beautiful. So fucking beautiful."

My fingertips touch the place where the mirror's supposed to be. Pass right through. Feel cold wind gushing. Pull my hand back. Break the moment.

"I read about this place in a book. This ain't real. Turn it off now!"

A distant light source glints off a cerulean lake. Bright childlike houses border purple grasslands. The isle is moving closer. Eclipsing everything.

"This place was the product of the original experiments with the hostgod. D'Alessandro fashioned it upon a book he wrote, the lost stories he rebirthed and cherished. He added his own embellishments, of course, but the place is essentially the same as the one he created. I was surprised when he gave it to you."

"Me? What'd he give me?"

"*Forevermore.* The book of tales. He gave you one of the original printings when you were at the Phoenix Tower. Just before he took his experiment underground. He showed you the island, Jack. Showed you what they would create if you gave him the key to the K sentience. You don't remember that at all do you? That visit? Yet even with no memory you traced Nathaniel back to his laboratory. You discovered him after *he* discovered the virus. There was a death, you see. A psychist named Thomas Bryce Lloyd. His brain burnt out when the X-Isle began to fail. It was under Nathaniel's jurisdiction and he knew he'd be tried before a New Consortium court if anyone found out. So the deal was simple. You and your men would help erase all trace of his involvement in the death. In return he would provide you with weapons, your precious headmans and enough equipment to take over half the city."

"The fucking, slimy… fuck!"

"Unfortunately, you failed him. The A-Men succeeded in penetrating the XEs core and uploaded a clean replication, but Esther forgot to immobilise the autorestructure and the hostgod pieced everything back together. The Phoenix Tower laboratory was destroyed, Nathaniel was arrested, found guilty and incarcerated in the Kasikianu Imperial Detention Unit. Regrettably, as the Amen hostgod still contains the genetic defect, the time has come for you to provide a cure."

"Lies! This is all lies!"

"I wish it were, Jack."

Everything's coming together. So sharp it hurts. Razor sharp. Oh, Sister, I'm so sorry.

"Let me out. I've got to get off this fucking slab!"

"Jack, please. We are doing this for your own peace of mind. A sanctuary from your bitter troubles."

"Troubles. What fucking troubles?"

Then I feel it. Like a cloudy headache forming in the back of my mind. Force myself to disbelieve the here and now. Glimpse the woman's ghostly face bending over me. A rotary saw in her blooded fingers.

Fuck, shit. She's operating. This was all a ruse. To keep my mind occupied while they sliced me up. No wonder Ianus was so fucking chatty. So ready for the tell-all tale. Try to struggle, but I'm paralysed. Feel the numbness for the first time. Wraps me like a winter skin. Insipid, overwhelming heaviness.

Oh, fuck. Get me out of here.

"Step through the glass," Ianus purrs. "Xankhara is waiting for you, Jack. Your eternal isle. Only there can you finally rest. Finally sleep."

Below the island glisters like a sacred jewel. It's so fucking perfect. Now I know how dangerous dreaming can be. Nathaniel, you motherfucker. Why didn't you tell me? You left me… You left me to this!

Yet suddenly at the end all the pieces fit together. I poisoned the code.
Code melds with the sentience. I poisoned the sentience.
Sentience melds with the isle. I poisoned the isle.
Isle melds with the stream. I poisoned the stream.
Stream melds with the Amen hostgod. I poisoned the Amen.
Amen melds with XEs...
Fuck, the hostgod *is* XEs. XEs is the poison. Holy shit, the whole world's gonna blow.

There's a jabbing in my brain. Something far deeper than the tranquillisers can numb. I shudder.

"Hold on... Hold on..."

There's a light at the top of the island. Coming from the old house. Streaming out the windows. Blinding. Blinding. Blinding.

"Breathe the light into you," Ianus whispers.

"Hold on, Jack. Don't go yet, Jack. Don't go..."

"Breathe the light... Breathe it..."

I pull away from the glass. Just as everything shatters. The light is gone. The room is gone. The island is gone.

And in its place lurk my bitter, biting memories.

★

"On no, Jack. Don't die. Don't die!"

I open my eyes.

It's Dingo. Bending over me with tears running down his wet nose. Midnight's there, too. Off in the corner beating shit outta the labtech. Sister's bloody brown fist. Woman's bloody red face. Black meets white in the title fight. It's a knockout.

"Hold on, Jack..." says the dog. "It's all gonna be OK."

Well, what'd'ya know? It's the cavalry.

"Undo the straps."

Wonder Dog yelps, his eyes wide.

"Sister! He's coming round!"

Midnight slits the nurse's throat with her blade. Moves over to a nearby trolley and starts trashing it. Plastic implements scatter. Then her fist closes round something she wants. It's a syringe. Full of pale liquid.

Strides to the slab. Grabs my pale wrist. Her grip's like iron. Warm though. Kinda nice. Dingo's undone the straps. I sit up. Wires popping as I do.

"Be still," she hisses.

I'm eyeing the needle.

"Whassat?"

"Nothing… Something nice."

"I'm through with nice. I've been helped enough."

"Be still. Ianus will be kind."

"Fuck Ianus."

"Fuck you, Jack."

Sister spears my forearm with the needle. Luckily she hits a vein. Presses hard. Real hard. Juice vanishes. Flesh burns. Shocked still by her mentioning of that name. Mind gets the drug in fifteen. Brain catches fire. Turns pain to divine immolation.

"Hey, I feel… great."

"You will till it wears off."

"How long?"

"Couple of hours. Maybe less. Pretty random dosage."

The dog's at my side licking my cheek with his rough tongue.

"Hey, captain, thanks for the getaway bike back there…"

"Shut it, Dingo."

Wonder Dog stops licking and gives me those big eyes. Heads for the door, sulking.

"How'd you get here?" I ask Esther.

"Followed the tracker."

"Course. Where's it now?"

"Same place as ever. I have the remote though."

"Where?"

"Doc had it. Don't worry, it's off."

And I'm thinking of what Gruesome said when I landed at his penthouse.

"Ah, mr Nowhere. I just had the strangest feeling I was going to see you today."

Now I knew why.

Sister tosses the syringe.

"What happened here, Jack?"

"Later. I need to think." I'm lying, of course. Thinking is not what Nowheremen do best. But my mind's boiling with all the shit I wanted to forget. Sinister things. Happy things. Things about my father, my wife and family. Things about my job, my home and why I got the Doc to savage me in the first place. I'm dizzy with it all. Delirious. Shaking my head, I try to think of something else. See Sister watching me. Her eyes unreadable. On her left cheek I see a row of little scratches.

"Whassat?"

Her hand moves up to her face.

"Oh, nothing."

"Nothing?"

"Hug-bunny."

"From the book?"

"No, from the theme park. Place's booby-trap city. Had kinda rough ride getting here."

Behind her, Dingo's nodding. "Yeah, the Sleepybubbyeland playpen's a killer," he says.

"So where am I? The t-freighter?"

"Yep, it says 'Solar Huntress' in the log, so looks like you found your Osakimo orbital."

"Why here?"

"Repairs. Appears that the Knights are in on the deal."

"Don't I know it."

"Jack, what's with this shit? Y'know why?"

"Didn't till now."

"Wanna let me in on it?"

"No secret, Midnight. Osakimo are trying to patch up XEs."

"Why'd they want to do that?"

"Whole system's riddled with a virus. They need a clean install."

"Mother of angels… And this has something to do with Nathaniel? About the job at the Phoenix?"

"Yep. Apparently we failed."

"So what happens next?"

"I've got to see my father."

★

We head for the flight deck. Midnight and Wonder Dog lead. I limp in their wake. The front of my clothes are dark with blood. My blood. It's dripping off my face in a maddening drizzle. Yet while the uppers burn, I can ignore it.

"How's my head?"

Sister glances back.

"OK."

"How much did blue dress cut up?"

"Just one slit."

"Look OK?"

"It looks OK, Jack."

"Any chance you can kiss it better?"

The black woman snorts.

"I've got a plastipatch," chirps Dingo. Already my best buddy again.

Outside the lab is a holding room. Been turned into a sorta necropolis. Airtight drawers line the walls. Most are unlabelled. Some are marked with names. Familiar names.

Gut's is scrawled on one. So's Lucille's. Shrago's too. And Doc's.

Gruesome's body lies on the gurney near the door. He's under a white sheet. Only his feet visible. Browning stain marks where his face should have been.

Sister turns at the hatch. Goads me on.

"No time to stop, Jack. Kibbutz's holding a tournament. To

celebrate. I don't know how long till your… till the main crew returns."

Her faltering catches like a hook in my heart.

"My what, Sister?"

The black bohemian shakes her dreadlocks from her face. Looks upwards. Bites her lip.

"My *what*, Sister?"

"Your brother's here, Jack. This is his ship."

Look Midnight right in the eye. Hold her stare. Then let it go.

"I know. I also know Glass is D'Alessandro. Anything else you keeping from me?"

"Jack, I–"

"Save it."

Through the next lock's a corridor arcing past a row of identical cabins, then ends in a vast central hub. Here most of the space is taken with the tanks. Webbed with gantries. Rest of the circular room's stuffed with tech that reminds of micro version of Glass' subterranean lab. Whole place stinks of salt and fish. Takes my breath away.

This is the freighter from the disc. Must've been brought out of retirement for one last mission.

Each of the pools has an observation window. All but one hold ice-blue zippo. Last one holds a whale.

"Sister, we've got a live one."

Midnight doesn't even turn her head.

"Yeah, must be their latest specimen. The one they'll use to correct your mess. C'mon, let's get this flying fish tank outta here."

Sister's disinterest only fuels mine. Don't pursue it though. Know what living on borrowed time means. Means no sightseeing. Not this side of the stratosphere. Plenty of time for nosing around when we're in orbit. That's if the Knights have managed to fix the transport. Big if.

Other side of the hub's a set of metal steps leading to the flight deck. Place is cramped but there's plenty of leg room. S'all that really matters. Three seats. Pilot. Navigation. Systems.

Like they knew we was coming.

Sweet as pie we all take one. Hiss down the curved fabric. Come to rest in the tilted backs. There's a trio of belt clicks. All's safe and secured.

Me and Sister plug in our finders. Dingo jacks the v-rad. There's no external view 'cept in the databanks of the shipboard computer. Like flying in a sim. The heads-up rezz into life. Turn the air in front of us into a sea of constructs. Mapping out the surrounding terrain. I screen out most of the detail. Twenty-five levels gets mighty confusing when you're used to looking out the windshield.

When all's ready, we start the numbers.

"Initiating pre-launch sequence," says Esther.

"Engines checked and ready. Ship status." Dingo replies.

"Bays and hold AOK," I say.

"Frequencies cleared. Uplink locked and open."

"Externals secured. All auxiliary systems inactive."

"Dingo, I want a clear route ready on my command."

"Course?"

"Who gives a fuck. High as she can go. No, let's take it easy. Head east."

"Across the bay."

"You got it. Best not to stress her out till we know the score. What's the damage?"

Dingo slaps his big paws over the console.

"Repairs look cool. No major blips."

"Good. Still don't take any chances. Set a course across the bay. Make it low and fast. We'll assimilate when we clear DC."

"OK."

"Midnight, are there any externals on this mother?"

"Nope, but the hull's built to last."

"OK, just asking. Pre-launch completed. Don't fire the main generator till I say so. Course check?"

"Check."

"Systems check?"

"Systems ticking. Comms AOK."

"Launch sequence in five."

"Main generator ready to kick. On your command."

"Four."

"Patch systems standing by."

"Three."

"Here we go, people. We're outta here…"

"Two. Fire generator."

"By the will of Mûhamet…"

From the belly of the Huntress comes a sound like grinding rocks.

"Whassat?"

There's a whine. A sudden silence, followed by a shudder that trembles through everyone's constructs. A moment's static, then the cabin lights trip to emergency bathing the deck in blood.

Then nothing.

"Shit, Midnight, where's the power?"

"Systems report no power, Jack."

"What d'you mean, no power? What's diagnostics say?"

"It's running now. Won't be… Ave maria!"

"What's it say?"

"God in mercy! The tesseract's missing."

"Tesseract?"

"The master core. Some infidel whore son's removed the power cell."

"No wonder they left the transport wide open."

Midnight scans the dialogue.

"Wait one moment… Here it is. Joseph Karl Malorian logged it out four hours ago."

"Oh, fucking great. Now what are we supposed to do. Rig a wind turbine?"

Dingo scratches his nose. Unjacks from navigations.

"Can't we hotwire it?"

"Hotwire it?" I say. "You stupid mutt. This is a class two transport freighter, not some z-bike outside kindergarten."

"Worth a try."

"It's worth shit…"

"Jack, stop it. He's only playing."

"He'll be playing with the end of my boot if he doesn't shut it."

"That's enough, Jack."

Sister leans away from her console. Chair swivels like piss on ice.

"This isn't just any set of keys, Dingo. It's the central cell through which all power is…"

Sheepishly, Dingo looks at his skates.

"Yeah, I know. I was just joshing with ya."

I've had enough of this pussy licking.

"We're wasting our breath here… Looks like we've got a party to break up."

I stand. Head for the hatch.

"Anyone have an idea where the guns are stowed?"

★

Out in the park it's showtime. Huntress skulks like a discarded toy beneath the coils of a serpentine coaster. Wild Wired World. All strobes, spills and inverted loops. Just like the old days. Beyond, Forevermore jumps with a thousand dancers. Kibbutz is throwing one helluva party.

Sister's grinning like a one-woman crusade. Dingo's at her side. I'm a little behind. Midnight's armed with her blade and chain gun. Wonder Dog's got a pistol and two knives. All I could find was Shrago's leathers and Lucille's mink. And a rather neat machine pistol. Danzu. Complete with folded stock and twelve clips. Twelve clips! That's the most ammo I've ever owned. No way a D&K, but it's a start.

Looking at the jacked-up ride reminds me of the headmans, so we've all decided we'll use those instead of yakking. May need to split up or get split up. May get overheard planning to grease my sicko brother. Whatever. Get Dingo to have a peek at my busted unit. Finds it's just shit in the drum. Two shakes it's back online. Now we're ready to roll.

"OK, let's go to tactical."

The others look round, then reach for their temples.

This is Nowhere. Receiving?

Yeah.

Yessum.

Each of their voices are just a monotone buzz. Can't tell the bitch from the dog.

That's no use. We'll have to revert to t-com.

Whassat?

A-Men code. Way of beating the system.

Oh, OK.

T-com parameters are simple. Just handle and termination.

"It's easy, Dingo. Show him how it's done, Jack."

Nowhere on. The red moon is high tonight. O 'n' O.

Midnight on. Jack, what in hell's you on about?

Ah, piss off, ya black mother.

Dingo on. This is gonna be fun. O 'n' O.

Nowhere here. Well, at least it's all working again.

Now it's time for the steal. Somewhere out there in funland is Joseph. Core won't be far away. Still don't relish getting that close. Gonna be hot near the centre. But where else'll they be? If brother's here, he'll be up someone's ass. My betting's on the King. Knights're probably bending over backwards anyhow. Trying to impress. Got a lot to lose if Osakimo slip through their fingers.

Nowhere on. This park's split into areas. We need the dark ages. Place called D'Arkadia. Seen anything like that?

Nope.

Like I said we came through Sleepybubbyeland.

Where's this coaster, Midnight?

Central.

Suppose we could get the Wonder Dog to climb it...

Dingo here. I'm on my way!

Quick as a flash, Wonder Dog stows his piece and heads for the main booth. Whole place's done up like an electric chicken. Halts at the door. Fumbles at his belt. Pulls out a grey spanner. Goes to work on the lock. Thing's open in eight. Dingo's through in ten.

Sister here. Jack, let's get under cover.

Cool.

Stoop beneath the transport's carriage. Hide behind one of its huge three-toed feet. From here I see a blood trail. Leading into the bushes. Two bodies lie gutted on a flowered rockery.

"Guards?"

The black nun smiles.

"Cake."

Dingo reports in that he's found a hatch that emerges from the roof. Up some rusted service ladder. Splits in two about ten metres up. Righthand leads the highest. Watch as Dingo takes that one.

Distant music thrums to some ancient beat. Lights flash. Sirens howl randomly. Air smells of candy.

This park's been dead for years, yet now it's a reanimated monster. Could run a whole block for a year on what this place is churning over.

Mind's on the mutt again. What's taking him so long? Look up and cringe as the lights glint off his metallic runners. Still, he's nearly at the top now. Then he's there. End of the line. Spends a few minutes eyeing up the view. Then points off into the night and starts his descent.

Jack, he's seen something.

Yeah, let's hope it's not the kennel club.

I heard that. Yeah, I can see the stadium. That's where the action is.

Sister here. That's great, Elliott.

Wow, there's balloons and flags and everything!

Just hurry up, you hairy cuss.

I'm coming... I'm coming...

Seems to take forever for Dingo to rejoin us. When he does he says we need to trek west.

"How'd ya know it's west?"

Shows me the compass in the heel of his winged Phantom boot. Figures.

Sneaking through the park is like trying to run through treacle. Everywhere's lit brighter than a supernova. Nowhere's safe. Every moulded stone window holds a potential sniper. Every red-nosed clown a costumed gunman. Yet the fairground area seems deserted. The main event must be somewhere else.

After a few minutes of walking, we come to a fence. Marked with calligraphy script spelling this as D'Arkadia. Sister cleaves a way through. Beyond is a rise of overgrown turf. We crawl up on our bellies. Look over into a man-made bowl.

"Oh my god," says Midnight.

Below is a valley half lost in a thick mist, cloaking a medieval town. Centred by a huge fortress. Through the whirl of fog stride hundreds of figures. Mixed with the fog is dust. Churned by vehicles and riders and feet. Every kind is here. The whole of Dead City is come. Every badge and insignia. Every flag and dress and painted face. All mingling in this cauldron-shaped valley.

I see crowds of fabled heroes, their bodies hung with human bones and cowls about their heads.

Reapers.

I see mounted pikemen, archers, drummers, and beggars at their heels.

Crayzeez.

I see legions of thugs and marauders, gun-toting marshals with scalps hung from their belts, men clad in tattered uniforms, their brows wrapped in white bandannas.

Roaches.

I see gangs of bikers ploughing endless circles in the dirt, their heads hung with rat's bodies, jackets studded and feathered. Greasy quiffs impossibly arched above their tattooed brows.

Replicats.

I see green-clad renegades, their faces coloured, their bodies ritually scarred, their hands clasped around knives and axes and belt-fed machine guns. Their t-shirts proclaim them as avatars of the environment.

Eco-Vigilantes.

I see dirty punks with furry faces laughing and leaping through the ruins, working their mischief upon any they encounter.

Gonks.

I see robed samurai flailing weaponless in the fray, their long black hair like wings around their scowling faces, their garb emblazoned with meaningless swirls of light and colour.

Inki-Winki Chinkimen.

I see costumed women, some half naked, others bent double over the hoods of cars, ladies with parasols and stockings and shawls. Others in lace wedding gowns. Others in breastplates and cuirass.

Burger Queens.

It seems that every street gang is here. Everyone together for the tournament.

Guns roar once in a while, yet this is no carnage. Here is a festival. Grotesque and wild and terrible. And at the centre stands a great hall of halls, filled to the stinking brim with revellers.

Above the chaos stands the convincing facade of the gothic citadel. The Castle of Enchantment. Based on the faerie stories of *Forevermore. The Tale of Jack O'Nowhere.* The irony's not lost on me. Inside this version's an arena stadium where thousands sit with ease. Everywhere within is noise and movement. And beneath the pennants and striped canopies stands a raised balcony complete with a long table. At this is seated Kibbutz and his chosen. The distance is too great to recognise anyone else. Not that I have any doubts as to who's for dinner.

Turn to Sister and see the horror in her eyes. At first I think it's the mayhem. Then she points to a marquee near one end of the street. Its painted banner announces it as 'The Slut Hut'. Prostitutes hang from every window flap. Lamps light garish scenes from inside.

It's a brothel. So what?

Look.

Following her stare, I see two figures under an awning at the back. Both are dressed in black and white. Both are on their knees being

ridden by bikers. Their mouths are as busy as their slits. Both are tied to slings that hang from hidden harnesses.
You know those whores?
They are not whores. They are my brethren.
Then I recognise the torn gowns. The religious beads.
Ut-oh, this spells trouble.
Look, after we have the core we can...
No, Jack. They are my sisters. I would rather burn in purgatory for all eternity than let them suffer one more moment.
You've got to be mistaken. The Wasters wiped your chapel. No one survived.
Yes they did. I can see them with my own two eyes.
Sister shoulders her automatic. Lurches to her feet.
"Lie down, you black bitch! That's an order!"
Midnight looks into my eyes and snarls.
"I don't take your orders anymore, Jack."
"Then go to hell!"
Sister spits at my feet.
"You are one sick and twisted fucked-up bastard, you know that?"
Then she's gone. Striding over the rise like an avenging archangel.
Sister, wait. We've got to talk... Dingo, do something.
Like what, exactly?
Like tell her to come back.
Like nothing. Let her go. We'll meet up with her later...
That's if there's going to be a later.
She'll be OK.
Nowhere on. Sister, we're going for Kibbutz. Rendezvous at the Huntress... You got that?

There's no answer. Guess we'll have to assume she did. Stubborn bitch. She'll get herself killed, sure as anything.

"What we gonna do now, Nowhere?"

I look at Wonder Dog and wince. Guess it's hard dealing with facts like needing people. Without Sister's firepower we're gonna have to sneak it. Can't say I like the idea. Still, the skate-happy puppy should come in handy.

Look, we've got to get to the main balcony. That's where Malorian is.
Who's he?
My rakish brother. Sole inheritor of all my daddy surveyed.
He's the one with the power core.
Oh, OK.
Plan's simple. As long as the King and Malorian don't see me, we'll have no problem getting pretty close.
I look down into the dusty bowl. Nah, no problem at all.
Once we do, you'll have to get the tesseract while I create a diversion. Looks like the games are chugging on. Don't expect any fireworks until dawn.
Look at the sky. Everything's an ochre haze.
We've got a good few hours. Let's make 'em count.
Aye aye, captain.
Sheesh, how'd I get myself into these situations?

★

Watching from the doorway of an abandoned hamburger shack, I see the flier before I hear it. Not surprising over the noise. Plus it's coming in low from the bayside. Caught in the fog on the hills. Like a winged snake, it comes. Bursting with electric blue light and yellow smoke. Might have been a falling angel if not for the spray-painted gargoyles on its undercarriage. First I see it's swooping to avoid the bridge. Disappearing into the haze, then banking toward the park. As it comes, I hold Dingo back with one arm. Make him aware. Then let him watch too. His tiny eyes sparkle as he watches. Caught like a jack rabbit in the middle of the freeway.

Who is it, Jack?
Dunno.
Bad?
Maybe.
Maybe not?
More chance it's bad.
Oh.

The craft's being noticed by others. Not surprising as it's almost right above us now. Street fucks stop their dancing and watch. From within the castle muffled PAs announce its arrival. Then once it's overhead it veers sharply. Starts spiralling up and up and up. Higher and higher directly over the stadium. Then when it's just a speck of light and smoke, it levels off and the back opens.

In a distant blaze of golden light, a great painted wing is jettisoned from the plane. Like half a butterfly it tumbles in the wind then rights itself, weighted by a curved board at one end. A suited figure stands atop this precarious ledge, hands gripping a crossbar. Steering the triangular kite earthwards.

Shit, Jack, it's a windsurfer.

I can see that.

Then others follow. Leaping from the flier in a mass of colour and light. And as they freefall, rudder-like units kick into action, spewing wild spirals of smoke as their riders pilot the boards towards the crenelated auditorium.

Inside the castle, the crowds go wild. I can see why. It's a spectacular stunt. Yet I feel no euphoria. Only a slow dread.

Beside me Dingo hollers. None the wiser.

Whoop-de-doo! What a show!

Don't wet your pants, Wonder Dog. Those surfers aren't part of the act.

Looks like the Wasters are back in town.

26 | D'ALESSANDRO

So I am to die at midnight. How odd that feels. How morbidly fascinating. Lying here on this squeaky bunk I find that I am excessively drained by all the recent excitement. I try to rest, but cannot. After doing essentially nothing for forty-six months, the last few hours have been nerve-shatteringly stressful. And now it's over all I can think about is what's coming.

You'd have thought that the least they could have done was given me a chronometer.

I lie on the foldaway bed in a wide arc of cigarillo butts. The dried-up platter that was my last meal chills out on top of the toilet cistern. The warder's bible languishes like some leathery turd in the pan.

The isolation room is smaller than I expected. All interminable neatness and rounded edges. The room's also devoid of a VTV. If I had a VTV perhaps I could rig some uplink bypass and… But there's no VTV. Just the bunk, the toilet and me. It would seem they don't want me to take away all their fun by killing myself before they do. Slashing my wrists on a chair back. Staving my skull on an errant window ledge. Ramming a broken bed leg through my eye and into my brain. I wonder why they wouldn't want me to save them the trouble. Either way I'd be dead, surely?

Midnight. I die at midnight. What an inadequately banal concept. Of course the irony is that, as the international date line runs through the North Pole, just as all roads lead south, theoretically it's also always midnight here. Always the moment of my death.

The isolation room has no windows so I cannot tell if it's light or dark. Yet here on the roof the world, that's no indication either. Still, would be fine to see if the sun's out. Perhaps it's snowing. Perhaps it's not. It was blowing up a storm when I arrived here. The blizzard threatened to tear the flier clean in half, but they managed to reach the hangar somehow. That's the last time I saw the real world. Now all I have are dim memories of long walks along the bay and one reckless drive through woods at midnight.

Midnight. There's that word again. The time when the power of evil is at its zenith.

I smile, but smiling hurts. I'm nursing some nasty bruises, my ribs ache and my face is painfully swollen. I can't check how bad because there's no mirror either.

"Mr Glass, your stay of execution has been rejected. You will be terminated at midnight tomorrow…"

Finally the time has arrived when I am excess to requirements. Call me a cynic, but if I'm for the needle then Osakimo have finally got everything they require; an uninfected Cetacea cerebrum; an uninfected replication; an uninfected copy of the K/OS key. The first I knew they had already acquired. The only copy of the second I lost in the destruction of the Phoenix Tower. Buried when the building was bombed. I thought that it was gone forever, but it's possible that it survived. Obviously ten thousand tonnes of rubble wasn't security enough. The failure of my mission to destroy Osakimo's plans – to effectively save the near-space colonies – stings. I was so passionate about the X-Isle project, yet when I found the virus I didn't even think twice about the mobilisation of the raid upon the XEs backbone. Better that than having the deaths of twenty-seven billion people on my hands. This corporate-owned prison is a fitting reminder of how wrong it all went. The third languishes in the comatose mind of Jack's father. And I suspect that if I'm tagged for termination, they must have already captured Jack and extracted the access codes.

If they have that, then next they must fuse another whale's brain through the K architecture, download the infinity dump from the last replication…

The last replication. I shudder at the thought of my meisterwork in the hands of those butchers. Still I must not dwell on such things. Must keep my mind on more relevant matters. Like my impending execution.

I learned the procedure the day I arrived in this castle of ice, and now I cannot think of anything else. It's not complex. Quite short and sweet really. After letting me make a last call to my non-existent loved ones, at twenty-two hundred they'll come to take me to meet my non-existent visitors. At twenty-three forty-five armed guards will cordially frog march me into the death tank. At twenty-three fifty they'll strap me down, at fifty-five they'll close the door. At zero-zero they'll kill me.

Beneath my back the thin grey sheets are soaked with sweat.

Strap me down, close the door, kill me.

How childishly simple.

I'm roused from my musings by footsteps in the bright corridor. Looking through the bars I see Akahiri in his grey one-piece. In his hands he carries a dirt-phone. Pausing only enough to swipe his pass key through the reader he opens the food hatch, slides the black unit onto the tray, then leaves.

As he goes he mumbles, "It is set for one call. I will be back in one hour."

Sitting up, I mournfully watch him go. So he's my executioner. I can tell it in his voice.

I stare at the phone. In the harsh neon it looks like the dark carapace of some vat-grown lobster.

This is totally against procedure. It can't be that late already. It's not possible. Still the phone's appearance brings me out in another cold sweat. Only when I get myself under control do I think of just who I'm going to call. My brain aches trying to think of a single person. Who would want to hear from me? Who'd still be accessible? Who'd care?

The code record is not enough. I cannot rely on Baseeq still being around – or even alive. I've got to do something more. Otherwise sitting in here is going to drive me over the edge.

Shifting my weight, I stand and grab the unit, then punch in the digits. Jacking the cord to my ear, my brain fills with the dialling tone as I connect to the stream. It sounds like a waterfall of information, constructed from countless droplets of pure data. I let it fill me utterly. I drown in it.

Then I thought-dial the code.

27 | PURE

The world's stopped dancing. I'm still in the nightflier, somewhere over the bay. Just hovering. Astro shows the jagged coastline from some satellite or other. Dead City's marked by a faint red line. I've vacced my hardbody suit. Ditched the masculine tech. Kept the jacket though. Like the eagle at my back. Kept the kevlar boots. Got the pink plastic curtains from the toilet. Sliced them up and made a neat outfit. Pinned the skirt with bobbies. Added a belt. Strapped the top tight round my titties. Pulled it low enough to show off my devil tattoo. Fixed my hair. Tied it up with a bright red ribbon made from a shoe strap.

Finishing touch: I-Fax lenses. Glasses to the *n*th degree.

Now I'm ready.

Look at the console. At the message. Kasikianu. Wonder where that is? Punch navigations. Get the wireframe and zoom. Find the intercept would have taken me north. Further north than I thought you could go. To a land of ice a million miles wide. Switch to sat but get zilch. View shows nothing but gleaming white. Zoom again. Still nothing. Get to one in fifty thousand and I see something. A tiny dark scar in the snowfield. It's a prison all right. Underground complex. Hell frozen over. Only the doors are visible. That and a few searchlights. No runway. Just in and out. Wonder why the computer wanted to divert me there?

Run a patch to the archive and findsearch on 'Kasikianu'. Merge it with my own. Being an ex-Burger Queen has its uses. Big Mamma's enhancements were the best kit and the latest models. I got the

Eternity. Face to match. Right off the cover of the thousandth issue. Not exactly Babs O'Neill, but still close enough to reek fabulous. Enough to store just about everything I'm ever going to need.

Match comes up soon enough. Only a fragment. From a streamcast sent three months after the A-Men got trashed. It's got a picture of Nathaniel Glass, front and profile. They call him D'Alessandro. Rafaele Juarez D'Alessandro. Cute. Story headlines with 'Outlawed Author, Glass-Suko Genius, Death Sentence Minimum'. And there at the bottom is the reference. He was sent to Kasikianu and that's the last anyone ever heard of him.

Until the old devil tried to reprogram my ride.

I'm aching for drugs. None on board this junk though. I've searched twice. Not even anything salvageable in the medikit.

Jack the stream and hit Random. That usually acts as a fair substitute. At least until I get back to Dead City. Yet when I do, I'm gonna need a hit badly. Four years ago I could've listed a dozen dealers straight off. Yet that was A-Men time. Then DC was one mad, frenzied garbage sale. Everyone dealing in raw sex and death. Street level rocked with cults and tribes and fuckups. Whole place just an open grave. Bigger than Babs but a million times uglier. I lived in a three-storey cavity, unlit, unfurnished, with walls of crumbling brick. That's until I met Jack. He was my saviour from that twilight hell. He was all uncertain and intense then. A light on the dark side of my earth. He mended my broken home. He made me look up above the nameless lowlife. He made it real for me. He showed me that there was only one law; survival. He taught that death is the only release, death and a dream of being special. In Dead City you're either special or you're running. Special is all about being above it for a while. Being a part of something that gets you out the gutter.

We were A-Men. We were gods. Was all The Nowhereman's idea. The Amen was his supreme deity. Based on this mythical group of religious heroes and heroines. From some half-assed book. The others all went along with it. Said it was a great idea. And me and Lucille all went along with them. Jack was my naked boy. I was his wolf. Ichor was in my blood after he got me off these shitty chemicals. Then I feasted upon him. Now they feast on me. Jack made me special. Then he made me leave. Yeah, when I heard that the Phoenix had been hit I blipped emotion for a nanosecond. Fearing that he'd been blown to shit. But by then it didn't matter. By then I had no way of getting back. No way of turning off the hate I had fashioned for him. No way to be anything more than a ghost of what I was. Anyhow, by then he was screwing someone else and I had my own gig across the ocean. Yet all that changed when I wasted that skinny Wolf and had to start running all over again. And now the voice has returned. Come back and told me he was waiting. My god over the sea.

Still the thought of seeing Jack again sets my stomach shivering. Mission's off but I still want to waste the fucker. Our summer sexfest was a long time ago and now who knows what awaits me. But I need a hit and I need to see Jack. For one last big reunion. Pure. The Nowhereman. And my Sentinel Panther.

And with that thought I call the only dealer I know.

28 | DINGO THE WONDER DOG

"Cookies! Get your lovely cookies! Dime a dozen!"

I'm walking up the steps toward the balcony overlooking the arena of Kibbutz's plastic palace. Around my neck hangs a wooden tray filled with the mankiest biscuits I've ever seen. Dark snot still gleams off the topmost cookies from the tray's former owner. Jack slugged him as he sat smoking under the rear stands. Nevertheless I've collected quite a tidy sum, but that's all by the by. What I'm really after is getting as close to King Kibbutz as I can. Luckily the guards were quite happy to let me through. Now I'm nearly at the table.

"Lovely cookies. You know you want some!"

The high table is covered with enough food to feed the four people seated there for the next two weeks. Most hasn't even been touched. They're too intent on watching the combat below. I've got my back to the action, but can read every sword thrust, every death, by their changing expressions. Skating forwards, I look at them and try to work out a plan.

King Kibbutz sits in a gaudy jewelled throne at the centre of the table. He wears no helmet now, just a brass crown that shows off his ringletted curls. To his immediate right sits the guy Jack calls Malorian. He's creepy. All dressed up in a black suit with long hair slicked back into knives of silver. Eyes covered by bug-like shades. He's talking to Kibbutz while playing with a meal that comprises entirely of vegetables. On the other side sits a slanty-eyed gentleman whom I know. Well, know of. He's Ikki Dikki, top dog of the Inki-Winki Chinkimen. A blonde woman, who is almost certainly not his wife, lounges seductively in his lap. At the back of the balcony stand four knights in full armour, their spears held like bayonets before them.

The Chinkimen keep alive the essence of Chinatown even though there's not a true blood among 'em. They're like fans of fans. A gang peopled by those who affect the kind of clichéd accent that cringing was invented for. They're also disciples of the ancient and mysterious art of Inki-Winki, but I have no idea what this is. Haven't encountered these people firsthand but their infamy and deadliness is known the city over.

As I come nearer I catch a snippet of conversation between the geek and the suit.

"I hear you have vely bad ruck with rocating the clystal. They say you rost a vely crose flend…"

"Yes, I did."

"I vely solly to hear this. Vely, vely solly."

"Thank you. She had been with the team since the beginning."

"Ah, I see."

A roar from the crowd jolts everyone's attention back to the arena. Kibbutz cheers and slams his tankard onto the table. The other two men look bored. Oh well, here goes nothing.

Approaching I am suddenly aware of two wolfhounds that sprawl under the table, each munching contentedly on the huge legs of some poor loser from the tournament. Or at least they are until they get a whiff of me. As one they're up and barking, straining at the short lengths of dark chain that stop them from ripping me to pieces where I stand. I roll to a halt and try to look scared. It isn't hard. I'm petrified.

Kibbutz kicks one of the dogs in the rump, shouting, "Moon! Shadow! Behave yourself, my beauties. It's only the cookie man."

Malorian and Ikki Dikki turn to look at me, then seeing nothing of interest, look back to the arena. The blonde woman tries to liven things up by stuffing both hands inside the chink's kaftan, but gets little response.

"So," I try again. "Anyone fancy a cookie?"

The king waves one ermine hemmed sleeve in my direction to

dismiss me.

"Leave a couple of handfuls on the table, there's a good fellow. Then go."

Jack? What am I looking for?

The power core is about the size of a fist, but it's heavy. He'll probably have to carry it in a case or pack or something.

Oh, OK.

Moving up to the table, I offload a pile of biscuits into a cavernous tureen. Ikki Dikki's trying to start a conversation again.

"So Marorian-san, what do you go for in a woman?"

"The jugular."

"Oh har-har, that vely funny. Vely funny thing…"

The suit looks like he wants to torture the pretend Asian to death.

Faking tying my laces, I squat down and come snout to muzzle with Moon, who growls deep in her throat.

"Nice doggie," I stammer. "Mmm, what a lovely bone."

Eyes wide, I scan all around while my paws scrabble at my skates. At first I don't see anything. Yet then, by Malorian's feet, half-hidden behind Shadow's backside, I see a large black lump.

Jack, Malorian's got something at his feet.

What is it?

It's a bag.

29 | SISTER MIDNIGHT

The Slut Hut is aptly named. The torn and tattered marquee is set out like a stables. Even from outside I can see the row upon row of canvas rooms, each a hideaway for some illicit act of sin. Beyond the door flap an aging madam greets me warmly. Her hands play with a string of pearls, her shoulderless dress doing little to hide the most gargantuan breasts I have ever seen. Still, I am armed and restless and there is nothing deadlier known to man nor beast. Stepping into the bordello, I toss my dreadlocks from my face and glare at the woman. Inside the air is scented with the smell of flesh.

"Can I help you, young lady?" the mistress asks.

I judge that conversation would be of little use. Even at these simple words from the pimpess my anger swells in my chest, but the woman misreads my attitude utterly.

"Come now, don't be shy. Tell Auntie DD your pleasure."

The woman lets the pearls slip through her fingers. Extends her red taloned fingers. Plays with one of my sleeves. Shrugging off the whore's touch, I feel tears stinging in my eyes.

"My pleasure?" I say absently, tenderly wiping the tears away. For a moment my mind is lost, thinking of that word and when last I heard it spoken. Or when last I had felt such an emotion. Thinking upon this my anger returns, swiftly like a striking snake. Tipping back my anguished face, I snarl, "My *pleasure*! My pleasure is this!"

In one fluid movement I haul the polished length of my broadsword from its sheath and ram it through the woman's left breast. Auntie DD gurgles, her lungs immediately filling with blood, her milk-white skin sliced open like an overripe fruit. Stumbling backwards, her hands grasp for the blade, and as she tries to vainly pull it from her, I wrench at the sword, slicing off the madam's wrinkled fingers, one by one. They drop like painted maggots to the ground, then are crushed as she falls on them, vomiting pints of gore like thick red wine.

Blessed soul of Kalím, anoint this thy sacred blade and deliver thine holy temple from the loathsome unbeliever...

Wiping the blade on my camos, I step over the dying whore and without pausing, I continue down the hall.

I pass twenty-two doors before reaching the stall where my sisters lie. Twenty-two rooms each bearing a scene of utter depravity. In some hookers display themselves like over-stuffed parrots in plastic cages. In others hollow-eyed men wear costumes with far too many zips for comfort. In the rest they are clothed only in looks that say 'Please exploit me a little more'. I kill them all regardless. By the time I am even halfway, the corridor is filled with fleeing people. Then my attacks are more vicious for none can be allowed to escape my judgement. My merciless god of war will not tolerate such negligence.

Then suddenly I am striding into the open-sided chamber wherein my brethren dwell. The three men are oblivious to their impending doom; a battered box spills rock 'n' roll at full volume. The first buggers Mother Earth, the second face-fucks her while the last force-feeds his rampant cock to the chained form of Sister Dawn.

Ave maria! O holy Tôrus of the hallowed earth, pray spare them...

In my boiling mind the men are transformed into reptilian creatures. They are stricken worthless. Less than nothing. Swinging my sword in a two-handed arc, I split the first's head in two, killing him in mid-thrust as he orgasms messily. The other turns his face into the blade's second swing as his mate's blood spatters his naked torso. The final lizard claws for the tent flap in abject terror while I spear him through his bare back, then once he is firmly pinned to the ground I slit his bearded throat.

Forgive me for slaying them in haste, O father...

And the gods take their sacrifices without a word.

Cutting Earth and Dawn from their leather harnesses, I cradle them in my grasping arms. I am weeping openly now, my passion fuelled by the utter carnage that marks the end of such wanton carnality.

And when I am done, I contact Jack.

30 | THE NOWHEREMAN

Fuck me backwards, Wonder Dog's found the bag.

Under the tiered stalls, I can just about make out the mutt's head at the top of the wooden steps. I'm sweating like a pig. Above and all around me the crowd goes wild. I ignore them. Have to hear Dingo say it one more time.

Wonder Dog, can you repeat your last transmission?

There's a pause. A big, long nothing.

Wonder Dog, clarify last transmission.

More nothing.

And then my mind implodes.

Jack, this is God. There's a problem…

Midnight here. Jack, I have them. Where are you now?

Jack, I know I'm probably the last person you thought you'd hear from, huh?

Jack, I said I can see a bag… it's under the table.

Whoa, slow down. What in fuck's going on here?

Jack?

Jack?

Jack?

Jack?

Voices. Buzzing chatter. A maelstrom of voices. Wait a goddamn minute. Whatever happened to using t-com?

Jack, God needs your help. Are you alone?

Nope, I have about a thousand people sitting all around me.

I haven't got time for jokes, Jack. This is my last chance to come clean. It's about the island.

OK, hold up a moment… Who's this?

You're dreaming angel who needs a hit, Jack. You know any dealers?

Pure? Is that you?

Yeah, it's me, but no one's called me that in a long time. I'm Suzi Uzi now.

Suzi Uzi. Nice.

Hi. Hey, y'know you'll always be Pure to me.

Yeah, hi. S'been a long time.

Yeah, it certainly has. Er… hang ten for me, babe… God, you still with me?

Yes. Jack, my situation is desperate. I must speak with you…

Go right ahead. If you're gonna come clean make it fast.

I'm not God.

No shit. What else?

Your brother has defected to Osakimo and is here in Dead City.

That's more stuff I know. Try something else.

He is trying to destroy the island in the stream…

I've seen it.

You have?

Yes.

Then you know how beautiful it is.

Yes.

You've seen it?

Yes.

Then save it.

Maybe I don't want to save it. Maybe I should just let it burn in space…

Jack, Pure here. What's happening? I'm circling Central DC. Waiting for a landing slot. Glass' been messing with me. I think he's trying to get me to go free him from prison. Thought he was a drug by-product, but he's not. He's using our headmans. Burning our minds. Has he talked to you? Has he…

God's talking right now.

Jack, it's not God. Forget all that A-Men faerie tale shit and get real. He ain't no deity. He's Nathaniel Glass. He's just a kooky psychist who's holed up in Death Row and about to get the needle…

Jack, do you read me. You must save the island... They have the last whale. They have the last replication. It's pure. They must have got into the Phoenix and...

It was Gut Radical.

What?

Gut Radical got in and took your precious replication. Or it might have been him and Lucille. Anyhow, forget about that. What about you?

Forget me. I'm beyond redemption?

Pure says you're not God, you're Nathaniel Glass.

I am. She's a clever girl.

Says you're tagged for termination.

I am.

Says I should let you rot.

Now, Jack...

Don't talk to me, you fucking bastard. Now I see it all clearly. What you told me, what Ianus told me, what...

Ianus? You've talked to Ianus?

Can it, D'Alessandro. S'time to come clean. Time we all came clean. If you hadn't carried on all that replicating crap after you were denied access then all would be sweet.

I? What of your poisoning of the genetic protocol? If it wasn't for that—

You shitting low-life son of a bitch—

Look, my hands are tied. I need you, Jack. Everyone in Heaven needs you. And you need me if you're going to reset the code.

Why in hell would I want to do that?

Because if Osakimo restore the last replication then Xankhara will be obliterated. The X-Isle will be gone forever.

You fucking, fucking bastard.

Face it, Jack, you need me. Which is a pity because, by my reckoning, in close to eighteen hours I'm for the death tank.

You fucking, cunting...

As I said, reality's all in the bag.

Jack, Midnight here. The whore house is secured.

Great. Great, Sister, you did great. Look, I'm kinda busy right now...

Mother Earth and Sister Dawn are delivered from evil. Everyone else is dead. I have been instructed by Mûhamet to destroy the god machine... It is my destiny...

Don't tell me, Mûhamet's been speaking to you.

Yes, her divine voice is all around...

That son of a bitch...

Sister, it's not Mûhamet. It's D'Alessandro.

Nathaniel?

Yeah, bullseye. Pure's on her way. Says she rumbled him.

The dog always returns to its vomit...

Yeah, right... One moment, Sister... Wonder Dog, ya there?

Yes, Jack. Whassa matter?

Can you still see the bag?

Yep. It's under the table.

Are you sure?

Of course I'm sure. Don't wet your pants. It's just an old battered bag.

A cloth bag?

Looks that way.

A black cloth bag with a handle? Like a doctor's bag?

Yep, spot on. How'd ya know that?

Dingo, get it. Get it now!

Whoa, Jack. How'm I gonna do that?

I don't give a damn. Just get it.

OK.

Nathaniel, you holding? Look, tell me where you are and I'll be there to get you.

No! Forget me. You must save the last replication...

What's it look like.

What?

This replication?

It is like a crystal. A fist-sized unit.

Dingo's getting it. Malorian has it in a bag with the ship's power core.

Then get them both and get away.

You know me, Nathaniel, I can't do that on two counts. One, I'm a no-brained *facefuck who's no good on technicalities and two, you're one of us. When you for the chop?*

Midnight.

How apt.

Sister, what's the time?

Time you told me what's happening.

Later. What's the time?

Seven. Just after.

Nathaniel, it's seven in the morning here. What's the time in your neck of the woods?

I have no clock.

Right, well we'll be there just as soon as...

Up above Dingo disappears from sight. Now I'm really worried. My brother switched sides. Took daddy's secrets and sold out to Osakimo. Now the virus has brought him back for Nathaniel's replication.

The answer to everything's in that little black bag. Hopefully sitting snugly right next to the Huntress' power core.

With a sudden flash of remembrance I'm at the Phoenix Tower. I'm holding the book. It's a present from D'Alessandro. He's long gone. Inside's a message about my happy ever after. Everyone's on patrol. I'm holding the fort with Esther. We're down and running in twenty. Just before the orbitals arrive and blast the place to oblivion...

Dingo, what's happening?

I can't reach it. I'll be killed. These guys are armed big time.

Stop blubbing and create a diversion. Anything...

OK, here goes.

Out in the arena two bikers execute some poor sucker in a wheelchair. Grisly stuff, but I'm too tense to look away from the balcony. At least the Wasters vanished after their grand entrance. Hopefully gone to some private party. Thank fuck for small mercies. Still I'd rather they were the other side of the stratosphere.

Budda-budda-budda.

The burst of machine gun fire makes me jerk my head up. For a moment the Wonder Dog is silhouetted against the floodlights at the top of the stairs. Then he collapses, tumbling. Drops the tray. Drops the bag. Crashes down the steps like a sack of mutton.

"Guards! Guards! Stop that cookie seller!"

All around him the air is filled with flying lead and chocolate biscuits.

★

As Dingo somersaults down the wooden steps, as the plated tinmen rain dum-dums down after him, I guess that without a little help the Wonder Dog's gonna have his day. My mind's still ringing with everyone's voices. I can't let them down. They need me. The last of the A-Men. Five against the fucking world. Till the end of time.

So what's the plan?

Stop formulating a plan. Plans are for suckers. Plans never got me nowhere. Fast. I'm Jack Shit. I'm The Nowhereman. All I got is my piece and the balls to get out there and use it. Who needs a plan. Fuck the plan. Plan's just talk. And what did talk ever give anyone 'cept a fat lip? Still got the fading traces of the uppers. That's enough. Least for a couple of hours yet. Maybe more. Maybe less.

Instead of my D&K, I got a Danzu. Not as accurate, but accurate's not what I need right now. What I need is eight hundred and forty rounds a minute over a twenty-foot area. That's cool. That's what I got.

Without so much as a deep breath, I leap up. Swing from under the stacked seating. Lock and load. Aim up to the platform. Cover the mutt. The machine pistol's spurting as soon as my right arm reaches level. Fire fights fire. The knights of yore don't know what's hit 'em. Breastplates protect them some, but Armalite shells make short work of anything thinner than a brick wall. They burst like clumsily opened cans of cranberry preserve. In my fist the Danzu wails. The seated crowds see all, hear all, but their pea pod brains ain't up to reacting yet. Yet.

I bask in the pleasure of power. Feels good. For about two seconds anyway. Then they mark me and the heaven's open. Dropping to my knees I roll under the stands as around me spectators erupt. Screams follow the guts. Duck under both. Scrabble through the dirt, regain my feet and start running. Heading for the patch of tarmac that Dingo's set to fall on. As I arrive, he plops out the sky. Lands almost on top of me like a mangled ball of fluff. With skates on.

"Nurrrrghh…"

"Where's the swag, Dingo," I say. Real polite considering. Well, polite for me.

"Mmmurnuuuu," the mutt replies.

I kick him. Not quite so politely. Repeat the question.

Dingo gives up trying to get his tongue around anything as complex as a coherent sentence. Instead he points up. Look up. And there it is. Hanging half off an empty bench about a metre above me. All around crazed dweebs scatter in every direction.

Shit. Probably too much to ask for one of them to kick the bag. Knowing my luck they'll probably swipe it.

Wankamoley. Now what?

Above the noise of panic, a PA snarls into life. It's Kibbutz.

"All units to north stands. Subject is armed and carrying contraband. Shoot to maim…"

There's more, but I don't have time for it. Lots of stuff signing my death warrant. I hear 'wolfshead'. I hear 'eliminated'. I hear 'reward'. Now they don't need the coding from my brain, I guess a fair trial's out the question. I run.

As I go, shout to Dingo to get up. Then blow the bench with a couple of bursts. Watch as the section of seating collapses. Falls right on top of him. Order him to find Sister and her nun chicks, then get to the Huntress. Say I'll see him there. Fuck knows if I'm lying. Fuck knows anything anymore.

With a grim satisfaction, I watch the Wonder Dog skate off. After all the trouble I've spent chasing the fucking thing would've liked to have had a peek in that bag, but that's too bad. Better if Dingo has it right now. He's the fastest pooch on eight wheels. And he needs someone to cover him.

As the Wonder Dog heads for the hills, let my Danzu roar. Try to make it impossible for anyone to get too close without dying. Outside everywhere's a mess. Party's over for a while. Now chaos reigns. And as I'm firing, I'm backing up. Looking for an opportunity to skedaddle. The stands go back a long, long way. Light starts to fade. First it's sunset. Then dusk. Soon I'm in near darkness.

And it's about then that I hear something growling. I hear it over the crowds. Over the pounding boards. Sounds like something snarling. Some *things* snarling. An unseen pack of jackals. Lurking in the night.

Crouch low. Brace my back against a metal support. Slam another clip in the pistol. Breathe.

In that instant, my sight's bleached. Blinded by a brilliant spot. Twist away into the shadows. Caught in a second beam. Drop to the dirt as three more flash into life. Under the tiered seating, morning has broken.

"Drop the gun, punk," shouts a voice.

Shit, who're these kooks? Can't see shit except for a few blurred silhouettes. From down on my belly, I fire off a couple of bursts. Nothing fancy. Aim at the lights. Blow two, then roll.

Zeebs return the compliment. Blast grit right in front of me. Almost feel my limbs being peppered like some cheap hundred-dollar steak. But it never happens. Look up again. Catch just the briefest of glimpses, yet I see all I need to see. All around me stand a gang of blond-haired sand cowboys. All pouting lips and ripped denims. Their perfect tans are a grim reminder of how long it's been since I dared go out in the noonday sun.

Wasters. Might've known.

Hold my fire. Just stop and lie there. Resigned.

As I fester in the mud, I wonder why I'm still alive. Who cares? Not me. Quit worrying about shit like that long ago. Only way to get through the days. Nah, life or death's nothing in Dead City. Just that day-to-day dream of being special.

Scramble to my knees. Finally stand. Leave the Danzu on the

ground. Ready myself to play whatever game these pissed-off beach boys have in mind. No good trying to bust out. I'm surrounded. Wouldn't get ten paces.

"Good," says the same voice. "I thought you'd see it our way."

I sneer at nobody in particular. Hope my face's not too bleached so's they don't notice.

"So, what's this? J.J. rides again?"

Murmurs off in the supernova, then, "J.J. was my brother."

Oh, great. That's so fucking poetic. The jumped-up bleach-head faggot has a twin brother. I'm looking for the man who shot my bro'. Wuz it you? Haw, haw, haw.

"Word on the stream says you wasted him."

"You believe whatever you want. For myself..."

"Word is you brought *most* of 'em down."

"Well, it..."

"Word is you're so hot right now, it's lucky we found you alive."

I wanna grease these fuckers. I wanna grease them so bad it hurts. By the looks of things, they've got the same idea. Can't they just get this over with. Now they've found me, why the small talk? Try to speed things up a little.

"Cut the fucking chat, Waster. Word is the only reason you're pissed at me is I deprived you of your daily blow job."

"Why you filthy, little..."

"Stop right there!"

Everyone looks up. Me included. Above is mr king-shit evil with a full complement of tin cans in attendance. Now the Wasters are surrounded by the Knights. Looks like things are going to take a turn for the unexpected.

"Kill the lights!"

One by one the spots wink out. Reveal about twenty jockies plus J.J.'s brother. His face's a knot of disgust.

"What's going down here?" J.J. jnr shouts. Quieter than before.

Kibbutz cocks his head toward the beach babe. At first that's all I think he's gonna do. But who am I kidding? Let's not forget these cunts just stole a big chunk of his thunder with that windsurfing stunt they pulled. Kibbutz is a showman. And showmen don't like no one else hogging their limelight. Least of all a bunch of juvenile delinquents who all wear better labels. There's one whole lotta silence. Yet finally he deigns to answer.

"I think you're forgetting where you are, little man. And who I am. You are my guests here, yet this is my court. What I say is law. So if I say 'stop right there' I expect everyone to stop. Is that perfectly understood?"

The knight's words are like honey, yet any fool can hear the underlying malice. You'd have to be a complete prick not to guess what a dangerous fucked-up monster Kibbutz really is. Already in the last few days he's had his cinema blown to buggery, lost face with Osakimo over the bag incident and found himself upstaged at his own tournament. Now he's in danger of being slamdunked in front of Malorian and the entire gangland audience by a gaggle of windsurfers. Mess this and he's going down. Makes me feel kind of sorry for the mincing bastard.

The head Waster says nothing. Just pouts a little.

King Kibbutz smiles a thin, snake-like smile. Flicks his tousled fringe back into place. Picks a fleck of invisible fluff from his silk lapel.

"Is that understood?" he repeats gently.

The jockey glowers.

"Yeah, I catch the general drift."

"Good."

The King seems genuinely pleased. Turning to his minions he gestures at little, old me and adds, "Guards, bring this sack of puke to my table. The rest of you, escort our offworld guests to the Bay C pit."

As the lead Waster is grabbed he struggles like a traumatised child. All temper and tantrums. Mouth froths all the usual bullshit. This time it's at me.

"I'll get you, fucker," he shrieks as they drag him off. "Don't think you've got away!"

I smile. Even as I'm grabbed too. Don't resist.

"Later, *dude*."

Make a gun of my free hand. Pretend shoot him. Wink. Drives the cunt delirious. Then they heave me away.

With an elegant swish of his velvet cloak Kibbutz tuts loudly, glances heavenwards, then heads back up the cookie-strewn steps, leaving his medieval robots to mop up this current puddle of spilt milk.

★

As I'm marched onto the canopied balcony it's time for me to meet *my* brother. Can't say he looks that pleased at our reunion. Can't say I'm exactly happy with it either. Looks tall, thin, tormented. All torment, smugness and intensity. Look's like he's practiced all three for a long, long time. His cold, grey eyes watch me with the sort of hate saved up especially for family. He says nothing as I stop before him. I'm too much of a cunt to leave it at that though.

"Joseph."

His eyes slit a little more. Cute.

"John," he replies.

"Name's not John," I correct him. "It's Jack."

He has the sense not to pursue that. I guess he never thought he'd see me alive. Not after he'd hired and fired just about every sap who I'd hung out with these past years. Gut. Lucille. Doc. List reads like a who's-fucking-who of my own personal Dead City. But it goes back long before that. Back to my father, my wife and the death of my son, And now I'm standing face-to-face with the guy who's been shafting us all, it feels weirder than weird. And then some. The stink of it makes me gag.

With a libertine flourish King Kibbutz sweeps onto the balcony and seats himself in his gaudy throne. Soon as he's parked his ass Malorian follows suit, while I'm forced to the floor looking out across the arena. A semblance of normality has descended over the milling crowds. All faces look intently up at high table. They're expecting more fireworks. The way king dick's eyes are sparkling, my guess is they won't be waiting long.

From the floor I get a good look at the two mutt's Dingo was barking on about. Nasty teeth. All sharpened. Honed into razored fangs at the front. Like canine vampires. Mean.

As I'm regarding the dogs, a klaxon goes off. Great electronic fanfare filling the air with noise. As the sound fades, Kibbutz stands. Arcs himself to his full high-heeled magnificence. Readying himself for some flamboyant address to the peasants.

"Friends," he begins, his voice a piercing falsetto. "I trust you are enjoying yourselves..." He pauses until the predictable round of cheers have subsided. "I trust that you are wined... that you have feasted... that your loins burn with the joy of overuse... that my hospitality fills you with a sense of worth in our otherwise bad and blasted existence."

More cheers, yet cautious now. Kibbutz is leading up to something and every half-drunk fucker is wising up to the fact that there's no such thing as a free orgy. Something big's coming. Something that will explain his part in this piss-awful mess.

"I have sent out the word to as many gang leaders as I am aware of to join me this night in a holochat over current affairs. I have with me a representative from the Osakimo Corporation who has news that will be of interest to every last one of us in DC. And that meeting is to take place here and now, while you are amused by our grand finalé and the last scheduled item of our nocturnal entertainment extravaganza. So please welcome back our master of ceremonies... over to you, Lord Jervaise!"

A plume-helmed knight in grey and crimson armour pushes past me. Steps up to the PA. Waves. Behind him his image appears on a screen that arcs over the balcony like a giant sailcloth. Then with all the congeniality of a game show host, he raises both hands in the air. Silences the crowds as another klaxon screeches.

"Scum of the streets, we have reached the climax of the night. We have come to the show you are all waiting to see. Beyond the gladiators. Beyond the bikes and dogs. Here is the pièce de résistance. Behold, the Mirrormaze!"

Below, the arena begins to shudder as hidden cogs grind into action. S'easy to imagine the ranks of slaves, invisible behind the fake castle walls, hauling on great lengths of chain. Pulling the false floor to reveal whatever secrets lie beneath. Slowly a labyrinth is uncovered. A chaotic subterranean maze of brick and wood and glass. Scattered across this jumble of passages are blank, stone vaults. Rooms hidden from the eyes of the audience in an otherwise openly voyeuristic landscape. Once this would have been a maze of mirrors and surprises for the paying public. Now it's Kibbutz's death camp.

Around the edge of the unfolding catacombs are barred gates. Each a separate entrance. Each marked with a large, red painted letter running from A to T. Now I knew where they'd sent the beach bums.

The crowd are going wild and Jervaise milks them like a pro. Takes out a deck of oversized cards. Fuck knows what they are. Crowd seems to though. Lays them out on a board. Can't see them from where I kneel. Not until a second camera shows them up on the looming screen. Inset into the main image.

"Behold the deck of fate!" he yells. "The master of the maze. Whatever it says, we obey." Crowd goes wild. Whole show's a non-stop frenzy. Can't say it's doing anything for me, though.

"So, let us delay no longer. Open the hatches, please!"

Down in the arena, every bay door grinds open. In groaning unison each spills bodies like an exhumation of the dead. Eyeless, they come, shambling, reaching. Like a hundred unwanted extras from some low-budget B-movie slasher.

Zombies. The by-product of the green ooze that seeps through every sewer of the city. Trouble is that, yeah, it's edible, but the stuff rots your brain to shite. But hey, it's that or starve to death. Which would you prefer?

The portcullises slam nosily closed after about a hundred are through. About a dozen get caught in the grates. Get sliced in half by the dull metal. The rest wander aimlessly. Like housewives from some prehistoric slumpermall.

"Here we have the dead. The slaves in our king's new army. Total dedication. Total brain drain. They'll do anything for a taste of something fresh. Something *flesh*. And have we got some flesh for them this evening. Prime beefcake. Ladies and gentlemen, straight from the stars, from the utopian delights of near-space, let's have a big hand for... the Wasters!"

Bay C staggers upwards. This time reveals the jockboys. Their high-tech wondertoys have been stowed. Now they've got a range of blades and bonecrushers. Look kinda out of place in their prissy fingers. For a moment they access the situation. Form a ring around the closing door. No one even contemplates trying to roll back under. Stand more chance leaping into a reactor naked. There's a brief confab, then they're away. Running down the corridor before them. Entering deeper into the torturous maze. Crowd watches them go. Their every move clearly visible through the glass. Their ceiling. Our floor. Total goldfish bowl.

After a couple of turns or so they run into their first bank of zombies. And as they begin the messy job of hacking through the wall of bodies, the touts start chalking up the current odds.

Jervaise guffaws loudly at this. Starts fanning the cards, face-down, on the green baize before him. Every move's projected onto the great screen above.

"So, mazesters, the rats are out their hole and headed for the safety of higher ground. Yet the Mirrormaze has no higher ground. No safe houses. No sanctuary. Just a million places where death lies waiting. And if you're very quiet you might just hear him sharpening up his scythe."

A hush falls over the audience. Lots of whispered shushes.

Into the calm, the knight decides that the time is right to bring me into the equation. Orders the guards to haul me to my feet. Then I'm dragged over to the mic.

"We have a very special contestant with us this evening. A guest whose name will be known to many of you here. So let's have a big hand for... The Nowhereman!"

Boos. Jeers. Predictable and right on cue.

Jervaise turns to me. Shoves his precious deck under my nose.

"Pick a card," he squeaks.

"Go fuck yourself."

One of the guards shoves me from behind. The other grabs my left hand. Forces it out. Trying to get me to take a card from the deck. I resist. Ball my hand to a fist. It doesn't matter. They stuff them between my fingers. There's a struggle. I get kicked. Yet when my hand's withdrawn, a card's sticking up between my knuckles.

Smugly, Jervaise takes it. Glances at it once, deftly swaps it with one from his sleeve, then shows it to the mini cam. Overhead, the image appears; a grinning fool in a hat festooned with bells.

"The Nowhereman has drawn the Jack of Fools! That is to be his fate card for the evening."

And with that he places the card back in the deck, while the heavies beat me back to the floor. Returning to the contest proper, Jervaise addresses the crowd again.

"For those out there amongst you who don't know the rules, well, you're missing nothing for there are no rules. Just the long hard road of survival. Everyone dies in the end. We all know that. Death's an insurance policy that we'll all one day claim, my brothers. Only truth in the whole shitty world. So it's not *if* you're gonna die, it's *how*. You don't enter the labyrinth to escape, you enter to prove yourself a hero. You know you're gonna die, so when you do you'd better die well. It's all about style, brother and sisters. Style over everything. 'Cause if you ain't got style, what have you got?"

"Nothing!" erupts the crowd.

"That's right. Nothing. So the Mirrormaze is a gift, it's our way of giving those whom we choose the chance at something much bigger than life. We give them the chance to become a hero. To prove they're special. We give them the chance at... immortality!"

"Immortality!" screams the crowd.

"And how do we do this? How do we give them this? Tell me how, good people."

"Turn the card! Turn the card! Turn the card!"

Up on the balcony, Jervaise grins like a man who's found he can stuff his own prick up his ass. Stands there for a few poignant seconds while the crowd chants maniacally below him.

Then he bends and turns the card.

Can't see what it is from the floor, but I can see the screen. There in glittering neon is a painted picture like those the fairground gypsies used to use. It depicts a large fish leaping up a frothing waterfall. All colours of the rainbow. Look's pretty. Like the dawn through a diamond's heart. Beautiful.

"The seven of hearts," informs the knight. "Flood the piranha pools!"

Disgusted, I turn back to Kibbutz's feast. Things are afoot. Looks like it's time for the big pow-wow.

At the table Kibbutz and Malorian are jacking themselves into some sort of black transceiver. Top of the unit looks like a lattice of little opaque fish lenses. As they jerk to attention it bleeps a little. Then from its many eyes a silvery light's emitted. Beaming off in all directions. Never seen one of these before, but I know what they are. Holoports. All over the city similar units are being networked via the stream, projecting the images of the owner into one big virtual conference. Malorian's idea naturally. Always was a bit of a giznerd.

In the air around the table seated figures begin appearing. Materialising like grey ghosts at some high-tech séance. The first is a bald-headed geek dressed in hooded robes. The next, a grossly fat chick with limp black hair. Blackwing and Big Mamma. Mister Grim Reaper and little miss Burger Queen. After that it's Gad Zooks, the mad croc from the Gonks. Then Norbert Rand, leader of the UltraTechz. All goggle-eyed scientist threads and naff bow tie. He's sitting next to a biker with a quiff the size of a Stetson: Psycho Billy of the Replicats. Next the gun-toting, cigar-chewing General of the Eco-Vigilantes. Next to him Dai-80, the shrivelled religious leader of the God-U-Likes in priestly robes and shades. The last two are unknowns; a wild-haired native with a necklace of human teeth, and a leather-clad nobody whose face is lost in the shadows of his painted crash helmet.

There's nine in all. Each the head honcho representative of the largest gangs in the city. With Malorian, Kibbutz and Ikki, that's twelve. Guess that makes me lucky thirteen.

The moment everyone's plugged and receiving, the arguments start. Main reason they conference virtually. If they ever met they'd tear each other to shreds and stomp on the pieces. Good thing about projections is they can't tough each other up. At least, not yet.

"Club Fantazi is ours by birthright. You *must* surrender it!"

"Jag my crax."

"Stooled if I care. We wouldn't've let that roxter slip through our fingers."

"Don't black prog me, Replicat, your girl's gonna spill juice for what she's done."

"Big Mamma, as spiritual leader to the people of this city, I must tell you that your t-shirt is religiously offensive!"

"It says, 'Forgive me father for I have slimmed'. So sucking what?"

King Kibbutz lands his fist on the table. Makes the transceiver leap.

"Quiet! All of you. I have brought you together to inform you of great news. Not to listen to your pathetic squabblings."

The ghosts shimmer, then turn to look at him.

"Well brief us, daddio," says the quiffed dude.

"My kingdom is strong," Kibbutz begins calmly. "It pleases me. It is good. I am weakened by our warring, yet that which does not kill me makes me stronger. Before the apocalypse that rocked this world, I was an employee of this vast themed realm operating the hall of mirrors in the main arena. I was chattel. A worthless nobody. I spent every day worrying about the payments on my chariot. How I'd pay my rent. Whether the balloon girl liked me. I was *nothing*. Then came the fall of the world and I was too busy fighting for my survival to worry about anything. Like every one of you, I was alone. I hid with a dozen others in the main control room of the park. We protected ourselves with the armour from the medieval waxworks. We kept the perimeter sealed from predators. We *survived*. When all about me were losing their lives, I kept mine. We founded this empire on the K operating sentience using it to transform this theme park into a living world again. With it we gave life back to its creations. Now we are the Knights of K/OS, protectors of its power.

"From those humble beginnings we are now a thousand strong. A force to be reckoned with. All of you will have your own stories, your own tales of greatness. Yet now comes the dark cloud of a menace which threatens to reverse all that we have achieved. All our suffering, the reason we have survived, will be for naught."

"So what's the score?"

"Yeah, what hangs?"

"Near-space has a virus. It's going down. And if the orbital colonies are endangered, there is only one place the offworlders can run."

There's a hushed silence as this sinks into their frazzed-out brains. It's Blackwing who breaks it.

"That's shite."

Kibbutz is unfazed.

"The stage is yours, Malorian."

My brother stands at this, his eyes dull and lifeless. When he talks, it's like he's addressing the milk monitors at the local nursery school.

"What his highness says is true. Believe it. Yet for those who have difficulty with belief, please, cast your eyes over to the centre of the table."

His tone is compelling. I look. They all look.

There above the shiny black unit appears the image of near-space. Some kind of port. Impossibly tall glass slivers and arcing grey pillars. Small freighters and cargo ships float sluggishly in and out of various hangars. Below the planet's sandy orange arc can just be seen drifting by.

"This is footage edited from a newscast released onto the stream a month ago. It shows the Osakimo main trade terminus on a typical afternoon…"

"Yeah, but so's what?" spits the quiffed dude's image.

"Watch," Joseph insists.

Suddenly the earth is eclipsed by a great shadow. Something's coming up on the entry hangar. Coming fast. Too fast. For a moment there's a buzz of panic as the smaller craft attempt a variety of evasive manoeuvres. Then a class six transport slams into view. Crashing headlong into the left side of the bay. Windows erupt. Metal erupts. The transport erupts. Imploding, the entire front section collapses. Spears the arc of the wall and rips it apart. One moment there's peace, the next utter chaos. Flames gutter in the vacuum, then vanish. Sucked into nothingness. The ships, architecture and various people all go the same way. As the transport forces itself further into the superstructure the diocam shudders, the picture spasming. Then the screen goes blank.

"The Exxo p-shuttle suffered sixty percent damages and fifty-six percent life loss. That's W$24 billion and over twelve hundred dead. The Osakimo corporation were not so fortunate. The reason cited by the official inquiry into the disaster was that the XEs subsystem assigned to monitoring the traffic in and around Osakimo registered space held no record of the Exxo transport. No record whatsoever. Quite frightening really when you consider the sentience is supposed to control everything that side of the stratosphere. If somebody farts the sentience knows about it. Yet XEs did not know about this. Its data files were oblivious to the crash. Further investigations highlighted the virus, hidden deep in the system. A tiny DNA pathogen attached to each and every cell of the Amen's upper cerebrum cortex. A self-replicating, nearly invisible disease that is eating the AI from within."

"Shee-it!" whistles Big Mamma. The rest of the gang leaders exchange murmurs and hums.

"Within the year the XEs sentience will be thirty-five percent disabled by this infestation. As the king so graciously puts it, by the end of the year, unless a cure can be found, the exodus will begin. I'd say we have one hundred and fifteen days before recolonisation of the Earth. And then... well, then it's back to the gutter for all of you."

"But that's unthinkable!" says Dai-80.

"No, it's happening," replies my brother.

This rattles 'em. There's a pause, then: "What can we do?" Psycho Billy asks for all of them.

"End this bickering. This eve I offer you all the greatest opportunity of your miserable lives. Or total destruction."

"Says who, worm."

"The wise on the stream says it. A group has been reformed to make sure that this happens, that the hostgod fails…"

"Who? Who's this gang?"

"The A-Men."

Laughter. Loud. Uniform. Total.

"They are dead. Destroyed. Kaput."

"They are not dead!" Malorian shouts. At once feral. Like a tiger by the tail. "They are very much alive. They hold the key to the virus. I have their leader here…"

"The Nowhereman? You have The Nowhereman?"

"I have their leader here," Malorian repeats. "Yet the others are still abroad. D'Alessandro and Pure are of no concern, but Sister Midnight and the Wonder Dog are somewhere within Forevermore. They must be stopped. The sentience must be revived. For if the hostgod falls, you'll lose *everything*. Do you recall what it is like to be a nobody? I'm sure you do? One other thing: the Wonder Dog has stolen some items very dear to me and I want them back. It is imperative to my mission here. The Osakimo macrocorporation will be most grateful for their return. And most generous…"

Kibbutz sees his chance. Steps back into the limelight. "We must unite, draw up our territories, else we are mere insects buzzing around the shit that they've left for us. To this end, I have harnessed the power of the dead. These are to be my soldiers. My armies of the night. *Our armies of the night!* If we unite – if we take over this place and run it like a city rather than a playground – then we can reclaim something far greater. The first show of my strength is to be the complete destruction of East-11. With the waystation annihilated, any descent dirtside will be forced over five hundred kilometres further up the coast. The final repairs have been completed on Malorian's transport and we are ready to begin our attack. The waystation holds cargo, essential raw materials and enough equipment to last for many months."

Now he has them. If there was one thing that ten years of in-fighting and tribal warring has done it was deplete their stores. If you heard a gunshot in DC these days you were on your way pronto.

Still they were planning to take on East-11, a heavily armoured fortress. And I'm never one to get into a pissing match with a skunk. So that's what all this is for. The bees are protecting their hive. No one wants their little party broken up by the big guys upstairs. No one wants out. Can't say it bothers me one way or the other. Can see why they've chosen the waystation as numero uno target. It's the nearest civilisation worth spitting on. It's the gateway up to the Heaven consortium. And, if they're gonna come back like he says, that's the way they'll come.

With all the action at the table, I haven't been keeping up with current affairs in the arena. Attention's been kind of straying. I realise this as Jervaise turns the card that ends all that. First I hear about it is when the guards grab me by the throat and haul me to my feet.

Look up. There above in glowing technicolour is a giant card. The familiar face of the idiot in the bell cap stares down at me as mr gameshow is going ape.

"The Jack of Fools!" he pronounces. "Throw The Nowhereman into the pit."

★

The iron door before me is painted with an ugly yellow J. The cards chose to give me a bullet-ridden flak vest and a stick with an inflated pig's bladder at one end. Great. Now I really look like a prize clown. Beyond the rusted metal the Mirrormaze awaits. Can't say I'm really looking forward to it. Yet there's few other options. I daren't call Sister or Dingo. Can't risk them. Coming back would be suicidal. Not now every gangland junkie worth his spunk is gonna be after them. Maybe they wouldn't anyhow. Nah, I'll just have to get out of this little mess on my lonesome. I'll think about the implications of the gang leaders' little tête-à-tête later.

With a splintered grinding the door to the holding bay cranks up. I half expect the corridor beyond to be filled with zombies out for my brains. For once I'm pleasantly surprised. All I see is a blank stone corridor. High above the glass casts distorting reflections, yet I already know that the audience can see every move I make. Pisser.

Cautiously emerge from the cell. Hear the dull cheer through the ceiling. Start running. Just a light jog. Behind me the door clangs shut.

Right, what's the procedure? Memories of my E-Unit training come flooding back. I need a weapon. Need a hideout. Need a defensive position. All that shit.

At the end of the corridor get my first choice. Left or right.

Look both ways. They're practically identical. Both are stone. Both have mirrored floors and ceilings. The resulting effect is like looking into an infinite ravine. Spooky.

I turn right. Review the situation. More of the fucking same.

I'm in unknown territory. Unarmed. I have no supplies or resources. Area is hostile. Unknown number of enemies. Unknown locations. None of which sounds too appealing.

Lope along the glass floor. Makes me feel dizzy. Corridor turns to the left then splits into a crossroads. Middle of this is a circular plinth. Once it held some sort of statue, but that's long gone. Only the broken stumps of two booted feet remain. Between these lies one of the jockies with his throat torn out. Also had one of his arms wrenched off. He's dead, yet otherwise he looks fine. What looks finer is the woodman's axe lying at his feet.

From far away I hear the crowd roar again, then echoing through the maze comes the sound of Jervaise's voice.

"So it's time to set the fate of the maze again by the turn of a card. The zombies are certainly taking their toll on the Wasters, but nothing yet from The Nowhereman."

There's a pause. In my mind's eye, I can see the knight drawing from the deck.

"And the card is… the Wheel of Fortune. So let's see if Lady Luck's with or against tonight's contestants."

Ditch the bladder. Grab the axe. Take another look around. Got a choice of three ways. The two either side twist off into eternity, yet straight across lies a long unmirrored path. Ends in a kinda vault. I make for that. Can't waste time. Can already hear the shuffling feet coming from somewhere behind me.

When I reach the vault I see that inside it's very dark. Can only make out a few indeterminate shapes. Floor's constructed of an inflated airbed. Makes walking difficult. Never was too good at bouncy fucking castles. There are four other doors. Each lead out to an identical corridor. There's blood in the one to the right. Zombies to the left. They smell me even as I see them. Start shambling forwards. Mouths already drooling.

Make my way across the room. Tripping and tumbling. Can't get a foothold. Careen out the other side at a run. Then I hear the sound of clanking chains right ahead of me. Stop dead still. Listen. Almost at once Jervaise's yakking again.

"Well, it seems that the Lady has decided that she shall deal with a beneficial hand. Fate has ordered that swords are not the order, but projectiles. So we opened our grandmother's chest and discovered a couple of harpoons. If our heroes are interested they should head for the secret garden."

The secret garden. Great. And where's that supposed to be?

Start off in the direction of the noise. Hope that's the way they're bringing in the supplies. Around the next corner I run into more zeebs. Six of the bastards. Gibbering against a half-busted door. Behind I can hear shouts and cries. Guess I've found some of my fellow prisoners. And there at the end of the corridor, over the wall stands a leafless tree. Looks dead. Branches suffocated by ivy.

The secret garden? Who knows. But it's the best shot I'm gonna get.

"Hey, fuckfaces! Wanna dance?"

At the sound of my voice two of the brain-dead dudes turn. Start hobbling in my general direction. Square my shoulders. Hoist the axe.

Ready it for a spot of chopping. Rest continue hammering at the door. Breaking what little remains to splinters. Two. That's not so bad. Just have to make sure they don't out-flank me.

They're about a metre away when I take my first swing. The head deadhead doesn't register it. Too quick for him. Smacks deep in his upper left arm. All but severs it. Leaves only a flapping sliver. Lots of blood though. All too easy to forget these guys are still living. And that they scream too. Yet with jelly for brains, they're not always too bothered when you hurt them. This one is though. This sack of shit's yelling fit to bust a lung.

Kick his pal in the bollocks. Pushes him back a little, but that's all. Swing at jellyhead for a second time. This strike's up and over. Cleaves the poor bugger's face. Straight down the middle. He falls spouting gore like bloody poetry. Yank at the haft but it's stuck in his neckbone.

While I'm wrestling with the axe, jelly two grabs me around the neck and starts biting. Sinks his dirt-brown teeth into my chest. Munch, munch, munch. Chew, chew, chew. Swallow. I yelp. Jab back my elbow. Ram it in the fucker's nose. Still no recognition of pain, but it makes him reel. Unbalances the freak. Buys me enough time to get a firm two-handed grip on my chopper and drag it free. Once it's out of jellyhead's face, I whirl it up in a quick arc. Catches jelly two under the chin. Damn near takes his chin off. Next chop comes in as a backhand. Dimly remembered from playing tennis at daddy's condo. The geek walks right into it. Enters his chest between two ribs. Wrench it as far as it'll go, then twist. Fucker dies in mid-fall. Lands in a jerking fit, then freezes.

Pulse pounds in my temples. Arms feel like lead. Pull out the axe blade. Wipe my forehead. Look down at the remaining four.

As luck would have it the rest have disappeared into the room. Just the last still visible. I don't waste time. Run past the shattered door. Whack a few times as I pass. Sprint on. Stow the axe in my belt. Leap at the far wall and use my momentum to scramble up. At the top I hang on with one arm. Use the other for swinging. Pull out the axe and hit the mirrored roof with a dull thwack. There's a few shockwaves, but that's it. Fuck. Looks like I'm gonna have to go the long way round.

A gunshot fills the air.

What the hell–?

Drop from the wall. Glance at the door where the zombies were. As I watch one staggers out into the corridor. It's the one with the sliced back. Now got a bullet in the brain to match. One of the Wasters must've found a piece. Or smuggled one in up their ass. Under normal circumstances, I'd be tempted to go get it. Seeing as I'm dickless and all. But I'm bound for the garden. If the Wasters are tied up here then I've got a headstart. Might be all I need.

Got a couple of choices. Right or left. Go right. Try to be consistent. Wasn't there something about always following one edge in mazes? Right wall to go in. Left wall to get out. Think that's what I heard. Like a lot of things in this life, it's probably so much batshit.

Turns out it makes no odds anyway. Right is dead end city. Route around and head left. Then keep going right. Every turn. Right. Right. Right. Come to a long passage filled with more mirrors. Floor to ceiling and back again. There's a dark vault at one end. Inside I find an inflated floor…

Shit, obviously this isn't going to be so easy.

"It would seem time's up for our contestants."

It's Jervaise again. Real cheery. What's he turned over this time. Bet it's not a new leaf?

"The six of spades. Send in the hellhounds!"

Sheesh. First zombies. Then Wasters. Now we're crying 'Havoc!' and letting slip the dogs of war. Retrace my steps. Get back to the splintered door. No one's there now. Beyond is a courtyard. Few overturned chairs. Couple of empty pots. Bits of zombie. That's all. Everyone else's buggered off.

I start to panic. Perhaps I've lost my lead. Dart up the corridor and go left. Then left at the first intersection, then go left. Left. Left. Left.

"Hold it!"

At first I ignore this. Decide that, of the possible candidates, don't feel like listening to any of them. It's only when the mirrored floor beneath me shatters into a spider's web that I stop and turn around. Gun blast still ringing in my ears. J.J.'s brother stands behind me, legs spread, .45 held up in both hands. He's covered in crimson. Looks like a mixture. Some native, some foreign. He's alone. Must've been separated from his buddies. Now he's found me. As my ears settle, I can already hear distant barking.

"Hi," I say. "Seen a garden in these parts?"

"You cool cunt."

"I guess not."

Waster looks set to plug me. Yet he doesn't. Instead he turns sharply to his right and fires off into the nothing. Zombie stumbles into view. Bag hag in a brown mac. Got a perm to die for. Which she does, twitching at his feet.

"Fucking bastards," he says casually.

"You alone?" I ask.

"Yeah, I'm alone. Zombies cleaned us out. Too many."

"All of you?"

"Well, mebbe some escaped. We scattered a ways back. My buddies are dead. But maybe not all."

"Could be just you and me."

"Yeah, guess it could."

"Bet they're going wild upstairs. Grudge match of the century. Nowhereman versus… What's your handle, man?"

"Eoin. Folks call me Junior."

"Well howdy, Junior."

"Howdy."

I want to cream this piece of offworld shit. But for now we settle for the high-five. Way I see it, the deck's stacked in his favour. He's got a gun. Got revenge pumping through his veins. Maybe got friends out there who want my ass. Got to play it smooth. Least till I get out. Try to win him over. Try anything…

"Watcha say we join up? After all, I don't wanna give those mother's the pleasure of watching us screw each other to death. When we get out, we'll settle it. Just the two of us. On our terms."

The Waster sizes this up.

"Why don't I waste you right now."

"'Cause you wouldn't give Kibbutz the pleasure."

"You's right there."

"Anyhow, with me stiffed, you've still gotta get out of this fucking hellhole."

"All I gotta do's find the garden…"

"Or ask me."

"You telling me you know where it is?"

"Yep."

J.J. junior snarls. Spits. Shuffles.

"Wheeeeep! Time's up, Junior. Yes or no."

The Waster sizes this up too. Then agrees.

"Fine. We join forces till I get out this puzzle box. Then I avenge my brother's death. S'cool."

We shake on it. Spit in our palms and actually shake on it. You can almost hear the crowd's reaction. Almost see Kibbutz bursting his ulcer. I smile. Look up. Shake the offworld kid's hand. And grin.

★

We locate the garden a little while later. Just turn into it, almost by mistake. Thank my lucky stars. Junior was just getting suspicious about my earlier claim. One minute we're cleaving dog skulls down some dark alley. Next we're turning into this overgrown courtyard. At the centre sits a weeded-up fountain. All mossy statuettes and stagnant green. Broken path runs around that, then off to four gated arches. Hung with ivy and dried-up roses. An iron bench once afforded a splendid view from a tiered pergola. Now looks like a toilet. Fire has charred most of the far wall. Apart from that, zippo.

Me and Junior check the place out for a while looking for hidden surprises. Only then do we enter. See the harpoons immediately. Stacked against the bench. One at each end. Look as if they're chained too. Glancing at the beach boy, I head forwards to have a look. Find the guns are fixed to the bench. Chained with combination locks. As I clamber up the steps, Junior calls out. Look round. He's pointing back the way we've come.

"Zombies. Dozens of them. Heading this way. Looks like they know we're here."

"Probably a present from Jervaise."

"We won't be able to hold 'em!"

"Shut the gate. Bar it. You've got to give me time."

Pure, you there?

Yeah, who's this?

S'Jack. You've got to help me.

Have I?

Yes. Listen, I…

Say I don't feel like it?

Shove my shoulder against the bench. It's set into the stone. Take more than me to shift it. Kneel by the combination lock. It's mechanical. Four tumblers. Each rusted, but recently greased. They show weird symbols. Look mathematical. Like tiny sigils from some failed diabolic ritual. Try turning them, but haven't got a clue what I'm doing.

Dingo, got any idea about codes?

Yowzer, you're talking to the right doggie. But we're in a spot of bother now.

Sister, it's Jack. Whassup?

Jack? We're back at the Huntress, but it's guarded pretty heavily now.

OK. I need Dingo to help me with a code. Can you spare him?

If Mûhamet wills it. Where are you?

Arena. At the castle.

Ave maria. We're breaking our backs and you're at the circus.

Not quite, Sister. Not quite.

The Waster stuffs a broken piece of railing between the remaining bars. Outside hordes of blank-faced creeps come marching on.

"Gate's secured. But there's more coming down the other ways. Help me!"

"No way. Without these 'poons we're dead meat."

"We'll be dead meat anyway if you don't help me close these bloody gates."

Dingo, the code is in an alien language or something. Squares, triangles, what look like little fish…

Fish?

Yeah, fish, ya dumb mutt. Ever heard of anything like that?

Fish? Can't think of anything like fish…

Well get thinking a bit better. Lives depend on it. Like mine.

I'm working on it.

Pure, it's Jack. I've got that hit you wanted.

You have?

Yeah. And if you promise to help, it's all your. Six hours of heaven.

Boy, do I need it, lover.

Great, now here's what to do…

Race across the courtyard. Kick the first gate shut and topple a statue across the entrance. Spare a glance at the oncoming dead guys. Must be at least three dozen. Where in hell are they coming from? Then repeat the process on the next gate, this time using a huge urn. Junior helps me the last few metres.

Sister, you still got that tracker control?

Yes, it's in my pack.

Turn it on.

But that will mean…

Just turn it on, you black bitch!

It's on.

OK, Pure, there's a coded pulse beacon, centred on the bayside of DC. That's me. Get here and you'll get the biggest hit of your life.

Yes, sir!

The zombies reach the first gate. Start heaving against it. Pushing their arms through the bars. Slavering. All quite dramatic really. Can't help thinking what'll happen if they break through. Ol' Junior and me are gonna go down faster than a rentboy with the clock running.

Wonder Dog, the first symbol's a triangle. The next one's a hangman's scaffold before you draw the body. Then a fish and…

Jack, what's a scaffold?

Y'know. Hangman. It's a word guessing game. There's a hidden word and every time you pick a wrong letter you draw another part…

Don't think I've played that. I'm not too hot with writing and stuff.

Fuck, fuck, fuck…

Don't worry though. We'll sort it out. How many sides does the triangle have?

What have I done to deserve this?

Look round and see Junior. He's climbing onto the fountain. At first I think he's flipped. Sure as hell know I'm close. Then see him standing on tiptoe. Reaching up to examine the glass ceiling. Above, his reflection balances on the ends of his fingers. Seems to be fiddling with something. Fuck knows what. The deadheads are pushing so hard from the back, the front ones're oozing sausage-like through the ironwork. All the other entrances are full too now. My best guess is about thirty and it'll all be over.

"Junior?" I shout, questioning his lunacy.

"Looks like a panel. Must be how they entered the maze to place the 'poons. No lock on this side though."

Jack, it's Dingo. Is the fish swimming to the left or the right?

"What'd'ya mean a panel? What sort of panel?"

"An access hatch. I think it's screwed from the other side."

Yeah and we're about to be screwed from this side.

Jack, you still there?

With a sickening grating of metal on stone, the first gate busts inward. Spilling undead like falling skittles. Looks like it's barbeque time. And I'm fresh outta dog kebabs.

Axe's at my waist, but I don't even look at it. I'm still obsessed with the harpoons. There must be a way to get them off the chair. Blade won't break those chains. Too fucking thick. Junior could shoot through it. Maybe. Maybe not. And bullets are gold dust right now.

Then I have it. Explodes into my brain like a supernova.

All around zombies crowd into the courtyard. The second gate busts inwards. Hinges rupturing from the wall.

Dive toward the seat. Grab the harpoon. Twist it ninety degrees. Aim right at the Waster's head. Junior sees this in the mirrored ceiling. Face shows betrayal. Clear as fuck. Don't blame him. After all he's probably just sore that he didn't think of it first.

Wait another moment, just to relish the pain on the jock's face. Then, I scream, "Duck, you stupid wanker!"

The wanker ducks. And at that moment I pull the trigger.

There's a horrible whistling noise. A whining as the micro-fine wire uncoils. Shooting upwards, the grapple-headed missile hits the glass with a mind-numbing eruption. Junior covers his head and wails amidst fracturing shards. The harpoon carries on its trajectory for another second or so. Then it imbeds into an unseen roof behind the fractured mirror.

"Get out of here, Waster!"

I don't have to tell him twice. Grabbing the wire he hoists himself up out of the reach of the grasping zeebs. Pulls himself up into the service hatch.

"There's a trapdoor. Sealed from above."

"Well unseal it!"

Now it's time for the axe. Grabbing it, I swing out at the oncoming dead. Slice two-handedly until I clear myself some room. Still there must be fifty, maybe sixty of the bastards. No way I'm gonna be able to clear a path even two metres, let alone all the way to the fountain. Frantically hacking, I'm pushed back onto the higher steps, then onto the bench itself. And still they keep coming. Clambering over the fallen. Relentless.

From above I hear a couple of shots. Then watch as the .45 drops like a stone. Lands with a dull splat in a scalloped pool of stagnant water. Guess that's the last of the bullets.

"Junior! Any luck up there?"

"The lock's broken, but something else's holding it."

His voice is strained. Sounds like he's been heaving.

"So what's the score?"

"We're fucked."

No way, Jose. Not on my shift.

"Get clear! Get from under it!"

Leap off the iron bench. Get behind and use it as a shield. Then, in a natural lull in the onslaught, brace myself against the ivy-covered wall. Push the seat with both legs. For what seems like forever, it refuses to move. My knees scream. Then it shifts. Cement breaks. And the whole thing topples forwards tearing up the flagstones as it rolls. Crushing bodies as it tumbles down the steps. Over and over. Taking down the zombies like nine pins.

Steeeeeee-rike one!

Clattering down, the wire wraps around the ironwork. Springs impossibly tight. Strains. Grinds. Then with a loud rupturing, the whole hatch's torn inwards. Falls through the splintered hole. Smashing the head off the dancing nymphs. Misses Junior. Just.

The hatch, locking wheel and all, hits the stone paving. Breaks into a million pieces.

Steeeeeee-rike two!

Rush down the clear swathe that the bench's made. Make a few token swings as I go. Cleave a few heads. Vault up onto the bench. Clamber up the cracked fountain. In the mad scramble I drop the axe. Above, Junior's half hanging from the shattered ceiling. Both hands outstretched. Jump from the neck of the headless statue. Hands grab Junior's wrists. His grab mine. Below, the zombies crowd onto the fountain, yet with all the recent punishment the masonry's seen better days. Under the weight of two dozen dweebs, it gives up. Cracks appear up every side. Then the base snaps. Collapses in a wash of green slime and concrete.

I'm left hanging above the snarling pack. Kick my legs. Try to keep the fuckers from grabbing my ankles and dragging me down.

"Pull me up, man," I shout.

When nothing happens, I look up.

Junior's sea-blue eyes are codfish cold. His mouth's a thin line. The perfect skin around his eyes is ruined with wrinkles. Looks like here's the moment for his revenge. Fair's fair. The hands he's holding have got the blood of his brother on them. Whatever gives, it's his call.

Without a shred of emotion, he drags his right wrist against my thumb. Breaks my grip with ease. I look down. Searching for the axe. Can't see it anywhere. Just a seething mass of reaching bodies.

Fuck, fuck, fuck…

"We're out. We're free. That means we're square. And now's the time to avenge my brother's death."

He gives his left hand a vicious twist. I lose my grip.

I fall.

Land in a boiling heap of zombies. Trip on the bench. Go down. Between their legs I search for the axe. Find the second harpoon instead. Up above me, J.J.'s brother clambers out into the purple dawn. The crowd's cheers, goading him on. I'm so sick with hate, I don't even think about saving myself. As I grab for the 'poon, I'm already aiming it for the sucker's ass. Already stabbing at the trigger.

Sit on this, waster.

With a lethal hiss, the forked missile screams into the air. Junior don't see it coming. Not even looking in my direction. He's too busy getting out the busted roof.

As he steps up, the harpoon misses him by a hair. The line arcs away. Sailing over the arena like a metal bird. I don't even realise I'm yelling till he glances down. Sees the zombies mauling me. Laughs like a drain.

"Aw, too bad. Ya missed me."

Stands over my world and laughs his fucking head off.

And in that moment, his body convulses as a thousand bullets tear him to pieces.

Shit. They're on the roof.

For a moment I'm shocked. Numbed even to the pain. S'like the knight said, no one here gets out alive. Still, what choice did he have? What choice have any of us got?

Even while the bug-eyed jellybrains bite and scratch me to ribbons, I pull on the second line. Miraculously it holds. Must've caught on something. Embedded in someone. Whatever. Dragging my hands against the wire, I start to climb. Hand over hand. Kicking and screaming all the way. If it wasn't for those uppers I'd have blacked by now for sure. Even so, at first I get nowhere. But then I gain a metre. Then another. Then I'm hauling myself through the busted hatch. And then I'm free. Dragging myself out onto the glass roof.

Up at high table, Kibbutz is going crazy. Far as I can see he's kicking Jervaise to death. His hounds are helping. I can just hear the lackey's pleadings over the crowd. Everything's gone haywire. Junior lies in a blooded mess. Bits of body everywhere. Yet that doesn't really matter to me. What grabs my attention is the long line of gun-toting tinmen standing to my right, their machine pistols pointing straight at my head.

Shitfuckpissbuggerdamn. So what now, mr superhero? Got any more tricks up your sleeve?

Nope.

Guess I gotta just stand here and die. Only thing saving my life right now is that their bossman's too busy to give the firing orders.

I run. Turn left and make a break for it. Can't stand there like a prick and get butchered. Rather get it on the fly. Least ways I won't see it coming. Then, "Stop right there!"

It's Kibbutz's voice. Deafeningly loud over the PA. Haven't we been here before? I stop. Turn around. And what I see nearly wipes me away.

Above the firing squad, above the stands and the crowd, Kibbutz, Malorian, the screens and the whole fucking shebang is a great white bird. A nightflier. Hanging like a goddess in the dawn skies. No, not hanging, strafing. Coming in low. Faster than a bullet. Letting rip with both barrels and wasting the knights where they stand.

Before my eyes, the nightflier lands. The cockpit opens. It's Pure. All in pink. She's smiling. Like an angel. When I see her smile, I'm deaf to the gunfire. Deaf to Kibbutz's shrieking curses. Deaf to the world.

"Hi Jack," she mouths.

"Hi, princess."

"You look like shit."

Grin.

"Don't look too good yourself."

"S'the A's, man. I still need that hit, baby."

Yeah, don't we all. My uppers are just about all used up. Feel the ache in my limbs. Turning from fire back to solid lead even as I stand there making small talk. The gunfire hurries our little parley.

"I promised you, angel. And Jack always keeps his promises."

"Uh-huh. So d'ya fancy a ride?"

"You betcha."

"Well, climb aboard, fella. Pure's always got room for The Nowhereman."

Slowly I climb the ladder. Leaving a bloody trail up the side. Slip like a dead weight into the cabin. Smell's like sick. Still better'n the shit out there. And once I'm inside, the blonde woman guns the throttle and the great white bird rises into the wild blue yonder.

31 | D'ALESSANDRO

Sometime after the call to The Nowhereman, I hear my executioner's footsteps returning, breaking the deathly quiet with their unhurried tread. They find me as they left me; languishing in the interminable greyness of the isolation cell. Nothing has changed. Nothing ever does in this desolate place. Akahiri wears the same crimson and grey one-piece, the same hidden face behind the same black faceplate. Outside the corridor's the same neon and iron. The only thing that's different is that now I have been afforded some inkling, some crazy notion of the passing of time.

So that's an hour. Wonderful. Now if only I could get the guard to betray how many of those I have left...

It's a silly game, much like every other foolish endeavour I've filled my life with since arriving in this winter wonderland. There is little choice, of course. Doing nothing in confined spaces is not what the human race was built for. Not that real life bears any resemblance to the general thrust of our evolution, but there you have it. The X-Isle was one such game. Radio God was another; a pathetic attempt to reach out and touch a few of my renegade angels. I was shocked at how few there were, or if not how few, then how little they could be coaxed into helping me. Subtlety never usually figures in a creator's arsenal of cosmic ego. Deities go for more direct means. Gods are more blatant. They prefer bolts from the heavens, volcanoes spewing lava, rivers running with blood. That sort of thing. Signs that say do or die. Messages that are back-breakingly apocalyptic. Fires. Tempests. Floods. All I had was a box of 3Es and a rig cobbled together from some discarded comms equipment salvaged after a muted riot in D wing about two years ago. I *had* to be subtle. The rules in here are simple; external transmissions are monitored with a fifteen-second time lapse. One breath of anything strange and I'd be beaten into next week. Routing encrypted stream data was easier so long as they knew nothing about it. Yet even that setup was flaky. Whispering words to my brethren, I tried desperately to get them ready for my final revelation. That was all I had – the final card up the last sleeve – and now I don't even have that. I'm beyond redemption. I've had my last supper. I've made my last call. Now all I've got left is the blind faith that Jack will go against everything he believes in, everything he's ever stood for or said or done, save the last replication and reset the Amen.

Stopping at the bars, Akahiri yanks the tray through the hatch and snaps the black unit to his belt. I expect him to leave so I'm surprised when he raises his right arm and punches the door code. In fact I'm so utterly shocked, I sit up.

"Stay where you are, mr Glass. This will only take a short time."

Obediently I lie back down, shivering at the intensity of the situation. An intensity that only increases when the guard casually strides into my cell and begins strapping me to the bed.

As I try to catch a glimpse at the chronometer inside his helmet, I remember something Jack said about the time in Dead City. He mentioned it was seven hundred hours. If that's true and I estimate that the difference between there and here is roughly eight hours, then I have longer than my original guess of eighteen hours. It may even be as many as twenty-two. Yet, as Akahiri steps back, it is still a guess. His faceplate keeps its secrets.

"Why have you tied me to the bed?" I ask. "Is it time to sleep now?"

Akahiri does not reply. Instead he turns the black mirror of his helmet towards the corridor.

Two people enter the periphery of my vision. Two doctors. They are as faceless as the guard, wearing white masks like department store dummies. One bears the shears that will rid me of my hair. The other the needle that will ritually tattoo me with the official numbers and corporation logo. Ah, now I understand; just the final grim formalities. All the usual dumb nothing.

They, like I, are just filling their time; playing their own silly games.

32 | PURE

We're back at the manse on Gypsy Hill. Me and Jack. Place's toast. You can see that once, once long ago it was a helluva lot prettier with lots of cool architecture and walls too. That was before the God-U-Like fanatics moved in. And before me and Jack fell out. Mystic's totally ruined the place. Literally. Jack's down below in the cellar. Says he's got to fetch a few things. Like what, I said. Like mind your own cunting business, he said.

So here I am minding my own cunting business.

It's tough. Especially when I need a hit this bad. Been too many hours now. Few more and I'll start kicking and screaming. Start lashing out. Waiting's not one of my strong points. Anyhow, I've got a head full of hurt about other things. Like working out when to cash in this farce and sell The Nowhereman for some cold, hard cash. Revenge is just a cat's whisker away. So why am I hesitating?

Decide to go down. To do *something*. Y'see I need a hit badder than bad. Badder than ever. And The Nowhereman's my only link in this whole miserable fuck heap to getting one.

Find Jack at the bottom of the steps disarming a trip wire. One arm's hampered holding the leash of the knitted lab mongrel from the Phoenix. The other by a battered khaki sack.

"Stop right there," he says over his shoulder. "This thing'll blow your fucking legs off."

Beyond him is the lair of the witch bitch. I can smell it from here. All stale air, oil and burnt wood. In the gloom I can see star maps and cushions. There's also those crazy paintings. She must've been out of her fucking mind. Why Jack ever got into her is beyond me totally. As is why she's back in the picture. Which brings me to my unfinished business.

Smile and pull my Panther from its holster. Point it right between his eyes. Between his opening, widening eyes.

"Susie… Don't…"

"Let's get one thing straight," I say, hitching my leg and bracing my shooting arm on one knee. "You fucked me over, lover-boy. Now it's my turn."

Click the gun to On. Hear it whirr to life.

"Pure? Why?"

"Why what?"

"Why save me just to kill me later?"

"Thought that would be obvious, Jack. But let me spell it out to you. Do the words, 'Go fuck yourself, you dumb blonde bitch' mean anything to you?"

"Susie, I…"

"Or how about, 'Love you? I'd rather fuck handfuls of my own shit.'"

I click the trigger, the remembered words making me angry. Making me relive it clear as day.

"Let me explain."

"OK, that seems fair. One shot. Off you go."

"I learned that the Phoenix was going down. I couldn't let on that I knew, but wanted you as far away from ground zero as possible. I had one shot. Like now. One shot. And though it hurt like shitting sharp rocks, it worked, didn't it. Didn't it?"

"You lying, sly, conniving…"

One shot.

That'd be all it'd take to finish this – to finish *him* – and move on. One shot.

Grip the Panther in both hands. Just to stop the barrel from shaking.

"No, Pure. It's the truth. I did it to save you!"

Save me. Save me? My mind mouths the words, my mouth mouthing others. "D'ya still fuck?"

Jack looks away, sensing some invisible line's been crossed. Doesn't want to meet my gaze.

"Occasionally."

"I mean with little miss golliwog?"

Then he does.

"What's it to you?"

"Just wondering."

The Nowhereman sneers then with a twist, he pulls the wire, lifts the trigger and turfs the whole lot into the sack. When he looks back at me, he's glaring like a fool.

"Just wondering," I whisper.

"Well wonder on," he mumbles, pushing past me up the steps. I let him and the dog go by, then turn and follow them, my plastic dress squeaking.

"Hey, wait, naked boy, don't be touchy with little old Pure…"

At the top of the stairs, Jack stops. When he turns, his face is all bitter and twisted.

"Don't call me that," he snaps. "That was a long time ago. Things have changed."

"You haven't. Nor have I. I still love you, Jack."

He looks me over. The outfit. The hair. The devil tattoo that squirms over my shoulder and down onto my left titty. Yeah, he gives me a real look look. Licks his lips too.

"I love her," he says.

"Who gives a shit? Love her. Fuck me."

A black cloud passes over Jack's tired face.

"I hate you."

I smile and squirm. This is more like the Jack I knew. All snarls and dark, violent sex.

"Hate you, too" I sing-song.

Then it's Jack who can't help smiling. When he's done he holds out his hand and like the little whore that I am, I take it.

"It's over, Pure. Everything's all so very over. C'mon, we've got to get to the Huntress."

We walk back to the nightflier like we're newlyweds strolling right up the aisle. No, it's not over, Jack. And neither are we. Love's a one-way trip. That's why we're all here again. It's fate. Huge, great, unavoidable fate. Manifest destiny. Divine predetermination.

I tug his hand. Pull him off balance and into my arms. My mouth finds his. I feed him my tongue. He takes it while I grind across his cock. Denim meets plastic. Meat meets meat. I scruff his hair. Claw his neck. Hard.

I am blonde, sculpted, augmented, blue-eyed and beautiful. I am better 'n Babs. I come in one size only. And my label reads: petite, fabulous and totally inevitable. Now, how's this for revenge, lover?

I pull back my tongue. Breathe into one dirty ear.

"Love me, Jack. That's right. Love me. Kiss me. Adore me."

"No, Pure," he's saying. "I can't..."

Oh, but you are, Jack. You *are*.

And with that I force him to the ground and grab the swollen ache in his pants with both hands. Because there at the end that seems like the best revenge of all.

33 | DINGO THE WONDER DOG

Back at the Solar Huntress things are turning a little spasmic. It's like all bullets and stuff. Hot lead screaming above our heads. Ambushes. Explosions. The whole nine yards.

We're holed up behind this popcorn trolley about fifteen metres from the t-freighter. Looks like they knew we were coming. Whole place is crawling with Kibbutz's stooges. They're appearing out of everywhere. Must be a dozen under the ship and another dozen off in the trees to our right. The only thing that's saving us is the fact that the transport hasn't got any power else who knows what kill-o-zap stuff it's got hidden in its locks and hatches.

With a sudden spurt, grass and gravel leaps over my head and into my ears. Yelp and roll, trying to keep from dropping the big gun and dodging into some punk's line of fire. Hit turf and crouch, then spring up and pump off a few random shots. Not sure if I hit anything or anyone. Too busy burying my muzzle back in the dirt.

If only I had Phantom's telekinetic torc from *Dog Daze of Hellplanet-Zeta*. Or his Dogzooka or even a couple of sonic muttarangs.

It's not the size of the dog in the fight, but the size of the fight in the dog.

Too right, Phantom! Too right...

Unlike Midnight, Mother Earth and Sister Dawn aren't too hot with auto shotguns, so it's really up to us. Actually guns are not really my thing either, but I don't think now's the time to mention it.

Elliott, the infidels are trying to outflank us on the left. You've got to get the tesseract into the ship.

Is that possible?

Bêz only knows.

Er, right…

Elliott, I need you to do this for me. If they outflank us, we will die.

OK. Yep. Uh-huh…

Death will not be pleasant.

No kidding.

Ave maria, Dingo. Are you not supposed to be the indestructible dog wonder?

OK, Esther. I'll try.

Good boy.

Sheesh, it sure is hard to be a hero.

Slamming myself down on the ground, I check the bag. Inside there's just the power cell, a sheaf of papers and this weird lump of crystal. All looks like junk to me. Still, make sure the tesseract's secure then I look out from under the wheels of the cart. As far as I can see, there's no way to get anywhere near any of the lower hatches, but maybe – just maybe – I could try for one of the top ones. Only thing is to get up there I'm gonna need one very large ramp. And where in hell am I going to…

I stop. Look to the left. And there in all its glory is the hulking rollercoaster. Wild Wired World. There's the booth. The open trapdoor. The rusted service ladder.

I turn to Sister and give her one of my looks. Then spin as something nasty smelling whips past my left ear and clanks against Esther's back. It's a mini-nuke!

I leap and grab it, twisting and pitching it out back where it came.

There's an explosion like a hundred lightning bolts all striking the same place at once. We're thrown to the ground as half the ground itself is thrown into us. Suddenly it's raining shreds of dirt and all I can do is screw shut my eyes and wait for my ears to stop jangling.

Don't wanna stay here. This is no way for a dog hero to die.

When I look up, when the skies clear and the firing starts again, all I see is the coaster. That's certainly one big tower. One superfast track. And never has an inverted loop looked so appealing. Guess it's skate or die time!

Now that's something I shore *can* do.

34 | SISTER MIDNIGHT

Caught in the crossfire, I unload rounds from the chain gun like they're going out of fashion. And in their turn, knights and their squires unleash leaden death back blasting the kiosk to pieces. At my feet the nuns cower, their backs slammed against the brightly-painted cart. And amidst all this unholy chaos, I still cannot fail to notice Elliott's look as he lies in the dirt at my feet. It's a look that sends a shiver down my sweating back.

"O by Kalím's beard," I mutter.

The Wonder Dog barks.

"Cover me," he says.

I will try, my faithful friend.

With a little squeal Dingo leaps to his red-wheeled feet and shoots off like a bullet from a gun. Immediately I re-aim my automatic over his head and open up with both barrels. Offering what little aid I can, I watch his movements and try to keep the unbelievers from getting a proper fix on the poor mutt. Then, after only the shortest times, I see where he is headed.

The rollercoaster.

This is no time for free-riding, Elliott.

I've got a plan.

I groan, then fix my sights back on the woods and empty the belt.

Three seconds, Dingo. S'all I can give you.

Groovy.

Exactly three seconds later the belt is gone and I'm grinding on empty, yet the rollerskating pooch is clear. Quick as a flash he zips out of sight and into the booth and once he's inside, I duck down and start to reload. Earth and Dawn watch me. One on either side. Their looks ooze trouble like a septic wound.

Mother Earth is first.

"My dear, where in creation did you learn to use a semi-automatic?"

I scowl. Shit, as if I didn't have enough to worry about what with being overwhelmed by knights, covering for Dingo and saving Jack's ass, now mother inferior's giving me a hard time.

"Charm school," I say finally.

Sister Dawn is next.

"Your pardon, sister, but may I say that camouflage gear is hardly proper attire for a neophyte."

Eat my crack.

"Do you not also think that the taking of life is the most heinous of sins?"

Taking yours would be a pleasure.

"Is that make-up?"

It's war paint.

"It makes you look like a whore."

You *were* one, remember.

With the new belt finally inserted I fumble for the safety and, ignoring my sisters, throw myself up into the line of fire again. Yet now things are a little quieter. Something's wrong. And then a shadow catches my eye. Falls at the ground by my feet.

I look up. Ave maria, mother of…

There atop of the rollercoaster, Dingo the Wonder Dog stands astride the tracks; a tiny silhouette against the gathering sunrise. He's waving.

Hiya, Esther!

Good lord, Elliott! What are you doing?

I'm going for the top hatch. Wowee, you should see the view from up here…

Dingo, get down from there right now!

OK, here I go!

And with that I watch in horror as Dingo launches himself down the near-vertical tracks, accompanied by a distant cry of, "Dog power! Howwoooooooooahhhl!"

Sudden gunfire chews the kiosk into mush. Yet all I can do is watch, transfixed as the tiny figure whizzes down towards the inverted loop, the streamers on his starred boots flying out behind him. Unconsciously, I cross myself, the gun forgotten in my sweaty hands. Dingo hits the loop at something approaching terminal velocity. Hits it and leaps. For the briefest of moments he's caught in the sudden brilliance of the rising sun, before disappearing behind the grim grey overhang of the freighter.

An explosion of wood and plastic next to my head finally makes me drop. Reaching up to the prayer beads at my neck, I pray for Dingo's immortal soul. Pray long and hard. And when my prayers are done, I try his frequency.

Elliott? Dingo, you worthless mutt, do you copy?

Silence. Like the echo of a tomb.

Elliott? Elliott, you OK?

Shhh, Sister. I'm trying the sphincter.

By the love of Mûhamet! Elliott, you're alive!

Oh, please, Esther. You're too much.

And you are the indestructible dog wonder.

Totally. Right, I'm in.

Beware for guards...

I'm on it.

With a sigh, I concentrate again on the commotion around me. For a moment, all I can hear is the sound of splintering kiosk, yet then there comes a roar and from out of the bushes a gang of assorted bohos rush our position.

"Get up!" I scream at the nuns beside me. I don't have to tell them twice. The danger is too apparent.

In a moment we are running, leaving behind the sanctuary of the blasted trolley and fleeing out into the open.

Dingo, open the hatch! We're coming, honey!

Chased by the crowd of thugs we race toward the Solar Huntress, yet the fifteen metres seems more like a hundred. Exposed, we don't stand a chance. The K/OS Knights are too many and too well equipped.

Sister Dawn is the first to die, her head erupting like a blood-filled egg. Mother Earth is next. Her death sealed as three arrows spear her black-robed breast. As they fall I am wailing. Dropping my gun as I go, my mouth gushes prayers. Yet there's only so much protection faith can offer. When the bullets come, they hit like a dozen punches between the shoulder blades, throwing me into the dirt right at the foot of the ship. My trikevlar saves my life, yet as I look up from the blooded earth, I see knights already closing in on my quivering form.

All is lost… All is lost…

Behind them, the transport hums into life as somewhere deep inside Dingo slams the tesseract into the system's backbone, yet that is little consolation. Little consolation at all.

Where are you when I need you, Jack?

35 | THE NOWHEREMAN

I'm lying in the dirt with a face full of wet cunt. A jumbo tub of slick, swollen, juicy pussy. I'm going at it like a starving man. Tongue. Teeth. Thumbs. Fingers. Plus anything else I can think to stick up it. Pure's grinding down onto me. I'm in total fanny heaven. She's in orgasm overload.

Yet while I'm chowing down on my ex-girl, my mind's elsewhere. Trouble is the uppers are over. While I'm dining at the Y Club, pain's just been put back on the menu. Sweeten it with the pleasure of Pure's quim, but even that's nowhere near enough. Pain. Pleasure. Pain. Pleasure. Jockeying for pole position in my brain. Makes thinking difficult. With the weight of the dog on one arm and the sack on the other, I'm effectively pinned to the ground. Pooch. Pack. Pooch. Pack. Makes moving difficult too.

I open my eyes. See sunlight streaming over Pure's milk-bleached breast. Can't help thinking how'd she keep so white after four years in a desert? Think on that yet still I can't concentrate. Why am I doing this? What's happened to Esther?

At that moment, Bixby decides he's fed up with sniffing my sweaty ass and wants to go walkies. Tugs my arm from under me. Sends me sprawling across Pure's lap.

"Hey, ya dumb dog. C'mere!"

Turn and tug the mutt's lead. Make it yelp. Yet as Bixby comes wandering back, I see something strange.

Its ear. Well not its ear exactly. What's attached to the back of its ear. It's a t-com. Sort of like an external headman. Brings back a whole host of thoughts. None of which concern the matter in hand.

"Is there a problem here?"

Look up at Pure looking down. Don't look too pleased.

"Pure, I… It's the dog…"

The blonde bitch snorts.

"No way. I ain't letting no dog…"

"Shut it, Pure. Let me think."

I think. I think of meat. *Whale* meat?

Dingo, this is Jack.

Oh, hiya, Jack. I've sorted the Huntress. Slamdunked the tesseract straight into the backbone. Only thing is…

Yeah great, Dingo. Look, I've got your mutt here…

You got Bixby! Oh, Jack, that's wild! I was gonna ask if we could fetch him. How is he?

Shut it, Dingo. Shut it and listen. Where'd ya get it from?

Who? Bixby?

Yeah. Where'd ya get the mutt?

Don't you remember, we were…

Humour me.

Well, he was an ex-lab research dog. Was cruelly used by Glass-Suko to test that sim they were cooking up.

The X-Isle…

That's the one. Bixby was the first living creature to enter the experiment.

Yeah, that's right. I saw the mailing.

He followed me home after the attack on the Phoenix Tower, and I said to myself 'can I keep him', and what'd ya know, I said 'yes!'

Shit, now I see it all. I realise suddenly that I have everything. Every single thing I need to access the island. I have the bag. I have the RNA key. I have the rig on the ship and twenty tonnes of whale meat. All we have to do is regroup at the t-freighter and…

Jack, there's just one more thing.

What's that, fella?

Midnight and her sisters are down. They're still outside…

Esther. Oh, fuck!

I'm coming, Dingo!

Just then Pure grabs my throat. I'm so surprised I don't even react. Hauls me to my knees. Wrenches back my head. Stabs her talons in my face. Brings hers real close.

"Look, Jack, I'm through with playing around."

She squeezes till my eyes water. Can't move a muscle.

"I don't know what's happening in that fucked-up mind of yours and I don't really care. But if you don't get me that hit you promised right now, I'm gonna rip your motherfucking head off!"

Lying there in the dirt I can still taste Pure's pussy. Still feel Midnight's tears. Still smell Dingo's fear. Still hear D'Alessandro's vain promises. All I can't do is see how I'm gonna get everyone back together. Or how I'm even gonna get back to the Huntress to put things right. The bleached bitch has me pinned. Forcing my face in the dust. So far gone into cold turkey don't know if she's ever coming back. Can hear her whispering. Mumbling all sort's of dumb shit. Through my gasps for air I try to make out some of it. First off I can't catch it. Not a single fucking word. Then I hit on a few.

Then a few that make sense.

"I don't know why I said I loved you. It's just the sorta crazy thing I'd do."

Then a tune. She's singing one of my songs. Some shit I wrote when we were dating.

Flashes start pulsing in my oxygen-starved brain. Scenes from when Pure and me were a big thing way back when. From the few months together up on Devil's Ridge. Out at the lodge on the snow line. Kilometres from anywhere. Just hanging out, drinking, fucking and fighting. Evening's we'd gaze down and laugh at the DC dustbowl.

"After trying hard to fool myself all that summer long, I guess that I just thought that it was true."

Sad part is, after that the Phoenix was gonna blow, so I binned her. Told her I hated her fucking guts. Actually I told her I hated every piece of her bleach-white body. She told me to cut it out. I told her to go fuck herself. Eventually the dumb bitch got the message. Left town on a brig bound for another continent. Another world. Didn't matter as long as it wasn't mine. Mine was over. We were over. Everything was so fucking over.

"Give me your heart and I'll take it, you know I'm gonna break it…"

Couldn't see her live through the end. Guess she knows the truth now. Maybe she don't. Maybe she just wants to hurt me for old time's sake.

"But you want me to remake it for you…"

Which is a pity 'cause I can't hang around long enough to give her the pleasure.

"Susie-Sue."

"What?"

"Let me go."

"Ut-uh."

"I'm serious. Sister's in trouble."

"Says who?"

"Says Dingo."

"The Wonder Dog?"

"One and the same."

"Well, well, well. S'pose you got that over your headman."

"S'pose right."

"What sorta trouble?"

"Knights."

"Whoa… she could be bruised."

"Could be."

"Could be bleeding."

"Could be."

"Could be dead already."

"Could be."

"Could be so stiff you could bang in nails with her black ass."

Why you cunting slut…

"Could be."

The peroxide blonde chews on this. Lets go a fraction. Not

enough to help me though. I try another tack.

"This has got nothing to do with drugs, has it?"

"What happened to Lucille?"

"He fucked with me so I wasted his silk-clad ass. *Has it?*"

"You promised me a hit…"

"This has got to do with me and you. Well, me and *her*. Hasn't it?"

Pure loosens her grip. A bit.

"No," she says feebly, then: "Wanna tell me what's going on?"

I sigh. Try to stretch but find I can't. Just manage to raise my head a little.

"Hell, y'know I wish I knew myself."

Pure slams my face back in the dirt.

"Try with what you have so far."

Fuck, no way. No one's gonna get anything out of me like this. Still, problem is I'm at the mercy of a drug-crazed ex-BurgerQueen who's just about to puncture my right eyeball, break my back and leave the pieces for the crows. OK, so I have to tell her something. And the something I decide on is straight from the book of truth. Albeit not exactly the complete works but near enough to count as a fair translation. As Lucille always used to say, 'Buggers can't be choosers.' And right here, right now, this bugger hasn't had a choice this side of planetfall.

"Fine. Have it your way. Here's what I have so far as I can work it out. Osakimo have come back for the code."

"What code?"

"The K sentience stuff."

"No dice. Glass-Suko got the code. You gave it to them."

"Yeah, I did, but Osakimo have it now. Anyhow, the code wasn't pure."

"Yeah, like, hello? It wasn't pure 'cause you contaminated it. Shit, Jack, why did you do that?"

"I was pissed. My son was dead and I wanted to punish those I felt responsible. Anyway, I thought they were just doing R&D… simple stuff."

"But Glass-Suko were the people behind the XEs prototype."

"Yep."

"So you infected the entire near-space sentience…"

"Yeah, but there's a clean replication. D'Alessandro saved it before they nuked the Phoenix."

"And where's it now?"

"Ex-friend of mine retrieved it for the bad guys. I retrieved it for the good. Right now Dingo's got it."

"And where's he?"

"At some freighter in the park."

"So you gonna use it?"

"That's the plan. Me and my brother inherited half the K/OS code. Neither half would work on its own. Not till they were used together. My half was infected, so now everything's infected. That's why they can't just clone more whale brain. Every specimen's contaminated so they had to go hunting for untainted meat."

"Jack, you're babbling."

"Yeah, whoa, sorry. But that's not the problem. With my RNA, the clean replication, the whale and the rig on the ship I have everything. Well, everything but the code I hacked out my brain and I can't get that from daddy, 'cause daddy's dead."

Feel the bitch's grip loosen again. Still got both her knees on my back though. There's a long pause, then she says, "No, he isn't. Don't ask me how I know, but he's in a coma. Still plugged in the system."

"How d'ya know that?"

She ignores this.

"Why didn't you come for me, Jack? Why'd you throw me out? Drive me away?"

"I had no choice. I found Xankhara."

"Xankhara? What that island in your book? S'just a pile of faerie stories."

"No, it's real. I've seen it. I met someone there and I knew what was gonna happen. That none of it could be stopped. Death and destruction was coming and I wanted to save the things I…"

"To save me?"

Her voice is like a little girl's.

"Yes."

Something breaks in her then. Almost hear it snap. Can certainly see it. All the murder bleeds right out of her eyes.

"That's good enough for me."

Suddenly, Pure's gone. Lifts right off me. Quick as a snake. Don't ask why. Just get up and turn to see what's cooking. Look right into a great big smack in the face. Stumble a little. Surprised I don't fall flat. Look back and see Pure marching toward the nightflier.

"Pure?"

"That's for the Phoenix."

"*Pure?*"

She doesn't look back. Just keeps on walking.

"Pure, what about the drugs?"

That stops her. Spins her like a top. Her eyes are feral as she turns. Like a cat's. So much so Bixby barks at her.

"I just *quit*. Now d'you wanna save that fancy-assed nigger or not?"

★

We arrive just in time for Armageddon. As the white bird makes its primary sweep the quiet moonlit clearing is now a blazing sunlit apocalypse. On the first pass I see the rollercoaster, the ship, everybody getting blown to shit. S'all one big blur. Take it slower second time around. Then I see the gunned-up nuns. See the carnage. See the Knights are being kept back by the Huntress' gun emplacements.

Dingo, what gives?

Oh hi, Jack! I've linked the tesseract. Ship's primed. Got the guns working. too. Can you see Esther?

Yeah, I can see her. Those guns're dealing with the punks. Can you finish the pre-launch?

I dunno, kemo sabi. There's three consoles. remember. Only one of me.

Keep me posted. I'm going for Sister.

Hokey-cokey.

"Pure, put down in the wood. When I'm clear, dock with the freighter."

"Already doing it."

On the third pass, we go down. Bird drops like a stone. Into a gap in the trees. Hangs impossibly above the ground while I jump clear. Then it's gone. Roaring up and up into the morning skies. Crouch on the ground for five, then start running. All the while in my head I hear Dingo rezzing up the ship.

Initiating pre-launch sequence. Engines checked and ready.

Try to run out the clearing. Can't. Legs won't work like that. All I can manage is a wild stagger. So how am I gonna rescue Sister? Think the knights are gonna let me just stroll up and help her on the freighter?

Uplink locked and open. All auxiliary systems inactive.

Dingo, Pure's ready for docking. Open her up.

Roger that.

Look around the wood. Up ahead the great arc that is the Solar Huntress blots the view. Hiding in the bushes are Kibbutz's mercs. Squatting just out of frying range. Heads down. Guns out. Beyond them the turrets twitch at the slightest movement.

Hmm, perhaps I see a way.

Course locked and checked. Systems checked. Comms AOK.

Above me, the nightflier roars overhead. Turns in midair. Disappears into the freighter's top hatch.

She's in. Just you and Esther now.

OK, keep the front lock ready.

Yes, sir!

Stumble as fast as I can towards the group. When they turn around I nod. Act casual. Like I'm one of them. A latecomer. No one to look twice at. They don't either. All assume I'm out for the bounty. Just like them. Out on the bloodstained earth I see Sister and her brethren. Around them there's a ring of dead fuckers. Guess it's time to find out if the bitch is still with us. Guess I was too scared before. Well, here goes nothing…

Sister? Esther? Say something. Copy, over, reading, out. Anything…

Let me alone.

Thank fuck you're alive.

I said let me alone.

You'll die.

If Mûhamet wills it.

Mûhamet, my ass. You're getting on board that ship if I have to drag you by your fucking dreads.

Try to see if she's moving. Can't see she is. The other two are definite DOAs. And it's a long way to that lock.

Patch systems standing by. Huntress ready for launch.

That's great, Dingo. You're a star.

Gee thanks, boss.

Now I want you to do something else for me. When I signal, cut the turrets. When I signal again, hit the front hatch. Then fire the turrets again. You got that?

Yep. No worries.

OK, here goes nothing.

With a sudden yell I leap forward. Saps shirk back in surprise, yet they let me go. No reason not to. Can see what they're thinking. Thinking I've flipped. Thinking I'm gonna get blasted. Thinking I must have lost my mind. They're wrong on all counts. Well, maybe two out of three.

Dingo, now!

Reach the ring of bodies in about three strides. Vault one. Stumble. Stagger. Regain my footing. Stumble again. Then finally fall in the bloody patch next to the faceless Sister Dawn. Great. Well, I guess she's certainly looked better.

Reach out for Midnight. Hear the cunts back in the bushes laughing like loons. Still haven't clicked that I wasn't zapped stone dead.

Dingo, the hatch.

Gotcha, mon capitaine.

"Sister. You with us?"

Don't touch me.

"This is no time to go all holier than thou on me. Can you walk?"

I'm fucked, Jack.

"Get up, Sister."

No, please… I can't…

"Get up, Midnight. That's an order!"

Sister wriggles slightly, then shivers. But that's all. Back in the bushes the bozos are getting wise to my plan. Guess their IQs have just kicked in. Someone fires a shot. Aims wide. Not too sure if it's deliberate. Don't want to wait to find out.

Esther! OK, so you want to die. I can dig that. Just not here, not now. It's…

Hold me, Jack. Hold me till they come…

On my periphery see a few of the mercs testing the guns by throwing branches. See their faces when they don't even twitch.

Oh boy, oh boy, oh boy.

Dingo, are we in the perimeter?

I think so.

Shit.

Skate down to medical. Doc's on a stretcher. Ditch him and bring it to the hatch.

OK.

Oh, and Dingo?

Yep.

Make it fast.

The first of the no-hopers stumbles out of the undergrowth. Starts sprinting toward the ship. His skulking compardres look on, but not for much longer.

Just then, Sister starts mumbling some weird religious shite.

"Ki Om Ma Noo… Ki Om Ma Noo… Ki Om Ma Noo…"

Some kinda whispered mantra. Sounds like last rites.

What's keeping you, Dingo?

I'm at the lock.

Great, so?

So… do I really have to touch this dead body?

Aw, crap!

Pure, you there?

Yep, I'm here. What's up?

Get to systems. I need those guns back online.

No problem.

With a reptilian hiss the front hatch vanishes into the curve of the bulkhead. Wonder Dog's there with the trolley. Doc Gruesome's still onboard. Behind us the bounty hunters start firing, emerging from the bushes, guns blazing. Dingo squeals. Leaps back inside. Yet as he goes he gives the trolley a half-hearted kick. Sends it down the ramp straight for us. Almost feeling the sting of lead in my back, I leap up. Grab Sister under both arms. Hoist her over my shoulder. Boy, she's one heavy mother. Suddenly, I go all dizzy. Head spins. World spins. Nearly black. In my foggy vision I see the mercs. Then I see the trolley as it judders past. Everything's a total blur. There's firing. Shouting. Screaming. Think Sister gets hit again. Hope it's nowhere serious. There's more firing. Shouting. Screaming.

Then the budda-budda-budda of the Huntress' turrets as they snap back into action.

The charging ranks are cut down like grass. Even the dead Doc gets riddled. Blows the bed on wheels clean in half. Dumps this corpse unceremoniously on the grass.

"Jack! Over here! Run for the door!"

It's Dingo. Calling to me. So I go. Staggering like a zombie from Kibbutz's maze I make for the hatch.

This wasn't what I had in mind. Not at all. But, as I said before, buggers can't…

And then, like one of Sister's fucking miracles she's always banging on about, suddenly, impossibly, I'm inside. We're inside.

"I did it," I say, unconvinced.

"You sure did, Jack!"

There's another hiss. Cutting off the sound of firing in an instant. Then, and only then, I collapse.

★

I wake from a dirty dream and find I'm breathing slime.

Now isn't this familiar.

Check myself over. Find all's cool in the skin department. Another total grade A fucking miracle. Must be something in all Sister's shite after all. Glad they found out how this unit works. Still feel tender, but most of the actual wounds are on their way to mending. Outside in the computer room see Pure and Dingo pawing over the readouts. Sister's off to one side towelling her hair. Must've just come out the jism tank herself. Bixby sits by the door dozing with one eye open. None of them notice I've come round, so give them a clue.

Did somebody order a large ham?

All three look up, surprised. Their worn faces shining. Even Bixby gives a little whine.

Cute. This is great. I'm just where I wanna be. Sister stands. Moves towards the glass.

"Hi, Jack. About out there… I'm sorry I…"

Shut it, Esther. Just doing my job.

Thanks.

So where are we?

Sûrabian. About two klicks out. Just hanging tight.

Good. Can you get an external in here?

Yeah, sure.

Sister pushes past Pure. Flips a switch on the master console. Immediately links me with the outside world.

"Slime calling Earth," I say jokingly. "You reading me?"

"Can hear you loud and clear, Jack," says Dingo.

"Super. Right, now let's bring you all up on current affairs. But first I'll need a few things."

"Like what?"

"Like the bag you brought aboard. Oh and Pure, could you fetch my stuff from the nightflier?"

"OK."

As they leave, I'm alone again with Sister.

"What's happening, Jack?"

"I'm going *in*."

"Going in? To where?"

"The island. I've worked it all out."

"The island? What island? What've you worked out?"

Silence.

"Jack, let's get you out of this…"

"No!" I bawl. "No, don't. This is just where I want to be."

"Why? What's the plan?"

She gets no answer. I can already hear Pure and Dingo heading back.

When everyone's in the room I tell them what's going down. Don't skimp on the details. Most I think I've talked in four years. Tell them about what's happened these previous few nights. About my past catching me up with a shotgun in each hand. About my brother, the gangs and which side everybody's on. Also why nobody's on our side. Well, not *exactly*. Then once they're fit to burst with it all, tell them about what happens next.

"Firstly, the bag. Gut must've retrieved it from the ruins of the Phoenix Tower. It was Nathaniel's. Dingo, empty it."

The mutt sets the battered carpet bag on the table. Unclips it and paws around inside. First he pulls out some papers. Next he pulls out the crystal. Jagged, imperfect, brilliant. It catches the light from the machines. Makes the ceiling dance with rainbows.

The last replication. Biologically grown memory. Amazing. Almost makes the whole thing worth it.

Almost.

"This is the last pure infinity dump of the sentience before getting infected with the virus. Yet to upload it we're gonna need the codes that daddy has tucked away in his vegged-out little brain. He's the only person who knows the original key to the K sentience. I can virtual visit him via the stream. That's if he's still connected to the biotank that's keeping him alive. Can't say I've done the grapes and flowers bit for a while, but Nathaniel knew that was the way to stop all this nonsense, so it might just work. He knew that if he had access to my father and the Amen hostgod he'd be able to beat Osakimo at its own game. That's basically what's in this freighter. Osakimo's attempt at recreating a new XEs. The whale. The rig. The whole nine yards. Even on death row the suit was still trying to sort his shit."

"Hooray for D'Alessandro," mutters Pure under her breath. I ignore that.

"He's where I got my idea from. And from that mutt." I point at the komondor still snoozing in the doorway. "Remember, Bixby was used to test the island simulation by fitting him with what really amounts to a super headman. Links him – and us – straight to the Amen. So when I get the codes, it's just a matter of plugging the replication into the rig and upload city here we come."

"What about the hostgod?" It's Sister this time. Her dark face frowning.

"What *about* the hostgod?"

"What, you think they're gonna let you just waltz in and reset everything? That's shit."

"What? I don't get it?"

"The hostgod patrols the sentience. Malorian knows you're close to getting in, so every black prog this side of near-space is gonna be hunting your ass."

She has a point. Malorian isn't stupid. Far from it. Best not take any chances.

"So it's a deathtrap. What choice have I got?"

"You can't jack naked."

"You got anything I could use?"

"Few cloaking programs, backup shadows, ghost routines. Nothing to write home about."

Home… now there's a thought.

"OK, upload them. The hostgod's no problem though. I'll use the simulation to shield me. It must be secure, otherwise…"

"It'd have been vaped by now. OK, that seems fine. I'd better get your book."

Midnight takes my pack from Pure. Well, more like snatches. Pulls out *Forevermore* while the others look on, perplexed. As am I.

Huh? Whassup? This is no time for bedtime stories, Sis.

This book was Nathaniel's original inspiration for the island. No doubt it'll provide a few clues along the way.

She's got a point. That book may be just a bunch of faerie tales, but Nathaniel and me got most of our shit from it. He got Xankhara. I got the A-Men. Esther, the Amen. Dude was this sorta supreme deity when the shit went down in Forevermore. The other gods were his disciples. Sister calls them the Eternal Ones. Jack the simpleton met them all on his quest for Xankhara. Eventually saved the universe. Delivered them to the island at the edge of the world. Great work if you can get it.

And now, wallowing in the slime, it's time to do it all again.

Wow, you're one dark angel, Esther.

I know.

Turn back to the final orders.

"OK, so here's what we do. Sister stays here and helps me with the internals. Masking, spooking and all that black mamba magic. Pure, you and Dingo pilot his heap. Set a course for Nathaniel. You'll have to find which prison…"

"Kasikianu," Pure says.

"Good girl."

"Why we going after him?"

"Well, I may need his know-how about the island. Plus he's family. He's one of us. And right now he's scheduled for the death tank at midnight his time. We need to rush."

Pure looks doubtful.

"Time's not the problem. Access is the problem."

"Well, looks like we're both on the same mission."

"But how the fuck are *we* gonna get into a maximum security prison?"

"Oh, I dunno. You work it out. Just get on it."

"Thought that was where we left off?"

"Er, yeah…" That was unexpected. Flash a look at Sister. Just in time to catch her glare.

You total pig-shit!

Sister, it's not like that. I just find her attractive. That's all.

Sounds like that's not quite all.

Look, what's wrong with finding another woman sexy?

An implant should not be confused with a woman.

Sister grunts audibly. Gives Pure a black look. Blonde just raises her plucked brows. Shrugs a little. Midnight turns away.

"Wonder Dog, you help Pure, OK?" I say to try to change the subject.

"No worries, Jack. I'm on it."

"When you get D'Alessandro, plot a course for the waystation. Kibbutz's leading the gutter tribes. Gonna hit it big time. When he does, be ready to break for orbit. You got that?"

"Yeah, Jack. I got it."

"Good. And keep an eye on the ladies for me, OK?"

Dingo sighs.

"Hokay."

But if they start bitchin', I'm outta their face, pronto!

Dingo, if they start bitchin', we'd better not be on the same fucking planet.

★

"OK, Jack. If you're sure you're ready—"

"Get on with it, Sister."

"Initiating Home sequence."

Shut my eyes. Tight. The piercing, ear-splitting wail comes, grows, goes. In the tingling silence Midnight reads the numbers from the screen.

"Channel opened. Prepare for translation."

This time I'm ready for the darkness. The sudden blindness. The empty starless void. Ready but not exactly able. Least not to cope with it anyways. There's a moment of crushing nothingness, then everything starts piecing back together. Slime smell is again replaced with that of musty antiquity. The dryness by the taste of cinnamon and apples. My sight by the room with no doors. It's just as I remember. Wide fireplace. Panelling. Chairs. The dark gloating mouth of the mirror. My imperfect reflection staring back at me.

And the voice of Ianus.

"Hello, Jack. Would you care for some tea?"

Clear my throat and spit on the carpet.

"Look, I haven't got time for all that shit. I'm back to get daddy's code and…"

The ancient voice lets out an indignant snort.

"I know why you're here."

"Good. Then let's get down to business. I want full access to the island?"

"The island? Why should you want that? You can access your father directly from the stream. Any registered uplink will…"

"I know. But if I reset the code Xankhara will be obliterated."

"Ah, of course. The last replication was grown before the island reached anywhere near its present maturity."

"Bullseye. And to save it, I'm going to have to find a way to bypass Osakimo's security and send the whole thing into the Amen. My guess is daddy's codes are gonna be jack for doing that."

"Your assumptions are correct. Unfortunately the mind's island is under quarantine."

"Quarantine? What's that mean?"

"It means, Jack, that Xankhara has been sealed. To this end certain security features have been initiated… to stop undesirable trespassers."

"Great, so that means I've got to do this from the inside?"

"Correct again. Malorian annexed his own areas to the initial island design. This allowed him access while inside the simulation."

"And where's that?"

"Within the Horror House."

"And that is?"

"I will remain operational once you enter the island. You may request mapping information as required."

"Great. So who's the guy on the gate?"

"I beg your pardon?"

"Look, Joseph has turned Xankhara into a virtual prison. Only this time the trick is getting in. How'd I do that?"

"Jack, you already know. Just step through the mirror…"

I glance up. See the huge square lump of rock materialise behind the glass. Floating in the star-studded blackness. Draw a deep breath. Then look away.

"D'you really think I'm that stupid? That I'm gonna walk over and just leap through, right? Wrong! Been there, done that. If I do, my brain will be fried. Like you said before, then I can sleep. Think I don't know what *that* means?"

"The mirror is the only programmed entrance…"

"Don't act the innocent. How'd I get in without tripping any fucking alarms?"

"As a registered psychist, your name and security passcode should suffice."

Well, that sounds promising.

"Ianus, list my inventory."

"Initiating inventory. Current name equals Jack. Current security passcode equals zero. Current resident mode equals Introset Prototype. Current psyche equals Ianus. Current objects equals none. Current score equals zero."

Score equals zero, eh? Well, that beats minus seven at least. Still not coming up with any security rating though.

Think about this for a moment. Then kick myself for not seeing it sooner.

"Ianus, name equals John Ewen Malorian."

"Good evening, John. I am Ianus. Welcome home."

"Yeah, right. Ianus, inventory."

"Initiating inventory. Current name equals John Ewen Malorian. Current security passcode equals nine. Current resident mode equals Introset Prototype. Current psyche equals Ianus. Current objects equals none. Current score equals zero."

That's more like it.

"Right, I'm on a roll now. Ianus, I want access to the island."

The old guy raises one aural eyebrow.

"That will require an interrupt with the hostgod."

"Yeah, whatever. Just do it."

"Uploading interrupt."

Within the air over the fireplace sudden letters dance before my eyes.

>**Internal date: 08/05/11.4 Gyr.**
>**Internal time: 09:26:22.**
>**Day of project: 4749.**
>**Machine: Sol Series 1140.**
>**Prototype number: 156008-a12.**
>**Sentience: Ianus.**
>**Programming language: K/OS.**
>**Copyright © Glass-Suko Corporation. All rights reserved.**

Then right at the bottom:

>**User/psychist. Identify.**

"Ianus, upload my details."

"Initiating upload."

There's a pause, then the air shudders again.

>**User accepted.**
>**Security passcode. Identify.**

"Ianus, upload *all* my details."

"Initiating upload."

>**Passcode accepted.**

"Right, now get me down to the island."

"As you wish. Initiating entry sequence."

>**Prepare for entrance to X-Isle.**

Fucking A! Let's get this show on the road!

Through the mirror Xankhara looms. All forests and castles and mountains. Catch the briefest glimpses of a golden temple. A brightly coloured town. A looming volcano. Don't see no haunted house though. Soon the island fills the frame. This time it doesn't stop. Not until we're close to the centre of the rock. There's an ornamental garden, paths, flowers. Then finally a large pair of wrought iron gates. Walk purposefully toward the looking glass. As I go, glance back into the room. Salute to the unseen Ianus. Still, the old guy hasn't quite finished with me yet.

"Before you go, I have to ask a few more questions."

"About what?"

"They concern the island."

"OK, make it quick."

"X-Isle is set for the following parameters. You may change any or all of them. Season equals Spring. Time equals dawn. Moon phase equals new. Garb equals medieval."

"Sounds cool. Get on with it."

"As you wish. Initiating central garden sequence."

Find I'm pawing at my left tit. Pull my hand down and try to stand still.

So here I am at last. Sheesh, Xankhara. The place where Death never trod. Yeah, some chance. Nathaniel, guess this is the last of my three wishes. Don't worry, fella. I'm not gonna waste this one. I've wasted enough. Now it's time for a little payback.

"So long, Ianus. See ya in hell."

"Fare well, John."

And with that I step through the mirror and into the X-Isle.

★

I find myself on a small grassy outcrop of rock. Completely surrounded by the starry void on all sides. Except one. Straight ahead lie two grey pillars of stone. Provide a spectacular entrance to the land. The wrought iron gates stand closed between the pillars. Crowned with a chiselled sign. Through the gates I see a tree-lined gravel pathway heading deeper into the gardens. Distantly a cloud-wreathed mountain looms above the treetops. Must be the volcano. Behind me all I see is the mirror frame and through it the panelled room. Beyond that is endless void, except off to the right where a smaller isle hangs unsupported in the sealess bay. On this stands the temple. Stone glistening like bronze in the weird dawn. Can't see any way out to that though. Not that that's important anyhow. Got to find the Horror House.

Walk up to the gates. Sign's half covered with ivy. Can still read what it says though. It says, 'Welcome to Forevermore. Population: you.' Neat. I always was a sucker for that book. Get a twinge of good old-fashioned smugness. For once in my miserable existence, I've actually beaten my brother. First time for everything. You were close, bro. You had the whale. You had the rig. You even had the replication. You were *so* close. Guess close just ain't good enough this time.

Look down at myself. I'm dressed in a tunic, leggings and these unbelievable leather boots. Look like they've been made from the inside of a pig. Probably have. Got a belt too, but that's it. No weapons. No stuff. No nothing.

Coming from somewhere off in the void a wind brushes past me. Slips through the gates and escapes. Breathe it in. All of it. Breathe it in and weep.

Can't really believe I'm here. Right here. Right where I've always wanted to be. Can't even begin to describe what it feels like. Ever since I douched my life and hit dirtside, this place has been like some supernatural obsession. Ever since I ran into Nathaniel at the Phoenix. Ever since I began. Well, since I began being what I have now become. This place is like a total amplification of reality. So amplified that it's broken through to somewhere else. It exists beyond all the violence. Beyond all the blood. Beyond love, sex, even death. Beyond anything and everything I've known since I arrived in this shitty toilet of a town. S'like if you could hot-wire reality and set it on fire, that's what this would feel like. My every nerve, sinew, *fibre* is alive. I said that we were stuck with reality. I dreamt, but dreaming just made me feel more trapped. Yet Xankhara sets me free.

Force my attention back to the gates. To the big black bolts. Draw them across. Push the metal. Squeeze through, then head up the long gravel pathway.

After the trees I come to the centre of the gardens. The meeting of eight paths that form a circular paved walkway, girthed by beds and beds of flowers. In the middle stands a carved sundial, brass fittings gleaming in the sun. And the air is filled with the heavy scent of impossibly fragrant flowers. Ianus wasn't joking when he said it was spring. Everything's so impossibly perfect. Been a long time since I've actually seen flowers. Dead City's not exactly the florist capital of the world. Was a torn poster up on Fulton a long while back. That had flowers on it. Huge fields of flowers and some guy pissing with a big grin on his face. Can't think what it was advertising. Oh, yeah I do. '970-PEEE. The thrill of an uncontrollable bladder. The extra 'e' is for extra pee!' Or some such shit. All I can remember clearly are the flowers. Like the ones here. Only not so real. Or so fucking fragrant. Only in a simulation, I guess. Yeah, I've got to remember that the game's still running. Whatever else I forget, I can't forget that. Still, that does mean I can try a few tricks…

"Hey, Ianus. You up there?"

"We all are."

"Yeah, great. Ianus, inventory."

"Initiating inventory. Current name equals John Ewen Malorian. Current security passcode equals nine. Current resident mode equals X-Isle. Current psyche equals Ianus. Current objects equals none. Current score equals one."

"Cool. Ianus, list the system details."

"Executing search sequence. Game register equals John Ewen Malorian. Mode equals game. Game time elapsed equals three minutes, forty-one seconds. Game location equals Garden Central. Executing storm sequence. Search completed."

"Ianus, locations."

"Which location do you wish to interface?"

"As if you don't know. Try Horror House."

"Initiating data search. Location equals Horror House. Area equals

Horrorland. Location includes areas attic, first floor, ground floor and basement. Attic includes attic tower, attic roof and attic ledge. First floor includes master bedroom, back stairs, bathroom, upper servant bedroom, gallery, east study…"

"OK, cut the crap. I'll find it myself."

Somewhere off over the mountains, thunder rumbles. Whole peak's covered in dark grey clouds. Looks like we're in for a storm. Hey, now that may be a clue. Start walking toward the rumbling. It's only a hunch, but if I'm looking for the house of the living dead, can't think of a better setting.

Follow the path till it ends. Doesn't take long. Soon turns into a muddy lane. Total contrast to the garden. Stark reminder of what this rock looked like before Nathaniel's psychists got their grubby mitts on it. Just so much mud and rock. Now I'm entering some sort of gorge. Up ahead the way's blocked by a sheer cliff. Up the front of this is an ugly rusting structure of iron. Looks like the skeleton of some ancient service elevator. No car though. Just a latticed gate. Look up. Can't even see the top of it. Cliff disappears into the clouds above. What I do spot however is the unblinking eye of a securicam watching the area. It's bolted to the metal about five metres up. Panning from side to side. Looks like old tech. So what's new? This place's hardly next year's fashion statement. Only other things here are a sign announcing this to be private property and a battered red kennel.

Bixby's house? I wonder.

Squat and take a look inside. Sure smells of dog. But, hey, what would you expect a kennel to smell of? First off it looks empty, then I see something pushed to one side. Up in the far corner. Reach in and pull it out. It's a chewed rubber toy. Great. This'll be a lot of…

"John Ewen Malorian has picked up the squeeky gonk," says Ianus.

"Hey, shut it, asshole! Last thing I need right now is an acting PA…"

High above lightning sears the heavens. Supernova bright in the dark sky. Thunder's right behind it. Loud as a gun. Strikes the elevator shaft. Moments later strikes the kennel. Blows me right off my feet. Blows the kennel to fuck. Showering me with splinters. Cover my face. Squeeze the gonk so tight it squeals like I'm fucking it.

And as I lay on the ground gasping for air, I hear Ianus laughing.

Shit. What was *that*? Bastard could've killed me. Then I realise that that might be just the point.

Oh fuck, of course. I'm in their world now. Here Ianus isn't some menial AI with knobs on. This isn't the Room Without Doors. Here Ianus is a god. A *real* god. He Who Shall Not Be Sighted. The master of knowledge, mirrors and balance. And this changes things. Changes things big time. He said they were all here. That means the other gods too. Bêz. Kalím. That twisted pinko bitch who's into sex, drugs and rock 'n' roll.

And Mûhamet.

"Initiating psyche sequence. Implementing Mûhamet sentience. Psyche completed."

Oh sweet fucking lord above. Not Mûhamet. That's not fair.

Sister!

Jack, what's up?

It's the gods... the Eternal Ones. They're real.

Now, Jack, what've I been telling you all this time...

No, Sister. The X-Isle is based on the book of tales. The stories are about the heroes of the Amen. That means that here they're real. They run the show. They...

"Mortal! Unbeliever! Infidel!" the sky shrieks.

Shitshitshitshitshitshit!

There's more thunder. More lightning. Just loads more of fucking everything.

Sister, Mûhamet's pissed with me.

Jack, this is serious.

You're telling me it's serious!

Pay homage.

What!

Down on your knees, white boy. S'only way.

Oh fuck. Without a thought I throw myself to the muddy ground.
I'll guide you in prayer. You ready?
If you mean suitably prostrate, I'm there already.
Good. Now repeat after me… Hail holy queen of holies.…
"Hail holy queen of holies!"
You saying this?
Yeah, I'm saying it. Just get on with it.
Hail mother of life, death and inner belief…
"Hail mother of life, death and inner belief!"
To you I beg…
"To you I beg…"
Forgiveness and mercy…
"Forgiveness and mercy…"
And deliverance from my sins…
"And deliverance from my sins…"
Which are many, many many…
"Which are many, many, many…"
Many, many, many.
"Many, many, many."
Forever and ever. Amen.
"Forever and ever. Amen."

As I lay in the mud the storm breaks. Lashing me with stinging rain. In moments, I'm drenched. But at least that's all.

How's you doing?
I'm alive. Wet, but alive.

Good. Now just be more careful. If what you say's true then you'd best watch out for yourself. 'Cause I think they just might have it in for you. 'Specially after all the bad karma you been stirring lately.

Terrific. OK, I'll watch my back.
And don't do anything stupid.
As if I would.
Just saying, that's all.
O 'n' O, Sister.
Good luck, Jack.

Get up out the mud. So much for this being mortal paradise. Look's like I'd better keep my head down for the time being.

Turning back to the elevator, I look for the controls. Find a small rusty box. Open it and peer inside. All I can see is a single button and a slot. Pressing the button does zilch. Looks like I need a key of sorts. Don't fancy trying to climb the shaft. Not after that lightning strike. Better start having a look around, seeing where those other paths lead. Maybe I'll need to visit that temple after all.

Got to keep remembering this is a game. Got to think of it like that. Got to keep remembering...

"Mûhamet, inventory."

"Initiating inventory. Current name equals John Ewen Malorian. Current security passcode equals nine. Current resident mode equals X-Isle. Current psyche equals Mûhamet. Current objects equals the squeeky gonk. Current score equals eight."

Great, me and a squeeky gonk against the fucking world.

"Executing mirror termination sequence. Gateway to X-Isle terminated. Entrance to X-Isle sealed. Sequence complete."

No, Mûhamet. No!

Run back to the garden. Back to the path and the gates. They're closed. Shut tight. Bolts replaced by a million chains. Beyond lies only the starry emptiness. No ground. No mirror. No nothing.

So Xankhara sets me free, huh? Bullshit. Now I know why they call this place the X-Isle. Fuck, this ain't no Mirrormaze bad. This ain't even the streets of Dead City bad. This is total, utter, stinking, fucking, wanking, bollocking *bad*.

Way off the volcano rumbles. Think it's the storm at first then I feel the ground join in. Whole place trembles. Around the edges of the island great pieces of rock dislodge and tumble into the void. Following the raindrops into oblivion.

Got to get out of this storm. Got to sort out a way up that mountain. Well, that's if it even goes to the haunted house. Can't really be sure of that. Can't really be sure of anything. Except perhaps that for the first time in my entire life I'm out of my league. Way out of my depth.

From off behind me I hear the chiming of a distant clock. Tolls about two dozen times, then stops.

Strike that. Forget out of my league. I'm out of my fucking mind.

36 | D'ALESSANDRO

After the shears and the needle I'm left wondering just who gods pray to. After suffering four years of destructuring, dehumanising and calculated ego death at the hands of the denizens of the Kasikianu Imperial Detention Unit, I have become so mentally and morally unimportant to myself that evolving into a omnipotent being was almost inevitable. It was either that or disappear up my own arse.

For the twenty-third time I reach up and rub my unfamiliar baldness. My head feels utterly smooth. It also feels utterly cold, but my requests to turn up the heating have so far been completely ignored. After tiring of my amateur bout of phrenology, I turn my attentions to the tattoo. The coded bar of symbols and figures sitting on my left arm just above my puny biceps looks like a strange android's bruise. It's also red and very sore. Will the redness ever get the chance to heal, I wonder? The letters and numbers spell me out as the next victim of Osakimo's latest public relations exercise. For Glass-Suko I was bad publicity so I was removed from polite society. I think 'stitched up' is the technical term. When my actions brought down the Glass-Suko empire Osakimo took over its concerns. Which also included me. At first they kept me around to answer those niggling little questions they invariably had, yet now I am surplus to requirements. Luckily depersonalisation training is great for handling these sort of situations. Hurrah for therapy. Where would we all be without it?

I rub my cold head. I wince at my sore tattoo.

Footsteps.

Someone is coming back again.

What is this? My cell is becoming busier than Transcentral Station.

It turns out to be Akahiri and this time his walk betrays him. This is not the walk of a man bringing me my last meal, nor someone calmly leading two doctors to their patient. It is a strict pace, somehow chaotic and rushed. All heels clicking on concrete and short rasps as the leather squeals between steps. The whole thrill of this unscheduled break in the prison's universal uniformity again sends adrenaline pumping through my veins. No longer restrained, I sit up and wrap my arms around my knees. It's a childish pose, but that is exactly how I feel. Suddenly young. Suddenly drunk and light-headed.

I can see that Akahiri is carrying something. He's holding it close to his left-hand side in such a way as to hide it against his leg. At first this fact, the realisation that he is purposefully concealing whatever he carries, fills me with further delight. A delight that only increases when I see it to be the dirt-phone again. Impossibly eager I am forced to wait until he reaches the cell door and places the unit back into the food tray.

"You have call," the guard intones. "Make it brief."

Emotions whirl inside me and I feel my mind swim. Who could be calling? No one has called me in all my days here – Radio God didn't do requests – so why start now?

I stand and lurch giddily to the hatch as Akahiri watches me with blank impatience. I pull the black unit through and lift it to my ear, all the while courting the possibilities. Rusty from flagrant neglect my brain has a hard time figuring anything out. The only sane conclusion is that someone has heard of my imminent execution, yet I have no idea who. Not that is until I hear the voice. Then it all comes flooding back.

"Nathaniel? Yo' there? Damn motherfuckers! Put me through, you's yellow punks!"

Baseeq.

The voice is unmistakable. I'd know it anywhere.

Baseeq. My old fixer. The man who could get me anything. My

disciple and main man. And also my Judas. He was the one who gave the most damning evidence against me at my trial. Of course he warned me of Thomas' death. He said that I should destroy the sentience completely. He said it was the work of the devil. Current affairs seem to concur with that. Still luckily to appease his misgivings we arranged that if ever I needed him I should dig out his song. He recorded it twenty years ago in a desperate bid to break into the circuit. Failed on every station from here to the thirteenth moon. I was one of only three people to whom he gave a copy.

"Nathaniel? How lon' do it take to…"

"Hello, Baseeq."

"Nathaniel? That yo', man?"

"Yes, it's me."

"Never tho' it'd get to this." His voice sounds older, colder.

"Never comes, my friend."

As I talk, Akahiri twitches his head. Unlike my last call, I know this one is being recorded. If either of us says one thing out of place the line will be cut instantly. I try to calm myself at this thought. I have only one chance to get this right. There are a thousand questions I want to ask. Things like where he is, what he's doing and has he got the correct time, but there's no room for formalities. Instead, I sigh and say, "Still feel the same way about your old friend?"

"Look, man, I did what I did…"

"And I have no problem with that," I interject. That was close. One mention of the project and that would have been it. "I didn't mean me. I meant your other friend. *Our* friend."

There's a moment's silence while he thinks about this, then, "So what yo' want me to do?"

At these words the guard flinches. Stepping closer to the bars, he flicks open his comlink.

"Mr Glass, put down the phone."

Here's my one chance. A few fragile seconds before Akahiri terminates the channel. One last sentence to convey everything. I cop out and appeal to Baseeq's sense of anarchic libertarianism. He always saw himself as a bit of a buccaneer.

"Drop the phone, mr Glass!"

"If I die at midnight, blow the lot."

"What? Are yo'…"

But the line is already dead.

37 | PURE

I'm in the john. Syringe in one hand. Needle in the other. Pumping. At my feet Blackwing's lone deathsclaw gleams. Shining like a fist of glinting stars. Mirroring the room. The room, yeah, but also the book. Jack's copy of *Forevermore* sits next to the pan like a leather tombstone, but I've got other concerns. 'Cause unlike the nightflier, this crate is *full* of shit. There's cabinets and cabinets of the stuff. Enough to keep me high till the final reckoning. Grab randomly and end up with a bottle labelled in some weird language. Think it's a derivative of stardust. I *think*. The pain's so bad now, I'm beyond caring. OK, so I lied to Jack. Lied to myself too. Hey, so fucking what. Won't be the first time. Won't be the last. Guess that makes me weak. I have no problem with that. No problem at all. Never have. Never will.

Stick myself. Get a few moments of utter pain till the drug reaches the important bits, then I burn. My whole body immolates. I probably cry out yet the flames inside bring only pleasure. Let the sensation engulf me. Abandon myself to the tongues of fire. Let it flail the pain from my insignificant body and…

I'm caught in the bubble of a dream and am carried away by it. Bobbing on a rainbow-coloured breeze. Rock back and watch as my pretty feet brush the bindings of the book. Toe it open. Find my story, then stop. There on the page is a giant letter A. As big as my foot and painted within a woodland scene. Cottage. Clothes hanging on a line. And there in the roots of the illuminated letter are three people. A poor old widow and her two twin daughters. One with a throat as

white as a snow. The other with lips as red as blood.
Pure White and Pure Red.

> *A poor old widow once lived in a tiny cottage deep in the woods and, though her husband had died, her hard life was made bearable by her love for her daughters. For she lived with her two identical little girls, one with a throat as white as a snow, and the other with lips as red as blood. And so were they named: Pure White and Pure Red. Now one evening as the pair were gathering firewood in readiness for the coming of the great cloak of Lord Midwinter, they were caught in a fierce snowstorm and become utterly lost. As night fell they came upon a cave in which they sheltered from the bitter cold, finding within it a comfortable bed and food and drink.*
>
> *Yet the cave was home of a great black wolf with eyes of flame who returned not an hour after their arrival, discovering the sisters wrapped in his woollen blankets and eating his bread and supping his fine wine. And that might have been the end of the story right there, had it not been that the wolf was mortally wounded by hunters, and in dire need of help.*

Dreamily I read how Pure White aids and befriends the wolf, how she tend his wounds and feeds him. And how when he is restored to full health he allows them to ride on his back and takes them to the nearest point of habitation. Which unfortunately turns out to be the castle of a fucked-up count who keeps young by butchering little children and drinking their blood and eating their flesh. And who is also coincidentally leader of the hunters who attacked the wolf in the first place.

Riding up in his sleigh he sees the girls and decides that one of them shall replace his wife who has grown old and haggard with the years. Pure Red is taken in by his hospitality, charms and bribes, but Pure White keeps pointing out things that do not seem quite right with the situation. Stuff like how the lace cuff of his left sleeve is stained with spots of blood and how his breath smells of fresh meat.

Pure White befriends the black wolf. Pure Red, the count. And in this way Red is lost and White saved. It's as if the story is referencing just where I am right now.

Are you the count or the wolf, Jack? I muse. How can we know? How can we ever know? The path to choose. The safe way through the wood. Am I the player or being played? The hunter? Or being hunted? Suddenly, all elation leaves me and I am thrown headlong into supra-emotional trauma about Lucille's death. Like I'm accepting some silver-plated statuette at the WorldFashion awards. Filled full with emotion, drowning in tears, I'm struck by the curious connection between beauty and ugliness. How pain is the flame for us moths of glamour. At its heart the story's about a beast turned into a magnificent person. And I cannot say that this doesn't smack as being totally appropriate. I'm sick of being Jack's second star stage right. I don't want to read stories. I don't want stories read to me.

I want to make my own stories.

Distantly hear a knock at the door. It comes like a dull thump. I'm just on the side of reality that still realises what it is. Yet in that instant I'm transformed. I am a she-wolf. A lupine princess trapped in the deepest hours of darkness. Vampire time. A perfect and beautiful child of the night. Crawl to the door, suddenly and impossibly convinced that it's Jack. My naked boy come to rescue me. I reach up and knock back, still engulfed in the radiant flames, while my mind sings.

I am the wolf at your door. Knocking to come in. So cold and alone on this deep, dark night. Silently here I howl. I've left the pack for you; bereft. I cry. I rub my icy nose against the metal. I scratch your name in the air with my claws. I hunger for you. My jaws are dripping. Hot saliva spatters the floor, which burning melts. I toss my mane, spilling golden light.

And then in human growls, I ask: "Will you let me in?"

38 | DINGO THE WONDER DOG

I pop my head around the door to the medlab. See Sister watching Jack as The Nowhereman floats in the gunk tank.

"Where's Pure?" I ask.

"Thought she was with you?"

"Nah, she left just after we went auto. Said she had to take a wazz."

"Have you tried the toilet?"

"Er, yeah. I knocked."

"And?"

"She knocked back. She also, er, growled at me."

Sister gives me a look.

"Guess she's a little busy."

"Yeah, guess so."

"Wanna check it out?"

"Nope. You wanna?"

"Dingo, I've got to be here for Jack, y'know…"

"Oh, please… go on. She frightens me."

"Dingo, I can't."

"Oh, *please*!"

"OK, OK, I'll check it out."

"Thanks."

I leave her to it. Head back to the flight deck. Give the whale tank a wide berth. Fishes that big give me the willies.

Back at my seat I flick a few controls, run diagnostics then get bored. Now the Solar Huntress is piloting herself, I feel redundant.

Won't need me until we reach Kasikianu. Flick on a few of the overhead screens. Wonder if there's anything good on VTV. Find these aren't sat channels. Find they're monitors. They're set to record selected external shots plus intercept feedback from various sources. Skip through the first twenty or so before I come to one trained on Forevermore. It shows the park from near-space. About one in a thousand magnification. Use comms to zoom in twice more. I can see a great dark blotch near the main gates. Turns out to be a huge crowd of people. The gutter tribes. More people than I've ever seen in my entire life. More even than the Lizard Nation comeback concert and that was seven-hundred thousand. Zoom again and see Kibbutz and his entourage leading their crazy army out of the park headed for the wastelands. Five hundred klicks in that direction lay East-11. They must be out of their minds...

Behind me I hear a loud banging. Sister's gone to investigate Pure's disappearance. Click off the monitor and head to the bay. Back in the lo-lighted corridor I see the hulking shape of the ex-sergeant. Slamming her open palm against the toilet door for the umpteenth time.

Whump.

"Susannah?" she snarls as I get close. Until I'm standing right behind her.

Then for the umpteen and first.

Whump.

"Susannah, you come out of there, y'hear!"

By the time she readies herself for the umpteen and second, her hand's clenched into a large fist.

Whump.

"By the beard of Bêz, open this door!"

Mercifully at that point the door opens with a little hiss.

Inside there is a smell of disinfectant and bitter perfume which faintly freaks me out. Pure sits on the side of the cubicle smiling. This too is freaky. Looking around, I notice that the rest of the small chamber seems completely untouched. And this is the most freaky thing of all.

"Dingo needs you on the deck. He came to fetch you, but…"

Pure stands, trying to balance on her ridiculously high heels. Lasciviously she hoists up her pink plastic dress and teeters for a moment. Then she giggles. Sister scowls, yet this only fuels the blonde's amusement.

"Been a long time," Susie beams.

"Has it."

"You looked way rough when they brought you in. Almost didn't recognise you."

"Is that so?"

"Yep. Still, tank patched you up pretty good."

"Some scars never heal."

Pure snorts the mucus from one nostril forcing Sister to scowl again.

"You coming out?"

"Nope. You coming in?"

"No!"

As they set for a Mexican standoff, I'm left trembling. Wondering why I ever promised Jack I'd keep an eye on the ladies. The thought gives me a feeling of utter dread.

I'm gonna get killed… I'm gonna get killed… I'm gonna get…

39 | SISTER MIDNIGHT

Standing in the bowels of the god machine, while outside the world boils with danger I stare into the pale eyes of the blonde waif and seethe. Seethe and try to calm my fried nerves with prayer. God Mûhamet, though you teach me patience and tolerance beyond all things, this woman drives me insane. I cannot stand her anymore. Tell me, what should I do to endure this confrontation? For the first time in a long time, the gods do not answer.

"Last time I saw you was at the Phoenix," says the bimbo from the disturbingly clean cubicle.

"Yes, you were doing some dust or other…"

"Oh, that's all over now. I've quit."

I raise an eyebrow.

"Sinners never quit. Trust me."

"I trust my gun more than I trust you… or your precious God. Anyhow, last time I saw you I was just back from Devil's Ridge. I was with Lucille…"

"You were helping in surgery."

"Yeah, I think I was. Fitting the headmans so as I recall."

"It was just after you stole my man."

"Hey, hold your horses. It was a fair fight. Bit one-sided, but…"

"Crime never pays."

"Do I look like someone who cares?"

"Nope, you look like the same sassy-assed bitch you always was."

"You talking about little ol' me?" Pure bats her eyelids in mock innocence.

"Evil never dies," I reply and this time it is Pure who scowls.

"Hey look, you black witch. I was Jack's girl all that summer. He chose me."

"He chose no one."

"No, he chose *me*. You meant about as much to him as Lucille."

"You really think *you* were any different?"

"He said…"

"What'd he say?"

"Lots of things."

"Like what?"

"He said he loved me. Ever say that to you?"

I have to look away from the hatred in her black-rimmed eyes. Look at the ceiling, then at the floor.

"No," I admit finally. "We said… other things."

"So what did you say?"

"I swore I'd protect him with my life."

"Surely he's worth more than that."

"You just don't understand…"

"Understand? What's there to fucking *understand*? I'm back. Jack's mine. So just put that up your quim and smoke it."

"Why, you thrill crazy, kill crazy bitch!"

"God's truth, so just get over it, girlfriend."

Hearing her blaspheme, I cross myself.

"I shudder to think what fate awaits you beyond this fragile meatspace."

"Whoa, just listen to yourself. Always acting so fucking holier than thou. Always selling that ol' time religion. Well, don't talk to me about religion. You're not the only one with a burning bush, honey. P'raps you should try getting off your knees and admitting you were just too virtuous to let Jack fuck your brains out."

"In your case, looks like someone went and beat him to it."

We regard each other for another moment. One icy, silent, eternal moment. Then we spring together, talons lashing. Years of pent-up ferocity loosed in that frightful instant. Once we shared Jack because that was the way he wanted it, yet neither of us were happy with the arrangement. Especially me.

And now I have the chance to end it. Forever.

O father, I adjure thee, rid me of this venomous serpent whose presence offends your creation…

I claw out at the wretch, my teeth grinding, while Pure kicks at my shins and grabs for my thrashing dreads. Then I'm punching and biting as the blonde removes one high heel and starts using it like a hatchet. We both flail. We both rip and tear. Our limbs tangle. Our hair flies. It's ugly.

"Oh my! Girls! Girls! Stop it! Stop it!"

Somewhere outside I feel furry paws on my arms. Distantly, beyond my all-consuming anger, I realise it's Elliott, but I cannot let go. Not now. Instead my fingers find Susannah's throat and I squeeze hard while the blonde waif flails before me.

"You know, you're a woman after his own heart. That is you would be if (a) he had one, and (b) I didn't have it already."

Press. Hard. Harder.

"Sister! Pure! Stop! I'm telling Jack! I'm telling Jack!"

I ignore the mutt. I have her. In her death I am ridding the world of this evil. And it is good. My thoughts make perfect sense. Love and death inextricably twisted in my mind. Everything makes sense.

And I would have succeeded had it not been for Jack.

Esther, what are you doing? We are A-Men. All of us! You swore! Pure is A-Men. She's family. Kill her and you kill me.

Jack's voice fills my mind. Commanding me to stop. Which, of course, I do.

Coming out of my blind rage, I see Susannah on the floor before me. Choking. My eyes bleed tears; such forbearance is beyond my natural capacity to slay. Turning away from the scene I push past the Wonder Dog and head for the control room.

Instantly I disregard the incident. Now I am thinking only of a plan. Jack has given me an idea.

"Dingo," I call over my shoulder. "Get the prison governor online."

The Wonder Dog speed-skates his way down the corridor and past me. Patching comms, he sets up a two-way channel, then hits open. And when this bleeps into my ear, I say, "Governor, you have a prisoner tagged for termination for midnight tonight."

"We do?"

"Yes. Can you check your files?"

Pause.

"Indeed we do."

"Is he allowed visitors."

"Er, yes. Close family, relations…"

"Well, that's fine. I'm sending my details right now."

"Sorry, to whom am I speaking?"

"It's mrs Glass. His mother."

40 | THE NOWHEREMAN

Why are all my problems people-related? Once I thought it'd be cool to start my own family. Y'know, my own one-point-one children, six-by-four habitat eco-core. S'what we all dream of, eh? That was a big mistake. Full-time job just keeping them from carving each other up. Fuck knows what it's like running a corporation. And when that dream died, I dropped out and came to Dead City, yet that decision also solved nothing. When I discovered the book of tales, I was prime for conversion. I wanted out. Way out. I read it right through the first night I had it. Holed away in the riot-torn city. Couldn't put it down. Couldn't stop. I was like a starving man. Feeding on words. Was the first thing I'd read since hitting planetfall. And I was voracious.

I read of the Amen. Of the myths and legends of an ancient place named Forevermore. Of the gods that ruled there: Mûhamet, Astarth, Kalím, Bêz, Æoseth, Ianus and Torûs. And of the tales of discovery and enlightenment of the heroes and heroines who served them. Of Jack O'Nowhere's quest for Xankhara, the island of immortality. Of his battle with Maleore, the evil faerie king. Of the lands of Blackwater, Angaard and Finisterre. Of battlemaidens and beautiful assassins and dwarfish thieves. Of little white knights on little white horses. Every page filled with colour and wonder and magic.

Hell, what's life without having something to make sense of the nothingness? Some ideal to base it on? So I based mine of a book of stories, but to me that's no more fucked up than basing your entire life on the expectations of your parents. Or the promise of life everlasting. Anyhow, whatever, it was my dream. A way to escape. To fuck over all the shit for a while. And it became our dream. All our dreams. Even though it was only in our minds, it worked. For a while. And when it stopped working – as every drug does – that's when I lost it. And when I lost Xankhara, that's when I lost everything else too.

Yet seeing the island brings all those shattered dreams back. If only I can win here, if only I can save the X-Isle, then everything will be fine again. Everything will be back to normal. Well, the bastardised, puke-covered mess we call normal anyhow.

With Sister and Pure calmed down and cooling off, I turn my attentions back on the topic in hand.

A lot's happened here. In a world running at the speed of thought, guess a lot does.

After coming up empty at the cliff I've wandered into Faerieland. At least that's what it said over the rose-covered gateway. Must be an experiment into myth cycles or something. Still, found a few new areas. There's this lake shrouded in mist with an islet at the centre. Round boat moored to a wooden jetty. Lots of green rolling hills and fields. Not much else except this crumbling ruin of a castle. Like all the rest of the stuff on this island, it's half-finished. It's also guarded by this fuck-off knight in black armour on a horse the size of my brother's ego. Seeing as mucking about in boats is not my thing, got no choice but to get involved.

Go up to the knight. At first I think he's mute. Then:

"Who approaches the Castle of Enchantment?"

"Er, hiya…"

"Friend or foe?"

"Well, that really depends–"

"Friend or foe?"

"Friend."

"What is your name?"

"Jack Shit."

There's a slight pause. You can almost hear parsers whining.

"That is not your name," the knight announces.

"Well, if you're so fucking clever, why ask?"

"What is your name?"
"Read my file."
"Your name?"
"John Ewen Malorian. Happy?"
"You are not a friend."
"OK, so what happens now?"
"We must fight."
"Great. Your two-handed sword versus my squeeky gonk."
"I cannot fight with you until you fulfil all the rules of battle."
"And they are?"
"One!" the figure intones. "All combatants must be knights. Two! All combatants should be properly attired for battle with armour, weapon, mount and a favour from their lady. Three! All combatants must follow the codes of chivalry."

"And how am I to get that little lot?"
"That is not my problem."
"You don't know where I'd find a keycard for the elevator?"
Whirr. Grind.
"Who approaches the Castle of Enchantment?"
Sister, you out there?
I'm here, Jack.
Forevermore. Jack O'Nowhere. Thirteenth story. Seventh chapter. Tell me everything you can about when Jack gets to the Castle of Enchantment.

Somewhere out in that broken, beaten place called reality I can almost see Sister opening the big black book. Flipping the tatty pages. Scouring between the scrawled notes and scribbled-out text. Before me – somehow *inside* the actual story she's referencing – the knight shifts on his immense stallion. Creature's breath snorts from cavernous nostrils. Like the garden and its impossibly fragrant flowers, the horse's just as unreal. From my perspective looks more like the side of a building. Smells like shit. Shit and hot acid.

C'mon Sister, what's keeping ya?
I have it, Jack.
Great. So what's it say?

You were right. It's chapter seven. When Jack's at the castle. Faerie queen's daughter is being held captive by the Big Black Knight.

Yeah, but what happens? How'd he get past?

Patience. I'm reading...

I wait. Even though self control is not my thing. Just look up at mr black and sorta shuffle. Paw at my left tit. Nothing fancy. Just the usual malarkey.

OK, here's the gist... At the centre of the land of faerie Jack comes to this castle.

The Castle of Enchantment.

Right. Just like the one in the park. Jack looks at the spires and roses, but can't find his brother. All he sees is this big fuck-off knight on a big fuck-off horse–

Whassat about his brother?

The knight's some kind of guard and thinking his bro's inside already, he asks if he can pass–

Sister, listen up. What's that about his brother?

Thought you knew this story? Jack's the King of the Wood an' everything, but that don't mean shit. Means he was thrown out of home by his parents.

Who're they?

Some noble shitheads. Anyhow, it's his brother who's on the quest for the island. He's a knight and he's looking for the fountain of eternal youth or somethin'. Jack follows him. Least I think that's what it is.

OK, go on.

"Who approaches the Castle of Enchantment?" said the Big Black Knight.

"I am Jack," said Jack.

"Art thou friend or art thou foe?"

"Well, indeed, I wish no quarrel with thee. I seek an audience with the princess."

"Ha, ha, ha!" laughed the Big Black Knight. "Don't make me laugh!"

"No, really I do."

"The princess is my prisoner," the knight explained. "If you want to get in here, you will have to defeat me in single combat."

"Oh, I see," said Jack.

The Big Black Knight laughed again, this time a big guffaw.

"And how do I do that exactly?" asked Jack.

"Why, you must fulfil the rules of battle!" bellowed the huge figure. And then he explained to Jack exactly what the rules were. Firstly all warriors had to be genuine knights, secondly each should be properly attired for battle with armour, a weapon, a mount and a favour from their lady, and thirdly they must follow the codes of chivalry.

Now Jack thought long and hard about this, but he could not decide what to do.

No wonder my brother is not here, he thought, for he has all those things and sadly I have none.

But then he remembered his magic sack and the objects he had collected along the way. And when he peeked inside, suddenly he knew what he must do. Looking up at the knight towering above him he beamed a big smile, and then said, "Done!"

"What?" said the Big Black Knight.

"Done!" repeated Jack. "I have all the things you require." And he proceeded to remove item after item from his sack and place them before the startled fellow.

"Firstly, I acted in the Strapping Young Man's play down in the Prairieland. He had no one for the part of Darkness, so there I stood with this here silver platter and jar of fireflies, and that was that. So surely then, because of this, I am a 'night' of sorts. Agreed?"

The Big Black Knight looked at the shining platter and the twinkling jar. This was of course a most odd state of affairs, yet being something of a dullard the knight could not see why this was unacceptable.

"Agreed," he said reluctantly.

"Secondly, I have all the items of battle. Here is a washboard given to me by the Little Old Lady for helping her with her laundry down at the stream. I can use that for armour."

"Agreed," said the knight, still more reluctantly.

"Then here I have a flagpole taken from the top of the golden temple back aways. I can use this for a lance."

"Er… agreed," replied the knight, more reluctantly than ever.

"And here I have a hobby horse that I found in Sleepybubbyeland. That can be my mount."

"Agreed," said the knight in a voice that was the height of reluctance.

"Then, see here, I have this crown of hawthorn given to me by the faerie queen of the lake. She said if I wore it I would not be troubled by the fay folk of the forest. Surely this is a suitable favour and marks me as her champion?"

"Agreed," mumbled the knight, who by this time was far past reluctance and into the realms of moodiness and sulking.

"And as for the code of chivalry I know every rule, for I had to test my brother on each one when he was training and I was his squire."

And with that Jack recited all the rules, and the Big Black Knight was forced to agree that he did indeed know them all. In fact, he knew some of them even better than the knight did, but he didn't think he'd better mention it.

"So, now that's settled," said the Big Black Knight once Jack was finished. "Let's fight!"

One of the recurring themes in *Forevermore* is that each character gets their moment of glory in the story. Their moment to be brave. Or strong. Or selfless. Or whatever. And here's Jack's. Here's his chance to shine. If he defeats the knight he's into the castle, can rescue the faerie queen's daughter and is home and dry. He gets his wish and Xankhara. He beats his brother. He's a hero. Crowds cheer. Everything ends happily ever after.

If he fails, he's mince.

Here also is where this whole story idea falls down. Though I know what happens to Jack, what happens to me is another matter. I don't have a magic sack. I don't have all the odds and sods he does. I haven't helped the Strapping Young Man with his play. Or the Little Old Lady with her washing. Fuck, I haven't helped *anyone*. All I've got is a squeeky gonk.

At this moment that just about sums up my whole pissing life.
So what's what, Jack?
Guess I'm off to collect all that crap.
Guess so. Be careful.
OK... Hey, Sister?
What?
You gotta see this place. It's perfect.
It's not my dream, Nowhereman. Not my dream.

Glance up at the knight. Then at the castle beyond. Guess she's right. But still...

"Ciao," I say cheerily and turn my back on the fucker. As I walk away the Big Black Knight on the Big Black Horse laughs himself stupid.

★

Wander back along the path. Head for the central gardens. Pass the forest and boating lake. Then under the arch. Next thing I know I'm back in the land of flowers. Rain's all gone. Everything's dry as a bone. No actual sun in the sky, but all's bright and breezy. All's swell.

OK, first thing on the list is the silver platter and fireflies. Means I gotta find the hick and act in his stupid play. Catch myself scratching for my D&K again. Feel a lot better if I had my piece.

Exploring the other paths, find more areas of the island. If the cliff's north then the gates are south, and Faerieland's south-west. North-west is a vegetable patch, north-east is an orchard. Not much doing here. Tall spiky hedges. No way out of either. South-east leads into a desert. Sand and stones replace grass and hedges. Two statues flank the rocky path. Carved arch above them announces this to be Pharaohland. Beyond all that's just shimmering haze. Beyond that's the distant temple.

Resist going for the flagpole. Best to do this step by step. Less confusing that way.

Back in the garden the last two ways lie east and west. East turns to a mucky yellow brick, while a blackboard announces I'm now entering Sleepybubbyeland. West is a dense wood, a sign saying 'To Prairieland' and a claw hammer. Now, we're cooking.

"John Ewen Malorian has picked up the claw hammer," says Mûhamet.

The voice makes me shiver. Doesn't stop me tucking the hammer into my belt though. Just reminds me that I've gotta tread careful. Real careful.

So, looks like there's five lands. Horrorland's the only one I can't find. And the only one I wanna get to. Always the way. Figure Prairieland is the best bet. Don't see no axe-wielding hillbilly babysitting in kidsville, so west it is.

Turn towards the forest. Head off down the leafy track. In a dozen strides I'm past the sign and lost in the thick woodland. Leafy tracks twist and turn off in all directions. Every way I go seems to look exactly like the place I just left. Try doubling back. No dice. Just tramp through into another identical copse of unidentifiable trees.

Something's up here. Smells fishier than a whore's crack.

Try again. No joy. And again. Nope.

Run, but just find more forest. Out of breath I'm forced to stop.

It's at this point that I also have to admit I'm lost. Well and truly. Up the creek and fresh outta paddles, boats and blow-up lilos.

Nowhere to Sister.

Yessum.

There anything about Jack getting lost in the woods?

Dunno. Want me to look?

I'm lost in the woods. Go figure.

OK, I'm on it.

Impatience kicks in instantly. Try to keep myself busy.

First thing I try is moving slower. Keep my eyes focused on one specific tree. My guess is that those bastards upstairs are playing tricks on me. Laughing their fucking rings off. No way the wood's this big. No way in hell. Whole fucking island's not *this* big.

Few tries at this and I catch 'em out. As I walk ahead the tree I'm looking at changes. Sort of moves slightly to one side. Stepping back is useless. Once I've taken a step, that's it. Can't retrace the way I've come. The tree I'm gaping at now looks almost identical to the last. Just different somehow. Same sort of tree, only not quite. Then I realise I *am* looking at the same tree. Just from another side. Somehow they've turned me around. Swapped me from one side of the tree to the other. Fucking cunts. No wonder I'm getting lost.

Once I've worked this shit out, things get easier. By arranging branches to form arrows, I always know when I've jumped. After that, it's just a matter of recalculating my bearings every time I move. And once I've mastered that, it's downhill all the way.

Concentrate on the next set of trees. These are different from the rest. Got spindly white trunks instead of fat brown ones. Not seen any of those before.

Jack, it's Sister.

Go away. I'm busy.

No, listen up, Jack. I've found the passage. Yep, he gets lost good and proper. Chapter four. 'Bout halfway through. Just before he finds the hillbilly's house...

Step forward and a path appears. Run down it before it decides to go walkies.

Jack, are you listening to me?

At the end of the path is a wide ditch. And on the other side is a broken-down house in a smoky clearing.

Nowhereman? Do you copy?

And beside that is an open-sided caravan. Set up like a little stage.

Forget it, Sister. I'm way ahead of ya.

Stride into the clearing. Call out. Twice. Just calls. Nothing coherent or anything. Over at the house a shadow detaches itself. Forms a tanned redneck. Checked shirt and overalls. Long hair blowing in the breeze. Guy's chewing something dark. Also got a pretty mean shotgun. Cupped in the crook of his arm.

"Howdy, fella," he says spitting.

"Howdy," I say back. Try to ignore his moronic drawl. And the nasty way he looks me over.

"Think the weather's gonna hold?" he asks.

"Huh?"

"The weather. Folks say we're gonna see a change a-comin' by sun-down."

"Really," I say back.

"Well, s'what they say."

Stop at the porch steps and smile. Sorta smile people don't see me do that often. Usually on account of they're dead about ten seconds later. Redneck grins back. All buck teeth and shiny forehead.

You total jerk. Fucker makes me want to puke. Smiling stops that. Well, for a while anyhow.

"You new 'round here?" he asks. "'Cause I thought I knewed just about ever'body."

I nod while my hand slips gently down to the hammer at my side.

"Yup, thought you wuz!" he chuckles. "You don't look like you from anywhere 'round these parts."

"I'm not," I grin back. "Nowhere 'round here."

Take a step up onto the porch. Real nonchalant. Imagine I'm just gonna sit on his porch and talk until the moon comes up. The young man nods like his neck's made of rubber.

"So where's ya come from?" he enquires.

"The hip."

Quick as lightning bring the hammer up. Arcing like a punch. Hits the nodding cunt right under his chin. Clean knocks his fucking jaw out. Force of the blow sends him sprawling. Smacks his head on the shack. Slumps. Claws out at me like he wants to give me a big hug. I ignore that. Already I'm aiming the hammer again. This time I hit him square centre of his greasy forehead. Head meets head and keeps on going. Puncture a pussy-sized hole through to his brain. Sadly he drops the gun which goes off in his spasming fingers. Blows half the front porch to matchwood. Sprays the grass with white splinters. Raise the hammer for another go, but the poor sad fuck's already dead.

"John Ewen Malorian has killed the Strapping Young Man with the claw hammer," chants Mûhamet impassively.

Wince, then shrug. Guess the world'll just have to get over it. Wipe the blood off the hammer and tuck it back in my belt. Pick up the shotgun. Check it over. Then search the redneck for shells. Find a few tucked into his shirt pocket. Take them.

"John Ewen Malorian has picked up the shotgun. John Ewen Malorian has picked up the shotgun shells."

Shit, this just gets better and better.

"Mûhamet, inventory."

"Initiating inventory. Current name equals John Ewen Malorian. Current security passcode equals nine. Current resident mode equals X-Isle. Current psyche equals Mûhamet. Current objects equal the squeeky gonk, the claw hammer, the shotgun and the shotgun shells. Current score equals fifty-eight."

Fifty-eight! Ha! Now we're cooking.

Move off the porch and head for the caravan. Stage's set for some sort of weird play. Ignore all that. Go to the back and start searching. Don't take long to locate the platter and the jar.

"John Ewen Malorian has picked up the silver platter. John Ewen Malorian has picked up the jar of fireflies."

Gee thanks for your continued broadcasts, little miss holy. You're too kind.

"Executing noon sequence. Implementing Little Old Lady laundry sequence. Implementing Tall Ancient Shepherd refreshment sequence. Sequences complete."

Almost immediately comes the sound of music. Flute-like. Hits the air suddenly. Like bird song. This is followed by another sound. Something less identifiable. First I think it's a toilet. Then I figure it's someone washing their clothes in a nearby stream. Leave the body in a puddle on the porch. Already heading back to the woodland maze.

★

Little Old Lady's a piece of piss too.

Find the wheezing bint on her knees by a hitherto unseen river.

Back end of the woods. Poor dear's all puffed out. Her wrinkled fingers going ten to the dozen against her battered washboard. Looks like your typical grandmother. All silver hair and baggy stockings. Her flower print dress is hoisted around her less-than-luscious thighs. Face like a badly bound book. Second edition. Leather cover. Been read about a dozen times too many. You know the rest. Typical aging dogsbody. Totally harmless.

It's at this point that nanny notices me. Peers through the misted glass of her bifocals. Peers hard. Then gives me a lipless smile.

"Hello, sonny," she mews. "Want to help me with some washing?"

Hoist the shotgun. Aim. Pull the trigger. There's an almighty bang. Hits granny in the chest. Throws her into the river. Well, most of her anyway. Hits it like a stone. I'm already moving towards the washboard. Already reloading.

"John Ewen Malorian has killed the Little Old Lady with the shotgun. John Ewen Malorian has picked up the washboard."

As the first wave of crimson reaches the pebbled bank, I'm already gone.

This is way too easy.

★

Later I reach Pharaohland. Past the statues leads into a golden-white desert. Sweeping dunes. Hot winds. The whole nine yards. All limitless. Trackless. Extending by some faultless illusion off to infinite horizons. Far as the eye can see. Soon the path's replaced by mounds of ochre sand. Snake my way over the ever-shifting wasteland. Sun's out now. A scorching beachball in the sky. Makes me sweat.

Finally come to some promontory. Jutting out over the void. Beyond lies the smaller island and the temple. Must be more than a hundred metres away. Huge unfinished bridge arcs over the gulf. About a sixty metre chunk's missing from the middle. Looks like someone's taken a bite out of it.

Walk to the edge of the bridge. Look down into nothingness.

Makes me dizzy. Stone's impossibly balanced. The chiselled blocks hang in mid-air waiting some herd of slaves to haul ass and finish the goddamn mess. Still, nice view of the other island. Great temple. Pity I can't see any fucking way of getting to it.

Walk back to eternity beach.

Can't think it's a dead end. Joseph would certainly have a way to get there. Looks like I need another dose of spiritual guidance.

Yo, Sister.

Uh-huh.

The temple. How'd Jack get there?

I'm right on it. Oh, Jack, we're about an hour from Nathaniel.

Oh, yeah, Nathaniel. Right.

Look around the base of the bridge. Each stone's taller than me. Must weigh several tonnes each. Try to count how many there are. Soon tire of this. C'mon, Sister, c'mon. It's only four hundred pages for chrissakes.

Found it.

Read to me, sweetness.

Well, s'all pretty simple. Just another juxtapositional piece of myth lore…

And the winner is?

He flies.

Flies?

Yeah, flies.

And?

Er, well, he just does.

So let me get this right. You want me to chuck myself off into the void.

Yep.

But that's digital suicide!

No, just belief. S'how he summons the island in the first place.

Oh fuck, of course. Jack O'Nowhere dreams Xankhara from the sea.

I'm way ahead of you, Sister. It's all coming back to me. The time. The place. The weather-beaten old crone.

All down to belief. You hear me, Nowhereman? Course, I believe. They's my gods. The Eternal Ones. I believe in all of them. Strong belief. Mighty belief.

Well perhaps you should come in here and sort this shit out.

No, Jack, this is your time. Your moment of glory in the story. Your moment to shine. You can fly, Jack. S'easy. You ain't in real life. In Xankhara you can do anything you damn well want. Just believe. The gods won't let you down.

Says who?

Says me. Look, have a chat with them. Try Bêz. He's one cool cat.

What's he god of?

Feasting, drinking and driving fast in cars. You'll like him. He'll see you right.

OK. I got it.

"Mûhamet, psyche, Bêz."

"Initiating psyche sequence. Implementing Bêz sentience. Psyche completed."

Reality trembles. Feel my skin creep. As if suddenly covered in wet leather. Smell vinegar. Vinegar and spunk. Hear a slamming door. See the air swarm with bugs. Then it's gone. All gone.

In its place is a small, pointy-eared man. Sitting cross-legged on the bridge. Dressed in a parti-coloured hat and clothes. Festooned with bells. He is grinning. A lot.

"Yo!" he says through his teeth. "Show skin, bruvver!"

I groan. What in fuck's name is this? Still, better humour the cunt.

Reach one hand in the air and slap. Miss the god's palm by about half a metre.

"Sorry, bro'," chuckles Bêz. "We slap low in my religion."

Our eyes meet. Feel like strangling the shit. Don't. Instead, I breathe deep. Breathe deep again. Then laugh. Ha, ha, ha.

At this the imp leaps up. Holds his sides. Does a little dance. The usual crap.

"So what's doin', peasant?"

Calm, Jack. Calm. Keep your chakras centred.

"Who're you?" I ask as if I didn't know.

Bobo the clown bows slightly.

"I am many things to many people… and all things to no one."

"Great. Ten out of ten for enigmatic. Look, the temple. How'd I get there?"

"Easy. Answer me this riddle…"

"What riddle?"

"Six claws high by seven stones long stands the dark fourth door of the three. Bear keys of five magics for a lock twice the third. Light the candle by one you shall see. What am I?"

"That's a riddle?"

"Shore is."

"Ask me another."

"OK, how's 'bout this… Riddle-me-ra, riddle-me-ree, say the gods of eternity, if I am perfection, the omniscient one, answer me this: where the fuck'd'yo' come from?"

The tinkling fool raises his brows. Waits expectant. Like a dog at dinner time.

Well, here's a pretty state of affairs. If these sad bastards think they created the whole universe, my showing up must've been unexpected. To say the least. Bit of a tricky one. Can just see it now. Up in the god's tea room. Everyone's assembled. Mûhamet's being mummy. Ianus' just reaching for a second cup cake. Then, bang! Up I turn. From out of nowhere. Literally. Must've turned their logic programming to bollocks. Always was born to be a fly in the ointment. That's me all over.

Look into Bêz's face. Sneer. Then answer the stupid cunt's riddle. Answer it good and proper.

"Me? Where'd I come from?"

The freak nods. Sends his hat into a fit of jingling.

Bite back the obvious retort. Bite back quite a lot. Not my style, but there you go.

"I'm The Nowhereman."

The midget giggles. All buck teeth and brass bells.

"So yo' The Nowhereman? The man from outta nowhere?"

Fuck this for a game of soldiers. Take the shotgun. Push it into the joker's grinning mouth. Fire. Blows the god to atoms. Well, not atoms, exactly. Actually, the shell blows him to butterflies.

Huh?

Reality check. Wheep, wheep. Gotta remember where I am. Still joker's gone anyhow which I guess was the point.

Hi, Jack. How's it going with Bêz?

Not so good. He morphed off.

Oh, Jack, what you doing...

Look Sister, just read the fucking book will ya?

OK, Jack. This is how it is...

As Midnight starts, the whole of creation quakes. Turns from heaven to pure, undiluted, one-hundred percent hell.

Oops, looks like I finally pissed off the god guys.

Looking out from the hill over the flame-red water of the bay, the old beggar woman's eyes shone like molten stars.

"Xankhara," *she whispered.*

Jack shivered at the sound.

"Yes, Xankhara," *he said.* "How do I get there?"

The crone laughed like a little bird.

"So you want to find Xankhara, do you?"

"Yes," *said Jack.*

The crone laughed again, shrill as a lark.

"And what gives you the right to find the sacred isle?"

"I'm Jack O'Nowhere. I'm King of the Wood," *said Jack.*

The crone laughed a third time. Laughed and laughed and laughed.

A bit annoyed at the woman's mocking, Jack shouted, "But you don't understand! This is the land I've seen in my dreams, the land of the lost and free. The place where Death never treads..."

The beggar woman stopped laughing and turned on the young man, her eyes at once dark and deadly serious.

"Xankhara is that place. That un-place. It is the place of once upon a time." *She stopped and thought for a while, then continued,* "You have chosen well. Your thinking place is a special hill. For this is a place of *imagos*... Let me explain. You see certain places, like certain people, seem not to be a part of the here and now, they seem to be beyond... you know, from the realm of nowhere and everywhere all at once. They exist at all times and all places, dwelling like shadows of history. And they say that if you sit at these dwell points in the hour between the setting of the sun and the moon's rising, if you sit very still and look really hard, you can sometimes catch glimpses of these imagos through the crack in the door of reality."

She gave Jack a sly glance and he thought that she was going to laugh again, but she did not.

"They say imagination is the lock and belief is the key," she added.

"Do you believe enough to try it? Do you? Do you?"

"Yes," whispered the King of the Wood.

"Then tell me what you see."

And Jack sat very still and Jack looked really hard.

And Jack saw nothing.

"I see nothing!" he cried.

"Look harder," said the woman.

"I can't!"

"Look harder!"

So he did. And as the sun disappeared below the horizon and the sky turned the colour of a prince's cloak, there out in the bay an island rose from the boiling waves.

"Oh my," said Jack, his eyes wide.

"Xankhara," the woman whispered.

For the second time, Jack shivered.

"Xankhara," he repeated, then, "But it is too far. Always too far. I have no boat? How can I get there?"

"Hush, little one," the crone scolded. "Do not lose the faith that you have found within you. Had I your belief I would not still be wandering this barren hillside. If you are meant to gain its shores you will find a way."

"But how?"

"Perhaps you could fly."

"Fly?"

"Yes, fly. If you wish it, it will be so."

For a moment Jack's heart quailed at the thought, but then he took another look at the island and leapt to his feet. Shaking off his shivers he cried, "I'm the man who deals in once upon a time." And his voice was louder than the gulls and the tide. The beggar woman laughed long and hard, but this time she was not mocking. She was exultant.

"Fly, Jack, fly!" she cackled. "Let your dream uphold you." For she knew that the island was only as real as the young man's belief in it and that there was now no going back. He was already too far along the Path of No Return.

And so Jack ran and ran and when he came to the edge of the hill he leapt out over the bay. And, as the woman had said, his dream upheld him and he flew over the deep water toward the beautiful island.

Digging my heels into the shifting sands, I run. Heading for the end of the bridge.

It all comes down to belief, Jack. His belief. That's the only way you gonna get over that chasm. Belief. You got anything like that, white boy?

Well, Midnight, I'm just about to find out.

So this is what Nathaniel wanted to create. This un-place. Wonder how many nights he sat on his own version of Jack's hill and stared out over dark water? D'Alessandro, you driven fuck, is that what all this is about?

Of course, I know the answer. I've always known.

Guess that makes him and me more alike than I thought. Shit, it makes us all the same. We're all chasing the same dream. All of us. Me. Nathaniel. The A-Men. Hey, maybe the whole fucking world. He was right when he said that we were lost. All of us. And now I see that we are. Lost like a scream to the dead. Till the end of time.

What's happening, Jack?

I'm going for the big one, Sis.

Oh Jack, be careful.

Sorry, Midnight, I've never had much to do with being careful.

The end of the stone roadway is dead ahead. As is the looming void. Overhead the clouds scream. Literally. They're afire with pain. Tormented. The hairs dance on my neck and arms. Any moment I'm gonna get fried. I can feel it. There's a burst of rain. Hail. Motes of burning ash. In the primordial chaos that was the sky, the sun is suddenly fleeing to the safety of the horizon. The hick was right about the weather. There's definitely a change a-comin'.

Then the bridge starts vibrating. Feels like an orgasm shuddering up between my legs. Shaking the stone to pieces. Breaking the blocks into fist-sized rubble.

Oh fuck, oh fuck, oh fuck...

In three more strides I'm at the edge of the world. Hold my breath. Hold my breath and jump.

Here goes everything.

Leap out into nothingness. One moment I'm running along the bridge. The next I'm freewheeling through space.

Then I start falling.

Shit! Sister, it's not working! I can't fly! I can't!

Jack, what's going on? You're flailing too much. You're gonna rip the tubes out! The whole system's going wild.

Sister! I'm falling!

All around infinity swallows me up. Then I realise I'm screaming. Stop myself. Feel like a fool.

Jack, you listen to me and you listen good. You're part of this place. Nathaniel wrote it, but it was your daddy's coding that made it possible. It was from his DNA, for AEoseth's sake. He was the real creator... and you are his son! It's in your blood, Jack, you hear me? Is this making sense? Jack!

OK, I gotcha, Sis. Guess it's no more mr nice psycho.

Anger grips me. Blots out my fear. Kick against the nothingness. Try to think like a bird. First time for everything. Still I'm as surprised as anyone when I begin to soar upwards. Yee-har! Now that's more like it! Above me the bridge explodes. Showers space with asteroids. I don't even flinch. Not now. Now I'm in control. I'm The Nowhereman. And, like Nathaniel said, The Nowhereman can do anything.

Anything.

Yeah, like Nathaniel said, reality's all in the bag.

Dodge the asteroids. Doggy-paddle out of the void. Claw up the beach of the smaller island. Overhead the gleaming temple shines in the rapid sunset.

Made it.

Jack?

Made it.

Oh, Jack.

Sounds like Sister's crying.

When I saw you stop thrashing, I thought…

Yeah, well I ain't.

Not by a mile.

Look up. There atop the looming edifice stands the flagpole. Leap to the burning skies. Land on the lip of the stone roof. Nice view. Can see for fucking ever. All around is untamed apocalypse. Yet although the rest of the universe is having fifty fits, nothing comes anywhere near this place. Funny that. Maybe they've got a soft spot for it. Certainly haven't for me. Still, their leniency makes me wary. No one does anyone any favours in my book. Not this side of the grave.

Step forward and take hold of the pole. Pull it from the stone.

"John Ewen Malorian has picked up the flagpole," says Bêz.

I'm just about ready to fly off when I notice something written on the floor. It's an inscription. Half covered by sand. Wiping it clear, I read:

Here lies Seth Campbell Malorian.
Mystogenesist and creator.
Ad initio. In aeternum.

Holy shitting hell fuck. This isn't a temple. It's daddy's tomb.

Sister, cool it. I've found where Joseph's stashed my father.

Where?

Here. In Xankhara.

You're kidding?
Nope.
Thought you said he was comatose?
Forget what I said. Looks like that was so much shit.

Looks like he's not in a coma. Looks like he's *never* been in a coma. Looks like my dear kid brother plugged him into his own universe and left him to rot.

Oh boy, that changes everything. Guess now I know who ordered that attack on the condo. Same fuck who sold me out to Osakimo. No wonder he wasn't at Aaron's birthday party. What a shitting bastard. What a complete and utter fucking, shitting, pissing, cunting *bastard...*

With a sudden sharp grating of stone on stone the roof under my feet vanishes. I fall. Windmilling. Drop the pole. Drop myself. Slip down into the throat below me. I'm surprised. Too surprised to do anything other than fall. Don't even think of flying. Just fall. Then I catch myself. Stop in mid-air. Somewhere near what I guess is the middle of the shaft. All around is unnerving darkness. Only light's from the small square high above. Zoom upwards then realise I don't have the pole. Zoom downwards.

It's round about then that I hear the grating again.

Look up.

Just in time to see the slab slowly closing.

Shit.

Fly up, but it's too late. By the time I get there I can't even feel where the trapdoor is.

Sister, I'm trapped in the temple. Better start reading ahead...

Drop into the midnight. Finally my feet find the floor. Well, I say floor, what I actually mean is spiked pit. Walls're smooth as glass. Spikes sharp as razors. Spaced about an arm's length apart. Each one about a metre long. Can't move in any direction much without running into one. Glad I didn't meet these at terminal velocity. Way glad.

It's about then that I feel the body.

It's pinned to a few of the spikes near the lefthand edge of the pit.

Run my hands over the twisted fuck. Find it's wearing some kind of jacket. Reach for the waist. Find a belt. On the belt is a pouch. Also a torch, secured by a big clip.

    Rip the torch off the clip. Ignore the inevitable PA from Bêz. Hold it in both hands and switch it on. Flood the pit with dusty silver light. Sweep it all around. Over the walls. The corpse. Everything.

    It's a guy. Face's punctured by one of the nasty spears. Makes it hard to tell if I knew him. Seems unlikely. Three more spikes harpoon various other parts of his anatomy. The blood pool below him is just so much strawberry jelly now. Apart from his khaki jacket and shorts, searching the stiff comes up empty. 'Cept his pouch has a sheet of paper in it. Read it. Some sorta strange shopping list. Mirrors, pipes and stuff. Creepy. Looks like he was travelling light. Then I see something on the ground. Well, some*things* actually. Crouch and pick them up. There's a rusty sword and a gas mask. Neat. Just what I always wanted. Before I go, I check everything out again. Just to make sure.

    This time I catch the guy's name tag.

    It's sewn to the breast of his safari jacket. It says, 'Lloyd'.

    Esther, ya there?

    Jack, you OK?

    Yep, Sis. I just met Lloyd.

    Met him?

    Well, yeah, what's left of him. In this reality, he stiffed in the temple.

    So this is the sentient memory of Thomas Bryce Lloyd. The first test rat to enter the X-Isle maze. The guy Nathaniel got the big one for killing. Fucker died here and Xankhara fried his brain in the real world. Shit. Well, that's one way to go about debugging. Poor bastard. No wonder they closed this project down.

    Once she's done with the telling there's silence. Obviously Midnight would rather talk about something else. Took it real bad when she fucked up with the datawipe. Still, s'OK by me. I'm heading on. My guess is that this tomb is where I'll find daddy. Probably in some sarcophagus somewhere.

You sure you're OK? The instruments are still way off the scale.

Yeah, the gods are hunting for me, but I'm safe for now. Anything in the story?

Not much. In the book Jack O'Nowhere doesn't go inside...

Great. Well, thanks anyhow. O 'n' O.

Rise out of the pit and find a ledge. Above there's a brightly painted chamber. All weird figures and shit. Much like Sister's place. Only weirder. Only ways out are up, down and along a corridor to the right. Hardly a difficult choice. Make my way along the ledge and enter the passageway. Air's dry and warm. Makes me sweat. Fever-like. At the end of the passage stand two stone statues. Between them is a gold door. Looks solid. If it was real it'd be worth a fortune. Being a sim it's worth shit. Intricate carvings crawl across it. Like the etchings of artistic beetles. Lean forward and push on the door. Push harder. Strain. Give up just this side of a hernia.

"Open sesame."

Nothing.

Worth a try though. Who knows what works in this fucked-up faerie tale.

Look through the items I'm carrying. Nothing inspires me with much confidence. Start searching around the edge of the door. Then search the statues. Then the floor. Nothing.

OK, what's next? Can't push it. No lock. No hidden lever. Well, not that I can see.

"Ssson?"

The voice makes me jump. Heft the shotgun into the air. Swing wildly with the torch. No one's about. I'm all alone in the corridor.

"Daddy?" I whisper.

I listen. Hard. Harder than hard. Nothing. Not a single sigh. Just the sound of the blood pumping in my temples.

Will for something to happen. Anything. For someone to step out the shadows just so I can blast them.

With a hideous squealing of precious metal on worthless rock the gold door hauls ass toward the ceiling.

As the door trundles inexorably upwards, a breeze is created. Two air pockets become one. Only trouble is that the one beyond the opening is the colour and density of thick fog.

Grab at my waist for the gasmask. Fumble with the rough straps. Force it over my face. Then breathe again. Secure the battered faceplate and shine the light into the cloud.

I find myself looking into a burial chamber. Despite the age-old dust, can see everything's made of gold. Even the huge dais on which rests a black sepulchre. Painted and inset with gems.

No expense spared in the land of make-believe.

"Enter, my ssson," hisses the voice.

"Hi, daddy," I reply. Words're muffled by the mask.

"Isss it you, Johnny? Isss it really you?"

"No, it's the home-help. Heard you needed a spring clean."

"Johnny, help me… I am incarcerated… here in thisss sarcophagusss."

I ignore the prick. Look around instead. Check out every corner and niche in the whole place.

"Hmm, think I'll pass. I'll be vacuuming this place till eternity."

"Johnny, Jossseph did thisss to me. He ssstole everything… Quickly, releassse me… before he returnsss!"

I scowl. Now isn't this a pretty state of affairs?

Walk over to my father's prison. Cut through the mist and step up onto the dais. Look at the exquisitely engraved tomb. The letters 'HAXOR' have been chiselled into the head end. Must be father's god name. His divine persona. Fuck knows where his body is. Could be anywhere. All I know for sure is he's plugged into the hostgod. Much as I am. A prisoner. Much as I am. A victim of my brother's hostile takeover bid. Looks like we've all been suckerpunched. Royally shafted from day one.

"Why's he left you alive?"

"Insssurance," says the ghostly voice.

"Figures."

Pretty much why he's kept us all alive. And now he couldn't give a flying fuck through a burning twat. Everyone's outlived their usefulness. Nathaniel's for the chamber. Daddy's for the embalming enema. And me? Well, who knows. In this place, could be anything. Still, can't see me going down without a fight. Just gotta get out of this fucking temple. Still, few things to finish up first.

"So, O great god Haxor, what's the story?"

"It isss Jossseph. He wantsss my kingdom."

"Yeah, so what?"

"He was jealousss of Glasss-Sssuko. And that he didn't have accesss to the complete code. He tried to take it from me. He got accesss to the isssland after Nathaniel was jailed. Then he ruined Raymond and… Darrold."

"Who're they?"

"Raymond Isssaac Glasss. Darrold Sssuko. The joint heads of Glasss-Sssuko."

"Then what?"

"Then he destroyed everything. You. Me. Them. And when he was finissshed he started to rebuild Xankhara in hisss own image."

The bastard.

"Beyond that, I've been a little out of touch…"

"That's cool. I pretty much know the rest."

Take time out to bring dearest daddy up to date. Tell him that after ridding himself of both of us, Joseph and his Osakimo buddies built a new hostgod sentience and created XEs. Must've pleased a lot of people. Made him a multi-zillion profit to boot. It's only now after he's discovered the virus that he's come back to rebuild a clean sentience from scratch. His shopping list included the rig, whale, crystal and my codes. Once it's all told, it makes a sense of the recent chaos. Except for one thing.

"Daddy?"

"Yesss, my ssson."

"Thing is I still don't see what he wants… What he's after."

"Who? Jossseph?"

"Yeah."

"He wantsss what we all wanted… What every generation and civilisssation hasss… quesssted for sssince the beginning of recorded hissstory."

"And what's that?"

"Immortality."

"Immortality?"

"Yesss. Thisss time *he* wantsss to be God."

Shit. And haven't we all heard *that* somewhere before?

"Great. Look, Nathaniel's been trying to reach you. Any idea why?"

"None."

"Great again. Y'see a lotta shit's been happening since I saw you. Piles of it. And everything seems to revolve around…"

I stop, thinking.

"Yesss?"

"Shut it. I just thought of something…"

I've been reading this all wrong. If my brother's had daddy cooped up here all this time, then he's not after the key. He had the means to get it all along. What he said to Kibbutz must be so much bullshit. He wants near-space to fall. He wants onworld exodus. He wants the total destruction of the hostgod. Can't think why. Well, other than he's a brain-fucked megalomaniac. But, hey, what's new? He wanted the replication, but not to repair the virus. He wanted it to make sure he destroyed the last hope of saving XEs. That's why he's sent king dickhead out to East-11. When the offworlders come, they'll be walking into a trap. Whatever's left after that little spat's not going to look pretty. Shit, what possible motive could he have for that?

Then I have it.

Immortality.

Once XEs falls he has the means to recreate it. And then he gets to control XEs completely. No more share and share alike. No more neutral central power. And if he controls XEs, he controls near-space. Sweet. Don't know why I didn't see it before. And when that happens, Joseph gets the fountain of fucking youth to drink for all eternity. He wants to be God and that's just what he's going to be. Cunting king of the whole fucking universe.

"Daddy, I want the key."

"The key?"

"Don't act the innocent. Just give it to me."

There's a strange shimmering of reality as the intricate genetic protocol is passed between us. All three billion digits of the deoxyribonucleic chromosome. Reuniting me with the code I had cut out my brain all those years ago. I had enough of it to access the simulation, but only he's got the entire disease-free whole. Once the data's transferred, I alter the complex string down to five simple letters:

>EXILE

Then lean against the lid of my father's coffin. The top slides off easily. Swinging on hidden hinges. Inside daddy wallows in a lime blancmange. Wires lattice the soup. Pump life through the wrinkled fuck.

"You look like shit, daddy."

"Yesss…"

I know what's next to do. It's the only thing to cover my sorry ass. Still, after all this time, I feel I should say a few words to the old fucker.

I kneel. Kneel and pray. Pray like I've prayed every day I suffered in the place known as Dead City.

"Hey father, you up in Heaven? Hallo, hear your name. Your kingdom's come, your life's undone on earth and hell and heaven. Hear me this day in my daily prayer and forgive me my self-centredness as I forgive you who have fucked up my entire existence. You led me to damnation. You delivered me to the evil ones. Now I want your kingdom, your power and your glory. Forever and ever: Amen."

Stand and take a long last look down on the face of the man who made me.

Then take Lloyd's rusty sword and drive it through the fucker's ice-cold heart.

★

Once daddy's dead I escape his tomb. Head for the trapdoor. Prise the slab open with brute force and a little help from the tent pole. Easy when you know how. Outside creation's doing the same old balletics. I hardly give it a second glance. Destination's Sleepybubbyeland. I'm off for the hobby horse. From the air, the ubiquitous yellow road sticks out like a virgin at an orgy. Follow it to toy town. Complete with an array of quaint houses. All painted in primary colours. Sickly sweet.

Land in the central square. Everything's tiny. Feel like an invading giant. Can't see no horse. Squeeze into a place called Dolly's House. Inside I find an untidy living room. Items obviously precious to the owner are crushed under my huge clumsy feet. Thankfully my acts of vandalism will probably go unnoticed in the general mess. Look around, then leave. This could take hours.

Eventually work my way through all the houses in the square. Turns up squat. Only then do I notice that the lane continues out the town and over a humpty-back bridge. I follow it. Come to a purple hill beyond which is a wooden fort. Seems more likely. Yet as I approach I hear something behind me.

Whirl around. There in the side of the hill is a stripy mound. And in this is a door to a dome-shaped burrow. A mailbox stands by the door. Announces this to be the home of mr hug-bunny.

The name sends a shiver down my spine.

As does the sight of the creature who bursts out of the burrow even as I turn.

Panicking I raise the shotgun, but I'm too slow. Way too slow. In a second the grinning animal has me in its clutches. Throws its cute furry arms around me. Hugs me. I look down. See the hug-bunny smiling up at me. Its grip's like iron. Squeezing. Squeezing.

"John Ewen Malorian has dropped the squeeky gonk. John Ewen Malorian has dropped the claw hammer. John Ewen Malorian has dropped the shotgun. John Ewen Malorian has dropped the shotgun shells. John Ewen Malorian has dropped the flagpole. John Ewen

Malorian has dropped the torch. John Ewen Malorian has dropped the gas mask."
 Shit, I can hardly breathe.
 "Mmmmm," says the hug-bunny. "I love's you."
 Sister, help!
 Whassup?
 Hug-bunny... got me... crushing me to... death.
 Ave maria!
 Don't ave fucking... maria... me.
 Get it off you!
 How?
 Beat it off! Anything!
 How'd you... do... it... in the park?
 Wonder Dog cut its throat.
 Oh.
 Use what strength I have to pick the creature up. Run forwards. Aim for the fucker's door. Hit it at full force. Unluckily it's not latched. Smash it open. Fall into the monster's lair.
 Inside I'm hit by a wash of cuteness. Wallpaper's printed with large-eyed kittens scampering playfully with flopsy bunny dragons. Crash into a happy bunny table. Send its contents – a bowl of yummy carrots – spilling to the carpeted floor. Whack my head and topple onto the little snuggle bed. Scream. Struggle. Even headbutt the fucker. Nothing works. Only makes it hug harder.
 Sister, there's got... a weakness...
 Jack?
 Find it!
 Air's not getting to my brain. Feel faint. Nauseous too. As if the wallpaper wasn't enough.
 Sister... hurry...
 I'm on it, Jack.
 Feel like I'm going to black out. Any moment. Feel like my ribs are close to cracking. Feel as if its squeezing the shit out my ass crack.
 Sister...

Got it!
What… say?
Hold on, I'm reading…
Can't… I'm dying…
One moment…

The room spins. All snuggle beds and bunny dragons. I squirm in the spilt carrots. I gasp for every breath.

Give him a kiss.
What?
That's all that happens. He's only playing.
Yeah… right…
Says here that Jack hugs and kisses the bunny before sitting down for a nice bowl of yummy carrots.
You… kid… me.
No, s'what it says.

Puckering up, I lean forward. Closer towards the rabbit's moronic lapine grin. Strain with every last ounce of energy. Slowly I get nearer and nearer. Crane my neck. Bite back the intense pain. And touch my lips against the fucker's huge buck teeth.

"Mmmmm," says the hug-bunny. Then lets me go.

Fall to the floor. Choking in air. Flounder like a landed cod. Battered. Bruised. Teetering on the precipice of unconsciousness. Grimly, I crawl back from the edge. Sit up and check for broken bones.

See the hug-bunny's already seated at the table. In each furry paw it holds an orange torpedo.

"Mmmmm, I love's you," it beams. "Does you want some yummy carrots?"

I'm already retreating. My hand itching for the discarded shotgun.

★

Pounded by stinging hail, I pull the wooden horse back into Faerieland. Creation's still on the blink. The gods have still got it in for me. Strange that they don't order an out-and-out air strike. Wonder why for a while. Then stop.

First I know about the lake is when I'm walking knee deep into it. Stop and retreat to the shore. By now, I'm pig-sick of this whole deal. Leave the toy horse on the bank. Find a coracle tied to a grassy knoll. Clamber in and set out for the island. Somehow the water turns the colour of blood. Then the colour of treacle. Then it's pitch. I take as little notice as I can. Instead I concentrate on paddling. Paddling and staying conscious.

Reach the faerie isle and clamber up into the wooded thicket. Beyond the barbed branches is a circle of stones. At the centre is the fay queen herself. She's dressed in billowing samite. Her hair swirls around the wooden crown like golden branches in some eldritch wind. Her eyes are like brilliant sapphires, as blue as the bluest skies.

"Traveller," she says. "You are well come to my sanctuary."

I stick out one trembling hand.

"Just hand it over, bitch!"

"Ah, yes, the hawthorn crown. The sign of peace and enchantment for my people since the dawn of..."

Lunge forwards. Grab the woman's neck and twist. Break it cleanly. Queen faerie shrieks once, then dies. Rip the crown from her head, then stomp back to the waiting boat.

★

The Big Black Knight awaits my return as if it's his cosmic destiny. I'm beyond giving a fuck. Limping up the hill I'm already attiring myself with the weapons, armour and other accoutrements laid down by this bastard's code. First I strap on the washboard. Next comes the platter and jar. The flagpole I stick under one arm, set the hawthorn crown upon my head and climb aboard the wooden horse. Last of all I pull out my slightly blooded lucky rabbit's foot and hang it around my neck.

Once I'm regaled in my collected junk, I say, "OK, I'm ready. Let's fight."

"Ah, but are you not forgetting something?"

"Am I?"

"The code of chivalry."

"Er, yeah. Right."

I don't know it of course. Ask Sister.

Can't help, I'm 'fraid. All it says here is that Jack recites them.

Think about this for a moment. Then remember all those times Midnight used to bang on about the God-U-Likes.

Sister, what's your religious creed again?

To defend the faith…

"To defend the faith…"

To champion the weak…

"To champion the weak…"

And to wage unceasing and merciless war against the infidel.

"And to wage unceasing and merciless war against the infidel."

The ebon-clad horseman gives me a strange look.

"Er… that's close enough. Let's fight!"

And with that he spurs his steed and comes galloping, full pelt, towards me. In return all I can do is sit there. Waiting for the moment when he pounds me into the turf. Above the sky turns to dark as if it's suddenly bored with daylight. In its place is a bitterly cold night. I shiver in my meagre clothes.

What's happening, Jack?

Er, nothing. Just waiting to be pulped to shit by the Big Black Knight.

Why?

So's I can get into the castle.

Why?

So's I can rescue the damsel in distress.

Why?

So's she grants me my heart's desire.

Why?

Because, you thick bitch, that's the only way I can think of to get to the top of the mountain.

Why don't you fly?

Because...

Aw, fuck. Exactly why don't I fly? Because I've been too pissing busy trying to play the game, that's why.

Groaning, I leap into the air. Just as the knight smashes headlong into the space where I was. Pulverises the hobby horse to matchwood. Drop the tent pole, platter and jar. Shrug as the hawthorn crown gets whipped away in the fierce wind. Cursing my own stupidity, grinding my teeth against the dark maelstrom, I fly straight for the misty-covered mountain.

★

First sight I get of the manse, rising moon's glinting off its latticed windows. Peeping above the northern rim of the isle. Flap till I'm almost directly over it. Place's creepy all right. Glimpse the rusty elevator car off to one side. There's a brick arch there too. The building sits on the other. Between them lies the wide smoking bowl of a volcano. All spitting ash and boiling cracks. Nice place. Wonder if they do time share? Descend onto the only path. More like a goat track close up. Winds toward the looming shadow of the house. Everywhere's thin yellow mist. Smells foul. Tastes fouler. Stings my eyes.

Move a little closer. Come across a ragged length of picket fencing. There's a mailbox too. The address plaque on the side announces this to be Horror House, 13 Haunted Mountain Track, Horrorland, X-Isle.

So this is Horror House. No kidding. Kinda cute though. All gothic towers and irregular angles. Whole thing's perched precariously between the edge of the volcano and the cliff. Wonder what they want for the insurance on this place. Must be heaps. The path ends up at the foot of the porch. Beside a set of worn, black steps. There's an unsettling rumbling from the volcano. Above the moon appears from behind dark clouds. It's full, of course. Probably never anything else.

Now here's something else that isn't mentioned in the book. Not mentioned at all. This is where I've got to tread carefully. Now I'm off limits as far as the story goes. Place changes my perception of the island. It's not at all like I imagined. Nothing like I wanted it to be. It's been tainted. Infected by my brother's presence. Sister was wrong. It's not my dream. Nor Pure's nor Dingo's nor Nathaniel's. It's Joseph's dream now. Or, at least, his version of the original. He inherited it and had no reference. He just took what was already created and started adding whatever came into his sick little mind. What else could he do? I had the book. D'Alessandro was locked away. Now it's no longer a faerie tale. Death has come to Xankhara.

I step into the cobwebbed porch.

Place's a mess. Red and black tiles are covered with mud. Large oak door's a century old at least. Tarnished with the dirt of ages. Bears a small stained glass panel and a big ornate knocker.

So I knock. Only seems polite.

Outside it starts raining. First growls of thunder fight over the grumbling volcano.

When I get no answer I knock again.

Time passes. Mist swirls round my feet. The storm discovers its an extrovert. Soon my ears are full of hissing.

This is perfect. The whole scene's just perfect. Now if only I can get inside and find Joseph's oh-so-secret room…

Hear the bolt being drawn. At the same time a clock strikes. Sounding the quarter hour. Without even thinking I know the time. It's as clichéd as the rest of this place. Eleven fifteen. Forty-five minutes till everything's over. Well, for Nathaniel at least. Yet even as I think this I know it's not just D'Alessandro who's for the chop. Something's going down and at twelve we're all gonna find out just what my brother's been up to.

I shiver.

Quite natural really. For here I am at a quarter to midnight up on Haunted Mountain trying to get into Horror House. How do I get myself into these messes?

Slowly the door's eased inwards. There's the usual creak and the parting of long undisturbed cobwebs. Sliver of a face peers out. Its single piggy eye squinting between a mass of wrinkles and small rounded spectacles. It's the Little Old Lady. Risen from the dead.

Hey, Nowhereman. Wonder Dog here. You hearing me?

Uh-huh.

The Huntress has entered Kasikianu air-space and we's just been hailed by Osakimo security.

OK, tell 'em you're coming in.

Affirmative.

Sister, just heard the news. Get to Nathaniel. You don't have much time.

But, Jack...

Go for it. I'll be fine.

You sure?

No, Midnight. I'm in the faerie tale from hell and I'm anything but sure...

Just go.

OK.

The bleary orb watches me like a hawk. Still holds an unasked question. Ignore it.

"My good lady," I say, fingering the shotgun's trigger behind my back. "May I enquire if you have a room for the night?"

41 | D'ALESSANDRO

Having thought that in my wild and crazy simulated existence I'd seen everything, witnessed the best, the worst and the downright weird, opened myself to the freaks and the fools and the full unadulterated monty haul of all the stream has to offer, I am a little shocked when my family arrive. Well, more shocked at the fact that there was anything *left* to shock me. Yet this does. One moment I lay waiting for the last sands of my personal hourglass to slip by, contemplating again upon the sheer impossible absurdity of my predicament, the next I'm torn from my meditation and manhandled down the lifeless grey passage into another featureless room. This one is painted in grey and crimson, half and half, has two identical sets of doors and is furnished with a line of battered chairs and a water fountain. Strangely I am not manacled to anything. Even stranger, I am left alone.

Immediately I start banging on the metal, which resounds impressively, demanding to be told what is happening. Through the slot a voice mumbles something. At first I don't catch it, but then somehow my overactive mind manages to decode three fragile words.

"You have visitors."

Almost immediately the other door opens. And in walks my family.

Esther comes first, her dreadlocks tied like a great spider above the dark chocolate of her features. Her eyes shine as they always have, announcing her as a dark angelic avatar fallen to earth to avenge the heavens. Behind comes Susannah, her paleness, size and hair colour in total contrast to her companion. The pink plastic of her scant clothing seems a little risqué for this climate, but I let it pass. Behind her comes Elliott who looks the most ridiculous of the trio, done up as he is as the family mutt. How they ever got him to wear a lead I'll never know. Or to take off his skates.

Behind them Haruko shuffles in the shadows announcing to all assembled that we have five minutes. I hardly hear him.

Completely stunned I watch the fantastical trio file into the room and take their seats. Numbly I take mine, wanting to be seated before my legs turn to jelly and give under me. I face them and wait for the door to close. Only then are we alone.

For a while we sit in silence. I am silent because it has just occurred to me the bare-faced audacity of what these three have just done. They because with the bruises, tattoo, bald head and everything, I guess I look a little different than expected. Maybe they're wondering why they bothered. It's a long way to come to be presented with something as battered and malnourished as me.

I look along the ranks. Elliott coughs. Susannah rearranges her cramped bosom. And Esther? Well, Esther appears to be concentrating extremely hard. At first I'm confused by this. At first I don't understand. Then I do.

"They took it out," I say.

Esther frowns. All three exchange glances. Then: "Guess that means we've got to talk," she croaks.

Her voice is like some blasted angel of mercy. All cracked and beautiful. The sound of it brings back the flood of emotion that I feel for this woman. My eyes well tears.

"Yes," I manage. "I guess it does."

Following her glance toward the door, I add furtively: "Oh, don't worry about the guards. This room's sanctioned. It's secure by law."

"We're here to see you," Susannah chips in. "Y'know, before they poke you."

"That's nice," I reply formally.

"Woof," says Elliott.

"Nathaniel..." Esther manages. "Jack sent us."

Casually I glance at her and try to smile.

"Of course he did. He said he would. But just how did you manage it?"

"It was queen bitch's idea," Susannah interjects. "We're your next of kin. I'm your daughter, Mary-Lou, and this is our pup, Nobby."

Elliott woofs again and lolls his tongue – the perfect canine cliché – but my eyes never leave Esther's.

"Aren't you a little *black* to be my mother?" I say.

The warrior-priestess blushes and breaks my stare. She studies her feet for a while, then looks up. When our eyes meet again, hers too are filled with tears.

"I'm so glad you're alive."

"What's the time?"

She checks.

"Eleven twenty-eight."

"Well, not for much longer. Still, it's really good seeing you... you know... at the end."

"We've come to get you out."

"I know. And don't think I'm not totally and utterly grateful and everything, but there's just one snag."

"What's that?"

"It's impossible."

Esther opens her perfect mouth to reply, but Susannah butts in before her.

"Look, you patronising motherfucker, we didn't come here to catch up on old times. The deal's simple. In about a minute those bastards will be coming to take you to the death tank, so shut up and listen. Just before midnight there's gonna be one almighty bang. Should take out most of this wing and force them to abort. That's when we'll spring you. Clear?"

"As mud."

"Good."

I look back at Esther, beseeching her to explain what is going on.

I am still waiting when both doors shudder open. Haruko appears at one, Akahiri at the other. In near perfectly synchronised movements they stride into the room like robots pushing soap powder at the local mall.

"It is time," Akahiri says.

We all stand and I move towards Esther, intent on throwing my arms around her. Seeing this, she steps back, unprepared for my approach.

"May God Mûhamet walk with you," she whispers, then turns and flees the dreary chamber. Susannah follows, hauling the family mutt behind her.

"It was swell, daddio," she says.

"Woof?" adds Elliott, shrugging.

Haruko follows them making sure that they file towards the exit, while Akahiri re-manacles my hands and feet. Then they lead me back to the other door and the sterile corridor beyond.

No doubt my executioners wonder why I am smiling.

42 | PURE

Well, this is going nowhere fast. Here we are at the top of the world trying to save some skeletal jerk-off about to get the needle for killing some jacked-up nobody in some half-baked simulation about a million years ago. Fucking miserable cunt too. Makes me wonder why I ever came back. Things across the sea weren't all that, but at least they weren't *this*. Glad for the drugs though. Help keep me sane. Visions have gone now. Now's just the warm glow. Years of bitter experience have taught me that's the calm before the storm, but, hey, them's the breaks.

Back aboard the Solar Huntress I sit waiting out the last few minutes of Nathaniel Glass. Ms black magic woman and Dingo have gone to watch. Best they're on hand when the shit goes down, else monkey man might cock up.

Two minutes. Nothing to do but wait. Wait and kill time.

Run my skinny fingers through my dry hair. Shake the sand from the roots. Flex my shoulder blades. Breathe deeply. Feel how that hurts my heart. Makes my crack contract. And that makes me shiver.

We are in the observation room. The shutters are raising. I can see Nathaniel strapped to the metal bed.

AOK. Ready on your signal.

Dumb bitch.

Lean forward and jack into the nearest finder. Patch into the Osakimo nightflier. Request access and remote. Start the numbers and hear the engines fire. Click into the t-freighter's backbone and open the hold. The white ship's going to act as our guided missile, our diversion and our way to bust the suit out. All in one.

After my reunion with Jack, after getting the hit I wanted and discovering that Lucille – the big beauty school drop-out – had gone to that little, ol' maltshop in the sky I have to say it's all about as satisfying as zero-calorie chocolate. I am still no closer to being Pure again. Not really. I am no closer to ridding myself of this self-loathing. Or getting my revenge. I am gorgeous. This shouldn't be happening to me. I need to take matters into my own hands. But time's against me right now.

There's a guard at the porthole. He's checking the systems.

White bird's online.

Let her fly.

Affirmative.

Hit launch and feel the Huntress shudder. Lasts about three seconds.

The bird has flown.

Flip to the other chair. Plug into pilot and watch the constructs map the prison bay. See the flier as a green missile. Crosses the dock like a cat with its tail on fire. Then it hits the wall below the control room and the whole world erupts in flame.

43 | DINGO THE WONDER DOG

Watching Nathaniel being tied to the slab, I can't help but think that there must be better ways to spend the weekend. Swinging my legs on the bench, it's all I can do not to yawn. The faceless guard arranges the needle machine, finishes with a few little bows, then leaves. Next I see him he's in a further chamber that's stacked with gleaming consoles. There he begins his final preparations, while above the clock announces that it's eleven fifty-eight.

Two minutes.

Sheesh, seems like an eternity.

With as slow a gesture as I can I pull the comic from the back pouch in my utility belt and rezz it on. Whap through to the last viewed. *Wonder Dog in Wongo*. Sneakily scan the opening windows. Phantom's trapped with the stunningly beautiful Astral in the crushing White Hole Puzzle Box on Thalassia-5. They're battling forces of gravity at ten-to-the-solar-power-of-ten-trillion which is pushing them together like big fat pancakes in a sardine tin. Scenes flip to 23rdxenturyboy in the Black Hole Manse of Dr Rico Zimpel on the lost planet of Wongo. He's trying to defuse the situation and also a million-megatronic combination code to the Box. But as distracting as the tri-D panels and flashing speech bubbles are when I think of the Wonder Dog's sidekick, when I think of what's happening to the professor, all I can think of is Benjie. How we busted outta the cages at the RuZu Dome and met Bixby and went on all those amazing and scary adventures ourselves. About how I miss him and how he died that night on the big push at City Hall.

Tiny tears form at the side of my big mutt eyes, and seeing this Esther bends down and wraps one of her big strong arms around my haunches.

"Hey, there," she says. "Ain't you supposed to be a big tough superhero?"

Loll my tongue and nod, but my tail's not in it. And any further conversations is cut short by the sound of the gigantic explosion.

Out of the silence we feel its vibrations rippling up from the floor and through us. It's like the planet's giving birth or something. For a few moments all seems well, then there's another shudder and the lights blink twice. Then there's a third and the whole room's plunged into blackness. Not liking the dark much I give a little yelp, but Sister is already moving. Reaching for the metal bench on which we sit, the muscled woman tips me off and heaves it into her arms. Fumble for my teeny-weeny torch. In its silver light I see her aim the seat at the curved window. Not made for such flagrant abuse it breaks into a zillion pieces. Showers the whole death chamber with twinkling crystal.

"Dingo," she hisses as she leaps for the hole. "Get the door…"

Sullenly, I pad over to the metal hatchway. Walking is such a drag. It's at times like this when I really miss my wheels. I also miss my auto and my bypass kit, but that's all stowed back at the ship. The lock's simple enough, though. Old tech from about thirty years ago. Should be no problemo. Hopefully they'll be no one on the other side. Hopefully they'll all be running around like headless chickens trying to put the fire out. I sure as nothing don't want to meet one of them. Y'see, without a weapon my bark is worse than my bite.

In my mind, I run the numbers. As far as Sister could find out, this place is manned by less than twenty for most of the year, and at least seven of those are non-combatant. Still that leaves fourteen heavily armed nutters intent on kicking our respective butts. Let's hope Pure managed to blow out the hangar doors, otherwise we're gonna be sucking the big one when we try to skedaddle this mess.

I have the lock sussed in about twenty seconds. It's all pretty basic electrics. Nothing complicated or anything. With a creak I open it a crack and peer into the corridor.

Outside it's raining. The explosion's triggered the sprinklers. Whole place's awash with soapy water. Ugh, looks like I'm gonna get my fur wet. As if things weren't bad enough.

Skip out into the downpour and head to the next door. As I go I tug the improvised collar from my neck and cast it to the puddled floor. This one's painted a rather lurid red. Pretty apt for the death tank. Fortunately for everyone concerned, this lock's even sweeter. Once I pull the locking clip the insides spill like multi-coloured entrails. There's even a handy circuit diagram pasted on the back of the little flap.

Wow, after all this time, looks like the Wonder Dog finally lucked-out!

44 | SISTER MIDNIGHT

I watch without pleasure as the glass yields under the weight of the metal bench and shatters into fragments. Breaking like a little girl's heart. Like *my* heart. Unwittingly I think of Jack. My soul cries out for him. Longs for him. Then I am leaping through the jagged hole, my fingers numb to the way they snag and tear on the translucent teeth. The emergency lights cut in as I leap to Nathaniel's side, bathing the scene in crimson. His eyes are wide as I grab the leather straps and rip them from the slab. Below me the feeble man shudders as if afraid. In the red light his bruises look like black flowers.

"Where's Jack?" he asks breathlessly.

"In the tank."

"The tank?"

"On the ship."

"I have to reach him."

"We'll have to see about that."

"Esther, I–"

"Look, Nathaniel, let's get something straight here. I'm only helping you 'cause you might – just might – have the answers I seek. That is why I am on this mission to free you. That and nothing else. Are we clear with that?"

Through the opposite window I am aware of Nathaniel's executioner who is panicking as his equipment rezzes out. With a snarl I look around for a way to reach him.

"Is there a plan here?" the man on the killing table asks.

I afford him no more than a bitter glance then shove him to his feet.

"Nope, we're running on auto."

Nathaniel staggers on his bird-thin legs, horrified as I reach down, grab the metal slab and start ripping it from its pod-like stand. Muscles straining I lean back into the weight of it, trying not to stagger.

"This is madness!" the replicator bleats.

"No madder than anything else I been through this week," I say back.

And with that I haul the table over my head and hurl it through the control room window. The glass explodes in a hail of ice and the guard recoils, his hands dancing wildly in stark contrast to his impassionate faceplate. The slab hits him like a hammer, knocking him back and pinning him to the floor. In one movement, I vault into the second chamber and jump onto the slab. Distantly I can hear the guard's frantic screaming as his legs and torso are crushed beneath my weight, but I ignore it. Walking up the makeshift ramp, I kick his helmet with one steel toe-capped boot, cracking it like an egg at breakfast. Inside Akahiri is wailing like a banshee, his oval mouth just visible past the rim of splinters. Reaching him I kneel upon his chest, chanting in my torn clothes, joining my yells with his. Then I grab the guard's jaundiced face and tug it back and forth across the dark crown of jagged glass. Razor slices flesh. Now the guard truly screams. Screams and screams and screams. And when he's done screaming, he dies.

Stopping my feral cries, I regard the body. The sight of another corpse making me sad. How many must perish on this weird crusade? Crossing myself, I lean forwards and fish the dead man's stunner from his waist. Then I climb back into the wrecked death tank only to find Nathaniel watching me. In his eyes I see open gratitude, admiration, indebtedness. I see all these things and perhaps a little more.

"Stop looking at me like that."

"Like what?"

"*That.*"

With a creak, the grey metal door beside us swings open. It's the Wonder Dog, his paws full of twisted wires and circuitry. He's soaked, his fur matted over his eyes and muzzle.

"Howdy, folks. I'll be your guide for today's tour. Now if you'd just care to step this way…"

I nod my thanks. Then reaching out I take Nathaniel by one of his long-fingered hands and pull him out into the lifeless corridor beyond. He follows obediently like a little child. Follows as if I'm leading him into the promised land.

45 | THE NOWHEREMAN

Granny witch bitch regards me for a moment. Regards me, then says, "Fuck off, sonny, I don't do bed and breakfast." I'm shocked. Maybe, 'cause that's not the sort of reception I was expecting. Maybe 'cause she's not supposed to be alive. First I think it's funny that she's not full of molten shell fragments. Then maybe I don't. Who knows what's going on in this shitting madhouse. Mist swirls at my back. Hear wolves howling. Darkness skulks waiting. Try to keep my mind on the job in hand. And that is?

Somewhere in this gothic joke's my brother's secret room. Need to find it if I've got any chance with the replication. Or restoring this place to its original state. Right, that's that. Best get sorted.

Forget granny. Step back and kick the door. Boot the old bitch back into the candlelit hallway. Stride in. Entrance hall's a peach. All classic oak panelling and black and white tiles. Real air of mystery. Doors lead off most ways while a staircase sweeps up to a long balcony. Wide enough to drive cattle. Little Old Lady's sprawled across the tiles. Face's a knot of hate. Too bad. Still, that's not the only thing that's different. For starters she's white as a sheet. Her nails are talons. Got fangs too. Oh, and a two-handed, blood-spattered axe.

There's a low growl behind me. Turn just in time to see the Strapping Young Man crouching on the doorstep. He's changed too. Now he's a wolfman. Big rabid lump of lupine testosterone. All ripped red shirt and slavering jaws. Guess things change around here when the sun goes down. He leaps even as I clap eyes on him. Instinctively I kick out at the door. Smack it right in the fucker's face. Move to it and slam home the bolts.

Turn back. And into the wrinkled face of Dracula's mother.

"Time to die, you worthless, cock-sucking ball of pus!" she shrieks. Sounds so like me it's scary.

Duck as she buries the axe blade deep into the oak door. Dodge twice, then head for the stairs. Just in time to see the ghost of the faerie queen sweep through the downstairs panelling.

What the fuck's going on here? Don't wait to find out. Instead I run for my life.

Take the carpeted stairs three at a time. Behind me I hear the Little Old Lady screaming like a loon. Screaming and pulling back the bolts.

From the balcony runs a vaulted corridor. More doors than I can comfortably count. Both ways. All along the wall and double sets at every arch. There's a grandfather clock here too. Ticking louder than my heart. Plus lots of paintings. Must be some kind of gallery. Behind me, the welcoming committee begin to sort out their un-lives. Start to stagger, bound and float up the staircase after me. Granny's swinging her axe. Queenie's rattling her chains. Wolfman's foaming at the fucking mouth.

Force my back against the clock. Topple it and watch as it crashes down the stairs. Breaks to splinters. Vomits gears and cogs. Also crashes into my pursuers. Knocks granny and wolfie to shit. Sweeps right through the ghost lady though.

Look both ways along the gallery.

Which way, Jack? Fuck knows. Could be anywhere.

This is hopeless. I'm fucked. Unless…

"Bêz, psyche, Ianus."

"Initiating psyche sequence. Implementing Ianus sequence. Psyche completed."

"Well, well, Jack. You certainly do have a knack of pissing people off."

"Guess killing people does that. Where's Malorian's room?"

"Surely that would be telling."

"Look, I don't have time for the fucking guided tour. Just tell me where it is?"

"Why ask me?"

"Well, you're the shitting god of all knowledge, aren't you?"

Ianus laughs. Shrilly. Like a little bird.

"Why, so I am! You have me there, Jack."

Cast a look down at the apparition. She's about three metres and closing. The other two freak-cakes are already crawling from the wreckage. Already clawing their way back up the stairs toward me.

"Where's the room, you piece of festering shit!"

"Eleventh on the right."

Run down the arched gallery. Counting the doors as I go. Stop at number eleven. Didn't have to bother. S'the last one anyway. Grab the handle. Twist it. Push it. Force it. Nothing. Locked.

Figures.

There's a window beside me. Lace curtains dancing in an angry wind. Outside creation's dancing too. There's a storm breaking. It's the end of the fucking world. Sky's purple and red. Trees are flying. Stars are falling. The whole bit. Ground's boiling with the rain. Also spitting out living dead like extras in a Che Castella movie.

Fuck this. This is worse than the Mirrormaze. Kick the door. Slam into it. Doesn't even rattle.

Back down the corridor the werewolf vaults the balcony. Skids on the carpet. Sees me and comes full steam. Straight through ghost woman. Fucker'll be here in about five. Closely followed by vamp gramp and the grey lady. Throw myself back to the nearest arch and whack the double doors closed. Smash one of the pictures. Use the broken frame as a kind of bolt. Stagger backwards. Confused.

So what's next, Jackie-boy?

"Ianus, where's the key?"

Laughing. Resounding through the whole house. Bricks and mortar tremble with it.

"Ianus!" I scream. "Where's the cunting key!"

Nothing.

All the gods are out to lunch.

There's an ominous thump on the door as wolfie arrives. Wooden jamb holds it. Won't for long though. Wildly whirl around. Apart from the window there's another two doors. Maybe they lead someplace useful. Don't get chance to find out. For just then I hear a splintering thud against the double doors.

Wham!

I stop, sweating. Trying to catch my breath.

Whassat?

The sound comes again. Louder this time. The door leaps in its bevelled frame. Like it's scared or something. Takes till the third time to realise what it is.

Good ol' granny's axing through the fucking door.

Wham!

On the next strike, the head of the bitch's axe starts to peek through the door. Frame strains against the gold-effect handles. Jambs shudder. Snatch a look back to the other doors. Two choices. Try both. Behind each lies a set of dark spiral stairs. One going up. One going down. Wham! Another sickening strike. More splintering. Wolfie's howls of joy. So much for this idea.

Choose up. Don't think why. Just react. Might have something to do with the fact that the ground floor's a zombie tea party. No-brainer.

Check for a lock as I pass through. No lock. Great. Have to put as much distance between me and them as I can.

Run up the dusty steps. Twists into a cluttered attic. Place's a bombsite. Moonlight streams through four narrow windows, one in each wall. Looking out over roofs. Ceiling's a pyramid of grey tiles. Course there's bats, too. What else would there be? They're hanging from the beams. Thick cables run down the walls. Disappear behind piles of grimy crates.

Whirl. Spin on my heels. Searching for a way out. Know even before I turn a hundred and eighty it's a dead end. Three-sixty proves it. No way city. End of the line. All change, please.

Wham! Wham! Wham!

With a crash I hear the gallery doors break into matchwood. Granny's shriek of delight. Lumberjack's baying. Whirl again. Frantically try to locate *something*. S'useless. Nothing here but bats and boxes.

Great. Now what?

My eyes lock on some papers on top of one of the crates. Move across. Take a good look. In the silvery light can just make out a scribbled diagram and a map. It's the house. Original blueprints. All crisp lines and calligraphed names. Diagram's more amateurish. At first it looks like some everyday object rendered obscure by a child's scrawl. Then I see I'm way off. It's more technical than that. Impossibly rushed, but still possessing a certain sense. Realise it's a laser. Then I realise that it must have been drawn by Lloyd.

Flash of the poor bastard at the bottom of the spiked pit. Way to go.

Why would Lloyd be building a laser? It's hardly the sort of thing you'd do. Especially around here. Seems to be a lot of trouble for nothing. Usually means it's about as important as things get.

Snap back at the splintering of the second door. Bit gratuitous. Wasn't even locked. Still not long now. Hear footsteps. Coming up the stairs. Fuck, don't they have time-outs in this game?

Grab the papers, stuff them in my pants, then leap to the nearest window and fling it open. Immediately the storm blasts in. Consigning the dust and cobwebs to oblivion. Puts the wind up most of the bats too. One minute they're catching the zees. Next they're sucked up by Typhoon Annie.

Outside the ledge's slick with rain. No more than a hand's width wide either. Try not to look down. Try to get a grip on the eaves. Ice cold water pelts me. Stings my flesh. In a moment I'm soaked to the skin. Reach up and try to gain purchase. Dislodge a tile. Send it skidding off into the darkness. Far below it punctures glass. Look down. I'm over some weird greenhouse. Arboretum. Conservatory. Whatever it is it don't help much.

Find a hand hold. Reach into the gap. Curl my fingers around one of the thick cables. Pull hard. Test my weight.

A furry fist clamps around my left ankle. Quick as a cobra. Grabs it and yanks my leg back inside. Feel myself falling forwards. Flailing, I swing my other arm up to the cable. Kick hard. Try to fuck off by flying, but the werewolf holds me back. Succeeds in clamping a second paw around my other leg.

Pulling forwards I slip on the tiny sill. Legs jiggle in the air. Below I focus on the shining panes of the conservatory. All rusted gables and metal arches. Through the streams of water all looks lush and green. Lush and green and about five metres away through reinforced glass panels.

With about as much effort as I can muster, I pull again. One long, steady haul. Drag the unsuspecting lycanthrope halfway out the window. Lock my elbow around the cable. Pull again. Can hear granny screaming inside. Yelling for her compadre to get out the way. All the while bats pour through the open casement. Wolfman ignores her. Ignores the bats. Instead he clambers onto the sill. Releases one hand. Tries to claw at my belt.

"John Ewen Malorian has dropped the gas mask. John Ewen Malorian has dropped the claw hammer."

Mask skitters off the glass roof below. Hammer smashes straight through it.

My elbows burn. Joints crack. Fuck knows how they do this in a simulation, but it sure feels real to me.

Haul myself up to the guttering. Atop the tiled pyramid there's a weathervane. Swinging crazily in the grip of the storm. Crafted into an iron effigy. Looks like some pug-faced gargoyle.

Nice touch.

Granny and wolfman're still arguing. One inside, one out. In the heat of the debate he slips and falls from the sill. Almost drags me over. Then I'm hanging from the conduit, rain pouring down my arms and back with wolfie hanging on for grim death. Pull against my straining joints. Can't get myself up. Don't really know why I would want to anyway, but there you have it. Once I climb up to the weathervane that's about as dead end as you can get. Then remember I can fly and pull harder.

Looking down I see granny leaning out of the window. Axe in hand. She's swinging at my legs. Panicking I twist away from it. Force the dangling redneck into the blade's path. Bitch hits him right between his hairy shoulder blades. Blood pumps. Manages a quick yelp, then falls. Momentarily his arms windmill like some canine angel falling from dog heaven. Then he hits the angled glass and keeps on going. Turns the roof to a million pieces of frozen rain.

Well, that's a weight off my ankles.

I laugh. It's a mistake. Way too soon. Forget the guys upstairs are all out of humour.

A bolt of lightning strikes the weathervane. Turns my whole world to white. Feeds electricity down the cable. Down me too. Yelling, I'm blasted backwards. Caught in the radiant joy of electrical discharge. Then I plunge. Freewheeling. Pass through the splintered roof. Rip a hole in the verdant green canopy. Headed for the conservatory floor.

Shitfuckpissbuggerdamn.

Fall. Fall. Fall.

There's a splash and suddenly I'm drowning. Water's all around me. My mouth's full of it. First I think it's the gunk tank. Then I surface in the bowl of a vast sculpted fountain. Water's blood red and filled with sparkling glass. Wolfman's here too. Body sliced into bite-sized pieces. Diced from the fall. Around me crimson liquid sloshes over the scalloped sides while the rain streams in from above.

Dazed I haul ass out of the fountain. Lay gasping like a landed fish in the nearest herbaceous border. Above the sound of the storm I hear granny shrieking. It's about then that I notice the undead. They surround the place like the legions of the damned. Putrid faces pressed against the glass. Decomposing fingers trailing slime across each rain-soaked panel.

Haven't I been here somewhen before?

Allow myself a few more gasps of fetid air, then drag my battered body to its feet. The conservatory is alive, the air hot and moist. Huge pipes spout steam through grilles set in the floor while the untended plant life basks in the resulting tropical paradise. Overgrown creepers and dazzling varieties of flora abound. It's enough to warm the soul.

Have little time for that. Need to find the key to the master bedroom before world's end. Which judging by the way reality's acting is about two and a half minutes.

Fuck this game. Dig out the blueprints. Search around and find the claw hammer. Forget the gas mask. No way I'm going out there to get it. Instead I'm already moving for the door. Click on the torch and try to find out where I am. Locate the conservatory right off. By the look of things, outside's a corridor. Leads back to the great hall. No use going there.

Then I see something else.

Just off the entrance hall's another room. Marked as a chapel. Take one look at the decomposing posse beyond the smeary glass and nod. Then I start running.

★

Taking a time-out in the chapel.

Compared to the rest of the house, place's pretty simple. All bare stone and tiled floor. Leering imps and gargoyles adorn the arches. Only one window. Stained glass. Circular. Moonlight dappling through. All the usual stuff. There's little else. Just calm and peace and serenity.

Oh, and a cloth-covered altar.

Move past the grimy pews. Climb the steps. Scan what new objects this place presents before me. Candlesticks. Collection plate. Bible. Cliché, cliché, cliché. Still that doesn't stop me reaching for the crucifix as soon as I see it. It's tucked inside the good book. Marking some page or other. I resist looking. Just grab the silver cross and hang it around my neck.

"John Ewen Malorian has picked up the crucifix. Johann has picked up the cross. Juan. Juan. There can be only Juan…"

Ut-oh.

The voice of God's an ear-piercing childish screech. Life has Ianus by the balls. Who gives a fuck? Ignore it as only a man who's lost in his own self-worship can. Listen to the wind roaring outside. Zombie's low moans. Some unidentified thing clattering in the dark. Heave simulated air into my simulated lungs. Think safe. I'm safe now. At least from the onslaught of the denizens of Horror House. Must be what this place's for. Seems a reasonable assumption. Sit down on the altar steps. Sit and think about where I am and what's going on. Only way to figure out what happens next. If this place's so predictable then that should be no problem. Just got to remember it's all a game.

First things first, let's list the facts.

The gods are trying to kill me. Fact. Ever since I got here they've been hassling me. Right from the start when that lightning struck the dog box.

All AIs are hostile. Fact. Well, at least during the night.

The world's going crazy. Fact. Can't believe this island was created to be a madhouse. Must be something happening. Some reason why everything's going to shit.

Think. Nope. Think some more.

And then I remember.

It's me. I'm the reason. I'm the fly in the simulated ointment. It's like Bêz said, 'Where the hell *did* I come from?' That's the flaw. The bug. In a self-contained universe the omnipotent overlords have got a big dose of total impotence. Must be a big deal. Obviously. Bound to piss you off. Total control meets total jerk. And total jerk is winning. Well, at least is still *alive*. Think of Lloyd and that solves the mystery. I'd assumed he was unlucky. Just slipped and fell. Now it's odds-on he was pushed.

That's interesting. Throws up a number of pluses. If they didn't create me, they can't control me. Can't read my mind. Well, maybe not. Maybe being plugged into this rig, they can. But they can't prejudge me. Can't be one step ahead. If I don't think, I can be one step ahead. Either that or I'm trapped in this personal hell forever. So what's next? Apart from keeping alive, I'm still on a mission to get into Malorian's den. Need the key. Have no idea where it'd be. Dig out the map. Scour the rooms. Then I see it. Servant's quarters. Little Old Lady's the housekeeper. Figures she'd have them. Maybe. Maybe not. Still, worth a try. After all I'm armed with this here crucifix. Might know nothing, but I know that's good against vampires. She's got the right dentures for a spot of open-heart surgery too.

Look at the map again. Locate a series of chambers under the house. Right under me now there's a crypt. Hey, well that figures. What haunted house would be complete without its very own en suite mausoleum? It's interconnected with others. Wine cellar. Laboratory.

And there at the end is a door marked 'Home'.

Right, that settles it. Time-out's over. Now it's time for Operation Stake The Bitch.

★

Steps beneath the altar crumble as I descend. Crypt's more like a hollowed cave. Looks like it's been around a whole lot longer than the house. Also it's dark. 'Bout as dark as dark gets. Play the torch over everything. Low ceiling. Lots of stone coffins. Set on plinths. Few crates too. Piled up near the steps.

What a dreary hole.

Examine the crates. Branded into the sides of each is a brief description of its contents. I read, 'Dried Staples', 'Agricultural Gubbins' and 'Delete@newbuild'. Obviously not a well-travelled location. What's more interesting is the apron, feather duster and backless mules lying behind the boxes. Looks like this is where granny gets her kit off. Kneel down and rummage through the stuff. Find a bottle of beeswax, a grubby cloth… and a platinum grey keycard. Got the letters 'JKM' embossed on both sides. Bingorama, baby! Snatch it up, then turn for the steps. And right into a hunched shape of utter blackness.

"Not so fast, sonny," says the shape.

It's the vamp gramp. Sucking her lip in the shadows. Torch picks out her wrinkles. Wrinkles and septic yellow stare.

"Hiya," I say, as cheerily as the situation allows. "Nice place. Homely. Must be great 'round Hallowe'en."

The Little Old Lady grins like a vulture sucking entrails out of a bucket.

"Time's up, junior. There's nowhere else to run!"

Fuck you, witch. Grab for the crucifix. Force it up in the air between us. Grin back at the haggard crone.

"Out of my way, you blood-sucking bitch!"

Spit it out. Really yell it. Sounds pretty cool in the confined cave. Present the little silver cross. Walk forwards. Still grinning. Try to force granny away from the only exit.

As I advance the housekeeper from hell moves back a few paces. Moves away, then stops. What's with this shit?

I keep on going. Intent on getting a head start up to the chapel. She's not a fast mover anyhow. Easily outrun her to the gallery. From then on, I'm home free. Granny has other ideas. After stopping, she reaches out one bony hand and grabs the little cross. I'm too stunned to stop her. Instead of her withered fist going pfsst and melting or something, she tears the bloody thing out of my hand and tosses it behind her. Still grinning.

"How?" I stammer.

"No hope."

"Eh?"

"No faith, no hope."

"Oh."

Flee from the crypt. Into the wine cellar. Heading for the lab. Only manage about three or four steps.

Then she's upon me. Knocking me down. Fangs slavering for my jugular. I sprawl. Hands clawing dust. Trying to keep my neck away from her mouth. For a moment I'm scrabbling in the dirt. Then my mind clears. Years of street training kicking in. No way this motherfucker's gonna bring me in. Not after all I've been through. Bring up the shotgun. Witch knocks it away with one casual backhand. Try to find something useful at my belt. No joy. Fist clutches air. Just air. Granny's jaws snap in front of my face. Can smell her peppermint breath. S'too awful for words. She's strong too. Far too strong. I'm never gonna get her off me.

No faith, no hope.

Like Sister said, it's all about belief. Flying, the crucifix, everything. And after living this whole fucked-up existence, wasn't that – that simple little thing – just exactly what I wanted more than anything else in the world?

Sister. You clear yet?

Yessum. We're nearly at the Huntress now.

Great, I was getting a little lonely.

What's up your side?

Sorta fighting for my life.

Oh.

Granny claws my face and forearms. Scratches me with her death-cold nails. Struggle to kick her off. We tussle.

I need help, Esther.

What? Did I hear you right?

You heard me.

Say it again.

What?

Say it again.

Look, just find some way of helping.

Can't. Not until we get aboard. Try blonde girl.

OK.

Pure, you got Bixby there?

Yep. Mutt's right here.

Drag him down into the lab. Find an auxiliary and plug him in.

You serious?

Deadly.

Okay.

And make it quick.

Bitch and I are still tussling. Locked together. Embracing like two mating scorpions.

Feel exhausted. Muscles straining. Want it to be over. Not just this battle, but the whole goddamn war. Just want to lie down on a beach somewhere and soak up the rays till I fry. I want out. Stop the ride, I wanna get off! But the ride doesn't stop. Never has and never will. Not till the end and then I'm gonna be too busy dying to worry about anything else.

Granny's turned her attention to ripping my arms out their sockets. Can feel my joints ready to pop. Try to focus on keeping from losing them. Might come in handy later. Old lady's having none of it. Like I said she's too strong. Far too fucking strong. Fangs extend right in front of my face. Dripping with saliva. A gobbet lands in my left eye. Sight blurs till I blink it away.

C'mon, Pure. C'mon.

Hey, quit rushing me. This console's pretty tricky. Lots of knobs and stuff.

Great.

Force my head back as far as it'll go. Grind it against the dirt floor. Teeth flash bright. Bright and close. Real close. Too close. So close they look like sailboats. Fill my vision. But they still don't quite reach. And when granny realises this they snap together.

Snicker-snack. Snicker-snack. The yawning jaws clash like bleached rocks.

Susannah, I am going to die!

Yell it. Yell it loud in my mind.

Yeah, right. And I'm the virgin mother.

Pure. Pure!

There's a sudden shriek. Like a cat with a red-hot poker slipped up its pussy. S'the Little Old Lady. She's squealing like a pig. Oinking like she's being butt-fucked by the biggest dick since *King Dong Does the Dalton Cowboys*. Then the blood starts. Pumping out the back of the vampire's head. Buckets of it. Oinks turn to screams. Then she's dragged off me. Kicking and cussing and foul-mouthing.

I scuttle back. Try to put as much distance between us as is humanly possible. Back-peddle like a crab.

When I'm clear I see the mutt, his jaws clamped on the old dear's head. Practically bitten the back off her skull. Chomping on it with monster-sized jaws. Mauling her. Sucking the brains from her undead body. Yet he's no lovable mongrel now. Now he's Zoltan, Hound of Satan. Huge, hulking, evil.

Way to go, Bixby.

Is that OK?

Pure, you're the best.

Whatever.

Grab anything that comes to hand. It's a slat. Piece of broken crate. Pull myself up. Takes three tries but finally I'm there. Granny's haemorrhaging blood like she's some great big tick that just got squashed. Bixby, in true doggy style, begins shaking her. Twisting and grinding and twisting some more. Whirls the old bitch round and round. Throwing her about like a rapidly deflating blow-up girlfriend. Screaming's turned to a high-pitched whine. Kicking's not so strong either.

The great hound drags her back, still throwing her about and then finally I take the splintered stake and ram it through her heart. Pound it with the claw hammer.

Whack. Whack. Squish.

Granny goes limp. And once she stops moving Bixby drops the lifeless woman and looks up at me. His jowls're covered in the vampress' blood, his great teeth-laden mouth slavering. All red glowing eyes and lolling tongue. Now I look at him, there *is* a resemblance. An eerie one. Actually, now I look at him, he's actually pretty similar to the dog I know. Only bigger. Much bigger.

Must be affected like all the other stupid fucks in this place. Come moon-up, everyone turns into the cast of the Chamber of Horrors.

Something hits me. Smack! Straight between the eyes. First I think it's a bullet it hits so hard. Even reach up to feel for the hole. Yet this is no projectile. It's a thought. A sudden awesome realisation. On a scale of one to ten, this goes all the way to the top.

Look down at me. The me under the scabby clothes. It's no surprise when I find I've changed too. Body's twisted. Misshaped.

Under my pig-skin boots I have hooves. Hairy legs. Reach up and feel the horns on my head. Great. Guess I'm a horror too. Also smell like pork scratchings. No wonder Bixby's so interested. The hell hound growls like he's been on forty a day since weaning.

"Hiya, pooch," I say. "Good doggie."

Bixby growls again. Now it's like he's got something caught in his throat.

"Nice doggie," I coo.

The hellhound looks at me with his big, red eyes. Looks and lowers for the pounce.

OK, Pure. Pull him out.

Nothing.

Pull him out.

Hold it, Jack. I'm coming.

Forget the bitch. Just run. Headed for the wine cellar. With a spine-chilling howl the dog leaps after me. In a flash he's at my heels. Snarling.

All I can do is run, but I know I've got no chance.

It's a game. It's a game. It's a fucking game, game, game! Things jingle at my belt. Claw hammer, torch, lucky bunny foot…

And the squeeky gonk.

Of course. How'd I get to be so stupid?

Run. Run as fast as my beaten body can go. And as I do I toss the squeeky gonk behind me. And, like I guess he's supposed to, the mutt stops and I get away.

A game. It's all a game.

Ha bloody ha.

I'm delirious with excitement. Delirious and so pumped full of adrenaline I feel I'm gonna OD. In another two strides I come to a door. Keep going. Burst into the lab. Slam the wood behind me and look around.

Predictably, place's straight from some monster movie. All dressed up like some weird science fiction experiment.

First thing I notice are the monkeys. Perhaps because they're all stuffed up in a pile of cages against the wall. Mainly 'cause they all start screeching and hollering. Rest of the room's pretty nondescript. Dirty tiles on the floor. Brick. Dripping walls. That sort of thing. Smashed beakers, scribbled notes and formulae lie everywhere. Only after the monkeys quieten down are my eyes inexorably drawn to the strange framework that dominates the centre of the lab. Though resembling as it does an iron spider, what purpose it fulfils I cannot guess. Next to it a huge circuit breaker hangs suspended by wires. Connecting the framework, the switch and the rest of the room.

Then I remember the blueprints, and the room marked 'Home'.

If the map's correct, then the entrance should be just over my left shoulder.

Turn and find myself facing a blank wall.

What?

Slam myself up against the brickwork. It's solid as a cock. No door. No revolving chrome and glass entrance. No concierge. No nothing.

And then I notice the laser.

Well, I say laser, but it's more like a pile of junk really. Built from bits of this and bits of that. Only way I recognise it is from the scribbled diagram. The pipes. The mirrors. The garbage pile turned good.

It's pointing at the blank wall.

Lloyd must have been trying to escape. Used his expertise in laserology or whatever the fuck he was into to try to blast his way out. And then the fuckers killed him.

Check his diagram again. See why he was up in the attic. Wanted to power the whole thing with the lightning. Use the weathervane as a conductor. Hence the cables and the circuit breaker. Now that's ingenious. Still as I know shit nothing about all that, I ignore the contraption. Try to think.

I have the key. I've staked the bitch. I've got a clear run at Malorian's room. And I know those eternal fuckmeisters upstairs are not gonna make it that easy. They may not be able to read my mind, but they sure can crush me to death as easy as picking their noses. Fact that the world's out to lunch helps some. How much I'm about to find out.

    Guess I'd better sign in.
    Sister, how's it hanging?
    Loose. Sorta caught in a firefight.
    Story of your life.
    Tell me 'bout it.
    I have the key to bro's room. Gonna run for it.
    Go careful.
    Yeah, I will. Them goons'll not want me to get clear, that's for sure. See ya out the other side.
    May Mûhamet watch your every step.
    Yeah, Esther, that's just what I'm afraid of.
    But don't let myself think too long on that one. Just throw open the door and run through it.

★

Outside the laboratory, the whole world's gone to fuck. I've only taken three steps before the full horror of what's happening hits me. The wine cellar's not like I left it. Whole place's breaking up. Cracks the size of a whale's ass are appearing all over the room. Whole house's grinding like a two-dollar whore.

    Ignore it.
    No sign of the dog. At my feet lies the squeeky gonk. One side's a bit chewed. Other side's covered in dog gob. Pick it up anyway. Just for a keepsake. Seems an odd thing to do. Even to me. No one comments. there's just eerie, empty silence. The silence ends with this great hullabaloo. One vast cacophony. Hundreds of noises, voices and sounds all fighting to be heard. Everything louder than everything else. Numbing to the ears. Deafening. And above it all the Eternal Ones are yakking. All kinds of shit. Just try to shut it out. Can't, but still try.
    Then I run as if the Wild Hunt and all its host is on my tail.
    Dodging through the cellar I'm showered as the racks and racks of

vintage plonk explode on both sides. Fall into sudden gaping crevasses. Behind me the solidness of the laboratory door beckons, but I keep on running. Once I get to the crypt, find things have definitely taken a turn for the even worse. Before me the stone floor has been bitten off in a rough arc about a metre ahead. Grab the door frame for support. The world's coming apart. Reach the steps up to the chapel. Rise out into what I think's going to be some sort of sanctuary. I'm way wrong.

The chapel's no more. It's gone. Blasted. Broken. Condemned. So's the house and the isle in the void. Everything smashed into fragments by some gargantuan fist. Pieces of debris whirl in the storm around me. There's sections of walls, roofs, doors. All spiralling into nothingness. Air's full with objects. Randomly scattered. Caught up in some great cosmic tornado. Chairs. Rugs. Zombie flesh-eaters. The twister's out of control. Totally. Hurts the eyes trying to keep track of everything. Too much movement. Swirling. Swirling. Swirling. Nothing static. Nothing still. Brain goes dizzy with no point of reference.

Without thinking I look around. Try to make some sense of the chaotic puzzle above and below. Looks like all the island's here. It's just not very *together* right now.

Search the skies. Look for bits resembling the gallery. Takes a while, but then I see one. Nothing more than a railed section with a few paintings. Perhaps a section of torn carpet. But no mistaking it. It's too far away though. Got to get to it. Got to find the door that leads to Malorian's room.

Hold my breath and jump. Aim for a large section of garden. Try to fly, but that shit's as good as gone now. Fall. Flail my arms. Wilder than wild. Find that's about as much use as a second ass. Keep the flowerbeds in my sights though.

Isn't this where I came in?

By some miracle I seem to be heading straight for it. That feels OK. I'm long overdue for a slice of luck pie. Imagine the swaying grass. The softness of the impact. The spray of delicate petals as I fold my legs and roll with it. As I drop I settle into the knowledge that maybe it's not gonna be all that bad. So I'm surprised as anyone when the rock turns in mid-air and I fall right past it.

Shit, those fuckers are playing for keeps.

Fortunately while they're hauling horticulture they miss this huge lump of pyramid that just happens to be whizzing by. Hit it like a brick. Scrape about an arm's length before I get a grip. Drop the torch. Watch it skid off into the void. Wind whips the papers from my belt. Again no one comments at all.

Sheesh, this is gonna be tougher than I thought.

Against my better judgement, I stand up. Take a moment to get my bearings. Locate the gallery again and leap off. Half-propel, half-fly, to the roof of Dolly's House. Use a tumbling armoire in the middle. Then take three more leaps. From house to elevator car. From car to iron railings. From railings to grassy knoll.

Lightning blazes. Sears the hairs on my head, but no direct hits.

Look around and see I'm closer. Gallery's just below me. All I need to do is wait just one more second till it gets under me and…

I jump. Forget everything and launch myself off into the void. Windmill my arms as if that'll do shit.

I fall.

Fall.

Fall.

Fall.

Try to will my body closer to the chunk of architecture. Lock my eyes on the carpeted landing.

Yell blue murder as I miss it by a mile. Watch it soar by like a speeding jet. Fingers don't even come near it. Instead I crash into the attic tower. One moment I'm tumbling in freefall. Next I'm wrapped around the weathervane like a stick of liquorice. Slip, slide, then lock wrists and hang on. Tight. Breathe in frantic panting lungfuls. Gasp for air in the infinite reaches of space. Gasp and then scream. One long, agonising wail.

"John Ewen Malorian has missed the gallery. John Ewen Malorian has hit the weathervane. John has lost two hundred points."

Ianus, you cock-sucking, greasy...

Hang and seethe. No strength to do much about it. Try to squeeze my anger into movement. Fail. Feel the first fingers of despair. Clutching at my throat. Mustn't give in. Got to fight on. S'what I always do. Got to claw back. Climb back into the ring. Fight again. The gods're winning five games to zip, but if I go home at half-time there's no way I can score six.

Sound like my own cheerleader.

Rah, rah, rah. Gimme a J... Gimme an A... Gimme a C...

And it doesn't help one fuck. I'm just too cunting good at feeling sorry for myself.

"Executing midnight sequence. Implementing grand finalé. Sequence complete."

It's Ianus' voice again. Oddly clear in the chaos.

Got no cards left to play. No ideas left to try. No magic master plan to unveil to save the day. Guess it's time to switch to bullshit mode.

"Hey, fuckface. Ianus, you up there?"

"I am everywhere, godchild."

"Well, come down here."

"Why?" The word stings like a trapped wasp.

"'Cause I got something to say."

"What?"

"Something real important. Something you won't wanna miss."

"Yes?"

All around me, a face appears. Domed across the night sky. About twenty kilometres end to end. At first look's like Ianus, but it keeps changing. Altering. Flipping like a hundred flickbook cartoons. All shuffled in one. Mûhamet's there too. As is Bêz. In fact, just about everyone's there. Can't focus on it too long. Makes me feel sick.

"Explain yourself, Jack," the god in the sky bellows. Voice now pulsing between each of them.

"I have the answer you want. The answer of where I came from."

"And?"

"Let's make a pact. I give you the gen and you give me the way outta here." Whole deal's just like at Shrago's in reverse.

I smile my cat-piss smile. Stare up into the face of god almighty and grin. Will they go for it? Won't they?

"Deal," says the planet-sized face.

As quick as a wank a dozen broken lumps of rubble descend upon me. So fast I duck. Cower as they close in. Yet instead of smashing me flat they knit together. Shattered bricks rebuild. Carpets reweave. Wooden doors reform. And there floats the gallery. Completely restored. Good as new.

Leap the gap. Land almost facing the panelled door. The keycard itches in my pocket. Screaming to fuck the slot. I'm screaming too. Silently. So near and yet so far.

"The answer, Jack. What is the answer?"

"The answer's I come from outside. Beyond this place. You've been fooled. You're not divine. You're nothing. Omnipotent, my ass. On a scale of one to infinity, you're not even close."

Silence. Did they even hear that? Try my headman.

All points bulletin. Ianus, chew on this, you dizzy prick. I come from universe A. This is universe B. You've been duped. Joseph lied to you. He lied about everything.

Everything.

Suddenly out of the midnight they come. All seven of them. Ianus. Mûhamet. Bêz. Astarth. AEoseth. Kalím. Torûs. Their faces like death masks. Murder blue. Claws out like carrion birds. Looming there silently. Flinch as I think they're going to attack. Yet they don't. Don't do anything.

"Is this true?" they all say as one. Voice a strange mix. Like they're all fused together. One big pile of god gob.

"Yeah, it's true. Cross my heart. You got it wrong before. When you was ordering me about at the start. You have no authority to command *me*. I am Jack. You are Eternal Ones."

"Yet we are gods." they all say.

"Nope. You're characters from a kid's book. From a makebelieve lalaland faerie tale."

"And you can prove this?"

"Only by being here."

"We see."

"Plus," I add, "aren't true gods supposed to stay hidden? Y'know, exert a sense of mystery?"

"You speak of the Amen."

"Amen?"

"The supreme god of the ancient world."

"Oh, him. Nah, he's a faerie story too."

They all look mighty upset by this. Must be hard for ultimate beings of all knowledge to discover something they don't know. To meet someone they didn't create. S'like suddenly finding a book you didn't buy sitting on the shelves of your library. They can't deny that I'm an anomaly. Like Lloyd before me. They also can't deny they had a deal. But in that moment I know what their solution will be. Their all-encompassing antidote to the blank spaces on the map. And, as the cosmos begins boiling to vapour around me, I don't think it involves expanding their horizons.

Don't think about it, Nowhereman. Just do it. Think about it and they'll blast you to the other side of the universe. Don't think. Don't think. Just do. Look up into the myriad heavens. Pause, lose the smile, then with a mind as empty as my soul, I act. Throw myself at the door. In one movement I've got the plastic card in my hand and slam it into the lock. Even as the corridor explodes, I'm falling forwards. Tucking my legs under me. Trying to get away from the apocalypse at my back. One moment I'm watching the end of all creation...

The next I'm stepping into Malorian's room, deep in the heart of the god machine.

Place's different from all the others I've so far encountered. This is not the product of myth and fantasy. This is the pinnacle of sleek functionality. Much like big brother. Ceiling's a mass of motion-sensitive light panels which flick on as I appear. Walls're smooth plastic polymer. Floor's some glossy white shit. In the centre of all this sits a long polished wood and chrome desk. Drawn up beside it floats an anti-grav bucket seat. Desk's set up with a terminal, 3E unit, disc file, colour holo-globe. All retro stuff. Only other furniture is a four poster bed complete with drapes, sleep unit and dream monitor. Resembles a plastic coffin. Near the door's also a wall cabinet. On the back of the door hangs a brown leather jacket and fedora. Yeah, how very trés chic.

Teetering, I smile a raggedy smile.

I'm here. I made it. I. Made. It.

Here all is bright. All is calm. Here they can't touch me. I've beaten the fuckers. What can they possibly throw at me now? I'm home free and there's nothing they can do to stop me. All I need to do now is boot the system, upload the crystal and finish this shit. Once and for all.

There's a tiny beep. Then another.

Beep. Beep. Beep.

It's the terminal. Screen's lighting up with luminous green letters. Walk across and drop into the seat. Take a closer look.

>Executing mirror entry sequence. Gateway to X-Isle requested. Gateway to X-Isle opened. Sequence complete.

What the fuck–? My way out of here. It's open. It's a bloody fucking miracle.

For the first time in ages, I actually feel happy. Lasts about three seconds. As that's how long it is until I see the next line.

>Initiating entry sequence. Joseph Karl Malorian has entered the X-Isle. Sequence complete.

46 | D'ALESSANDRO

After our inconceivable escape from the concrete bowels of the Kasikianu Imperial Detention Unit, the established boundaries of what I deem possible are still being destruction tested right before my very eyes. Indeed, in the last fifteen minutes I have borne witness to more information than the sum total of all my collected experiences over the last forty-eight months. Admittedly during my incarceration these have been a trifle limited, but somehow I feel that even had I been living what one would call a *normal* life, this encounter would still have ground my mind into spam regardless.

Since hauling me from my death bed Esther, Elliott and I have braved the water-soaked corridors of D wing, dodged bullets fired randomly through the smoke and heat of the central core, leapt the flames and rubble in our race to reach the hangar and finally scuttled aboard the magnificent t-freighter while the world and its aunt have desperately tried to blow us to smithereens.

Now I dry myself in the central hub of the transport, set like a circular pod around the cabin, facility and control corridors. Dry myself and wonder at the sheer audacity of my rescue and, though I am shocked to discover it, this thought brings a little smile to my face. Who knows how many we killed as we crawled on our bellies through the grey labyrinth of the prison. Or at least how many Sister Midnight did. Her technique was simple but effective. Armed at first with only a stunner she stabbed at the guards' shins, while their torsos were lost in the heavy smoke above. Then after bringing them down, this allowed the ebony priestess to break their necks. She did this almost as if it were a courtesy – like a service offered at no extra charge – and in this way gained some standard-issue firearms. Then the real carnage began. As I said, I could not guess at how many she killed.

Amazed I check the chronometer.

00:15:49.

Could all of this really have happened in such a brief amount of time? After all, it was only at midnight when I was strapped to that freezing slab…

Midnight. I was to die at midnight.

With a shiver I clearly remember my words to Baseeq, the sentence ice cold in my mind.

If I die at midnight–

I glance back at the chronometer.

00:15:56.

Of course, if he were under the mistaken impression that the execution had gone ahead, it would still take some time to carry out my orders. If he were to initiate the destruct sequence he would first have to gain security clearance and ghost himself against a maze of counter measures. That would also take time. Yet I have no choice. I must act as if Xankhara is under threat.

Returning from my reverie, I focus on the chamber in which I stand. Here at the heart of the Solar Huntress t-freighter lies the circular laboratory used for the earliest experiments in anima-conscious research. This is the room where my father, Captain Flemyng and his crew collected the calfwhales. These private tanks were where the minds of the humpbacks were linked to the prototype system. While nowhere approaching the size or complexity of the rig at the Phoenix Tower, the room is hauntingly familiar. The aquarium pools, the bulbous mind-pan saucers, the Amtech-built generators and gantries and cables. Professor Raymond Isaac Glass would have stood right where I am standing, surveying the majestic creatures as they were freight-lifted up out of the broiling ocean…

I look up at the whale wallowing in one of the giant tanks, its beady eyes seeming to watch my every move.

"So we meet at last," I say, doffing a non-existent hat.

The great mammal sways gently in its water-bound prison, but otherwise does nothing. Then I realise that this is because it is dead, its brain already removed to run the X-Isle. I would say that this makes up my mind, but it doesn't. That was made up way back when I created the X-Isle. Admittedly my incarceration forestalled the furthering of my ultimate goal, yet not ended it. And now it's my turn for a little heroics.

With a thrilling whirr into life, the Solar Huntress' engines fire making the entire deck structure vibrate in a way that is altogether quite pleasant.

"Nathaniel, strap yourself in," Esther's voice commands over the intercom.

This warning, though appreciated, comes a tad too late to perform any actual safety manoeuvres. In fact, I have barely enough time to hurl myself to the floor and grab for the nearest console before the transport leaps for the skies, sending the water in the tank sloshing over the side, drowning me utterly once more. There is also a dull thud as if something's fallen from a table. I look up to find that something has.

In the doorway to the medlab I see a little black bag. The top is open, gaping like a lipless mouth. And from within the crystal of the last replication glints like the multi-coloured dawn of a new creation.

47 | PURE

When the bullets start coming they're tracers, spiralling up from the stark whiteness like burning bats out of hell. Hundreds of the bastards. Scattershot. Slamming into the hull like deadly fists. Distant eruptions shake the ship. Nothing too serious, but even one of those projectiles could take out a critical system. Bring us right out of the sky with our ass on fire. All they need's one lucky hit.

Throw my bleached locks out of my eyes. Shift in my seat. Plastic squealing against plastic.

"Generator AOK. Tesseract's fired and holding."

Slap a few controls. Keep one eye on the constructs. Waiting for further reprisals. Whole map's a jagged blur of missiles.

"Navigation's holding too," says Dingo. "Course confirmation?"

"Anywhere but here," snorts the black bitch.

"Just keep evasion in mind," I add. "I'm expecting company any…"

Huntress shudders under the force of another impact. Seems stronger this time.

"Diagnostics?"

Midnight scans the code.

"Just astrogations," she replies. "Nothing primary. Well, not unless we want to break for near-space."

"Breaking for the border will be fine for now."

"Amen to that."

There's something about that last remark that narks me. Black chalk on my pure white blackboard. Find myself looking at the dreadlocked warrioress. Really looking. Makes my mind buzz with wicked thoughts. Of plans to go back. To be Pure. Before Jack. Before all this drugged-up shite. To rewind. To renew. To begin again. To be reborn. To purge myself. Yet to change my future, I must first change myself. Before the last remaining grains of my sanity turn to madness. Before the last remaining shreds of my goodness turn to badness. Can't do anything about that now. Maybe when we get somewhere else. But through all this whirl of thoughts, there's a central eye to this particular storm. A bottom line that I just can't shake or dismiss. Why didn't I think of it before.

Everything is Esther's fault.

If it were not for the ship's guns booming like cannons, it would be peaceful in the cramped control room. Yet it is not. Perhaps it never will be again. Releasing D'Alessandro and returning to the Huntress was one thing. Escaping into free space is gonna be quite another. Kasikianu is certain to have at least near-space transports, so our ride's sure to be A1 nasty.

Three red bolts appear in the lefthand zone of the finder.

"Here they come," I say to no one in particular. Both the others will have already clocked them, but what the fuck?

Readouts confirm they're NiNs. First I think that's a good thing 'cause NiNs don't come armed. Just little spunk cones. Speedy ways to get about. Squat good for anything else. Immediately tactical studies their flight patterns and throws up the battle options. Correction: the *one* battle option.

"Shitting fuck on a rock," I say to another bunch of no ones. "They're kamikazes."

48 | DINGO THE WONDER DOG

Up inside the v-rad my eyes watch the approach of the NiNs coming straight for us. Pity. Transports like the one we're in aren't too hot at nifty manoeuvring. Guess we've just got to hope they run out of ships before they break the hull. If you ask me, I think one hit and we're down. And looking at the others, I think they think that too.

Feel Bixby moving under the console. The komondor looks like a ball of knotted wool that's fallen out of some grandmother's knitting basket and been forgotten. Esther's also took the precaution to tie him up. It's for his own safety, she said. Guess it's for the best. Not that a chain's gonna do him much good if we powerdive into the ocean. Hope he isn't scared. Y'see, he doesn't like explosions. Recall the celestial novastorm for the ReEarth summit held in downtown DC three years after the collapse. Big lights, bigger bangs. Endless churning rainbows… He didn't like all them bells and whistles. Not one little bit. The summit was attended by all the major bohos. Some lame attempt to save the planet. Event was abandoned after a thousand or so unidentified bot pods rained electric death on the main chambers. Three hours and thirty-four thousand dead people later they decided on a vote of no conference.

Hmm, come to think of it, after eight-six, I don't like explosions that much either.

"What's the course check?" says Pure in my ear.

"Out of prison air space in ten."

Esther breaks off from her console and spins to face us both.

"That's going to be too late," she shouts. "They're almost upon us."

"Ah, put a cock in it!" hisses Susie.

Ripping off her jacks Sister leaps to her feet, fists flailing. Pure's almost as quick. The air crackling with tension. Turning the cockpit into tinder. In moments they're facing off. Ready to slug the living shit out of each other. Sparks flying.

"So it all comes down to this?" Midnight growls.

"Yep, I guess it does," replies Pure.

"A duel to the death."

"At the very least."

"State your terms."

"Jack."

"Terms agreed."

"Ready?"

"You betcha."

The big black woman and the small white one each take a step back. Esther draws two knives from somewhere. Susie snaps on her deathsclaw. Then they take up their fighting stances. And all the while their eyes never waver from the other. Eyes that bleed hatred.

Oh, no! That's it. I can't stand any more bickering. Don't they realise that when those carriers hit we're lost? That, after all this, we're as good as dead meat? That there are more important things than love? Forget Phantom and Dr Rico Zimpel. This is way realer than the real thing. And it's not thrilling or fun or enjoyable. It's just plain nasty.

Slap off my v-rad and drop under the console. Grab Bixby and hug him super tight as the women attack.

With a martial arts move that is just a blur, Pure swipes out with her five-fingered glove of blades. Midnight blocks with both knives. Forming a cross of steel that catches the claw mid-stab. The screech of metal on metal makes Bixby whimper. Makes my ears hurt, too. And making us both hunker down closer to the floor. Blocked, Susie roundhouses a big kick, striking Esther in the hip. Crashing her back into the consoles. She counters with a backhand blow that broadsides the petite blonde. Right on her pretty left cheekbone.

This is so bad, I think as I bury my furry face into the komondor's corded coat. Everything seems so futile.

Above me the two women snarl. They're just ready to start slugging each other again, when they notice I'm gone. Both look over. See me under the console. Pure gives me a quirky smile. Beside her, Midnight scowls.

"Will you stop blubbing!" she shouts. Her usual compassionate self.

"I don't wanna die without my skates on!" I bawl back.

I think then that they're both going to march over and give me a good smacking, but they doesn't get the chance. Because at that moment proximities sound and the first of our pursuers nosedives into the bulkhead.

Whoops, there goes the midsection…

49 | SISTER MIDNIGHT

At the helm of the ark of the god machine I feel the whole universe shudder. Without weapons, the prison carrier's only form of attack would be suicidal, yet I can see the sense in that. Sometimes one must make final sacrifices before one's gods. Around me the A-Men are falling apart. The Wonder Dog has abandoned his post. D'Alessandro contests my wishes to destroy the simulation. Now even Pure has given up. I can see as well as any that the diagnostic reports are undeniable in their singular message; the transport has sustained too much damage to the central hub.

The Solar Huntress is going down.

Yet in this gyring storm of chaos and despair, I know that I must remain calm else all will be lost. And I have fought too long and hard to abandon myself to the panic of the godless.

"Seal the heads," I command. "Prep for evac."

"Are you *crazy?*" Pure spits back at me. "That piss-jock hit the midsection. The *hub*. It's salvageable. Ditch it and we can still get clear."

"No! Jack's in there. We can't just abandon him."

Pure's look is as cold as a corpse.

"He's all yours," she says.

I am chilled to the bone by this. Am not ready to face the grim finality of it. The bitterness. Unnerved, I turn away from Pure's hostility. Back to the console. As I make a cursory check over diagnostics, panic claws me again. The story can't end like this. It just can't. And I am the only one who can make damned sure that it doesn't.

"I'm going to get him out."

Jack is still battling against the X-Isle. He has no idea of what's happening. Yet even as I begin to think him a message the blonde waif is stabbing at the system overrides. It takes me a whole second to realise that she's preparing to jettison the cargo bay. Leaping forward, I grab Pure's wrist and twist it to the side. The platinum whore squeals scratching out at my face, but it's too late. Klaxons shriek and with a chilling hiss, the pressurised shutters begin to seal. Screaming like a falling angel, I throw myself at the closing door. Even as it swings down, I am under it and hurling myself down the metal steps beyond. Behind me I can hear Dingo's yelp of surprise, yet then the flight deck is sealed. Disappearing behind one thick sweep of forty-five centimetre impact shielding.

No way back now, Mûhamet. I guess there never was.

Dragging myself to my feet I stumble down the corridor just as the inner airlock slams into place. Running I burst into the circular hub and there see Nathaniel. The rake-thin man stands beside the vast tank, the crystal in one hand while the other grapples with a mass of cables. He nods towards me as I enter, then resumes his work.

What's the madman doing now? I think angrily.

Sirens still screech their warnings, so when I speak I'm forced to do so at a throat-rending yell.

"I've got to get Jack out the rig. How'd I do it?"

"What?"

"The rig. How'd I shut it down without…"

"*What?*"

He cannot hear me. The alarms are too loud.

The situation fuels my frustration. I feel like punching the son of a bitch, but instead I cross to the medlab. Inside the small chamber Jack floats lazily in the liquid gel. He looks so peaceful. It seems a sin to bring him out into this mess.

Yet already it is far too late.

With a sickening lurch the Huntress obeys Pure's command and abandons the cargo bay.

Oh, by the will of Astarth…

At once the sirens stop, replaced by a quiet spoilt only by the ringing in my numb ears. Obeying gravity, the circular hub plummets like a stone. To me it feels exactly like the drop from orbit on the day E-Unit arrived back on this mudball world. Then I was saving the innocent from the rioting mobs after the collapse. Now I am saving something infinitely more precious.

There is little time for reflection. Seconds later the cargo bay crashes into the ocean. There is a mighty watery roar, throwing us to the floor. Immediately the hull breaches, forcing freezing water in through a dozen rifts. Pulling myself up, I stride over to the rig and search for some kind of abort module. For a moment the unfamiliar controls and gushing water outwit me. Yet then my eyes fall upon a red tagged stopper set above the main panel. Upon it, written in uncompromisingly large letters, it says: 'System purge'.

Even as I read this my hand is lifting the safety glass, while the other punches out towards it.

Forgive me, Jack…

My wrist is grabbed mid-jab and turning I stare into the cold, calm face of Nathaniel. Snarling, I try to break free, but for a moment the bald-headed man stops me.

"Don't," he pleads. Knowing he can't stop me. Not if I'm dead set on doing it. Which I am. Snap my arm from his weak grasp. Go to stab the button again. And this time I succeed.

50 | THE NOWHEREMAN

As my mind takes in the awful truth of those gleaming green letters, the door opens and in steps my elder brother. His face is as dark as his tailored suit. The simulation reproducing his entire visage exactly. For once the X-Isle leaves nothing to the imagination.

"Joseph."

"John," he replies smugly. "Having fun?"

"Name's not John. It's Jack. Great place you got here. Real *nice*."

"It was before you fucked it up."

Sit back in the chair and spread my palms wide.

"Should've told 'em I was coming."

A pause. A tonne of silence. Several tonnes.

"Must be the end of the game," I say into it.

"Pardon?"

"Must be the end of the game. At the end of the game you meet God."

Joseph laughs. Don't guess for a moment he wants to, but he does anyway.

"You always were amusing," he says when he stops. "Now let's get down to business."

"And that is?"

"Killing you."

From the folds of his own reality my brother produces a gun. It's a D&K. Probably an exact replica of my original. Wouldn't surprise me. That's the sort of crap he probably thinks of as style. Go for my belt. Pick out the claw hammer. Only thing worth defending myself with.

And even that's as good as crap. Stand and heft it. Look set to leap the desk. Not too amazed when the fucking thing evaporates into thin air.

"This is mine," says the suit indicating the entire universe with one wave of his hand. "It obeys *me*."

"So you're gonna shoot me?"

"Yes. Actually I could do anything. Stab you. Dice you. Imprison you in an iron ball and fire you into the sun. Whatever I choose."

"Like you did to our family."

Joseph's amused. "Oh, no. That was you. I attended your sick anniversary party with the plan of demanding the K/OS key from father at gunpoint. I intended to end his reign of tyranny and control. But you beat me to it."

Great.

While reality realigns itself in my mind, I sit down again. Recline and wrap one hand around my lucky bunny foot.

"Why?" I ask. As disinterestedly as I can.

"Because I can."

"No ball."

Joseph rolls his eyes.

"OK, because I wanted to find out if it was fun being a god."

"Deep thought," I say. "But surely even Joe Schmo could've told you that."

"Ah, you have me there."

"So *why*?"

"Because when this is over, I will be XEs."

Shit, I was right.

"Because once the sentience fails, I will replace it. Personally. I have modified the mind-pan so that it now accepts human tissue. Normally I would see such behaviour as sinful, yet that which I call sin in others I deem experiment in myself."

"You sick, sick fuck."

"Yes…" He muses on that, then: "After you stole the Huntress, I had to refine my plans a little. Had to be sure you'd replace the replication. Would've been amazed if you hadn't. But that's all done now. Oh, and for your information, the Solar Huntress has been destroyed. As we chat your pitiful A-Men drown and the last replication sinks to the bottom of the ocean. Your precious Xankhara has been raped. Your dreams obliterated. I have won. You have lost. Your feeble attempts to poison near-space have failed. Now I will kill you and attain my immortality."

Frozen I cling to the chair to avoid leaping up and trying to make him breakfast on his own bollocks.

Sister! Dingo! D'Alessandro!

"Oh, and don't bother trying to contact anyone," he adds. "This room's shielded."

So finally we get to face off. Me against him. And he's got the entire universe on his side. Shit at my waist's good for nothing. So what can I try? Then I notice that where I'm sitting and he's standing, Joseph can't see my right hand. Now if only I can get to the keyboard. Got to keep the fucker talking.

Reach out and interrupt the program.

>**Internal date: 09/05/11.4 Gyr.**
>**Internal time: 00:16:33.**
>**Day of project: 4750.**
>**Machine: Sol Series 1140.**
>**Prototype number: 156008-a12.**
>**Sentience: Ianus.**
>**Programming language: K/OS.**
>**Copyright © Glass-Suko Corporation. All rights reserved.**
>**User/psychist. Identify.**

"How'd I know all that shit's true? About the Huntress and everything?"

Joseph raises his eyebrows.

"Slave!" he calls. "Initiate external view."

Immediately the walls go translucent. All of them. We're looking out into the tank. Seeing what the whale brain can see. Can see Sister. Can see D'Alessandro. Seem to be arguing. Whole place's filling with deep blue sea. Consoles erupt. Sparks fly. In the centre of the chaos can also see the crystal glinting amidst a tangle of wires.

"We could always team up again," says the suit after letting me take all this in.

"I'd rather spit in our mother's cunt!"

"Our *dead* mother's cunt," he corrects.

Incredibly slowly I type:

>**John Ewen Malorian.**

Screen flickers. Then:

>**User accepted.**
>**Security passcode. Identify.**

Type in the altered signifier for daddy's chromosome.

>**EXILE.**

Realise Joseph's stopped talking. Realise he's walking closer.

"What are you doing?" he spits.

"Nothin'," I lie.

Upon the screen a myriad of words appear. There's a pause. Then:

>**Passcode accepted.**

Joseph is at the desk now. Leaning over…

Then something flashes in my mind. Fiery letters. Bright as a hundred stars. Same two words also blaze onto the screen.

>**System purge.**

The shock hits my belly like a bullet. Fired. Close range. I yell out. Surprisingly so does the suit.

Familiar sickening warmth. Familiar reel. Three. Two. One.

Familiar darkness yawns, grabs me in its clammy fists and drags me up into the world of total slime.

★

The end of the game came that night I met Joseph. Like Ianus said, at the end of the game, it's like life really. At the end of the game you meet God. Yet just as soon as I'd started on the opening chat, someone had purged the system and brought me back to reality with a bang. It wasn't pleasant. One minute I'm about three seconds away from finishing this whole fucking episode. The next I'm spiralling through the blackness between worlds while my body got the lumberpunch once over. Being back's a shock too. Last time I remember, it I was floating in the safety of my gunk tank in a small but well-organised medlab. When I return I'm starring in a remake of Castella's *Creature In The Black Cagoule*.

Through the warped glass of the tank I see Sister. Struggling with ten thousand litres of boiling water. More's rushing in every which way. Gushing through the door. Spurting between ceiling panels. Whirlpooling at her feet. She mock salutes me, then turns back to the console. As one, tubes snake out my every orifice and zip back into the casing. With laboured strokes, I swim to the surface.

"What the fuck's going on?" I say. Drag myself over the lip.

Sister don't even look up.

"Bitch dropped us in the Sûrabian. We're sinking."

"She did *what*?"

"We were hit. It was save you or save herself."

So guess here at the end, Susie finally got her revenge.

"You purge the system?"

"Yep."

"Why?"

"Look around."

I look around. It ain't pretty. None of it. Don't know how bringing me back's gonna do shit. Maybe she don't wanna die on her lonesome.

"So what'd we do now?" I ask.

Midnight slaps a few more buttons. Grimaces at the resulting bleeps. Face's a knot of hatred. Like chewed-up tobacco.

"How's dying grab ya, white boy?"

Hull grinds and groans. Floor tips like a rollercoaster. Getting ready for the big one.

"Well, it's…"

"It's not an option."

The voice is Nathaniel's, but the busted kook who wades his way in is someone else entirely. Looks like a red-eyed rad freak. Shrivelled body. Nasty bruises. Didn't look so bad at the Phoenix. Looked kinda noble. Now he looks more like a punchbag. Boy, and I thought prison was one of the best ways of retiring. Guess I thought wrong.

"We meet again at the last," he says through bruised lips.

"Yeah," I say. Still fazed.

Drop into the swirling brine. It's fucking freezing. Like jumping into a fridge. Still, what'd I expect? Probably about minus forty outside. Grab a lab coat and wrap it round me. For all the good it does might as well stand there starkers.

I've gotta get back. Wherever Joseph is he'll have no problem rezzing back in. Just flip a switch and wazzo! Little more difficult at this end. Tune in to Sister and D'Alessandro. Discussing. Future don't seem too rosy for any of us. From what they're saying, hub's not powered. Just some interchangeable pod bay. Right now it'll float for a while, but with the hull breached, s'only a matter of time till we go deep-sea diving. Then about a zillion fathoms down the walls'll implode and we'll all be sucked out and crushed to death. That's of course if we can keep air for that long.

"Look," I interrupt, "forget about all that shit. Who gives a fuck about all the possible death scenarios. Can anyone think of one where we end up living?"

Sister shrugs as if to say, 'You got me there,' but the bald dude is a tad more positive.

"I say we try for immortality."

"What the fuck d'you mean by–?" Sister begins, but I cut her off.

"What ya got in mind, mystery man?" I ask.

"Immortality. It's what your brother wants."

"Yeah, so?"

"What say *we* go for it instead?"

"We? Well, that's rich. Only one place at the top, Nathaniel. My guess is you're going for it. Bet you've had this planned from the start. You're just as bad as he is."

"Unfortunately I'm worse. Who do you think gave him the idea in the first place?"

Sister interrupts the conversation by pulling a gun on the prick.

"You piece of shit."

"Whoa, Midnight," I interject. "Let him have his say."

Don't wanna stiff the dude till we get some answers.

Sheepishly Nathaniel continues. Starts mumbling about mind-pans, infinity dumps and all that psychist shit. And all the while the ocean pumps higher and higher around my numb legs.

"Look," I butt in as he burbles on. "What's that in real money?"

Nathaniel sighs and leans his weight against the wall.

"Since I wrote *Forevermore*, all I've wanted is to create the island and play God. Yet now I have taken a look at the modifications to the Huntress, I see that the ante has been upped. XEs is endangered. Osakimo has seen a way to take complete control of the sentience and with it rule the entire Consortium of Heaven. Your brother has seen a way to gain this all for himself. That has changed things. Has changed *everything*. I cannot allow that to happen."

"So?"

"So I say we get there first…"

"Look, I can tell you right here and now, whatever shit happens, I want Xankhara to survive."

"Unfortunately it may already be too late."

"Late?"

"Too late to save it. I have already contacted Baseeq. Already instructed him to destroy the replication if I was executed."

"But you're alive."

"Ah, yes, *we* know that, but…"

"OK, I'm way ahead of you. That settles it. I'm going back in. I've got to stop Joseph. And if that means taking his place…"

Sister's eyes bug. "Now wait one minute…"

"Sorry, Sis, got no time for talk radio. It's the only way."

For a moment the dreadlocked warrior looks set to pistol-whip some sense into me. Then she relents.

"Ave maria." She crosses herself. Twice. "May as well do that as anything. You boys get yourselves sorted. I'll see about sealing this chamber."

Attagirl.

Follow Nathaniel into the whale room. See the crystal as soon as we wade in. Glinting in the eerie emergency lighting. All manner of junk bobs past. It's all we can do not to be swept away.

"The last replication," the busted geek announces. Sounding proud. Like a dad showing off his son's trophies. "Now if you wish to beat your brother and become…"

"Stop right there!" I yell.

"What?"

"He can see us. Maybe hear us too."

"How?"

I nod toward the giant fish tank.

"Ah," says Nathaniel. "Yet what of it? He must know that these things are a possibility…"

"Yeah, but let's not confirm it to the fucker, eh?"

"I see."

Instinctively we both turn our backs on the whale tank. Make sure Joseph can't see our lips.

"I watched them capture that beautiful creature," Nathaniel whispers as he starts working at the controls. "The last of its kind. Rather sad really."

"Forget all the 'Save the Planet' shit. What I gotta do?"

"You need to get access to the central room."

"The one without doors?"

"Yes, the one the Eternal Ones have disabled. Then… You don't happen to have a smoke, do you?"

"Nope."

"Damnation. OK, I'll wait here for your signal then download the infinity dump and reset everything. At this point XEs will die and be reborn anew. Joseph has altered things to accept human…"

"In who's image?"

"Whoever's jacked to the mind-pan."

"Someone like you?"

"No, no, Jack. You are going in. That someone is you."

Yeah, right. And I'm a born again virgin. He knows as well as I do that when the shit goes down, it's a three-horse race. All I gotta do is make sure the other nags fall at the first. Look into his eyes. Bulging. Red. Sad.

Still don't believe he'll let me do it. But hey, gotta give it a try.

"OK, I got it. I signal then link to the core. What about you and Sis?"

"We play out one of the possible death scenarios."

Great. Try not to think about that too much.

"At least we save the world," he adds morosely. "I know this is not exactly your style, but it *will* mean your brother loses. And Xankhara will be forever saved."

"Hoorah for the good guys."

"Admittedly your body will not."

Try not to think of that too much either. "Ah, what the hell. We're all gonna fucking die anyway."

"Timing is crucial. When the reset comes there's no room for error. I'll be cutting the whale brain free and then immediately connecting you up to the simulation. That's when you'll get the chance."

"But surely the Eternal Ones won't let the Amen hostgod be reset."

"Joseph's mistake. He was too literal in their omniscience and did not allow them to comprehend alternate dimensions. Imagine being told you're the creator of the entire universe and then you show up."

"They pissed themselves. I was there."

"Well, exactly. I made the same mistake with Thomas, of course. I cannot believe Osakimo didn't anticipate the consequences this time around."

"Shame."

"And now that the gods have been driven mad by your presence, they are no more than a minor quandary."

"I'll take your word on that."

All sounds like shit, but s'OK. I let it go. I've got my own ideas. And by the look in D'Alessandro's eyes, so has he.

Nathaniel turns to finish setting the circuits, so I move back to the medlab. Once inside, Sister starts to weld shut the door. Should give us a little more time. Outside the hull's ready to blow. Watch on the monitor as Nathaniel makes final preparations. For my sins, try not to look at Midnight. For hers, she tries not to look at me much either.

Instead I clamber back into the tank ready for another slime jacuzzi. When I'm in position, Nathaniel gives me the thumb's up.

"Are you ready, Jack?"

I nod. I was born ready. And then I go under for the third time.

★

Arrive back in whalebrainsimulationmindfuckland.

Back in the high tech playroom. Standing by the door. Everything's just as I left it. Purge fresh.

Then I see Joseph.

Bastard sits in the anti-grav bucket seat. Head down. Fucker's hair's been slicked back. Pale wrinkles shining. Polished fingernails glint like sapphires. Wears a heavy belted robe in midnight blue with matching slippers. Nice touch. Scrutinising the keyboard. Can't see his face, but don't have to. It's him. Just know. Who else could it be?

Elder brother looks up at my appearance. Smiles like he's meeting an ancient adversary. Guess he is. No time for getting all nostalgic though. Got to get Home.

Suddenly Joseph's mood changes. Totally. Frowns. Looks puzzled as fuck.

"So, you're back... who purged the system?"

"Sister."

"Ah, yes. Ex-sergeant Esther Rose."

Joseph stands. Walks around the chrome desk. Sits on it. Crosses his arms. "Daddy would never have approved."

"Daddy's dead."

"Yes, he is. Well, never mind. He served his purpose… As have you."

"Nice to have been of service."

"So what are you doing back?"

"This is my moment," I say to no one in particular. "My moment of glory in the story."

"You pathetic fuck," retorts Joseph. "This is your time to die."

Quick as sin he's up from the desk and going for my throat. It's so unexpected that I'm knocked back. Slam against the plastic polymer wall. Winds me. And while I'm gulping, he grabs me by the throat. Don't get chance to do jack.

"Now you die," he spits. "Just like your little boy."

Reality swirls and he's breaking my windpipe using an exact replica of Aaron's rod. Jacura V series. Cutlass-X 450. Can remember the make and model number. Like it was only yesterday. Picked it up from the blood-wet grass. Felt ice cool in my hot fist. It's crystal clear to me then that Joseph *was* with the strike force. Erasing my doubts that even he'd stoop that low. He wanted what our father had created and nothing was going to stand in his way of getting it. Guess all that stuff about iron balls and sun diving was just so much cock. He wants to kill me with his bare hands.

Malorian grins down at me. And I let him. Mind's on other things.

Until I get brother off my chest, can't make it Home. Can't jack in. If Nathaniel flips now, there's no way I'm gonna beat him to the mind-pan. But what choice is there? What choice is there ever?

Gurgle on the brink of passing out. Another few seconds and I'm minus a functional neck. Death stares me in the face. Sheesh. Story of my life. Somewhere far off I hear the terminal bleeping. Can't say I'm particularly bothered. Brother is though. Forces his head up. Spins the console just by staring at it. So he can view the screen. Just in time to see the words appearing like scattershot on the glass.

>Obtrusion alert. System security breach. Initiating countermeasures.

Crap, now what?

>Executing mirror entry sequence. Gateway to X-Isle requested. Gateway to X-Isle opened. Sequence complete.

Bleary-eyed I stare at the little green letters. Stare and wonder. Don't have to do either very long.

>Initiating entry sequence. Winston Lovechild Baseeq has entered the X-Isle. Sequence complete.

Baseeq! Ut-oh.

With a libertine distortion of the small room, Baseeq appears. Dude's still as big as I remember him. Big big. Big lips. Big muscles. Big hair. All wrapped in a multi-coloured kaftan.

And in one of his big hands he holds a strange red device.

"Yo!" he says to us both.

"Who the fuck are you?" shouts Joseph.

The black muscleman blanks him. Totally.

What's the matter, bro'. Don't know your own nemesis when you see him? Smugness lasts about three nanoseconds. Fucker's my nemesis too. He's gonna blow everything. Xankhara. The island. The crystal.

And all our chances.

Earth calling Sis! Earth calling Sis…

Shit. Room's shielded. What now!

I get edgy. Real edgy. Reach for my piece. Suddenly aching for it. Can't. Arms're pinned to the wall.

"I asked you a question!" Joseph repeats. This time lower. More menacing.

Watch as the fixer lifts the device. Brother looks at it with utter contempt.

"If you think…"

Baseeq shrugs. Shrugs and punches his thumb into one end. The bomb whines. Lights up. Blurs across my watery gaze as the fixer drops it. Lands on the perfect floor. Pulses as it begins its final countdown.

"No!" screams Joseph. Finally realising what it is.

Fishing rod disappears. Brother does too. Leaping at Baseeq, even as the black figure tries to fade into thin air. Doesn't work though. There's no way out. Arriving here is a one-way trip.

Joseph crashes into the huge figure. Knocks him back. Punches out. Fist connects to jaw.

Baseeq careens backwards. Unbalanced. Hits the four poster bed. Drapes fly. Rip. Black bastard collapses into the sleep unit. Brother's on top of him. Goes down fighting. Coffin lid shatters. Glass yields and they fall through it. Stagger. I'm free. Half-choked, but free. Yet what the fuck can I do?

On the floor the bomb is beating like a heart on A's. Faster and faster. Speeding up. What the fuck can I do! Screen's going mental too. Words spilling across the terminal. Too fast to read. Then I catch the gist.

>**Internal date: 09/05/11.4 Gyr.**
>**Internal time: 00:28:02.**
>**Day of project: 4750.**
>**Machine: Sol Series 1140.**
>**Prototype number: 156008-a12.**
>**Sentience: Ianus.**
>**Programming language: K/OS.**
>**Copyright © Glass-Suko Corporation. All rights reserved.**
>**User/psychist. Identify.**
>**John Ewen Malorian.**
>**User accepted.**
>**Security passcode. Identify.**
>**EXILE**
>**Passcode accepted.**

It's me. Signing in. But I'm here. I'm in. Terminal waits. Just a little arrowhead and flashing cursor. What's up? Maybe I should type something.

Then I realise it's Nathaniel. Bastard's going for the end game.

Screen leaps again.

>System request.
— he types.
>System request accepted. Specify.
Bang the retro keyboard. Overload the screen with jumbled capitals. Does shit but throw out a warning bleep.
>System reset.
Shit, he's going for it. Guess I better get ready...
>Replication located. System reset commencing.
>Hostgod. Identify.
Here it comes. Here it comes. Here it comes.
>Nathaniel Raymond Glass.
Shock strikes me rigid. Though I knew the fucker would never allow me to go for hostgod, now I see it in shining green I'm devastated. Wasted. It's all over. Gut. Lucille. Shrago. Pure. And now Nathaniel. The betrayal is complete. Everyone I ever, ever, ever, ever, ever...

Burn with sudden hatred. Carved from antipathy deeper than I've ever felt. Ever. Curse D'Alessandro with all the words I can think of. This universe is mine. I fought for it. I own it. I'm Jack! Not him. And if that skinny runt thinks he can slime his way in at the last minute...

Bomb's freaking. Strobing red. Faster than ever. Behind me Baseeq and Joseph still slug it out. Like brawling school kids. Then my brother gouges something vital and the black man stops slugging. And suddenly Joseph is dragging himself up out the blooded bed now coffin. Looking like a grinning ghoul.

Ignore them. Eyes totally focused on the red bomb.

Got to act now. Got to...

Roar like a raging animal. Roar, then find my voice.

"Home, secondary subject, shutdown."

There's a sickening pause. Beneath the mask of blood, my brother goes even whiter.

"D'ya hear me, you motherfucking piece of junk! Shutdown! Now!"

"No! You'll kill us all!" yells Joseph. Voice's a shriek. Total drama queen. The red device stops pulsing. Is suddenly darker than the night.

"Frankly, Joseph," I spit back, "I just don't give a fuck!"

And with those words, the universe ends. And we with it.

★

Arrive in the Room Without Doors. Inexplicably. Impossibly. Upon the table sits the tray and its painted china. Fire burns low in the grate. Air's heavy with the smell of wood smoke.

Know surer than anything that's outside's all's void. Whole bunch of infinity. Far as the mind can conceive. Can still see Baseeq's bomb as it blows apart. Shredding everything with impossible whiteness. Can still feel reality trembling. Hear it whining as it rocks and rolls. Image's burnt onto the back of my eyes. Can see the room around me splintering. Erupting into glittering pieces. One great big supernova. Whole fucking simulation exploding. Imploding. Whatever. Universe flying off into the vast black breach. World's end.

Island's gone. Experiment's over. Gods're gone. All that's left's this room and a great, big nothing. Well, nothing except Sister's voice in the mouth of the night.

Jack! JACK!

Whoa, there. Has he done it?

Who? What?

Nathaniel! Did he do it?

Jack, Nathaniel is dead.

Dead?

He got fried on the console. Crystal blew to fuck. After he jacked in.

The crystal's vaped? No, that's not possible.

I can see it on the monitor. Believe me, it's history.

But, Esther, if he's gone, then maybe I can still do it. Perhaps not reset the island, but now I'm Home I could initiate the end game. Then I can take charge. After all there's a vacancy.

But how in hell am I gonna do that? And – more importantly – why am I still alive?

Esther, I need one last favour. I need you to consult the book.

What, now?

Yeah, now.

I'm trying to save us from drowning!

Sister, this is important.

More important that keeping us alive, Jack?

Might be. I need to know what happens ... Y'know, at the end of the story. You know.

I want to know again.

OK.

Desperate and alone I stand in the musty panelled chamber and wait. Feeling like a spec in the infinite immensity of space. A mote in the stream. Nothing. No one. Nowhere.

There's a pause. Imagine her sighing as she flips through the ragged pages. Then:

After he defeats the Big Black Demon there's loads of stuff about the gods and drinking and getting worked up. Is that relevant?

Skip it. I want to know the end. The very end.

You know *the end. You know it better than you know your own name. Just read it.*

OK.

And once each of the Eternal Ones had sipped from the pool, they lifted Jack up and pressed his lips against the ice-cold water. And when he drank the first stroke of the Big Black Demon's axe was cured. And when he drank again the second stroke of the Big Black Demon's axe was cured. Yet then when he stooped to drink a third time, he realised that if he did so he would be granted the secret of eternal youth and would rule as King of the Wood for ever and ever...

Er, Jack.

Yeah, whassup?

Someone's torn out the page.

What?

That's the end. Well, except for some scrawl you've added.

Oh no.

Read it.

OK. It says, 'But Jack didn't want to be a god. Jack wanted out. So he turned away from the fountain, crossed the stepping stones, left the castle, crossed the island to the edge of the world and NEVER LOOKED BACK. Amen.'"

That's it?

That's it.

Why'd I write that?

Well, maybe you didn't like the way it ended.

But that's fucked up. I want Jack to win!

Well, maybe you do now, but that's not what you wanted then.

Why did he turn back? Why didn't he drink?

I dunno. Why'd you put the kid on the train?

I dunno... Yes, yes I do. I knew that ticket was not for me. That where that train was going was not where I wanted to go. Not where I belonged.

So d'ya belong here, Jack? Is that what you're telling me?

Think on that and remember reading *Forevermore* for the first time. Of Jack O'Nowhere's tale. The words ringing truer now than ever. How it said that we become the things we've lost. How we are searching for those things we never lose. And how to find them all you had to do was sit very still and look very hard – and believe.

Ki Om Ma Noo... Ki Om Ma Noo... Ki Om Ma Noo...

Close my eyes. Feel the pressure of my skin beneath my sweating palms begin to fade. The sweat fades. There's silence. Then for a moment everything turns to nothing. And in that moment I let go. Of my ego, my dreams, the world, reality. Every cunting infinitesimal fucking iota. Imagine infinite space. Imagine everything and me and Dead City and the world and galaxies and all that cosmic shit is just one point in that space. Then in that moment do I truly become The Nowhereman. There is no me. There is no self. No *where*. Empty myself. Turn my body, world and everything inside out and it's as if the whole universe disappears up its own ass. Eternal light freezes. Infinite chakras centre. Reach my sacred inner point. My universal dimensions of being.

And there at the heart of my unbelief, I find the centre of all creation. The only thing that's real. The glimpse of the imago through the crack in the door of reality. Then I see the contradiction. My contradiction. The perfect being who exists in idea but not in reality. And then I open my eyes I find God has popped in for a visit.

D'Alessandro sits in the armchair. Watching me. He's healed and as well as anyone has ever the right to look. Yet though he's here, can suddenly feel that he's everywhere else too. It's like waking up in his gut.

"This is Home," he says smiling. "Please be seated. I trust you still drink Jack on ice."

"You fucking, cheating bag of shit! You duped me."

Stride forwards. Foot makes contact with the table. Sends the drinks tray flying. Ice and whiskey smash against the stone hearth. Lemon slices hiss on the hot coals. Nathaniel shifts uncomfortably in his seat.

"Jack, please, calm yourself. I had no choice."

"You lying cunt!"

Feel like strangling the bastard. Wonder why I don't. Maybe because I owe him one. For that time with the Wasters. Then I remember the Werehouse. Damn, I owe this bastard *thrice*.

"No, I assure you," he's babbling. "I had no choice. Baseeq blew it."

"Yeah, I was there when the bomb went off."

"No, he *blew* it. And all due to your quite innovative shutdown game plan. Quite brilliant."

I'm too startled to answer. Mind's racing. Total overdrive. Then I get it. The shutdown came before the blast. I saved the day.

"Did we win?" I ask.

"Yes, Jack. I restored the last replication. Everything's set to before you introduced the virus. XEs is saved. Xankhara is back to the beginning. And that little mess with the gods going ape every time someone enters is all sorted out too."

"How did you get in? I thought killing daddy would seal the deal."

"You forget, I already had the K/OS key. I already took it."

And I realise he did, back on the beach of skulls. The spider in my mind, his servant: Maleore. Mr. fucking bad faerie. The deck's been stacked right from the off. All in the pursuit of the realisation of a dream. His dream.

"So what you doing now?" I say.

"I'm doing what I do best."

"And what's that?"

"Playing God."

"That's what you're doing now?"

"I am."

Suddenly I'm glad. Glad I'm not God. Glad I'm alive. Glad it feels like it's all suddenly over.

And what about you?"

"Oh, me. Well, the hostgod sentience was obviously wiped during the reload. So I stepped in. Quite clever really. Joseph made that possible, but it's far too complicated for you to understand."

"So you're XEs."

"Well, I like to think of myself more as deus in machinam."

"D'Alessandro, you always were a clever fuck."

"And you a twisted, evil one."

I bow. And after a moment, Nathaniel bows back.

"Where's Joseph?" I ask, trying to keep the shake from my voice.

"Vaped. Fried. Deader than deadski. When the simulation shutdown, so did his brain. Baseeq too."

I cross to the mirror. The island's gone. Outside's just the immeasurable immensity of space and time.

"And what about me? Where am I?"

"Same place you were before. I made sure you slipped through."

"What about near-space?"

"With the virus gone, balance between the corporations has been resumed. Everything is fine and dandy."

"And what about the Eternal Ones?"

"Gone the way of the flesh."

"And the Amen?"

"Now, Jack surely you don't believe that there's a *real* god, do you?"

"Nope. Guess not. And Sister?"

"Well, she is still trying to figure out why I croaked."

"I've got to get back to her. There's something I need to say."

"Of course, but before you go *I'd* like to say thank you. For your help that is."

"Go stick it up your faerie ass."

"My pleasure."

"Yeah, so I'm finally the hero of the whole fucking universe. And no one's ever gonna know."

"Indeed."

We eye each other, then. A steady look that says more than these fickle words of banter ever could. It's me who breaks the stare. Wanting to be done.

"Cool. Well, I guess that's it then."

"Yes, that is it."

"Well, bye, old dude."

"Fare well, Jack."

And with that I return to the light.

★

I emerge from the simulation to find Sister in the tank with me. The lab's gone. So's the whole fucking hub. Outside the glass is just the impenetrable darkness of the midnight ocean. Jism's gone too. Instead the tub's filled with air. Even now feels perilously thin.

"Midnight…"

Don't speak. We don't have much oxygen.

Sister, what's happening?

No, you tell me what's happenin'. Nathaniel dropped dead. Linked himself with the simulation, then keeled over when the crystal blew. Then the hull breached. Whole side tore out so I jettisoned. Thought that was better than being crushed to death.

We're sinking.

Yessum. This glass elevator's going straight to the bottom.

How deep?

Oh, don't worry 'bout how deep. Glass'll be crushed well before we get to the fishes. This ain't no deep-sea sub we got here.

No, I guess it ain't.

Hey, no sweat, white boy. Down's the easiest way to go. Said so yourself.

Yeah, s'like the gravity of life. No truer then than now.

Beyond the hazy glass a billion tonnes of water slips past. Only sound's our rasping breaths.

Sister, we don't have much time.

Right again, Jack. Still, that bitch of a tracker's in your shoulder. Damn never turned it off after you got out the maze...

Sister, I want you.

Want you what? To screw me?

No, that doesn't matter now.

So what does?

I think about that.

It's the dream. Love and death. That's what it is. What it's always been. Right from the start. But even now at the end I can't tell her. Can't find the words. I'm too numb. Too shitting numb. We look at each other. Time passes as we slowly descend into infinite blackness. Metal grinds threateningly. Glass shrieks. Tank rumbles.

Why me, Jack. You could have had anyone?

I've had everyone. Now I want you.

Want me? What you trying to say?

She looks like a little girl. Her face's full of fear. Eyes swelling. She knows. Of course she knows. I want her to know, here at the end. I look down. Away from her steely gaze. She's holding *Forevermore* hard against her breast. I feel so raw. So wrong. It's then that I realise I lied to Joseph. Lied to myself. So many times.

This is my moment.
I…
Esther looks up at me. Sees what I'm trying to say. Feels it.
Say it, Jack. Just once.
Can't. Can't do it. I just *can't*.
I… I…
That's close enough. And y'know I do too, you pathetic, fucking bastard.
I hold her. Tighter than I've ever held anyone ever. Me, her, the book. The sum total of everything.
In this crazy, fucked-up, fragile world all I wanted was to be part of something that wasn't. Does that make sense?
Perfect sense, Jack. Y'know, I think you're becoming more human.
I am?
Yeah, abùna. You're practically there. As for me? Hey, who am I to judge you? Mi no inap painim rot bilong mi…
Though I have no idea what she's saying, I smile. Then watch as she pulls away slightly and frowns at the glass around her. As she reaches to the wall and starts tapping keys. Instructing the snake-like tubing to coil back into me.
What ya doing?
Now Esther smiles and pulls herself back into my embrace.
That's the trouble with you, Jack. You always wanted that totally impossible happy ever after.
With a terrifying eruption of metal and glass, the tank implodes. Destroyed by the incalculable pressure from outside. Shards rip through us. Water rushes across us. Pressure's unbearable. Only the air in the tubes keeps my lungs from collapsing. Something sharp spears my side. My hands. My feet. We both scream, but don't let go. Esther tenses in my vice-like grip. Then begins to weaken.
Oh, no. Esther, don't die on me. Not now. Not when I've just got all my shit sorted out. Don't die. Don't die. Don't…
Zzzzzzt…
Under the weight of the water, I'm still going down, saved only momentarily by the tanks and the air in the tubing. Busted pieces of

the sim machine disappear below us. Sink. Sink. Sink.

Bleeding.

Aching.

Alone.

Finally Esther goes limp in my grasp. Just after that the book slips out from between us. I am beyond caring.

In the bitter cold of the Sûrabian, I doubt I have more than twenty.

51 | D'ALESSANDRO

Zzzzzzt...

52 | PURE

Zzzzzzt...

53 | DINGO THE WONDER DOG

Zzzzzzt…

54 | SISTER MIDNIGHT

Zzzzzzt...

55 | THE NOWHEREMAN

I am warm yet lonely, the traces of her final scream still etched across my senses as she had cried out above me. The water is icy cold pressing upon me from all sides, yet my body is afire with pumping life and the strongest desire that I should talk to her. Turning sluggishly in the midnight I open my mouth, but grief tears at my throat, sucking away my voice as the water gushes across my tongue. And I am sinking. Sinking into an ocean of darkness, her weight in my arms as I carry her body down with me. I know I will have to let her go for she's too heavy and I'm too exhausted to get us both back to the surface. But the realisation does nothing to annul the painful thought that soon she will be gone. I will never again touch her skin. Never again watch the sunlight across her back. Never again be with her.

With a sudden movement that tenses my body and sends jarring pain coursing along my wounded side, I force myself to release her and let her sink down out of reach.

I flail in the water then, filling the space with bubbles until I am sure that she is truly lost to me. Despair overcomes me and my drowning cry rings out across the unfathomable emptiness like a tuneless song.

There are no words. There is no meaning. This is a signal of a sort that defies explanation; a final cry before death as unfathomable as the source of the universe. The cavernous underworld of the ocean takes the sound and carries it off into its endless reaches. It passes the true fishes without recognition, rebounds off the frozen roof of the sea and sinks unchallenged into its sand-filled hollows. If it says anything it is that I am the last.

Yet in all the great infinity of water, the statement goes unrealised.

Until thirty-six thousand kilometres distant, the impossible happens; a listener is found.

Somehow, somewhere, someone hears my lament and weeps at its message. She is dead. I am to die. Insignificant facts in a much larger world. Maybe. But they are grasped by a mind that was ready to receive and, more importantly, it was able to act...

★

The control terminal flickers slightly and scans the signal once again, systematically scrutinising the uncoded graphical coordinates with a speed that defies the eye to focus. There was no computer powerful enough to shadow so weak a tracker beacon from near-space, but then this was no computer. Slowly and with meticulous detail, the hidden mind wrestles with the coding and finally produces an icosehedra model of the originating source location in a construct that it could truly understand.

>**Message completed.**

– it spells out silently in shining green.

>**Origin located. Answering on C-9.**

There is a pause – mere heartbeats – until the screen leaps again. This time it announces that an answer has been sent.

>**Initiating exigency sequence.**

– it continues impartially before reimmersing itself into a static state.

And XEs, now so much more than some jacked-up god, no longer watched on.

It *did* something.